The Cosmopolites

The Cosmopolites

A NINETEENTH-CENTURY
FAMILY DRAMA

HARRY BREWSTER

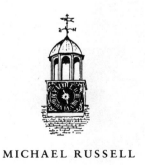

MICHAEL RUSSELL

© Harry Brewster 1994

First published in Great Britain 1994
by Michael Russell (Publishing) Ltd
Wilby Hall, Wilby, Norwich NR16 2JP

Typeset in Sabon
by The Typesetting Bureau, Wimborne, Dorset
Printed and bound in Great Britain by Biddles Ltd,
Guildford and King's Lynn

All rights reserved

ISBN 0 85955 204 7

Contents

	Acknowledgements	vii
	Preface	ix
	Family Trees	xii
1	In the City of Florence	1
2	San Francesco di Paola	4
3	Hildebrand	14
4	Fullness of Heart and Talent	26
5	The American Expatriate	38
6	The Stockhausens	49
7	The Early Years	55
8	The American Adventure	69
9	Metaphysical Courtship	79
10	The Sunflower at San Francesco	86
11	The Ivory Tower	101
12	The Breach	108
13	The Trio	113
14	Home and Friends	132
15	In America Again	156
16	'Anarchy and Law'	171
17	A New Life	178
18	Real Friends	190
19	'The Prison'	201
20	Ethel Resurgent	219

21	Henry James and H.B.	238
22	Julia	259
23	As Time Went On	268
24	A Widower's Free Life	279
25	Worldly Rome	289
26	The Mystification of Life	305
	Appendix: Germany in the 1860s	323
	Notes	327
	Index	331

Acknowledgements

My thanks are due to Lady Maclean for permission to reproduce the Maurice Baring material in the last chapter.

I am grateful to the Conway Library, Courtauld Institute of Art, for permission to reproduce the following illustrations: Hildebrand relief of Lisl von Herzogenberg playing the organ; Hildebrand relief portrait of Lisl von Herzogenberg; to the Kuntsthistorisches Institut Florenz for permission to reproduce: Hildebrand relief of Irene Hildebrand with their children; Hildebrand bust of H.B. Brewster.

[vii]

Preface

The second half of the nineteenth century and the early years of the twentieth, until the outbreak of the First World War, were the age of the cosmopolites – American, Russian, Polish, English and German expatriates on the European continent. They were to be found in Switzerland, Paris, Florence, Venice, Baden-Baden, and above all in Rome – a picture of that life in Rome is given at the end of this book. Multilingual, permeated with the various brands of culture from the same heritage, and of independent means, they were concerned with intellectual as well as social pursuits, without financial constraints but at the same time without ostentation. They prided themselves on what most would see as a highly civilized way of living. But it went with apparent unconcern for the troubles of the world; there was not much thought for famines and wars in Africa or Asia, disregard of human rights, colour prejudice and colonial exploitation – any more, indeed, than there had been among the great civilizations of the past. Civilization was not conceived in terms of relief from suffering. It had other qualities as well as faults.

Florence was of course outstanding for its British community, which included some remarkable personalities of the literary world, from the days of the Brownings to the turn of the century; but they remained very English and scarcely mixed with the other nationals – the expatriates who in a sense belonged to the Western world as a whole.

Towards the end of the century the fashionable French writer Paul Bourget poured out novel after novel – one of them (1891) called *Cosmopolis* – in which the main theme was cosmopolitanism. For Bourget the cosmopolites embodied the apogee of decadence, a set of monied people of different nationalities who spent their time in fashionable cities and spas, frequenting luxury hotels, country houses and villas, gambling, art collecting and museum trotting; and revelling in adultery. They were people without loyalties and without roots. In a context of burgeoning nationalism, not to say xenophobia, they constituted, for Bourget and others like him, a diaspora of dangerous sophisticates – metaphorical, and sometimes actual, Jews.

Henry James, who knew Bourget extremely well, reacted against this picture of Cosmopolis. In his tale 'Collaboration' he expressed his own view of that world, namely that it was a matter of cultivated and even creative people of different nationalities coming together constructively throughout Europe. They were not spending their whole time in adultery, nor were they leading the degenerate lives that Bourget pictured.

In this book I have set out to sketch the lives of a group of remarkable people who from different origins, European and American, came close together. Because of their cultural activities, range of interests, style of life and mobility across national boundaries that fell short of rootlessness, they embodied what Henry James meant by 'cosmopolite'. 'H.B.', my grandfather, is the most prominent cosmopolite of this collective biography

The main source of information I have used in reconstructing the lives of those who form the pattern of this book – a tapestry, as it were, depicting an age of our Western civilization – consists of many hundreds of letters and some diaries which have survived the vicissitudes of time. I have also had recourse to the testimony, wherever pertinent and appropriate, of published memoirs as well of the hitherto unrecorded stories and anecdotes which have been handed down orally from generation to generation within the circle of family and friends, inasmuch as they contribute to the liveliness or credibility of the picture or fill a gap in the continuity of the written records.

It is salutary that Virginia Woolf warned Ethel Smyth, who had flooded her with letters written to her by H.B. over the course of many years, against frequent quotation of lengthy extracts from them in her memoirs. H.B.'s letters are indeed remarkable – Henry James described him as 'the last of the great epistolarians'. They certainly impressed Virginia Woolf, although she was sometimes mystified by the personality of a man so different from herself. 'I can't catch him off his guard,' she exclaims in a letter to Ethel. But in a subsequent letter, about to Ethel's second instalment of memoirs, *As Time Went On*, which had been submitted to her for comment before publication, she writes:

[x]

I'm more seriously doubtful about the wisdom of such long extracts from letters. They tend to be facetious. Yet in part they are most effective, like the haul of live water, with crabs and sand in it, out of the real sea. I think H.B.'s letters come off very well, though I believe the scraps of him will whet the public appetite for more. But do be careful about letters; for one thing they break up the narrative so abruptly that the use of them without good reason is a danger.

Ethel, however, tended to reproduce long passages from these letters more for the sake of their literary quality than because they formed an essential part, which often they did not, of the story she was telling. 'I see what I miss – intimacy,' Virginia would remark at one point, and no wonder, since Ethel did not include the more intimate letters from her former lover, though she was far from reticent in relating the drama of her story with the only man with whom she had ever been to bed. ('Did you go to bed with more than one man?' Virginia asked her. I don't know whether the answer was given in writing or orally, but I am sure it would have been in the negative.) But because the extracts from the letters she chose lacked 'intimacy', and therefore did not form essential links in the chain of the story that dealt with a very close relationship, she heeded Virginia's advice and grouped them as appendices in the second volume.

The many extracts from letters I have incorporated in the text, some of them at length, have been quoted because they constitute an intrinsic part of the story, because they lead graphically from one stage to the next, because they actually tell the story, or because they illustrate a psychological situation far more eloquently than I could otherwise.

We are living in an age in which letter-writing is becoming a lost art; the biographer of the future will have to make do without them. How will 'intimacy' be brought back to life from the past? I hope the colours of the tapestry I have attempted to weave will be intense enough for the picture to come alive. They are drawn straight from that wealth of letters furnished by an age which still expressed itself in frequent, often daily, communication through the written word.

[xi]

SCHÄUFFELEN   HILDEBRAND

Gustav   Bruno
(1798-1848)   (1812-78)
Industrialist and inventor   Economist and
Founder of the Schäuffelen   liberal politician
Paper Company   ――――――|――――――
                        2 sisters Adolf Otto Richard

Irene   m. Adolf Hildebrand
(1846-1921)   (1847-1921)

――――――――――――――|――――――――――――――

Dietrich   Eva   Elizabeth   Susanne   Bertha   Sylvia

STOCKHAUSEN
Barons of Lewenhagen
Hanoverian family

Bodo Albrecht m. Clothilde Baudissin
    (1810-85)   (1818-91)
    diplomat

――――――――――――――|――――――――――――――

Ernst   Julia   Elizabeth (Lisl)
                    (1843-95)   (1847-92)
                  m. H.B.Brewster   m. Heinrich von
                                            Herzogenberg

BREWSTER

Elder William of the *Mayflower*
(1566-1644)
|
Love
2nd son of Elder William (crossed
with his father on the *Mayflower*)
|
Wrestling
|
Wrestling
|
Wrestling
|
Seabury
(the minute man)
(1754-1847)

William	Christopher Starr	Seabury
	(1799-1870)	New York banker
	m. Anna Bennet	

Louis	Henry Bennet (H.B.)	Katherine
	(1850-1908)	m. Baron de
	m. Julia von Stockhausen	Terouenne
	(1847-95)	

Clotilde	Christopher
m. Percy Feilding	(1879-1928)
	m. Elizabeth Hildebrand
	(1878-1957)

Ralph   Harry   Clotilde

I

In the City of Florence

The hallmark of Florence is its austerity of line, its sobriety of surface and colour. The puritanical architecture of the fourteenth and fifteenth centuries which here predominates and for which the city is famous can seem at first forbidding. It is not only all those stern proportions, but a sombre quality, too, in the ochre colours and texture of the walls, in the grey, in the pavements of stone, *pietra serena* as it is called, fine but far from serene. It can chill your heart, especially in the mist of a wet November or December day, when the mud oozes through from under the flagstones and the sky sinks with a perpetual and penetrating drizzle. Yet the close interplay of architecture with nature, the great wonder of Florence, soon stretches forth a conciliatory hand. It is the unique relationship between the city and its natural surroundings that still prevails, despite the onslaught of urban development.

One of the more austere and stately streets of Florence is Via de' Bardi where every house on one side of the flagstoned street is a fifteenth-century palace. On the other side there is a considerable gap in the line of buildings to make way for gardens that rise steeply to the south, up the side of the Costa San Giorgio hill, letting in light and sun to the benefit of the palaces on the opposite side. Some of these palaces stretch across to the Lungarno Torrigiani, running parallel to the north, one of the walks along the Arno river. Architecturally nothing much has changed over the last 120 years, though nowadays there are cars parked at every doorstep and invading every pavement space. Tourism is more rampant, but in the 1870s the city's attractions still exercised a considerable spell. Out of a total population of 200,000, there were nearly 30,000 Anglo-American inhabitants.

For a few years Florence was the capital of the newly founded kingdom of Italy and enjoyed a short-lived prosperity that came abruptly to an end in 1870 with the capture of Rome and the transfer

[1]

of the seat of government to that city. All the grandiose town-planning, demolition and reconstruction schemes of Florence date back to those few years. By 1873 the slummy but picturesque market centre had already been pulled down and the ugly arcades erected in what was to be called Piazza Vittorio Emanuele. The Viale de' Colli, the panoramic avenue of the hills, which was to encircle the city, had been planned and partly accomplished. One cannot help hoping it will never be prolonged, let alone completed, for it would irreparably spoil the few still untouched areas of the surrounding country.

Likewise other schemes had been started but not completed. The old city walls had scarcely been broken through to let the town expand. In 1873 there still remained standing long stretches of the walls that had been restored or rebuilt in 1530. The rhythm of renovation had by then slowed down to a lazy pulse and the city had reverted to a comfortable gait which suited both inhabitants and visitors. The community of well-to-do foreign residents enjoyed the atmosphere of the past, which prevails over the present with such splendour that one can readily understand its cultural allure.

One sunny day in the autumn of 1873 a young lady arrived in Florence and put up at a comfortable hotel in Lungarno Acciaioli with her mother, child, nurse, footman and a great deal of luggage. After a few days a visitor appeared on the scene, a fair-haired young man with a guitar and a violin. His visits became more frequent; soon he remained closeted with the young lady for hours on end in one of the rooms of her suite. The guitar would be heard and the man singing. The maid found that on a high wooden stool a bust of clay was taking shape. There was gossip in the hotel about the romance between Irene Schäufellen and Adolf Hildebrand, she a spirited Swabian lady of private means and he a young artist from Franconia on the threshold of success.

To give herself more privacy Irene Schäufellen removed herself and her attendant company from the hotel to a rented apartment in Lungarno Torrigiani across the river, with access in Via de' Bardi. And it was at the door of the flat in Via de' Bardi that Hildebrand one day found a young lady sitting on the doorstep who had sprained her ankle and could not move. She explained that she and her husband were living on the first floor, which was the floor below

Irene. So Hildebrand carried her up the stairs and into her apartment where she introduced him to her husband. This is how the friendship started between the Hildebrands and the Brewsters in Florence, protagonists of this biography.

2

San Francesco di Paola

There is a little hill in Florence covered with trees which rises a few hundred yards away from the southern city gate and overlooks the south-western walls. Access to the summit, scarcely more than 200 feet high, is only possible from the west, away from the city walls and the hemmed-in suburb, through a private park. You climb a steep path flanked by cypresses beyond clusters of linden, ilex and fig. When you are halfway up, the towers, belfries and domes of Florence begin to appear above the trees. Now thickets of bay, viburnum and phillyrea hug the stone path below the cypresses. A little further up the hill, as the climb becomes more gentle, there is an old wall on the left, behind the bushes. Its masonry up to the height of about five feet consists of an unusual material, a kind of concrete, neither Renaissance nor medieval, and certainly not Etruscan. It can only be Roman, probably of the third or fourth century AD, for only the Romans used this sort of masonry and were capable of the technique involved: rubble and pebbles held together by an extremely binding cement. Often there was a facing layer of bricks or stones, though, being less firmly held, they had not the staying power of the concrete core, which could endure for millennia. From this ancient base there rises another course of wall to the height of a few more feet, patently of the Middle Ages, which is simple stone masonry and is covered above with a tangle of shrubs and trees.

A few more steps and the path takes you to level ground covered with foliage. Some truncated ruins stand under overhanging oak and ilex trees. There is as yet no outward view because of the vegetation all around, but a couple of stone steps lead you up to a circular platform crowned by cypresses, pines and ilexes. From here you can look out on the whole of central, historic Florence; not a distorted aerial view, where the city lies far below at your feet, but a view where the buildings, standing up against the hills of the background, retain their architectural proportions. In the evening light

[4]

the cathedral dome looms huge, yet in harmony with other famous landmarks – the Campanile, Orsanmichele, San Lorenzo, the tower of the Palazzo Vecchio.

This is the hill of San Donato a Scopeto. It was crowned by the walls of a Roman fort nearly 2,000 years ago, the lower courses of which still encircle it. Then came the Dark Ages with little or no activity and the onset of decay, but then an early medieval building took shape on the Roman foundations, first in the form of a parish church and house. The earliest records go back to 2 June 1064.[1] The then rector of the church of San Donato, Ranieri by name, was summoned by John, Bishop of Florence, for having murdered a child in the neighbourhood, and was removed from the rectory. The Pilastri, 'an ancient and powerful family of Florence', were patrons of the church in those days and apparently became owners of it some years later. To this period belonged the porch of the church which was removed centuries later to within the city walls, where it is still to be seen.

The next surviving archives are of the thirteenth century, indicating a series of parish priests, several of whose names are recorded. Then in 1326 Monna Nese Pilastri donated the church to the monks of St Saviour at Settimo near Florence, of whose monastery it became a dependency.[2] On 30 May 1370 it was formally placed under the jurisdiction and care of this order by Peter, Bishop of Florence, its poverty and the scarcity of local population making it unsuitable to be continued as a parish. So it was entrusted to the direct care of the monks of St Saviour, in those days a prosperous and highly esteemed order, with the obligation to officiate regularly at divine service – *cultum divinum*. These monks held the church of San Donato a Scopeto, and the adjoining buildings they erected on the hill, till 1420.

For no obvious reason, Count Guido Antonio di Montefeltro, Duke of Urbino, succeeded in persuading Pope Martin V, who happened to be in Florence in the spring of 1420, to transfer the property of San Donato to the ownership of the canons regular of St Saviour at Bologna, a branch of the same Settimo order. The bull by which the donation was confirmed is dated 20 March 1420, and the new monks established there a fully fledged monastery. The Augustinian order of St Saviour is very ancient, but from that time onward this branch was locally known, and always referred to, as the

[5]

Scopetini – from the name of their monastery's location immediately outside the walls of Florence.

The Scopetini enjoyed a full century of peace and prosperity and the new era was ushered in by the first abbot of the monastery, a picturesque character, Sienese in origin and renowned for his holy life, who withdrew to the hill with a number of fellow monks. The event is recorded in the archives of the order of St Saviour at Bologna. Their aim was to instruct and educate young men to lead a holy life. A story is related about a novice who happened to trip over an old vine root, apparently dead and rotten, which lay loose on the ground. Irritated, he kicked it away. Father Stephen, the abbot, happened to see him. After rebuking him for his impatience he ordered him to pick it up, plant it and water it twice every day. It grew into a flourishing and productive vine which lasted as long as the monastery stood.

The city of Florence by various ordinances promoted the enlargement of the monastery and the prosperity of the estate.[3] At one time fifty *scudi* were spent on it, in those days a considerable sum, so that the monks were able to enlarge the building and 'make it into a magnificent monastery'. In the records of 1456 forty-six fathers are mentioned by name. Various other churches and similar monastic establishments were given to them or placed under their jurisdiction by, amongst others, Pope Eugenius IV in 1440.

In 1480 the monks commissioned Leonardo da Vinci to paint a great picture for their main altar. According to the monastery's records of the time, now in the State Archives of Florence,[4] the agreement was as follows: Leonardo pledged himself to paint a panel for their altar within two years, or at the very most thirty months. For his work he would receive from the monastery payment in kind – wood for burning and olive oil at regular intervals for a specific period, and on completion of the work the third of an estate located in Valdelsa, a country district some miles south of Florence, which had belonged to a certain Simon, father of one of the Scopetini monks named Francis. Simon had bequeathed his property to the monks for that purpose. If, however, Leonardo failed to complete the picture within the stipulated time, the monks held themselves free to do as they liked with the unfinished painting – which has been identified as the large unfinished panel, the *Adoration of the Kings*, now in the Uffizi gallery and one of Leonardo's major masterpieces.

[6]

Why Leonardo failed to finish it (he left Florence for Milan in 1484), whether or not the monks took the picture unfinished and what exactly befell the panel in subsequent years until well into the sixteenth century when we pick up trace of it again, are all questions which remain unanswered. No record has been found and we know nothing of it till Vasari mentions having seen it in Amerigo dei Benci's house. This is more than half a century after it had been painted. From then onwards there are definite records and we know how it found its way into the Medicean gallery.[5]

The monks of San Donato either rejected the panel because it had been left unfinished or, if they accepted it, did not retain it for long. In 1496, determined to obtain a suitably finished altarpiece, they commissioned Filippino Lippi to paint the same subject for them. Vasari, in his life of this painter, says: 'He painted for the monks of San Donato a Scopeto, now in ruin, a panel representing the Adoration of the Kings offering gifts to Christ, finished with great care ...' The panel is signed on the back and dated 29 March 1496. It remained at San Donato until 1529 and through Cardinal Carlo de' Medici, the celebrated collector, found its way to the Uffizi where it is still to be seen. The picture is fine but bears no comparison to the profundity of Leonardo's work.

The monks prospered till 1529. The Florentines had liberated their city from papal and Medicean rule, and had been enjoying a spell of freedom. But after the sack of Rome the Medici pope, Clement VII, came to terms with Charles V and, with the object of restoring the Medici dominion in Florence, agreed to the city's being besieged by the imperial troops under the leadership of the ambitious Prince of Orange. The odds against Florence being able to sustain such a siege were heavy, but the inhabitants were determined to put up a stiff resistance and took strenuous measures for its defence throughout the summer of 1529. The fortifications and walls of the city were strengthened under the supervision of Michelangelo himself, their best engineer. A scorched earth policy of defence was also decided upon. Every building within close reach of the city walls which could be used by the enemy as a vantage point of attack was earmarked for immediate demolition. The church and monastery of San Donato a Scopeto, perched as they were on a summit of a low hill that dominated the southern city fortifications at close range, came inevitably within the category of buildings to be destroyed.

[7]

The monks, who protested in vain, were ordered to vacate the premises. The Romanesque church and splendid monastery were brought crashing to the ground in a heap of charred stones, rubble and ash, although the monks, having been warned in time of their fate, had taken measures to remove to safety the works of art that could be carried away, including Filippino Lippi's *Adoration of the Kings*. With the assistance of the sympathetic Florentines they were able to dismantle in time the entire porch of the church which was taken into the city before the siege began.

The destruction of San Donato a Scopeto did not save Florence from its doom, any more than the barbarous blowing up of the beautiful Santa Trinita bridge four centuries later by the retreating German troops hampered the occupation of the city by the Allied forces. Besieged on all sides and gradually reduced to starvation, Florence held out heroically for nearly a year and finally capitulated on 12 August 1530. The Medicean faction secured control of the city once more and on 28 October the Emperor proclaimed that the rulers of Florence were to be the Medici for all time.

The Scopetini monks were allotted various temporary abodes within the city walls. Eventually in 1576 the Grand Duke Francis I conferred on the order the church and monastery of San Jacopo on the left bank of the Arno. Here they re-created the dismantled porch, which is still to be seen with an inscription stating that its stones came from the church on the hill of San Donato a Scopeto. The monks were ejected again in 1703 and from that time no more has been heard of them in Florence.

In addition to their hill, the Scopetini had owned considerable land which stretched around to the south, west and north west down a valley and up the hillside of Bellosguardo. The beauties and amenities of this area, as the years went by and the Renaissance world opened out, were sought after by the noblemen of Florence. They built their villas on the hillside and spent much of their leisure there. Until then the countryside had very nearly the same appearance as the background landscapes of Benozzo Gozzoli, a composition of cypress and pine, oak and ilex, vine and wheat. The change in the general character of the Tuscan scenery, which the introduction of the olive tree on a large scale was to bring about, had hardly started.

By the middle of the sixteenth century the powerful and prosperous Strozzi family owned a large section of the neighbourhood stretching from their own villa at St Vitus on the hillside, known as Lo Strozzino, to the city gate, Porta Romana, and further, skirting for a while the road to Siena before turning to the west to complete a loop. By then it embraced the hill of San Donato and all the land which used to belong to the Scopetini monks. Their vast estate included, in addition to a number of lesser buildings and farmhouses, a small medieval church which stood in the valley between the hills of San Donato and Bellosguardo. It had a shrine dedicated to the Holy Virgin, which was locally famous for being miraculous. So the church was known as Our Lady of the Miracles.

In 1589 Alessandro Strozzi, having returned from his travels in the East (bringing with him, incidentally, the artichoke – until then unknown to the West), donated part of his property in this neighbourhood to the friars of St Francis of Paola. The gift consisted of some fields, one or two lesser houses and possibly a villa, with at one end the medieval church of the Holy Virgin and, at the other, the site of San Donato.

These friars, the so-called Minims, had come to Florence from Calabria six years previously at the invitation of Bianca Cappello, wife of the Grand Duke Francis I. The Strozzi donation was made with certain stipulations, one of these being that within four years the friars should build a convent and a church. So, with a generous financial subsidy from the Grand Duke himself and the encouragement of Bianca Cappello, who was specially devoted to the order, the friars set about their task and by 1593 had completed the construction of both convent and church – or, more likely, reconstruction or transformation of existing buildings. The records are not clear on this point, but the medieval church was certainly still there when the friars came, since a fourteenth-century fresco was discovered a few years ago on one of the inside walls.

The convent as it now stands, a large two-storeyed building (original plans were on an even larger scale), was finished within the stipulated time limit, whereas many decades were spent refurbishing the completed structure of the church, a simple Latin cross. The task of renovation was entrusted to Gherardo Silvani, a young architect who was to become famous for his work in Florence during the seventeenth century. The church was adorned in a sober baroque style with cornices, pediments, pillars, pictures and sculptures by well-known artists of the day, among them Giovanni

Caccini, Valerio Cioli, Giovanozzo Giovanozzi, Giovanni Battista Vanni, Antonio Pillori and Alessandro Algardi.

As you enter the church, immediately on the left is a Deposition for a long time attributed to Filippo Lippi and on the opposite side a picture of St Joseph by Vanni (a much inferior work). One of the oval paintings above the cornice by Ignatius Hugford, an English eighteenth-century painter and collector, depicts a famous incident in the life of St Francis of Paola. The story goes that when stopping once in Florence on one of his journeys to France, the saint was visited by Lorenzo il Magnifico who had brought with him his little son Giovanni, whom he told to kiss the hand of the holy man. The saint said to the boy: 'Ego sanctus ero, cum tu eris sanctissimus.'[6] Giovanni was destined to become the supreme head of the Church as Leo X, who canonized St Francis.

A few years ago the walls of the interior of the church, which needed replastering and whitewashing, were scraped. In the process of this operation there came to light an old fresco of the Madonna pregnant which was identified with the original miraculous image. Perhaps it had ceased to be miraculous for it had been covered over with plaster by the over-zealous hand of baroque renovation and so had disappeared from sight for centuries. It transpired that the painter responsible for it was the fourteenth-century Florentine master Taddeo Gaddi. As the result of this discovery the fresco has been on tour at various exhibitions throughout Europe and the United States, and has only recently returned to San Francesco di Paola.

The order of Minims was founded in the fifteenth century by St Francis of Paola, a small Calabrian town. He spent many years of his life in France at the court of Louis XI whose confessor he became. Busy in this capacity as long as the king lived, he died in France at the age of ninety-one in the odour of sanctity.

The friars of the order were called 'Minimi' by their founder to distinguish them from the 'Minori' of St Francis of Assisi. They soon spread and multiplied over the entire south of Italy and little by little expanded northward, but not with the same momentum or lasting influence. In Florence they held the convent they founded, to which they gave the name of their saint, for two centuries. They were locally known as the Fathers of Good Rest – 'del Bel Riposo'. Although a mendicant order and 'The Least', which is what their name means, they started off, thanks to the generous support they were given, on a far from modest programme of expenditure, building on an ambitious scale and employing prominent artists of the time.

The convent was planned to be a very large edifice, containing a spacious arched cloister in the classical Florentine Renaissance style. However, funds must have run short for only one wing was completed, about one hundred feet long and nearly fifty wide. So only one side of the planned cloister stands, consisting of a high loggia which stretches the whole length of the house. It is undoubtedly the most striking feature of the building; the columns, in grey Florentine sandstone, are slim and tall, the arches well spaced and the vaulted ceiling gracefully spanned, creating the proportions from which the loggia derives its exceptional elegance and airiness. Who designed it is uncertain. It can hardly have been Gherardo Silvani, since he was only ten years old at that time.

The height of the whole ground floor is striking, about twenty-three feet, and the great rooms, originally refectory, chapter room and reception chambers, are all vaulted. From the loggia the stairs lead up to the first floor where a central gallery stretches the whole length of the house, with the cells giving into it, right and left, in true monastic fashion. The second floor virtually repeats the first-floor plan. The friars slept on the two upper storeys, prayed at set hours of the day and night in a little chapel with a window giving into the church, and congregated, ate, and attended to various business in the chambers of the ground floor.

In the early seventeenth century the entire back of the building was embellished on the outside by Gherardo Silvani, who redesigned the windows and cornices in a simple, pleasant Florentine *seicento* style. This side of the house rises harmoniously above the loggia which, however, is patently of an earlier date.

A back garden faces the loggia, which is shaded by tall ilex and cypress trees. Until the beginning of this century there was in the corner of the garden an arched entrance to an underground passage which led uphill to an old house about half a mile away. This used to be a dependency of the monastery. In the course of time the tunnel caved in and the entrance became blocked. So the arch was removed to improve the garden. It is said that the whole hill of Bellosguardo was honeycombed, and perhaps still is, with secret underground

[11]

passages whch were part of the city's medieval fortifications and later served in emergency as escape exits for the Medicean dynasty.

Today, as you come up the hill from the south-western city walls, Florence, after straggling on for a while, comes suddenly to an end in the square of St Francis of Paola, one side of which is bounded by a wall. On the other side of the wall are trees, fields and hills – the park, the open countryside.

Until the early 1890s the visitor was greeted by a tall marble statue of the saint with his hand raised to bless, which stood on a high pedestal in the centre of the square in front of the church. The statue was made in 1695 by the sculptor Piamontini who had been commissioned for the purpose by the Grand Duke. The records relate that Piamontini was instructed to place the statue on a particularly high base so that the Grand Duke could see it from his windows in the Pitti Palace.

At the north end of the square is the church. A few steps lead up to the door and bare façade; adjoining, to the left, rises the high front of the convent to which, in this corner of the square, a big green iron gate gives access.

In 1783 the Fathers of Good Rest were suppressed in Florence, for what reason is not known. The lease of both convent and church was obtained from the diocese, which now legally owned them, by the Federighi, an ancient family of Florence. They transferred to the church a magnificent sarcophagus made by Luca della Robbia in 1450 for Benozzo Federighi, Bishop of Fiesole. This remarkable tomb remained in the church of St Francis till 1895. On 9 January of that year it was removed to a more central and, admittedly, more important church of Florence, Santa Trinita, where it has since remained.

The Federighi occupied the convent as a villa and used the church as a private chapel till early in the nineteenth century when the estate was taken over by the confraternity of Misericordia, an association of voluntary bearers of the sick to hospital. They remained in charge of the property for a few decades and used as a cemetery not only the original churchyard of the friars, now a back garden, but the private fields which adjoined the square. More recently, however, the graves have been removed to make room for an orchard and a garden.

After the Misericordia confraternity had been in occupation for some years, the former convent became a chancery for the public

[12]

records of the commune of Galluzzo, a large village in the immediate vicinity of Florence, to whose ownership it passed in 1839. The church meanwhile was attached to the parish of St Vitus situated further up the hill and for many years remained a neglected appendage. Then, in 1874, by which time the former convent was not only used as public offices but partly inhabited by local paupers, there came about a dramatic change in its lethargic existence.

3
Hildebrand

In the late 1840s a gust of liberalism was sweeping through Continental Europe. In France Louis-Philippe was tottering, in Italy Mazzini was stirring up revolt against the Hapsburg rule and in Vienna Metternich himself, the champion of autocracy, was driven from power and made to flee from the Austrian capital. In Germany, where the paternal rule of princes and princelings had never before been seriously impugned, political life was suddenly in ferment, with elements in the smaller as well as in the bigger states striving to obtain constitutional rule and democratic freedom. Frederick William II of Prussia was a vacillating monarch who at one moment seemed prepared to come to terms with the newly formed National Assemblies of Berlin and Frankfort, which were pressing for a democratic constitution that would include and unite the whole of Germany. But the extremists who favoured a republic of Greater Germany provoked a reaction among the middle classes; so particularism under the rule of various princes prevailed again and with it a repressive, anti-liberal policy.

One of the most active liberal politicians in the state of Hesse at that time was Bruno Hildebrand, professor of economics at the University of Marburg. One of the foremost agitators of the 1848 struggle for democracy, he was elected a member of the National Assembly of Frankfort where he gave vigorous expression to his republican views.

When the extreme right came back to power Hildebrand managed to avoid imprisonment and continued his political activities as a member of the Hesse *Land* parliament. In 1850 this parliament was dissolved and Hildebrand impeached for high treason. Fleeing to Switzerland for safety, he spent the next ten years of his life as professor of economics first at the University of Zurich and then of Bern. Swiss nationality was conferred upon him in recognition of his work as one of the main organizers of the country's railways. Then,

[14]

with the declaration of a political amnesty, he was able to return to Germany and settled with his family at Jena where for many years he held the chair of economics at the university.

Bruno's fifth son, Adolf, who was born in Marburg in 1847, spent his childhood with his parents, brothers and sisters in Zurich and Bern. In his recollections of early childhood published forty years after his death,[1] he relates how even at the age of five his interest in the shape and proportions of the human body enthused him to strip the neighbours' four-year-old daughter; and having done so, he could not take his eyes off the sight of her naked body. He undressed her again on repeated occasions and would kiss her from top to toe – until he was one day observed by the cook and a stop was put to his innocent, if somewhat forward, pastime.

Years went by and in the late 1860s we find in Rome a promising group of young German and Swiss artists struggling to make their way, none of them well-off, some definitely poor, but encouraged and supported by a patron, Conrad Fiedler. Several of them were destined to make a name for themselves in the German-speaking art world before the close of the century, notably Böcklin, Feuerbach and above all Hans von Marées. The latter was an exceptionally talented painter in whom Fiedler placed great faith.

Adolf Hildebrand, handsome and nineteen, joined the group. He had come to Rome as a budding sculptor, after having studied for a while at a Nüremberg art school followed by some apprenticeship work in Munich. Before long a close friendship developed between him and Marées, a considerably older man. From the start Fiedler followed their careers, supporting Marées financially and Hildebrand intellectually, and though a rift later developed between his two protégés, he remained a lifelong friend of both. Many other young artists had reason to be grateful to him. As well as being a penetrating thinker and art critic, he was a rich, cultivated and intelligent collector of paintings and a patron of the arts. He is described by Ethel Smyth in her memoirs[2] as follows:

Conrad was a type you seldom meet in Germany, a fairly well known writer on philosophical subjects, an acknowledged writer on painting and sculpture, a generous patron of struggling talent, and yet ... O wonder! attached to no institution ... merely a gentleman at large. More than usually encased in a certain Saxon

[15]

frigidity that contrasts strangely with the geniality of the other brand of Saxon. I noticed that everyone secretly coveted his esteem and that his word always carried weight. His wife was one of those people whom all portrait painters pursue, more especially if the husband is a wealthy art patron. At that time she was quite young, tall and striking looking, with daring glorious blue eyes, yellow gold hair, and incomparable colouring. Unlike most of the friends mentioned in these pages she is still alive, therefore I will merely say that we were very fond of each other for years, although later on, after her first husband's death, when she and Frau Wagner became great friends, we gradually drifted apart. A gulf was bound to open up sooner or later between intimates of Wahnfried and people refractory to the Wagner cultus.

Fiedler's collection was very fine, and ranged from a superb Holbein to the early works of the great German sculptor Hildebrand whose first patron he was and whom he completely relieved from the necessity of prostituting his genius.[3] There were also plenty of modern German pictures (including about ten portraits of [his wife] Mary), Feuerbach and Böcklin, who by the way was Swiss, being the only names I can recall; but in the Museum, introducing me to Manet and the French school, he remarked: 'Of course we must encourage native talent but oh! for something on this level.' Feuerbach I thought the bore of bores and loathed Stuck, but Manet seemed impossible to take seriously. I marvelled at Conrad's enthusiasm though certain he was right, for one felt he knew.

Hildebrand's letters to Fiedler from the very outset of their friendship reveal an extroverted personality full of optimism, faith in life and a remarkable aptitude for rational objectivity in any form of discussion relating to art and aesthetics. Throughout his life he was actively interested in drawing, painting, architecture and music as well as in sculpture. Marées's letters, on the other hand, disclose a tormented soul, sensitive and delicate. He was a man preoccupied with himself and his work, though far from unresponsive.

The friendship between the two artists, begun in the stimulating atmosphere of Rome, was consolidated by a period of close collaboration in Naples. Marées had been commissioned to paint frescoes on the walls of the library in the newly founded aquarium of

[16]

Naples, and the director and founder, Dr Anton Dohrn, invited Hildebrand to assist in the work.

Writing to Fiedler in June 1873, Hildebrand provides a sketch of the carefree time they were having in Naples:

> About our life here in Naples Marées will have already written to you, also that your company is missed. It makes me very happy to think that at last I am finding an opportunity to paint. If only we could get on with things, I have been dawdling far too much. I have found Marées exceptionally well and we talk to each other mainly in Curiac,* when we wish to tell each other privately about the joys and pains of love. Dohrn is impatient, Grant is sullen and bathes in caves, Kleinberg is handsome and Dr Eisig silly and smart.† Marées keeps exerting a pleasant influence on our cuisine and is very busy with it.

In spite of this picture of leisurely life, the work was carried on at a feverish pace throughout the summer and autumn. By November Hildebrand had completed the busts of Charles Darwin and the zoologist Baer, and had given the last touches to the architectural features and decorative elements which framed the frescoes. These, consisting of seascapes and landscapes with figures, some of them nude, Marées had brought to completion after months of intensive work. Then the two friends decided to leave Naples for Florence.

So it was that Hildebrand saw the ex-convent of San Francesco di Paola for the first time. He and Marées had taken separate rooms in town and were walking one day up the hill of Bellosguardo. There they saw the large house on the square with its simple façade, its unassuming but dignified proportions. Curiosity took them further and, crossing the threshold, they came upon the sight of the loggia. They stood and gazed.

Marées immediately made arrangements to rent one of the large ground-floor rooms as his studio. Then, a few days later, they heard through an English acquaintance that the convent was going to be put up for sale. They had a vision of San Francesco as a home for active artists, as a centre of work in peaceful and harmonious

---

* An artificial language invented by Marées for fun.
† Charles Grant, Scotsman and stepson of a Methodist missionary, had been Hildebrand's tutor in Germany and became a lifelong friend. Kleinberg and Elsig were both assistants of Dr Dohrn.

[17]

surroundings. They decided to submit the plan to Fiedler, in the hope that he would accept their idea and buy the convent. The suggestion was tactfully conveyed to him by letter, but Fiedler failed to oblige. Marées had not a penny of his own and depended on Fiedler for his livelihood, whilst Hildebrand received a small allowance from his father, only enough to live on. Unless Fiedler stepped in, the convent could not be bought and the plan would have to be given up. As it happened, Fiedler had his reasons for not being the purchaser. He felt, as he says in his diary, too heavily burdened at that time with various other philanthropic commitments and he was not convinced that such close collaboration betwen the two young artists was in the interest of either.

When this became plain, Hildebrand appealed to his father at Jena whose response enabled him to buy San Francesco himself. At the auction sale it went for 29,255 Italian lire. The amount for the purchase Hildebrand got from his father was in the form of a loan on which he had to pay interest until the sum was returned. Most of the land, however, including the farm house and the hill of San Donato, which had been separated from the original estate earlier in the century, he bought from a separate landlord a few years later.

The first task was to make the house liveable and comfortable, as well as amenable to the respective needs of the two new occupiers. A great deal had to be done to the suite of offices and dilapidated rooms in which squatters had been living. Hildebrand decided to turn the ground-floor rooms into his studios and workshop, to use the first floor as his own residence and to do up the second floor to suit Marées's requirements.

Fiedler now came to their assistance with money and financed the very considerable structural modifications for Marées's studio on the second floor. Until these were completed the two friends agreed to share the first floor and Marées temporarily took over the management of the household.

Although the vaulted rooms on the ground floor could be used as studios after only a few minor changes, the first floor called for more careful planning if its monastic character was to be preserved as well as making the place adequately comfortable to live in. The problem was resolved by keeping the central gallery untouched – an important feature of the house – and by turning some of the rooms giving into it on each side – the original cells – into bigger rooms. A few separating walls were knocked down to make two drawing-rooms and a large dining-room, which still left enough bedrooms. Bathrooms were put in, and the kitchen and servants' rooms were organized upstairs on the second floor.

One of the drawing-rooms had its ceiling raised to almost twice its original height by the sacrifice of two rooms on the second floor. Then a large window was added to the two existing ones to let in more light, as well as the right kind of light, for Hildebrand's work. Central heating was put in on the first floor a few years later, the walls were frescoed by Hildebrand himself and subsequently by his daughters, and little by little both floors were fully furnished with Italian antiques. In the main bedroom he painted on the wall a view of the house in a Florentine landscape with a youth standing before it and holding a banner. On it is clearly written in Latin a verse Hildebrand took from an ode of Horace in praise of his farm near Rome: 'That corner of the world smiles for me beyond all others'.[4]

The major structural alteration was carried out on the second floor, where Hildebrand converted several small rooms into a large studio and other suitable accommodation for Marées. The roof was raised by three feet over nearly half the entire length of the house. This, in a way, was a mistake since it spoilt the proportions of the façade. Nor was it the only mistake that Hildebrand made in the course of forty years' structural adjustments, since he was inclined to look at the problems of his house solely from the angle of a sculptor's requirements. Nevertheless the damage done was small in proportion to the immense and lasting improvements. One of them, for instance, greatly enhanced the privacy of the approach to the house and the character of the grounds. When Hildebrand acquired San Francesco, the square extended, in its west corner, into an area right in front of the convent. Before long he was able to buy this corner of the square and incorporate it within the property walls, so only a gate, close to the church, gave access to what had become a private terrace in front of the building. Later he bought the statue of St Francis, which stood in the middle of the square, and had it placed within the walls in front of the house where it now stands flanked by two tall cypresses.

Shortly after the purchase of San Francesco Hildebrand and Marées moved in and then about a year later, early in 1875, by which time Marées had been able to settle in his own living quarters on the

[19]

second floor, Fiedler joined them. He occupied the first floor for several months and ran his own household. In the summer of that year, however, he decided to leave for various reasons, one of them being that, as Hildebrand owned the house, he felt that the young sculptor had every right to organize his own life on the premises without interference from too many friends. Fiedler was a man of tact and scruple.

Meanwhile Marées had been writing with enthusiasm to his friends about San Francesco. To his brother he wrote:

My apartment, which is in the course of being done up, will be ready in about two months. It will be very roomy: a huge studio, a drawing-room, a bedroom, a guest room, a room for the servant, kitchen, pantry, a large loggia and other rooms, and a wonderful view. I am temporarily living on the first floor and am looking forward immensely to your being able to share this splendour with me one day.[5]

To a girl friend he wrote:

Carissima, carina, . . . Hildebrand has bought himself a monastery where a permanent dwelling is being prepared for me too. Should you be coming to Florence and should you wish to see the famous view from Bellosguardo, you would not be able to avoid passing by the statue of St Francis . . . Immediately beyond the saint the gate opens to perdition. But enter without fear or anxiety, for awesome Hades will at once greet you as his mistress. Upstairs, from the former cells, a lovely view is to be enjoyed over the peaceful city to which we owe so much.[6]

But tensions were already clouding the apparent harmony of the Hildebrand-Marées relationship. The setting, the life of cooperation, indeed the friendship itself, were perhaps too perfect to last.

Whatever the reservations with which we may nowadays look back to Marées's paintings, he towers as an artist above his contemporary painters of the German-speaking world, including Feuerbach, Böcklin, Lanbach and even Thoma, a very gifted artist. Fiedler, the best connoisseur of the German art world of those days, had no doubts about his worth.

As a man, however, as a friend, Marées was difficult, even neurotic. He had wished to own San Francesco himself or at least be a partner in its ownership. He felt it was his discovery, for it seems he had seen it before they had visited it together. To find himself now the tenant of a much younger man, whom he had actually introduced to the place, was a bitter pill to swallow. When an attractive young woman, for whom he also had a soft spot, became the centre of Hildebrand's passionate attention, it was more than he could bear, since it was he who had introduced Hildebrand to Irene Schäufellen; and so the relationship between the two friends underwent further strain. In the end a break was inevitable and scarcely more than twelve months after San Francesco had been bought under such promising auspices, Marées reluctantly made up his mind to leave for good. He settled in Rome, where he died twelve years later having seen Hildebrand again only once.

San Francesco, no longer to become the collective home for young artists that had been originally planned, passed instead under the control and moulding hand of Hildebrand alone. He, with his wife, family and friends, was to give it new life, a new character of its own.

One of Hildebrand's qualities was the striking impression he made on people who were meeting him for the first time, an impression which was overwhelmingly positive and which never wore thin on closer acquaintance. His sculpture could affect people in the same way. This is how Ethel Smyth described him in her memoirs:

Hildebrand is, I am certain, one of the great artists of all time. Lisl* was rather shocked at my saying he impressed me more even than Brahms, but I think the remark was sound, for there are many great composers of modern times, but how many sculptors of Hildebrand's stature, I wonder? He was of a serene gay temperament, absolutely natural, and I think 'a-moral' is the term to express his complete detachment, in theory at least, from morality and current views on the conduct of life. Children, for instance, should not be brought up but left to grow like wild flowers; and the results of this principle in his own young family did not appeal to my English notions. Lisl once remarked that if he were not upright and kindly by nature – in fact a good man – he would be a very bad one, and this he allowed was true.

There was a queer mixture of simplicity and shrewdness about him – a lawyer's shrewdness I mean, not the peasant cunning of

* Elizabeth von Herzogenberg, sister of Julia Brewster.

[21]

Rodin, aware of the market and for all his genius never forgetting it. The public only existed for Hildebrand as a corrective. He used to ask what one thought of his statues, and once, when I said a certain arm looked to me too long, he explained that though as a matter of fact it was too short, the remark put him on the right track of the real error, which was due elsewhere; a thing I have often felt myself about the judgement of the man in the street. He was a tremendous arguer and theorizer, and would discourse till all hours of the night on a subject like *Raumvorstellung* for instance (concept of the cubic content is the nearest English I can find) and its connection with plastic art. His talk was so free from pedantry, so luminous, that any artist, or indeed any cultivated being, could listen to it with pleasure, and watch his clear laughing eyes become like pinpoints, as, with raised forefinger, he drove his argument home.

Like many 'picturing artists' as Germans call them, Hildebrand was deeply musical, played the violin and viola, and could transpose at sight, much to my admiration, whether from the alto, bass, or violin clef, with the greatest of ease; but it was impossible to get him beyond Haydn and Beethoven. In the same way all he knew or wanted to know of English literature was Shakespeare and *Tom Jones*, which he thought the finest novel in the world – no great compliment, for the only other novel he had read was *Elective Affinities*[7] . . .

I went to see him when passing through Munich in 1914; he had been very ill and the bounding vitality and loquaciousness of former years had gone, but he talked enthrallingly about modern work and said, with Hildebrand simplicity: 'Compared to these *artists* I feel like a mere workman' – nor I fancy did he wish to feel otherwise. I repeated to him a remark of Rodin's, whom he greatly admired – with reservations – about its being the office of the sculptor to transcend, in the interests of suggestiveness and mystery, the limitations of his models; and the old pinpoint look came back into his eyes as he said: 'It seems to me nothing can exceed the mystery and suggestiveness of Nature.'

Some people complain that his portrait busts copy Renaissance work, and on the other hand his treatment of the nude has been found classically cold. My own feeling is that everything he does is so intensely Hildebrand no matter who his progenitors may be, so absolutely free from concession to anything but his own artistic vision, that his work must surely be on the very first line. For many years taboo in Berlin, because when invited by the All Highest to collaborate in the *Sieges-allee* he freely spoke his mind on that terrible subject, he is as good as unknown in England; indeed I think the only originals of his in the United Kingdom are the busts of Baroness von Stockhausen I referred to,[8] and a portrait in high relief at Whittingehame.[9]

Not only did the very English Ethel Smyth fall under Hildebrand's spell, but so did the extremely German and rapturous poetess Isolde Kurz, who wrote a book about him after his death in 1921. In her account, after referring to Goethe's charm, she goes on to say:

Also Hildebrand was in his own way a charmer, into whose proximity nobody came without being captured. Wherever he happened to be everything around him would widen out and one would breathe, as it were, stimulating oxygen. Before he began to speak his listeners were already inclined to agree with him and with him alone. This was not only the effect of his astonishing intellect and the overwhelming directness of his approach; something else, inexplicable, contributed to it, a magnetic stream coming from him, cosmic as it were, which communicated to all around the sensation of a higher consciousness and order. The dejected would become cheerful, the timid bold, the mournful would take heart, for it was as if a more living bond would unite these people with the harmony of the all. . . Such influence, however, would take effect only between him and the individual; over a group of people he had no power; it was impossible to think of him as a speaker on a stand. The many disturbed him: he had neither the gift nor the wish to appeal to them collectively or to direct them spiritually.[10]

Amongst the younger generation, that is to say amongst Hildebrand's own unruly daughters, Isolde Kurz was something of a joke. Whenever an opportunity arose the girls would mimic her more ridiculous sides. Nevertheless she was an intelligent woman.

Hildebrand, as artist and man, lacked neither male nor female admirers in his lifetime. His male friends, such as Charles Grant, Henry Brewster, Rupert Wittelsbach of Bavaria and above all

[23]

Conrad Fiedler, were not maybe as panegyrical or as gushing as some of his female eulogizers, but certainly no less appreciative.

Ethel Smyth's enthusiasm about his greatness as an artist was perhaps exaggerated and nowadays, looking back to Hildebrand seventy odd years after his death, it is possible to make a more balanced and objective appraisal of his work. In attempting to size it up it is important to remember the times in which he worked; that he was able to detach himself to some extent from them shows in the way his successful output transcended the limitations of his period.

Hildebrand's good pieces of sculpture – and there are many – deserve far wider as well as more serious consideration than they have so far enjoyed. His weaker output, admittedly, which is no less abundant, is not immune from the imperfections of the period. His apparent classicism, however, is a stumbling block to critics who approach his work for the first time and Ethel Smyth was right in pointing out the danger of misunderstanding Hildebrand in this respect. In fact Hildebrand was not a classicist like Canova and many sculptors after him, nor was he a positivist as many others were in the last century who aimed at expressing the individual character or a specific aspect of their subject. Hildebrand, on the contrary, was an innovator insofar as he contrived to let the anonymity of his nudes prevail. His best pieces of sculpture transcend with healthy vigour any form of conventional classicism with which the critic might be inclined to associate him. His work bears little resemblance to the achievements of contemporary sculptors in Florence and Rome, local or foreign, all of whom delighted in classicism and snow-white Carrara marble. For it was not so much prettiness and purity, candour and 'beauty', or monumental grandeur with which Hildebrand was grappling, as the problem of containing and controlling, by means of form, the intensity, vitality and power of nature. When he succeeded, which happened not infrequently, he rose above the mediocrity of his age. Particularly interesting in this connection are his reliefs, where the problem of form is usually solved most harmoniously. An important feature of Hildebrand's sculpture, too, is the way in which so much of it is envisaged in the context of architecture and integrated as part of it. His faithfulness to nature was neither realism nor naturalism *per se*, but the result of his passionate interest in nature itself, of which, as he saw it, nothing could 'exceed the mystery and suggestiveness'. And those who have criticized Hildebrand's work as being pastiche have failed to understand that his creative success is in representing this very 'mystery and suggestiveness' of nature through form. Much of this is to be found not only in his reliefs and many of his drawings but also in his fountains, where the dynamic elements of his art find scope for expression.

Within a restricted circle of art critics and art historians Hildebrand is well known as the author of a thesis, *The Problem of Form*. This is a remarkable book which, together with the philosophical works of his friend Conrad Fiedler, has had considerable influence on modern thinkers in the field of aesthetics and art criticism, amongst others on Herbert Read. Nevertheless, eminently successful though he was in his lifetime, Hildebrand is still hardly known outside Germany and a small group of connoisseurs in Italy – though any traveller familiar with Munich will have seen some of his fountains, notably the Wittelsbach and the Hubertus fountains.

Documentary films have been made, exhibitions of his sculpture and drawings from time to time organized both in Germany and in Italy, and several PhD dissertations on his work have recently been written. A more comprehensive study of his achievement, long overdue, has now been published in Germany by Dr Sigrid Braunfels.

4
Fullness of Heart and Talent

Ethel Smyth was twenty-four when in the autumn of 1882 she arrived in Florence with two letters of introduction, one to the Hildebrands, the other to the Brewsters. She first approached the Hildebrands, who received her with open arms. The letter was from Elizabeth ('Lisl') von Herzogenberg, sister of their great friend Julia Brewster. Ethel had met her in Germany where she was studying music and had grown extremely attached to her.

When Hildebrand saw Ethel he was impressed. She had a trim figure, with bold blue eyes, a clear fair complexion and long blond hair tucked under a boater. Almost at once he invited her to come and sit for a bust. She accepted and came regularly over a prolonged period. Early in the morning she would arrive at his studio on the ground floor and, closeted there, they would work till late in the morning. Then, as though every day were an exception, Hildebrand would look at his watch, shake his head in dismay and exclaim: 'Good gracious, Ethel, I do apologize, it's past one o'clock – you'd better come up and have luncheon with us.'

Ethel protested, Hildebrand insisted, and finally Ethel gave in every day. They would leave the studio and begin to negotiate the steep monastic stairs to the first floor. Ethel was a strong, athletic girl, yet about half way up she developed a habit of turning pale and falling into a swoon. Hildebrand would obligingly lift her in his strong arms and carry her up the remaining steps. Then, as they got to the landing, the door would open and Frau Hildebrand would step forward to meet them. With a strained expression of concern, or possibly displeasure, she would receive a reviving Ethel from the arms of her smiling husband.

It was an unpromising basis for female friendship, and it is no secret that Ethel never took to Irene Hildebrand, though she had boundless admiration for her husband throughout her life. This is how she described her, somewhat condescendingly:

[26]

Frau Hildebrand was once a celebrated man-enslaver and was still gracious and desirable though no longer in her first youth. One almost regretted that such receptivity to the touch of life had been finally tamed to domestic uses, for nowadays she was rather by way of being fattish and motherly on principle. And yet I remember one evening of reminiscent youthful grace, when after some little domestic festival they all accompanied their guests as far as the Porta Romana; then suddenly she danced a step or two down the hill among the fireflies, and I saw a graceful Bacchante hanging aslant between me and the moon. She was a great dear, radiating warmth, kindness and hospitality, but I got on best with him.

Motherly and kindly though she was, Irene had a no-nonsense side. The little scene of her husband carrying Ethel up for luncheon kept recurring day after day until finally she could stand it no longer. So one morning, when her husband had taken Ethel out sightseeing, she mustered her three children and their little friend, Clotilde Brewster, gave them sticks and spears and told them they would go and attack Ethel's bust. The children were thrilled and Irene, herself brandishing a hammer, led them down into the studio. Together they pitched into Ethel's head which Hildebrand had almost finished and reduced it to fragments. When later he returned there were no comments on either side. Ethel remained a good friend, but the modelling was discontinued; and there was no more swooning on the stairs.[1]

The daughter of a British general, Ethel Smyth was brought up in the typical Victorian setting of her class. She would have been a staunch supporter of the Women's Liberation Movement, just as she was a militant suffragette at the beginning of this century. But in her early twenties it was music that kindled fire in her, for her talent was outstanding; and so it was music that brought her to Germany as a young girl. Sir George Henschel, the well-known singer and orchestra conductor of those days, described her in his memoirs as she was when he first saw her, a young girl of eighteen, in his native Germany where he was still living at that time.

Shall I ever forget that fine August day in 1877 when our little circle was suddenly brightened by the meteor-like appearance among us of a young and most attractive girl who was staying in

[27]

the neighbourhood, the daughter, we understood, of a British general? None of us knew what in her to admire most; her wonderful musical talent which she displayed to equal advantage at the piano as well as by singing, with a peculiarly sympathetic voice and in compositions of her own, or her astonishing prowess in athletic feats of agility and strength, showing us how to play lawn-tennis, only then introduced into Germany, or, to the utter bewilderment of the German young ladies, and young men, too, for that matter, how to jump over fences, chairs and even tables, thus altogether electrifying our pleasant but everyday life ... We were all agreed that we had among us an extraordinarily commanding personality, a woman that was sure to be famous one day.[2]

Another portrait of young Ethel, seen through very different though scarcely less appreciative eyes, is given to us by Conrad Fiedler in a letter he wrote to Irene Hildebrand in 1880, some time before the budding musician arrived in Florence:

We have spent Christmas quite happily; if not a herd of children we too had a child, an English girl of twenty-one. She is studying music in Leipzig under Herzogenberg and is on close terms of friendship with his wife. As they had left for Christmas and New Year she came to stay with us for a fortnight and has become very dear to us. As regards her musical talent I cannot but trust the very favourable opinion of Joachim who is here. I have been much impressed by the 'cello sonata she has composed, though I am no judge in such matters. But quite apart from this she is one of the cleverest and most remarkable persons I have come across for a long time, natural, lively and full of inner earnestness. I could write a good deal about her. You must get to know her some time. She has become very attached to my wife and our relationship has developed on a lasting basis. Sooner or later we shall no doubt all get together.

Joachim's opinion of her musical talent as a composer did not remain indefinitely so favourable and some years later Ethel took exception to his lukewarm reaction. Nor did her attachment to Mary Fiedler endure the test of time, as she herself points out in her memoirs.

[28]

Ethel's great discovery in Germany, however, where from 1877 she was spending recurrent periods for her studies in music, was neither George Henschel nor Conrad Fiedler, nor for that matter Brahms himself, but Elizabeth von Herzogenberg, Julia's sister and Brahms's most intimate friend. This is how Ethel describes Lisl, whom she had met for the first time in 1878 at Leipzig where the Herzogenbergs were living:

> If ever I worshipped a being on earth it was Lisl... The published correspondence between her and Brahms, and also various references to her in his biography, have given the world some idea of the personality of this remarkable woman, in whose house I became what he always called me, 'the child', till Fate violently and irrevocably parted us. At the time I first met her she was twenty-nine, not really beautiful but better than beautiful, at once dazzling and bewitching; the fairest of skins, fine-spun, wavy golden hair, curious arresting greenish-brown eyes, and a very noble rather low forehead, behind which you knew there must be an exceptional brain. I never saw a more beautiful neck and shoulders; so marvellously white were they, that on the very rare occasions on which the world had a chance of viewing them it was apt to stare – thereby greatly disconcerting their owner, whose modesty was of the type that used to be called maidenly. In fact the great problem was to prevent her swathing them in chiffon.
>
> About middle height, the figure was not good; she stooped slightly, yet the effect was graceful and ingratiating, rather as though she were bending forward to look at you through the haze of her own golden atmosphere. In spite of this ethereal quality there was a touch of homeliness about her – to use the word in its best sense – a combination I have never met with in any one else. Of great natural capacity rather than well informed, a brilliant, most original talker, very amusing, and an inimitable mimic, she managed in spite of all her gifts to retain the child-like spirit which is one of the most sympathetic traits in the German character – and what is more, to blend it with the strong pinioned fascination of one who could but know, like Phyllis in the song, that she never failed to please. And this surely is a remarkable achievement! It really was true that with

[29]

her sunshine came in at the door, and both sexes succumbed equally to her charm. As her marriage was notoriously happy, possibly too because her brilliant talents inspired a certain awe, men did not dare to make love to her, not at least the sort of men she met in Leipzig. But I fancy that in other circumstances a small flirtation would not have been disdained; I used to tell her that when talking to men she became a different woman – a difference which though slight was perceptible – but this mild accusation didn't fit in with her scheme of things and was eagerly repudiated.

In a burgher world it certainly went for something that this siren was an aristocrat. Sincerely as everyone in the artist set despised worldliness, I think her exploits in the kitchen (for among other things she was a heaven-inspired cook) gained a picturesqueness when you reflected that had the Court of Hanover not come crumbling about their ears in early youth, she and her sister Julia Brewster would have been Maids of Honour. . . . The essential point was of course her musical genius. Almost by instinct she read and played from score as do few routined conductors, and in judgement, critical faculty, and all-round knowledge was the perfect musician.

The enthusiasm was reciprocal; the extant records, published and unpublished, disclose a gushing passion mutually and equally felt. One might jump to the conclusion that there was a touch of lesbianism in this relationship, which may be true. But at the same time one should bear in mind that Lisl loved her husband dearly; her marriage, though childless, was an extremely happy one. Her enthusiasm for men, notably for Hildebrand's brother, Richard, and for Adolf himself, was no less demonstrative and was expressed with so little restraint as to arouse Irene's jealousy. Ethel, on the other hand, although women played a predominant part in her life, was to prove capable of forfeiting Lisl's friendship and attachment for the sake of a man.

The attraction Lisl exerted was evidently widespread. Ethel and Brahms were not the only ones to fall under her spell: many others, relations and friends, were entranced. The following is a description of her by her cousin Bernhard Prince Bülow, who was to become Imperial Chancellor of Germany many years later:

[30]

When I visited my uncle Baudissin[3] for the second time there came into the drawing-room an exceptionally beautiful girl. I stared at her as the poor shepherds of the valley stare at a girl from far away. I needn't be ashamed to say so even after the lapse of so many dozens of years; for she was my uncle's niece, my cousin Elizabeth von Stockhausen, who was to marry Henry Baron Herzogenberg, of Brahms's faithful supporters the most faithful. . . I see her still with her luminous golden hair, her gay, affable, enchanting, goddess-like expression and graceful carriage, a perfect reproduction of her wonderful inner self. . .[4]

Hildebrand was very fond of her and appreciated her immensely. He made a fine bust of her in her full bloom, an excellent but less flattering portrait drawing when she was a somewhat opulent middle-aged lady and, when she died somewhat prematurely, a charming relief portrait of her playing the piano, for her grave at San Remo.

As for Brewster, Hildebrand's friend, his Latin soul and Anglo-Saxon reserve recoiled from this brand of Germanic effusion. Julia was by nature the reverse, more Scandinavian, as Ethel Smyth points out.

In addition to all the qualities Ethel saw in Lisl, the fact that she stood at the centre of a whole world of musicians and knew everyone worth knowing, who did not belong to the Wagner cult, was an attractive asset. Lisl's amiable husband, a colourless though industrious composer, was president of the Leipzig Bach Union, an enthusiastic friend of Brahms and promoter of his work. Lisl's friendship, therefore, and Herzogenberg's appreciation were invaluable.

The letters which Ethel kept receiving from her passionate friend disclose not only Lisl's warm nature but also her frustrated motherhood. Some relevant passages are worth quoting. From Graz she wrote in 1879:

I sometimes feel as if the happiness bestowed upon me were almost too great, as if I were spoilt by Fate; and yet when I see Julia, to whom a second child will soon be born, I stretch out my arms for more happiness, have visions of that which I long for as if it had already belonged to me, and must come back again. But I do not feel it as a *pain*, my darling, or only sometimes. . . How I thank you for calling me Mother; do you know you have helped me, for since I have you I bear it more easily having no child of my own. . .

A few months later she wrote again:

I wonder how you will like Julia? What you think me so rich in, instincts, she does not possess at all. In a certain sense she is lifted high above the region where children of nature have certain things in common. For instance her feeling for the baby* is . . . mainly prophetic! Her eyes rest upon it with most affection when she has just been looking at its five-year-old sister, because she is saying to herself 'It will be like that some day.' The sense . . . of unconscious tenderness, the joy of feeling this little being dependent on one, all this is nothing to her. But in other directions she has acquired a freedom in loving, suffering and understanding, before which I bow down in shame. And what a heavenly absence of egotism! You never hear her speak of herself, and everyone who talks to her is persuaded of his own exquisite importance, though she never uses the conventional methods of the world. But this expenditure of kindness and sympathy fatigues her, and she flees the company of the others rather than seeks it. Both of them wish to live for themselves and the family only, and when they do associate with other people, it never gets beyond intellectual relations. They are kind – sympathize and awaken sympathy – but never embark on an intimacy that might fetter. What they demand above all things is . . . freedom. Intercourse with others makes Harry† positively ill, but no one who has any dealings with him imagines that *he* could possibly be that person!

Usually loving and anxious as a mother towards Ethel, who was twelve years younger, Lisl could be critical, possessive and even jealous. When she introduced Ethel to the Fiedlers, the young girl cultivated the friendship so eagerly and successfully that Lisl reacted somewhat petulantly:

There you are, perfectly happy in the house of the excellent Fiedlers who carried you off after knowing you just three days!

* Christopher, the author's father.
† sc. Brewster, 'H.B.', Julia's husband.

And though I am pleased I marvel again how that all rushed so quickly upon you, you little steamboat. What a talent to make friends you have, and to jump into relationships which I should want months to assimilate myself! I didn't tell you yesterday because really it is too childish, but I do feel jealous about the gladness and comfort you have in that house and which I can give you, things being as they are, so rarely in that opulent form which is so becoming to your health, my poor child! I seldom envy rich people but I do envy the Fiedlers in this case. . . I have nothing to give my child but my poor love – *no* my rich, rich love – and a little sadness to accompany it! I would like to have you near me, telling me that you feel happiest of all with

Your old Mother

From Florence a few months later, in April 1880, she writes again: 'I talk about you to Julia at her special request nearly all day! Send your Cello Sonata quick, quick; she wants to hear something of yours.' And about Hildebrand in May with gushing enthusiasm:

Hildebrand is doing a profile relief of me which takes up a lot of my time, but of course I am delighted and as proud as a peacock. The best part of it, however, is the intercourse with this delightful man himself. What with great cleverness and finesse, simple direct manners, and natural charm of intelligence, he is one of the most attractive of men. . . You know I have always admired his work, especially the Sleeping Shepherd-Boy, but this new group fills one with the sort of religious reverence that only perfect works of art inspire. You have no idea of the beauty of the young Bacchus – the languid perfection of the body, supported by a comfortable-looking, not at all revolting old Satyr – beauty that makes one think of one's best possessions, the C Major Symphony of Mozart for instance. Surely Hildebrand must win over his last opponents; can anyone dare to go on picking holes after this, or denying that there is an irresistible art-force before which one must do homage – in a word, a master?

Exuberant they might be, but her enthusiasms could be tempered with intelligent criticism, especially on the subject of music, where her appreciation tended to be objective and measured. This quality is delightfully shown in her letters to Brahms.

[33]

Lisl had met Brahms for the first time in Vienna when she was only fifteen. The Stockhausens were living in the Austrian capital at that time, where Brahms was also working, still giving piano lessons to make a living. When the Hanoverian minister Bodo von Stockhausen offered him the musical education of his daughter, he gladly accepted. Evidently her charms proved too great, however, for after a while he suddenly withdrew with the excuse that he did not want to hurt the feelings of Epstein, her former piano teacher who, as the records tell, had been quite willing, with a humble *cedo majori* bow, to hand over his gifted pupil to Brahms. Then another musician fell in love with her, Herzogenberg, to whose musical care the old diplomat entrusted the finishing touches of his daughter's education. The young man had a pedigree as well as academic training to recommend him for the task. Lisl fell in love in her turn and their marriage took place in 1868. The fact that it remained childless was a misfortune to which Lisl's strong motherly instincts could never reconcile themselves until the end of her life.

The Herzogenbergs lived at Graz for a while and then, in 1872, settled at Leipzig where they founded the city's Bach Union. Here it was that the friendship began with Brahms, who by then had become well known and had overcome most of his shyness. The relationship between Brahms and Lisl, which remained Platonic, was one of deep mutual esteem and affection. Brahms was seemingly a man unable to have a love affair with a woman of his own social and intellectual standing. The letters exchanged betwen them and published in 1907 cover a period of fifteen years ending with Lisl's death in 1891. The collection contains also Herzogenberg's own correspondence with Brahms which continues for a few more years till the composer's death in 1897. But it is Lisl's letters in particular which have the warmth, liveliness, humour and critical insight that give the publication its special interest.

Gentle by nature though she was, Lisl's indignation could be raised to a pitch over questions of taste. For instance the mere thought of a concert in which Brahms's D Major Symphony was to be followed by Wagner's 'Fire Magic' from the *Valkyrie* would stir up her wrath. Clara Schumann was to play Beethoven in the same concert, but was threatening to withdraw, quite rightly according to Lisl. 'Wüllner! O Wüllner!' she wrote to Brahms on 19 January 1878, inveighing against the conductor responsible for the miscegenation of the programme, 'you are a gentleman as a rule, but this programme is that of an impresario!'

Whether from her house in Leipzig or from Florence, where she would stay with her sister in Via de' Bardi, she kept writing to Brahms and receiving letters from him through the years. Her own letters were often enthusiastically appreciative of his compositions, sometimes subtly critical, analysing, quoting bar after bar and asking questions as to how exactly a relevant passage was to be played. Sometimes her mind would wander from the central theme of music to other forms of beauty. When, for instance, Brahms informed her in May 1880 of his decision to dedicate to her his newly composed *Two Rhapsodies for Piano* and asked her whether she could not think of a better title, she wrote back from the same balcony overlooking the Arno from which she had been writing to Ethel about Julia and Hildebrand in the course of that Florentine sojourn.

After thanking him warmly she discusses the question and says she would prefer the more simple *Klavierstücke* (Piano Pieces) as a title, because it suggests nothing, and the clearly delimited form of the two pieces practically contradicts the notion of a rhapsody. However, since it is possible to adopt different ways of interpretation in playing them she thinks that the misty garment the word 'rhapsody' conveys might do after all. She then describes with both perception and delight the view of the Arno and of the city seen from where she is sitting on the balcony:

How glad I am that you have been to Italy so that I don't have to tell you about it. I am sitting on an open balcony with a view of the Arno, almost midway between Ponte alle Grazie and Ponte Vecchio. You will know what this means, what a blue sky there is above, what dear soft mountains lie in the background and how overwhelmed I am when I gaze at all this splendour. I have already lived a hundred lives through the many wonderful experiences of beauty this week in which I have found myself unwittingly shifting from the single thing to the whole and from the whole back to every single thing. So my love for this heavenly place is always growing. How painful it is to realize that soon one has to leave and tear one's eyes away from all the things it has become a need for them to contemplate. I am so glad that

[35]

you have been here and that you have experienced the joy of discovering that no matter how far from such beauty one may have grown up, one has nonetheless eyes to see it, once one has stepped into its soul-stirring vicinity.[5]

Her meditations on Florence continue for a while, as she reflects on the glorious past of the city, on the modern Italians and civilization in general until, with a shock, she pulls herself back to the immediate, to news and musical facts.

In human relations, as well as in music and the contemplation of beauty, Lisl would plunge with the whole warmth of feeling of which she was capable, but not without critical discrimination. Her understanding and sympathy in this field, so greatly appreciated by her friends, are reflected in many of her letters. The following passage is an example which is extracted from a letter she wrote to Brahms, again from Florence, after a trip to the French Riviera with Clara Schumann whom the Herzogenbergs took with them to Italy.

We have been enjoying the company of Frau Schumann both at Nice and here, though we should have preferred to have been the cause of less trouble and more pleasure to her with all such beauty around. The dear one has ten years too many on her shoulders and she is losing the elasticity necessary for being happy in the face of local dirt, cheating and various other inconveniences. Also more time is required than her round-ticket – awful invention – permits her, in order to take in so much that is new, extremely fine though it is. It has happened a couple of times that we found her sitting on her stool before a Signorelli or a Verocchio looking very worried, rubbing her hands in fearful enthusiasm – she would not let herself be emotionally carried away or allow her soul, so capable of vibration, to stir. Everything however is won slowly and for certain things in life you have to serve your seven years. But then, if something touches her heart more quickly, how beautifully her grey eyes light up with that youthful strength we all love in this wonderful woman, and indeed one cannot begrudge her this pleasure seldom enjoyed. At San Francesco, in the company of our dear Hildebrand (whom you must absolutely meet and appreciate), she has always been happy and has enjoyed his splendid new productions.

You can well imagine how we have been talking about your

D Minor violin sonata and interrupting each other over it with mutual words of appreciation. Frau Schumann has played it with Amanda Röntgen, with whom she was very satisfied.

It was here, on this very same balcony, that in the autumn of 1883 Ethel, after her thwarted flirtation with Hildebrand, was received by the Brewsters for the first time. She writes in her memoirs:

Of the other couple of prospective friends, the Brewsters, I had learned a great deal from Lisl, her deep admiration for her extraordinary sister having been the theme of many letters. It appeared that these relations of hers were superhumans and that they lived in an Ivory Tower, knowing not a soul in Florence except the Hildebrands. This solitary frequentation was born of the fact that once, in pre-S. Francesco days, Hildebrand found the mysterious lady who lived on the floor below them sitting patiently on the stairs with a sprained ankle, whereupon he carried her into her apartment. Nothing short of that would have done it.

5
The American Expatriate

Henry James, once asked by a friend whether he knew Henry Bennet Brewster, replied: 'Why, I invented him.' And indeed 'H.B.' was for James the ideal American expatriate, urbane, cultivated and highly civilized, one of the most perfect examples of the cosmopolitan American type James had ever met. Yet the Brewster whom Ethel met in 1881 (when he was thirty-one) was in some significant respects a very different man – a complex nature, of which she saw only one side. This is how she described him and Julia in her memoirs:

My acquaintance with the man destined to become my greatest friend began, it is amusing to reflect, with a little aversion on my part, although his personality was delightful. Having for years had no intercourse with anyone save his wife, he was very shy – a shyness like that of a well-brought-up child, and which took the form of extreme simplicity, as though he were falling back on first principles to see him through. In one who was obviously what is called *une âme d'élite* this trait was of charming effect and in spite of it he managed to be witty, amusing and, when he felt like it, companionable. He seemed to have read all books, to have thought all thoughts; and last but not least was extremely good-looking, cleanshaven but for a moustache, a perfect nose and brow, brown eyes set curiously far apart, and fair fluffy hair. It was the face of a dreamer and yet of an acute observer, and his manner was the gentlest, kindest, most courteous manner imaginable. But alas! . . . as a thinker I found him detestable! Half American, half English, brought up in France, he was a passionate Latin, and the presence of an Anglo-maniac, loud in praise of the sportsman type of male, and what was worse, in love with Germany, goaded him into paradoxes and *boutades* it was impossible to listen to with equanimity: such as that Shakespeare was an agglomerate of bombast and bad writing; that Goethe's gush about Nature was positively indecent; that a work written without *de l'affectation* is coarse; that spontaneity is the death of inspiration, and so on.

His inveterate dislike of everything German was shared oddly enough by his wife... Julia was the strangest human being, if human she was, that I or anyone else ever came across, fascinating, enigmatic, unapproachable, with a Schiller-like profile and pale yellow hair; and though completely under the spell, I knew far less of her at the end of my two Italian winters than at the beginning. The home medium of this extraordinary couple was French – a fact that deeply impressed Lisl and me; they addressed each other in the second person plural, and though evidently the greatest of friends never uttered a word in the presence of others that could suggest anything as *bourgeois* as affection. Given their turn of mind it might be imagined that the matrimonial angle of the Herzogenbergs seemed to them comic, parochial and slightly redolent of Sauerkraut; moreover Julia spoke of Lisl as one might of some charming, very musical woman one had met somewhere and would be quite pleased to meet again if not pressed to fix the date. I was jealous for my friend, thinking of her uncritical worship of this gently critical sister, but the Brewsters were more amused at my enthusiasm than convinced that anyone who patted her husband's hand in public could be a relatively civilized human being...

To sum up, the Brewsters came under no known category; both of them stimulating, original talkers and quite ready to discuss their ethical scheme, including its application to domestic life, but of course only as a general thesis. On the other hand their friend Frau Hildebrand, human and natural to a fault, and who claimed for herself the wisdom of Sancho Panza, would privately maintain that all these fine theories must inevitably crumble at the first touch of the realities against which they so carefully fenced themselves in – a proposition I vehemently disputed, being quite carried off my feet by the impersonal magnificence and daring of their outlook. This readiness to cope with any and every turn of the wheel on your own terms went well with my views as to how life should be lived – but I had never dreamed of courage and love of adventure on such a scale as this.

[39]

H.B.'s English mother, Anna Bennet, belonged to an old Sussex family who had made their money in the wool trade. The main branch, to which they claimed to be related, were the Bennets of the earldom of Tankerville. Anna's brother Henry and his wife, with Anna and another sister, unmarried like herself, were in 1847 on a Continental tour which involved a visit to Paris, soon to be prolonged into a stay of several weeks. Their parents were dead, but brother and sisters still held together as a family in spite of the uneasiness caused by Henry's marital infidelities.

Dr Christopher Starr Brewster, H.B.'s father, a direct descendant of the Elder William Brewster of the *Mayflower*, was at that time a prosperous American dental surgeon in Paris. He is thought to have met Anna Bennet, his future wife and twenty years his junior, first in a professional capacity. A year later they were married, and appear to have been highly suited to each other despite the considerable difference in age. Both were pious but at the same time ambitious. The extant letters suggest that shortly after their marriage they were both courting the favours of Louis Napoleon Bonaparte, President of the French Republic, after the coup of 1848, and soon to become Emperor of the French.

These events took place at the height of Brewster's professional and social success in Paris. A portrait by a French painter shows him as impressive-looking, florid, blue-eyed and curly-haired. He had an unusual past of which we know only the outlines. The records tell us little until he settled in Paris under Louis Philippe:

Christopher Starr, one of Seabury Brewster's sons, was born at Norwich, Connecticut, in 1799. He graduated in medicine at Connecticut University in 1825 and after taking various postgraduate courses at other universities finally specialized in dental surgery which he practised for the next few years in the southern states. Then, about 1830, he left America to make his fortune in Europe, where he remained until his death in 1870, returning to New England only on occasional visits.

It is curious that he should have left the New World to earn his living. Movement across the Atlantic with this end in view has usually been in the opposite direction. His family had been settled in America for 200 years, his father was well-to-do, in the tanning business, and all his brothers were making their way in their

[40]

various occupations. Christopher, the youngest but one, decided – for whatever reason – not to persevere in what seemed a promising career in the States, and spent several years at St Petersburg, in the service of the Czar, Nicholas I, by whom he was made a knight of the Order of St Stanislas, as his death certificate attests. No letters survive from this period, so we are ignorant of why and exactly when he removed himself from Russia.

He must have settled in Paris in about 1840 and set up in practice as a dentist, having soon found out that his future success and likelihood of making more money lay in scientific dentistry, which the United States were the first nation to develop and introduce.

Dr Thomas W. Evans, Brewster's partner for some time, related in his memoirs many years later that until about the middle of the century 'those persons that made it their business to treat diseases of the teeth were ranked with barbers, cuppers and bleeders'. Tooth extractions were usually performed by 'mountebanks at street corners, or fakirs at fairs, where the howls of the victims were drowned by the beating of drums, the clash of cymbals, and the laughter and applause of the delighted and admiring crowd'.[1]

Once established in Paris, Brewster rented and furnished an apartment in rue St Dominique. He commissioned a fashionable French portraitist to paint his portrait, and had his crockery and silver embossed with the Brewster arms. Coming from the service of the Czars, he succeeded in becoming Louis Philippe's personal dentist; and through his position at court he expanded his circle of friends and began to entertain lavishly.

A little incongruously, he developed a close friendship with a German diplomat in Paris, Baron Stockhausen. However divergent their respective backgrounds, they both had a jovial temperament and were excellent raconteurs: Stockhausen was a master at embroidering on the fantastic adventures in Russia of his great-uncle Karl Friedrich Hieronymus Freiherr von Münchhausen.

It was in this aura of social and professional success that Anna Bennet joined Brewster as his wife. She was a woman of principle as well as of ambition, and though loving towards her husband and their children, she seems to have been of a thrifty disposition in running their domestic affairs. Nor would she hesitate to take firm action whenever she found it necessary, which was luckily not often. When a few years after their marriage Brewster ran into

[41]

psychological difficulties, Anna felt that his addiction to the bottle had grown excessive. So she extracted from him a written undertaking never to take spirits again.

For some years Brewster was the only dentist in Paris using the new American techniques and his success was unchallenged. Soon after the coup of 1848 he gained the favour of Charles Louis Napoleon, so his fortunes were not negatively affected by the fall of Louis Philippe. But in 1847, shortly before the coup, Brewster had taken what turned out to be an imprudent step, as far as his advantageous position at court was concerned. His practice had expanded so much that he felt in need of a partner. So he invited Dr Evans, a young dental surgeon in the United States, to come and join him in partnership. Dr Evans, who twenty years later was to become prominent as the rescuer of the Empress Eugénie when the empire collapsed, recorded in his memoirs: 'In November, 1847, I came to Paris with my wife, having accepted an invitation from Cyrus S. Brewster [sic], an American dentist of some repute then living in Paris, to associate myself with him professionally.'

At first all went well. Napoleon was soon to become President of the Republic. Brewster now had his assistant with him, whose business it was to attend to the lesser fry amongst the patients while he himself could devote his attention to the Prince. The latter appreciated Brewster, liked him personally, presented him with a silver dinner set heavily embossed in the style of the period and agreed to become godfather to Brewster's first-born son, who was christened 'Louis' after his own second name. Anna was thrilled.

At some point in this dental idyll, however, something went wrong. Evans succeeded in squeezing his senior partner out of the required weekly attendance on the Prince, who had very delicate teeth. He guardedly refers to this development in his memoirs:

My acquaintance with the Prince began very soon after I came to Paris. He had not long been at the Elysée when he sent a message to Dr Brewster, stating that he would like to have him to come to the palace, if convenient, as he had need of his services. It so happened, when the message came, that Dr Brewster was ill and unable to respond to the call himself. It fell to me, therefore, by good fortune, to take his place professionally . . .

[42]

He received me very kindly, without the least intimation that he had expected to see someone else... I found that a slight operation was necessary, which, when made, gave him great relief. From that time up to the day of his death, I visited him often – sometimes as often as twice a week.

The process, however, by which Brewster was ousted did not occur as abruptly as Evans relates. The letters which Anna wrote to her husband when absent on occasional visits to England suggest that a slow struggle took place against a background of intrigues. Brewster was evidently attempting to hold his own against these intrigues, while his younger partner was striving to replace him. This painful struggle went on for a few years, but in the end Evans won. Shortly after the final *coup d'état* of December 1851 he was invited by the Emperor to assume the duties of the only official dentist at the new court in the Tuileries. Brewster, on the other hand, disgusted by the court intrigues and the part Evans had played, gave up his Paris residence in 1852 and moved with his wife and children to Versailles, where he bought the old Hôtel des Princes de Poix at 52 avenue de St Cloud.

The new life at Versailles, though one of partial retirement, was far from being isolated, unpleasant or dull. Dr Brewster went on adding to his already moderately large fortune by continuing to practise in a more private though scarcely less lucrative capacity. Far from proving a social handicap, dentistry in its new form, when practised by a foreigner with special qualifications, was evidently regarded in France, though perhaps not in England, as an honourable profession. Admittedly money helped, but it was not socially inappropriate for Brewster's second son to marry the eldest daughter of a German aristocrat and for his only daughter to marry a Breton nobleman who had gambled away his fortune without losing his respectability.

The Brewsters led a social though not an ostentatious life at Versailles. Lady Chamberlain lived as their tenant on the second floor of their large house and their closest friends remained the Stockhausens in Paris who were destined to play an important part in the life of their son Henry.

Christopher Starr Brewster retained throughout his life a strong attachment to his home country and to his New England background. Although he spent most of his life in Europe, his links with

America and with the members of his family there remained close. He was highly conscious of being a direct descendant of William Brewster and greatly interested in his family history. In 1853, on one of his occasional visits home to the United States, he attended a meeting of a number of descendants of William Brewster which was held at Norwich, Connecticut, his own birthplace, chiefly to take measures for procuring a suitable written life of their eminent and revered ancestor. The following resolution was adopted:

> Whereas no Biography, containing even all the marked incidents of Elder Brewster's life, has ever been written; and, whereas additional facts have been lately brought to light, and faithful research may bring forth others, as materials for the purpose; therefore resolved, that
> James Brewster, Esq., New Haven, Conn., Chairman
> William Brewster, Esq., Rochester, New York
> Austin Brewster, Esq., Preston, Conn.
> Samuel Brewster, Esq., Syracuse, New York
> Sir Christopher S. Brewster, Paris, France
> (with ten other gentlemen named, of the connection) be a committee to devise a plan, and provide means as they may deem best for securing such Biographic History.

Following the adoption of these measures the Revd Ashbel Steel, A.M., assumed the task of making the necessary research and writing the biography. It was completed a few years later and published by J. B. Lippincott & Co. in 1857.

In the mid 1860s Christopher Starr retired from his practice but went on living at Versailles. From time to time he travelled, visiting England, Italy and Corsica, and whenever absent wrote letters to his sons in which he exhorted them towards thrift and economy. The letters disclose simplicity of mind and an affectionate disposition of heart, suitably invested with the fear of God his New England forebears had always cherished.

In one of these letters to his son Harry, after describing the 'shocking' behaviour of a drunkard at his hotel, he concludes as follows:

> Pursue diligently (as you do) your studies, but do not forget Holy God Almighty from whose blessings alone you can hope for either success or happiness.

Remember me in your prayers, and do not let amusement or cares allow your daily devotions to be neglected; that you may now be fortified and strengthened so that when in later life greater dangers and temptations beset you, then you may the more easily resist them, is the prayer of your affectionate father.

C.S.B.

The world of Elder William Brewster, where religion of a certain brand predominated, had scarcely altered. This descendant of his was still living in it 250 years later, and as long as he was alive the principles he had inherited had to be inculcated into his children. Nearly every surviving letter to his son Henry contains some such passage of advice on moral or devotional matters. Some of those he wrote from Menton, on the French Riviera, refer to his and his wife's attendance at Protestant mission services, and some speak of his repeatedly declining the pastor's requests that he himself lead the congregation in prayers. Several of the letters are also characterized by a kind of wry Yankee humour, usually applied to the changing weather, and by a somewhat whimsical partiality for all things American. During a fishing trip in England with his elder son Louis in the summer of 1866, for example, he writes that Louis and a friend caught three small fish apiece that day, but 'with a Yankee net and two Yankee Bays I think they would have caught 300 each time'. Likewise in a letter from Corsica dated 17 November 1867, he writes at some length about the beauties of a Corsican cave which a friend had taken him and Louis to see and then observes: '*Of course* we praised its beauty, but as I have seen some of those in America it did not astonish me.'

Anna, who shared her husband's piety as well as his practical approach to life, was more imaginative, more intellectually minded, and introduced an element of culture and sophistication into the family. To this her second-born child, Harry, was to prove particularly responsive.

At the outbreak of the Franco-Prussian War Christopher Starr felt far from optimistic about the French chances of success. On 17 July 1870 he wrote to the twenty-year-old Harry: 'I don't feel sure that Bismarck will not within ten days lodge at 52 Avenue St Cloud'; and within ten days his anticipation had virtually materialized. With the onset of the invading army he dispatched his wife, daughter and son

Louis to safety across the Channel and then returned to Versailles with Henry shortly before it was occupied by the Prussian forces on 20 September 1870.

Though doomed, Paris held out for a few more months. Bismarck was hoping that his blockade would induce the city to surrender from hunger without artillery having to be used. But the *francs-tireurs* – the guerrillas of those days – were proving a little more effective than they had been at first. Their sniping tactics made the immediate occupation of the city difficult without excessive destruction and therefore undesirable. So Bismarck gave orders to the Prussian Chief of Staff, Moltke, to establish the invading army's headquarters at Versailles and bide his time. Some of the Prussian generals complained that a more convenient locality in closer contact with the main lines of communication should have been chosen. Versailles was on the opposite side of Paris, but Bismarck insisted on it for reasons of prestige. A serious problem of billeting and administration soon developed. Not only Moltke's military staff had to be housed, but Bismarck's officials and a multitude of German princelings the Imperial Chancellor had succeeded in mustering to represent the budding German empire as a whole. Each of these had their own military and political staffs. So the crowd was soon to include not only Prince Charles and Prince Adalbert of Prussia, but also Prince Leopold of Bavaria – King Ludwig himself, much to Bismarck's disgust, preferred to stay at home in his fairy castles. There came also the Grand Dukes of Oldenburg, Saxe-Weimer, Baden and Mecklenburg-Schwerin, the Dukes of Holstein, Saxe-Meiningen, Saxe-Altenburg, Saxe-Coburg-Gotha and the Landgrave of Hesse. The Kingdom of Hanover was not represented for it had been abolished and its territory annexed by Prussia in 1866. The Stockhausens had at that time retired to Leipzig in bitter resentment against Bismarck. Other royalties, who had been invited to Versailles, were expected and the King of Prussia had given orders that the Trianon be reserved for them. In the Hôtel des Réservoirs a swarm of visitors on various missions, official and less official, kept coming and going – politicians, diplomatists, newspaper correspondents and even artists. Practically every building had to be requisitioned to provide quarters for the officers and men of the army.

Brewster and his son got back to Versailles not long before the Prussian army moved in. They found their house in the Avenue St

Cloud empty. Lady Chamberlain and her family had vacated the first floor and departed; the French family on the ground floor had also left. In the Brewsters' own apartment on the second floor there were only two old servants in addition to themselves. The house was big. Father and son felt uneasy about it, for they knew the Prussians' arrival was imminent. They tried to remove the more delicate furniture and pile it together in a small room, but there was too much else that should have been put away under lock and key. Food supplies were getting scarce and Christopher Starr was full of complaints.

There followed a few anxious days – troops marching in, horse-drawn army carts and guns rattling through the streets. On 28 September came the inevitable ring at the door, unusually prolonged. Old Dupont, the butler, came rushing up the stairs to announce that two Prussian officers wanted to see the proprietor. They were presently led in and old Brewster had to face them. He was fuming with rage and had no word of German. So Harry, who could speak the language, acted as interpreter.

The Prussian captain asked how many rooms the house contained and then curtly declared that the whole building would be requisitioned. After inspecting the house he announced that the officers would be billeted on the second floor. Dupont and his wife could cook for them. Brewster and his son could stay if they liked and occupy one single room. Other ranks would be accommodated on the other two floors and in the back-garden annexe. At this point Christopher Starr began storming with indignation, swearing and waving his American passport at them. He shouted at them in English that he was an American citizen, that Prussia was not at war with the United States and that therefore they had no right to requisition his property. Young Harry felt embarrassed and did his best to translate his father's outpourings in diplomatic language. The Prussian captain remained stiff, firm and polite. He stated that the requisitioning had nothing to do with nationality – they needed the house as long as the occupation lasted and they were going to have it.

The days that followed were both painful and difficult for Christopher Starr and his son, cooped up in an uncomfortable little room from which the sounds of Prussian occupation were all too evident. When women were brought in, the old Puritan could not help casting anathemas from behind the door which were greeted merely by

[47]

peals of laughter. Time and again he would burst indignantly in on the Prussian officers and poor Harry would have to use all his tact to soothe both his father and the angered officers in order to prevent their immediate eviction from their own house.

Death was soon to spare the old man further anguish. Years later H.B. described the circumstances in a letter to Ethel Smyth:

Have I ever told you about my father's death? I was with him alone at Versailles, and our house, like all others, was full of Prussians; sixteen officers, forty soldiers and twenty horses. My mother and the rest of them had been sent off to England with the jewelry and the moneybag (not so needless a precaution as your German friends would tell you; I saw a good many houses sacked; what is perfectly true is that the soldiers never did it without orders from their officers). Nothing could induce my father to leave his house, so I had to stay with him; he was seventy-one, and gouty, and hot-tempered, and he treated the Prussian officers outrageously. My time was spent in explaining 'spread eagle, and the land of the free and the home of the brave' to them, and soothing their feelings; they were on the point of arresting him time and again. But all the while I was burning inwardly with a sort of shame-fever at not being able to join my old schoolmates and enlist in the *francs-tireurs*. Often that seemed to me the higher duty; the commonwealth before the family. Then death came and struck my old father down and there was no one but me to hold his hand. That settled my opinion for life – first think of persons and then of ideas if you have the leisure; ideas can wait.

6

The Stockhausens

Perhaps the most brilliant period Paris experienced in the sphere of literature and the arts in the nineteenth century was during the reign of Louis-Philippe, the 1830s and '40s, a period of French political history far from sensational except, maybe, for the conquest of Algeria.

Compared with his predecessors the king was almost *bourgeois*, waddling about the capital, as he was seen doing, with his *embonpoint* and umbrella. Certainly he was no fool and he directed his country's affairs skilfully, like a business manager, eschewing foreign entanglements. So it proved a period of prosperity, with the industrial revolution forging ahead and the middle classes getting rich. It was also an age of relative stability, despite spells of local unrest. The growing *bourgeois* affluence brought in its wake leisure and generous patrons. Literature and the arts reacted against the humdrum materialism of life. In common with the intellectually minded 'children of the century' the students agitated at the university and in the streets for freedom and a less hypocritical way of life. The police charged and belaboured the demonstrators. Chopin, who had just come to settle in Paris, describes the situation in a letter to a friend:

> A huge crowd, not only of young people but of townsfolk, which had assembled in front of the Pantheon, made a rush for the right bank of the Seine. They came on like an avalanche, increasing their numbers with each street they passed through, until they reached the Pont Neuf where the mounted police began to break them up. Many were arrested, but all the same a huge body of people collected on the boulevards under my window, intending to join up with those coming from the other side of the town. The police could do nothing against the tightly packed throng; a company of infantry was brought up, hussars and mounted

[49]

gendarmes rode along the pavements, the national guard showed equal zeal in dispersing the inquisitive and murmuring populace. They seize and arrest free citizens – panic reigns – shops are closed – crowds gather at every corner of the boulevards – whistles are blown – reinforcements are rushed up – there are sightseers at every window (as there used to be at home on festive days). This went on from eleven in the morning until eleven at night. I was looking forward to seeing something happen, but it all came to an end at about eleven with their singing the 'Marseillaise' in a vast chorus.[1]

This was the Paris in which Bodo Freiherr von Stockhausen and Christopher Starr Brewster met and befriended each other. Stockhausen belonged to an old feudal family of Hanover and owned a vast estate near Göttingen. The medieval castle of his forebears, dating back to the twelfth century, was in ruins – only a tower remained standing; it was uninhabitable. He derived a sufficient income, however, from his estates to enable him to live at court in a manner appropriate to his social rank, as his parents had done. Highly accomplished, intelligent, lively and with a good sense of humour, he was chosen when still a young man to represent his country in Paris where he was sent in 1831 by the Hanovarian viceroy and accredited as minister plenipotentiary to the new King of the French, Louis Philippe.

Stockhausen spoke French as a Frenchman, having been brought up in the eighteenth-century tradition of the German aristocracy where French was the dominant language. Consequently he moved with ease in the Parisian high society leading the life of a diplomat and *un homme du monde*. Keenly interested in music, he was often to be seen in circles frequented by musicians as well as by lovers of music such as the Rothschilds.

Early in the 1830s a friendship developed between him and Chopin, who had recently settled in Paris and was virtually unknown. Stockhausen was one of the very first to notice the young Pole's talent and helped him become more generally recognized. He was also at pains to find him pupils who could pay generously for their lessons, for at that time Chopin was extremely hard up. The baron would invite him to dinner parties at which he would introduce him to members of the choicest Parisian society and urge

[50]

him to play the piano before them. From his early days in Paris onwards we find Stockhausen bracketed with the Rothschilds as the young composer's most devoted patron. In 1836 Chopin dedicated to him his Ballade in G minor, the first of the four he composed. The second was dedicated to Schumann.

A year later Stockhausen married a remarkable young girl, Clothilde, who had been living in Vienna for some years with her parents, Count and Countess Baudissin. She was both handsome and intellectually wideawake, and was soon to play a prominent part in those circles of Parisian society which were sensitive to music. The Baudissins were an old Huguenot family who had emigrated from France to the Rhineland in the seventeenth century and thence to Schleswig in the days when that province of Germany was still part of Denmark. She was reputed to have led a merry life in Vienna when barely grown-up. Indeed she had already written a memoir, an account of her life in that city, which was published years later. *The Memoirs of Countess C*, as the little book was entitled, not only intrigued her friends and relations but was also regarded by them as a most shocking account of Viennese society. Her nephew, Prince Bülow, later the German Imperial Chancellor, used to travel about with a copy of it. Shocking it may have been in those days, but it seems now quite an innocuous and rather touching little volume.

In addition to being bilingual in French and German, Clothilde could also speak English and Russian. She spent a number of years collecting and translating Russian fairy stories. Her appearance on the scene added a new dimension to Stockhausen's life in Paris; she was an excellent hostess, with striking looks and witty conversation.

In their eighteenth-century house in rue de Verneuil the Stockhausens would receive their friend Chopin. Well-dressed and of slight build, with blue eyes, fair hair and delicate looks, he was often to be seen among the habitués of Madame Stockhausen's salon – visitors such as Liszt, Comtesse Marie d'Agoult, Baroness Rothschild, Comte and Comtesse de Perthuis – but he came also to teach the piano. By 1845 Bodo and Clothilde had come to the conclusion that their four-year-old daughter, Julia, was musically so gifted that piano lessons from Chopin, by then well-known and highly successful, would be fully warranted as part of her education. So from that time until about the end of his life four years later Chopin taught Julia the piano. The lessons were far from cheap, about £15 an hour, but, so the Stockhausens felt, well worth the expense. They left an indelible mark on Julia's mind.

Not that Chopin was treated as an ordinary piano teacher, who in those days was apt to be ranked, as other teachers were, with servants and shop assistants and therefore let into the house by the back door and paid by the butler or a servant in charge of the household. Chopin was quite a different matter. His manners and general air of distinction were such as to render him acceptable to Parisian society on an equal footing. So when he called in the capacity of a teacher he would be received with the utmost tact and ushered straight into the drawing-room. The Stockhausens as well as the Rothschilds would leave the cash owed for the lesson in an envelope discreetly placed on the chimneypiece, peeping from behind a vase or a candlestick, for the musician to collect unobtrusively before leaving. It would be a mistake, however, to assume that Chopin went out of his way to curry favour with the conventional society from which he derived his income, though he recognized the importance of social contacts. His views on this matter were succinctly expressed in a letter to a friend about a year after his arrival in Paris:

> . . . I have found my way into the very best society; I have my place among ambassadors, princes, ministers – I don't know by what miracle it has come about for I have not pushed myself forward. But today all that sort of thing is indispensable to me; those circles are supposed to be the fountainhead of good taste. You at once have more talent if you have been heard at the English or Austrian embassies; you at once play better if Princess Vaudemont has patronized you. I can't write 'patronizes', for the poor old thing died a week ago. I have five lessons to give today . . . You will imagine that I am making a fortune – but my cabriolet and white gloves cost more than that, and without them I should not have *bon ton*. I am all for the Carlists, I hate their Louis-Philippe crowd; I'm a revolutionary myself so I care nothing for money, only for friendship, which I entreat you to give me.[2]

The other side of his nature, the unconventional, the romantic, individualistic facet, or 'revolutionary' as he terms it himself, was to find a happy reflection in the mirror of George Sand's world where the fastidious gentleman of society and the rebel could meet

[52]

and blend. A vivid picture of the peaceful domestic life Chopin and George Sand were leading during their period of cohabitation is given in a letter from Joseph Filtsch to his parents in Hungary. Joseph was the brother of the Hungarian pianist Karl Filtsch, a pupil of Chopin. In another letter he describes his brother's success with the Parisian society of that time. One day Stockhausen had the opportunity of hearing Karl Filtsch play the piano part of Chopin's concerto which the young pupil had been practising.

Baron Stockhausen enjoyed the concerto so much that when we were all at Count Apponyi's that same evening he pressed us to give the Count an opportunity of hearing it. Chopin came in shortly afterwards and had to promise that the concerto would be played at his house on Monday during Karl's lesson. And so the Count and Countess, their son and daughter-in-law, their daughter, the ambassadors of Saxony and Hanover, Baroness Rothschild, the great Meyerbeer, etc. came to hear the concerto. Karl played alternately like an angel and like a devil. Everyone was delighted, dear Chopin touched and flattered, myself happy, and Karl dignified and serene. The most striking moment was when Meyerbeer took him into his arms; this was more impressive than all the embraces of ladies, ambassadors, etc. who gazed wide-eyed at each other and flung themselves on Karl. M. Rothschild adores him and tries to win him away from our ambassador. I need hardly say that the Rothschild ladies have invited us. . .[3]

By the early 1840s Chopin was spending much of his time in the country with George Sand at Nohant, her château. It was a delightful house in an attractive locality. Life there was pleasant, there was privacy or company to suit the mood. Chopin could retire to his rooms and work whenever he liked. Often he and Sand would go for long walks into the country, but he had still to return to Paris at intervals to give piano lessons – both to produce the income he needed and to keep up his contacts in society. He writes to Sand, impatient for her to join him:

So you have finished your tour of inspection and the business of the outhouses has tired you. For God's sake husband your strength for the journey and bring us your lovely Nohant

[53]

weather, for we are having rain here. Nevertheless I hired a carriage yesterday, after waiting until three o'clock for it to clear up, and I went to see the Rothschilds and the Stockhausens; I am not the worse for it.[4]

Late in the afternoon of a cold winter day – it was Wednesday 23 December 1845 – Chopin called on the Stockhausens in rue de Verneuil, expecting to find in the drawing-room the usual group of guests attending Madame Stockhausen's salon. Instead he found her alone with a big Christmas tree in the centre of the room, busy decorating it and arranging presents around it and on nearby tables. She received him warmly, informally, with a note of apology. She was busy, she explained, preparing a Christmas party for the children and their friends to be held the following day. They were not in the habit of having it in the nursery, it was an occasion for the whole family to join in. By then Clothilde had had another child, a son called Ernst. To Chopin the Christmas tree was familiar enough, though it was practically unknown in the west of Europe at that time. Both the tree and the preparations for the event reminded him of home. The next day he wrote to his family in Warsaw:

The dear creature [George Sand] is unwell. Today is Christmas Eve, the feast of Our Lady. They take no notice of it here. As usual they have their dinner at six, seven or eight and it is only in a few foreign households that they keep up the old custom. For example Mme Stockhausen did not dine yesterday with the Perthuises (the lady to whom I dedicated my B minor Sonata) as she was busy with the arrangements for today's children's party. All the Protestant households keep Christmas Eve, but the ordinary Parisian feels no difference between today and yesterday. . .[5]

In the autumn of that year Chopin had completed his Barcarolle in F major, Op. 60, on which he had been working throughout the summer at Nohant and which he now dedicated to Clothilde Stockhausen in token of appreciation and friendship.

7
The Early Years

The friendship between Bodo von Stockhausen and Christopher Starr Brewster continued through the years on the basis of warm cordiality, so that Harry, Christopher's second son who was born in 1850, spent his childhood in close contact with the Stockhausen family where he was not only welcome but also greatly cherished. Clothilde von Stockhausen was his godmother. Brought up in the pious atmosphere of his father's home, he developed, as a small child, a religious fervour which could not only attract attention but also arouse amusement. There was, for instance, the story of the Zouaves which the author's Aunt Cloto, H.B.'s daughter, used to tell:

> 'Would you believe it,' Baroness Stockhausen, known to her friends more for her biting wit than for spurts of enthusiasm, broke in upon them one day, 'he goes out all alone to find the Imperial Band of the Zouaves and before the band master can get them to strike up a march for the patriotic entertainment of the passers-by, up has jumped little Harry on one of the great drums of the bandstand and standing erect has at once riveted the attention of the guards with the fiery outflow of his sermon on the fear of God and the danger of everlasting fire and brimstone in Hell. He has already made more than one convert to puritanism!' It would perhaps be comic, she went on to explain, if a grown-up were to tackle the Zouaves on the subject of the kind at such a juncture and in such a manner, but for a little boy of eight to climb onto a drum, stand up and preach with success, well, it was not only comic, it was wonderful.

The stance changed profoundly in the following years, influenced by Harry's childhood friend, Julia von Stockhausen.

Bodo's two daughters were both remarkable, but very different in disposition and temperament. Julia, who was five years older, had sharper features, a sharpness which became accentuated as years

[55]

went by, whereas Lisl had the mellower, blond looks which as a grown-up girl stirred, among others, the heart of her cousin Prince Bülow.[1] Both sisters were musical and played the piano extremely well. Julia had her lessons from Chopin, but her interests developed more in the direction of philosophy and literature, whereas for Lisl music became the dominant theme of her life.

Harry was a frequent visitor to the Stockhausens' house in Paris, and the affinity of mind he and Julia shared set them on terms of close friendship. For years to come he would always call her his 'godsister'. As she was seven years older, it was her influence which in those days prevailed. Under it his missionary zeal gave way to a very different outlook on all religious matters. Their *amitié amoureuse* went on happily for some years, but a couple of years before 1866, when Hanover was annexed by Prussia, Bodo von Stockhausen was transferred to Vienna as his country's minister accredited to the Austrian imperial court, and with him went his family.

In the years that followed Harry went to the Lycée, from which he emerged well-read and perfectly bilingual. At home he was exposed to the Anglo-American, neo-Calvinist and pious elements of the Brewsters' family life, an extension of New England in the large house at Versailles they often privately referred to as 'The Hole'. The other current of influence, which affected him increasingly, came from the eclectic, free-thinking world of nineteenth-century France reflected in the literature of the period. His Lycée schooling provided him with a fair knowledge of Graeco-Roman culture as well as of seventeenth- and eighteenth-century classics and the rationalist philosophy of those times. This formed, however, only the basis for absorbing the works of European writers and philosophers, for which he had an unbounded appetite. His letters and essays of the period are full of extensive cross-references and reveal the extent to which this current of influence was affecting his whole development and gradually shaping the man Henry James was to call the 'Gallo-American'. Although one of the results was a professed atheism, partly as a reaction against the excessively narrow piety of his upbringing, there remained a religious substratum which endured throughout his life and which was in keeping with his inmost nature.

The religious crisis came in his fifteenth year and affected him so deeply that it was probably the main cause of the partial deafness which afflicted him at that time for some months. 'When I was fourteen,' he wrote to Ethel Smyth many years later, 'I went very nearly stone deaf: people had to shout in my ears. And I believe it was due to great anxiety and trouble because I had lost my religion. I had been very intense on the subject for four years and had (heaven help me) converted Zouaves to Protestantism.' But harrowing as the experience must have been, there emerged within two years a perfectly balanced, self-composed, relaxed and in every sense normal young man who turned to face life with a fair amount of enthusiasm as well as a touch of irony, humour and Gallic rationalism. In disposition he was gentle, affable and kind-hearted, while physically he had grown into an exceptionally good-looking young man. Somewhat above medium height, he was well-built with regular, harmonious features, large brown eyes set far apart, a perfect nose, slightly aquiline, and very blond wavy hair. Throughout his life his friends and acquaintances were frequently to comment, both in conversation and in writing, on his striking good looks.

The letters he wrote at that time show already a remarkable aptitude for rational thinking as well as an intellectual approach to life. This free thinking, partially attributable to his Lycée schooling, partially to contact with his French friends, prevailed over the Protestant piety and simplicity of his parental home. Nevertheless he remained touchingly devoted and affectionate to both his father and mother. At the same time there can be no doubt that he greatly benefited from the Anglo-American culture in which he was brought up at home, where the language of everyday and the books about the house remained English. In their childhood he and his brother were regaled with books of adventure for boys, bound in those typical early and mid-Victorian bindings, solid and slightly embossed. They still bear the dates of donation scribbled in pencil or ink and ranging from 1856 and 1864, with the signatures of the donors – their father, mother, uncle Seabury, uncle Henry and other members of the family; books written by Captain Marryat, James Fenimore Cooper, Defoe and others. Soon Harry was fed with more serious literature, including not only the principal English classics from Shakespeare to his own days (with Byron figuring prominently), but particularly also American authors. Considerable attention, as the surviving papers in his handwriting show, was given to Bancroft's *History of the United States* and other works by American historians including Hildreth, Prescott and Motley. Nor were the poets and other American prose writers neglected such as Charles Brookden Brown, Crevecoeur, Alexander Hamilton, Frenan, Edgar Allan Poe, Longfellow, Hawthorne, Bryant, Emerson and James Lowell; even Herman Melville who was scarcely known at that time figured on his reading list. The essays in which he discusses these authors with considerable mental maturity for a boy of his age were probably written not for the Lycée, where Anglo-American literature scarcely came into consideration, but for a literary club which he, his friend Basil Chamberlain and other English-speaking boys had founded for the purpose of debate. No ordinary French boy at the Lycée had the opportunity of a double education such as Harry was able to have, just as no boy would have had it at any comparable school in England or America. In this respect he was indeed lucky.

At the Hôtel des Princes de Poix Lady Chamberlain had two grandsons living permanently with her on the first floor, Basil Hall Chamberlain and Houston Stewart Chamberlain, sons by a second marriage of her son Rear-Admiral William Chamberlain, whose wife had died when the two boys were still very small children. Basil, being of the same age, became a close companion and friend of Harry during their years at school. Like him he attended the Lycée. His brother Houston was five years his junior and therefore too young to take an intimate part in their lives. A few years later, after the Franco-Prussian War, both brothers seem to have drifted out of Harry's life. Basil settled in Japan where he was appointed professor at the Imperial University of Tokyo, while Houston settled in Germany where he became naturalized and married twice, the second time to Wagner's only daughter, Eva. He was to become notorious for a book he wrote entitled *Foundations of the Nineteenth Century*, wherein he contrived to prove the pre-eminence of the Aryan race with arguments which were years later used by the National Socialists to support their racial theories.

During the years shared at Versailles, however, Harry and Basil were constantly together, with Houston hanging on in the background – as did Kate, Harry's little sister. In addition to the literary club they organized theatricals which were performed in Lady Chamberlain's large drawing-room, or in the Brewster drawing-room immediately above, whenever Christopher Starr was away. Harry and Basil had friends and relations of their own age in

England and America who came to stay from time to time, and so of course had Louis, though he led a different life, being older and having other, mainly non-intellectual interests.

Harry also had a number of French friends, mostly schoolmates, who played an increasingly important part in his life at that time. Amongst these was Georges du Buisson, who became Harry's closest friend during the earliest years of his manhood and whose personality was to constitute, in the shaping of his mind, one of the most important currents of influence. Georges lived at Versailles with his mother, who also owned a country house at Claix, near Grenoble, where they both repaired during holidays, sometimes with Harry as a guest.

It was at the beginning of 1867 that Anna Brewster began seriously to consider the future of her second and favourite son. Through relations and friends in England, she took some initial steps for Harry to enter Oxford University, intending him to study there for three years reading Law or English Literature, then, after taking his degree, to prepare for the bar or a literary career. In fact Harry let himself be persuaded to go to Oxford early in 1867, where he succeeded in passing an entrance examination to Brasenose College. But before starting his university studies it was imperative, his mother felt, that he should finish his Lycée schooling satisfactorily and pass the final examination, the so-called *baccalauréat*. He was a bright boy, but had neglected certain subjects at school, particularly chemistry and natural history. She was of the opinion that some intensive coaching would help, but not in France where there were too many distractions, not all of them moral. Where better could he be sent to stay than with his godparents, the Stockhausens, at Dresden? They were now leading a private life in that city; Hanover's annexation by Prussia had brought about the old baron's retirement from diplomacy. True, Harry had not seen them for several years, but the Stockhausens regarded him as a nephew, almost a son. There he would not only learn German properly, but would also be coached by one or two tutors, under his godmother's supervision, in those very subjects in which he was weakest.

On 18 July 1867 Anna wrote to Clothilde von Stockhausen proposing this plan and adding that nowhere could there be a more ideally suited 'private family where a boy with a man's head on his shoulders would have proper instruction, protecting care, and plenty

[59]

of good solid food, above all where a right religious influence would be exercised'. Clothilde was delighted to accept. So in October of that year, shortly before his seventeenth birthday, Harry was dispatched to Dresden with the blessings of his devout and affectionate parents. But what happened there was perhaps not quite in accordance with Anna's wishes.

Shortly after his arrival he wrote to his friend Georges du Buisson as follows:

I leave for Germany, after many stirring vicissitudes I arrive at Dresden and fall in the bosom of a family... ah, my dear friend, what a family! A mother who has devoted her life to the upbringing of her two daughters, and who has achieved it against all accepted opinions and all the prejudices of society. At any rate from her hands have emerged two young girls who to begin with are as beautiful as the light of day; then, who without having ever learnt anything, know everything, have reasoned and reflected over everything, and, what's much rarer, have remained so natural, so simple, that I was bowled over. Imagine to yourself this mixture: a philosopher, a poet and a young girl who though perfectly sceptic is nonetheless the purest, the chastest I have ever seen – I shouldn't say seen, but dreamt of.

Dresden, 25 November 1867. Ten o'clock in the evening, on the left bank of the Elbe. The sky is overcast. The air is mild for the season. A smartly dressed young man is walking at a leisurely pace under the gas-lit lime trees, smoking a cigar and watching the people. He reaches the glass door of a nightclub by the river, Linkisches Bad, and enters with the ease of an habitué, though it is only the second time that he has come to this *Local* as the Germans call it. Men sit drinking beer with women of a doubtful background at tables which are placed mostly along the walls; there are some, too, in the recesses of the room where the ceiling is held up by pillars. A few people are drinking Rhine wine. The air is hot and laden with smoke. There are paraffin lamps on each table. The young man stands hesitantly at the edge of the large hall. In the middle couples are dancing to the tune of a Viennese waltz played on a set of string instruments and a piano placed on a slightly raised platform. He listens to the music which spins away in strains at times gay, at times mournful, and he looks across the floor at the girls who are lounging on the other side between the pillars, waiting – the *grisettes*, as he calls them in his French parlance – accommodating girls who, after a busy day laundering, sewing, or selling in a shop, are glad to be picked up and know how to put out the lamp at the right moment. There is one, on the other side of the room, who keeps eyeing him from across the floor and whose features intrigue him. She is not pretty, so he turns away. But soon he looks round at her again. . . he can't help it, there is something about her dark hair, white skin and sad eyes that draws him on. In the end he crosses the hall and accosts her. She laughs triumphantly as they stroll along arm in arm and sit down at a table. They drink, smoke and dance once or twice, then they leave the room and walk out into the street. It is late. The gas lamps have been turned down to a mere flicker. They cross the bridge and she takes him to her rooms on the fourth floor of a dim-looking building. They are simple, poor rooms but not sordid, the bed and sheets are scrupulously clean. The paraffin lamp is on the night-table ready to be put out. They lie naked, wrapped in each other's arms under the blankets, she extends her arm and turns the flame down which flickers out. But . . . he fails to be stirred by the contact of her body close against his, he remains *triste*, as the French more delicately say. He lights the lamp and looks at her again, puts it out, kisses her, strikes her all over, and hugs her again and again. No use, there is definitely something the matter. He lights the lamp again and this time lifts it up right over her, uncovers her completely and, pushing away her long dark hair which has been covering part of her face, examines every feature, then every fold of her limbs. He sighs and puts out the light again. He tries to comfort her with caresses, but she wants more. No, absolutely no use, he remains frigid. This has never happened to him before, he says to himself, though he is only seventeen and his experience is not unlimited. After a few more minutes he can't stand it any longer; he gets up precipitately, clutches his clothes and runs out of the room.

'C'était un roman!' Harry wrote to his friend Georges du Buisson a few days later. He had been unable to dispel his *tristesse* by the usual remedy, by lighting the lamp, he explains, by looking again and feasting his eyes, for his impotence was caused, he suddenly realized before rushing from the room, by his until then subconscious awareness of the girl's close resemblance to Rose. In fact the *éteigneuse* had turned out to be the very image of Rose.

[61]

Ah Rose, poor Rose! Do you remember that English girl whom you may have seen staying with us at Versailles, the consumptive girl my mother has been trying to cure for the last four years, whom I have always admired and loved like a sister, and who at that very minute was dying or dead? I left those rooms quite ill and had a fever all night. It was like having a dead girl in one's arms – Victor Hugo would say death itself. Well, thank God it's all over, anyhow an interesting psychological experience.

We do not know whether Harry went back to the Linkisches Bad. His mind was filled with increasing admiration for the Stockhausen girls, but however emotionally drawn to Julia he may have already been, this would not have stood in the way of little adventures of the kind that started on the banks of the Elbe and came to an end a few hours later. A French youth of his age – and indeed under du Buisson's influence Harry was very French at that time – had every right, if not duty, to establish his male prerogatives. Between exercising these and unlimited admiration for the chastity and purity of a girl, there was no inconsistency, and as time went on Harry was to prove far from intemperate.

For her part, Anna Brewster thought her son was living in an environment where the 'right religious influence' was being exerted, and must have known little or nothing about the atheism of the elder Stockhausen girl. Whatever Harry's father might have said if he had known – he would have probably regarded his son's way of life as outrageously un-American – Georges du Buisson, for one, must have approved. In a rakish frame of mind he would write to Harry:

> Your mother is glad that you are in Germany, she thinks that you will turn into a pipe, or a cigar, or a glass of beer. Lawson wants you to write to him very soon and let him know how your hair grows and if you have caught the clap (these are his own words, what a strange fellow!). Sixtine is sick on account of your departure, and is about to have a spider-web instead of a cunt, but she hopes you will remove it when you return. . .

And yet *au fond* there is a curious ambivalence about these two young men. Their correspondence, which discloses sentiments of almost passionate friendship for each other, is carried on in a highly intellectual tone, though with greater earnestness on the part of

[62]

du Buisson. On Harry's side there is often a touch of humour, if not flippancy, as well as youthful boastfulness. At one point Georges reproaches him for being too light-hearted and warns him against debauchery. Harry protests in a manner typical of a certain facet of his nature. Whether you walk out of a cathedral or a brothel, he says, it is the inner detachment with which you do so that keeps your soul untouched. He adds that anyhow the life he is leading is far from being as promiscuous as his friend is assuming.

When Harry arrived in Dresden he stayed with the Stockhausens for only a few days, after which he put up as a lodger with his tutors, Herr and Frau Meinardus. The reasons for this removal, which can have hardly been in accordance with Anna Brewster's plans, are unknown, for there is no explanation to be found in his letters, but one may suppose that they were of a practical nature – to enable him to study better under his tutors' direct supervision. Besides, he himself may have preferred this arrangement. Since his tutors were paid by him, he may have felt freer to come and go as he pleased, free to go out in the evening and come back late without explanation, than if he had stayed on as his godmother's guest.

In a letter to Georges, Harry describes the pattern of his daily life:

My life here flows on as gently as possible. I get up at half past seven in the morning; I have breakfast and a German lesson with Mrs Meinardus; then a lesson in harmony (*harmony*, do you grasp it?) from my cousin Stockhausen (Ernst) who is very good at it, or a lesson in Greek and Latin languages and literature from a professor by the name of Tancovius; then I go out to smoke a cigar on the banks of the Elbe or to a brasserie; I return for luncheon at 2 p.m. Then I work until 6.30, when it is time for the theatre from which I emerge at 9 o'clock. I dine and then until two in the morning I read Goethe, Lessing and Spinoza. And so on. When I don't go to the theatre I spend the evening at my godmother's house where I have tea with her two daughters whose praise I give up attempting to sing. To introduce some variety to my pleasures I am constantly having lessons in mathematics, physics and chemistry; quite often I drink punch with Stockhausen and one or two German females. You see, it's only you I am in a position to miss.

He goes to picture galleries, concerts and other performances. He

[63]

hardly seems short of pocket money, a good proportion of which he spends on buying books: Goethe, thirty volumes; *Histoire Générale de l'Allemagne*, by the Jesuit Father Barré, a set of twenty-five volumes which formerly belonged to the defunct King of Saxony, so Harry was told; *Ancient History* by Rollin, thirteen volumes; the whole lot being handsomely bound in leather. He mentions that the price turned out to be a real bargain.

He was busy observing, noting and drawing conclusions. After a few months, at the request of Georges, he sent a long account of life in Germany. This very long letter (see Appendix) is remarkable for the detailed description Harry gives of the customs and way of life of the different social classes, including the students. Of course there were many things Harry didn't see or experience, so the picture is in a way limited and somewhat one-sided, but nonetheless extremely vivid. The first page of the letter with its date is missing, and so is the envelope with the post mark, but one can deduce that it was written early in 1868.

It is hard to tell how far, after a separation of six years, the encounter between Harry and Julia evolved towards the binding relationship it was destined to become and how deep this mutual rediscovery went during the months of that winter. There was certainly no overt declaration, for Harry was still extremely young. But it did bring about a change in his plans for the future. He had gone to Germany on this visit having more or less promised his mother to follow her wishes – prepare himself for the *baccalauréat* and enter Oxford University immediately after.

Very soon, however, his letters to Georges disclose a modification in his intentions. We find that his *baccalauréat* is only vaguely aimed at, Oxford even more vaguely. His plans for life have taken a turning away from such time-serving aims. 'I have changed the objective of my studies,' he writes only a few weeks after his arrival in Dresden. 'The *bachot* stands no longer in the immediate foreground; what I now want to cultivate is ... my aesthetic sense.' This somewhat naive statement is not as priggish as it sounds when looked at in the light of his extreme youth and of what followed, no doubt under the influence of Julia – for better or worse. But much of what he says in this letter to his friend is genuinely his own.

My only objective is happiness [he goes on], but I ask myself

[64]

whether the way followed by the majority of men leads to it; from experience my answer is *no*. What does the beaten track consist of? Is it to complete your secondary education, to pass your *bachot*, then to enter into business, or study law or something similar? Once you have got there what do you do next? You certainly don't take full advantage of all these accomplishments in order to enjoy life during its short spell, but on the contrary, you work towards stultification and towards totally stupefying yourself in the struggle to achieve a post or a position in life.

Harry then proceeds in this long letter to enlarge on the futility of struggling to achieve a position, such as that of a university professor with a salary, a politician, an eminent lawyer, a Lord Chancellor or a station master. He adds:

I for one understand only that position where man feels himself to be above all positions, where he regards life as a bad joke and where his duty is to reject the 'bad' and retain only the joke, or rather — let me use a metaphor — it is like being at an outdoor night celebration at Versailles where the wisest thing to do is not to struggle in the crowd to reach the first row — for it is there that the lanterns stink and the smoke gets at your throat — but to climb one of the trees behind, to choose a good branch and look around at everything with ease. True, one might slip and fall, but what do you expect, in order to obtain everything one must risk everything.

He then says that what matters to him most is to improve his mind by closer intercourse with the works of great men.

This is what I am striving to do at present by studying Homer, Goethe, Shakespeare and Spinoza. Before coming here I didn't enjoy much in the field of painting; now, as the result of contemplating the works of art of all the schools of painting represented in the Dresden Gallery, I have come to appreciate this art with genuine love, however little I know about it as yet; for now I enjoy a fine picture almost as much as a good poem. In order to understand music better, which I have always loved by natural inclination, I am studying harmony. By frequently going to the opera I am learning to appreciate composers who are neglected

[65]

in Paris such as Gluck, Cherubini, Wagner and others. The excellent concerts I am able to attend are initiating me little by little into the various styles of Beethoven, Haydn, Schubert and many others.

You can see that by following this programme the *bachot* is receiving only half my attention; it is the half which includes Greek and Latin literature, science and history which I enjoy studying. As for Latin rhetoric, geography and everything to do with the technique of getting through the *bachot*, all this tends to be neglected. If absolutely necessary I shall apply myself to it later.

His mother, meanwhile, was reminding him of the purpose of his studies and the pursuit of a career. This he found both irksome and awkward, and so he resolved, before the end of the year, to write to her forthrightly about his feelings and intentions. The letter – in English, of course, and not in French, the language in which he always wrote to Georges – is the earliest to his mother that has survived. It is undated, but on the folder in which it has been kept we find written in Harry's writing: 'Letter to my mother from Dresden 1867'.

After referring to his life in Dresden and to his studies there, he plunges straight into the matter:

Life is short and time flies: no one doubts this. Now we have broached several times the bar question, and if I mistake not, the case stands as follows. You wish me to go to Oxford, to study for honours, for the sake of the éclat which they give; also to do there two years of law and finally be called to the bar after which I shall be free either to devote myself exclusively to law or to quit and become an author. The plan is very clear, quite reasonable and seems promising. Now try to put yourself *mon point de vue* without preformed opinions. I find myself at seventeen in the following position.

He goes on to explain how one is apt to absorb the prejudices or opinions of the world in the environment in which one lives, and how the only way by which it is possible to distinguish between truth and prejudice is to detach oneself from every belief and opinion and 'only admit as true those which the closest analysis and clearest evidence justify'.

After detailed examination of the steps his mother would have him

[66]

pass – distinction at Oxford, position at the bar, reputation or glory, crowned by the consciousness of having been 'useful to mankind', he dismisses them all as 'foolish'. Only 'le vrai, le beau et le bien' are to be sought after. His aim is to be like Socrates, Shakespeare, Descartes, Spinoza and Goethe. 'Such a one I will be,' he optimistically says, adding:

> Do not think me arrogant: I know perfectly well my own worth and my own capacity. I am born a poet and a philosopher, and am just as incapable of becoming a man of action as I am fitted to be one of thought; my field is purely speculative and it is in this sense that I said I would be a spectator not an actor in life. If you consider this kind of spectatorship inferior to the petty struggles and ambitions of the herd, I am sorry, but you will never make a sow's ear out of a silken purse.

Harry then spells out his proposal, which is to abandon the course his mother is urging upon him, to pursue the study of philosophy, to acquire the habit of long and serious meditation – 'a life to be passed in hard and obscure labour, in the search of truth and in the contemplation of the Beautiful and the Right. . . If a man in pursuit so noble as that of ennobling himself voluntarily renounces the world, fame, fortune, and all the joys of the crowd, who shall dare to condemn that man?'. . .

> You perhaps don't know what it is to feel oneself between life and death, attached to the former by two bonds only held by one person. The first bond is yourself, your love for me, and the immense unspeakable gratitude of a son for a mother who is devotion itself. The second bond is the aim in life which I have exposed in this letter and the success of which may depend on decision: may this decision then be calm and matured.
> Ever your affectionate son,
>
> HENRY BREWSTER

If we compare the exalted style, earnest content and moral posture of this letter with the somewhat lighthearted and often bantering flourish of most of what he was writing to Georges at about the same time, there appears to be a contradiction. But the basic gist of Harry's feelings are the same. Certainly he had not given up the world and its pleasures to the extent he was eager that his mother

[67]

should believe. Yet his motives in wishing to be allowed to give up the plans she had laid down for him were not so that he could lead an idle life, but so that he could pursue an inner spiritual activity of the mind which he felt was in keeping with his nature. Which is what, little by little, he achieved, though later in life he would have laughed at his youthful outpouring of conviction. At least he knew, even at that early age, exactly what he wanted.

To some extent Julia may have been at the back of it, and Anna must have felt and resented her influence: it would account for the touch of hostility she developed against her from then onwards. But whatever the extent of Julia's influence in so short a time – Harry was no doubt seeing her frequently – her views found an echo in his natural disposition. If she already had time to sow some seeds, they were falling on the right soil. The two of them developed – for the next few years, after his departure from Germany, exclusively by correspondence – a spirit of detachment from the external things of the world. This was quite in keeping with the plan set forth in Harry's letter to his mother. He and Julia rationalized their attitude in a sustained dialogue of a highly intellectual character dealing with life through the dialectics of philosophy. And indeed this inner detachment was to permeate Harry's thinking throughout his life, even when years later, through the influence of another woman, he came to terms with a worldly way of living. The contradiction then developed more pronouncedly between the introspective, retiring, contemplative side of his nature and the enjoyment of friends and life evident in his letters to Georges du Buisson at the age of seventeen.

After four months in Dresden discussing art and philosophy with Julia over cups of tea, and frequenting not only galleries and the opera but no doubt also brasseries and nightclubs where an *éteigneuse* could be picked up from time to time, Harry joined his parents in Florence in March 1868, and went back to Versailles with them in May.

Lisl had receded from the foreground. The letters he set about writing to Dresden were soon all addressed to Julia alone, no longer to the two sisters jointly. It was then, in the course of 1868, that the younger sister got engaged and married to her Austrian composer, Heinrich Freiherr von Herzogenberg. Harry meanwhile concentrated on Julia and the five years that followed were to prove a period of courtship of a very extraordinary kind.

[68]

8

The American Adventure

The *bachot* was bungled. Harry came under severe criticism from his parents who reproached him for having spent his time playing about with metaphysics instead of coming down to the realities of life and keeping a level head. There, by his side, stood his brother Louis, they pointed out, healthy in body and mind, free from intellectual pretensions and ready to cross the ocean and settle in America, the land of their forebears. He would enter business there or run a farm. Why shouldn't Harry do the same and go with him? Funds to give them a good start would be forthcoming. His parents would see to that and moreover there was in New York their prosperous uncle Seabury, the banker, with whom they could live for a while and who was always willing to be of assistance. They might even join his bank as junior partners. But perhaps now that stability had returned after those dreadful years of civil war, some extensive travelling in the United States might be advisable before binding themselves to a specific career, so that they could look around and discover what they really wanted to do. They would not be under any pressure to start on something at once, for they were both extremely young.

So Harry let himself be persuaded and a significant lull in his correspondence with Julia soon followed. The disgust at having failed in the examinations made him feel, for the time being at any rate, unfit for a life of the mind and spirit. Banking or a career in business did not appeal to him, but perhaps there was something to be said for farming and besides he was eager to travel. His father, who had spent his early manhood in the southern states, kept giving a glowing description of nature and life in that part of America. In fact, Yankee though he was, he had left his heart there, so much so that his feelings had been horribly torn during the Civil War. A cotton or sugar plantation might be the right answer to Harry's problems. The young man accepted the suggestion with an open mind and agreed that the best thing for him would be to travel in America and see for himself. In his last letter to

[69]

Julia before his departure he declared that on 6 October he would be sailing for America where he would spend a year 'travelling, hunting and dreaming'.

So in October 1868 Harry and his brother sailed from London, where their mother saw them off, on their first visit to the land of their ancestors – which could have been the beginning of a permanent return home. For Louis it was: he was integrated and swallowed up. Harry stayed only nine months. Unfortunately not one of the many letters he wrote from America on this visit, most of which were to his mother giving a regular account of his travels, has survived. Anna's letters to him, on the other hand, and a few from his father, have been preserved and so, at least by inference, we can obtain an idea of what was happening to Harry as he travelled south-westward across the country after a sojourn of three months in New York.

He and his brother stayed with Seabury, their bachelor uncle, at 535 Broadway, until 21 January. On New Year's Day Harry apparently had an unpleasant experience, the nature of which remains obscure. His father, writing to Anna, expressed sympathy for what Harry had called a 'terrible day', adding that Harry was about to leave New York alone, Louis having 'cast anchor' there.

Some weeks previously Harry had received a letter from Kate, his fifteen-year-old sister at home in Versailles, which contained a lively description of a party they had given – a rumbustious period piece.

Last Tuesday we gave a very jolly party (dancing of course). All went smoothly till nearly eleven o'clock when a dreadful accident occurred, namely the splitting of the pants. No, first let me tell you whom we had; of gentlemen two Minens, one de Villard, two Otlys, one Lane and a few others I think; of ladies one Julia Girardet, one Madame Minsen, one Madame Lambert, one Ellen Joubert, one Mlle Girardin, one Kate Brewster. We were not *very* many, but had jolly fun. Well then, in a figure of the cotillion where the gentlemen were to fall on their knees before the ladies, when de Villard did this his pants gave a crack and a crack, and there the size of a hand was to be seen. He however did not notice it. Mrs Minsen and Mama did and were shaking their sides most heartily. However something had to be done, for there was nothing under his trousers but his skin; it was rather 'shocking' for the young ladies who were aware of the

[70]

misfortune – Mlle Lambert above all who was his partner – and the best of it all was that he was leading the cotillion! So Mama asks Lane what to do. He thereupon goes and fetches Mlle Lambert away from M. de Villard and informs him of the accident he has caused by being so gallant and falling with such vigour at the feet of the ladies. Mama would have sent a maid to him, but the slit was in a region where it was impossible for anybody to tell him but one of the men. However, after having told his distress to Ellen who was sitting near him, he went into the little study where Eugène sewed his pants up for him and he came and danced with renewed vigour.

But Harry was busy with other matters of greater importance than cotillions and splitting pants. He was being pressed to enter his uncle's banking business in New York. He was not happy there, however, and soon developed a strong aversion to the city. The alternative plan of buying and farming a plantation in one of the southern states appealed to him far more and gave him a good excuse for travelling throughout the country, which was what he really wanted to do. His father was encouraging him to visit the South, but he also wanted to travel west, right across to California. So on 21 January 1869 Harry set off on his ambitious tour alone, his brother having decided to stay behind in New York for the time being. The letters his parents wrote enable us to follow him more or less on his south-westward course, which might have included a detour to Havana. First comes a letter from his mother written early in February:

> I am not surprised you did not like New York. Boston and Norwich will be the only towns you will feel comfortable in, or am I greatly mistaken in your tastes, the former because business there does not literally knock everything else on the head, the latter from its natural beauties. I hope you saw the museum at Washington – it is worth a visit, but you would soon have enough of the town or city, since you much object to towns.
>
> I was rather amused with Kate's observation on your wishes. She listened to your remarks upon slavery fast fading into an institution of the past. 'That sounds very grand,' says Missis, 'but I know what he wants to study slavery for – it is to get at the cigars!' Your father says that in his days the expenses at Havana

were more than double the New York expenses now. If they have kept pace with their neighbours your purse will suffer, supposing you are able to get there. Cuba has been your father's dream and like most dreams never realized.

After reaching Virginia his progress was relatively slow; evidently he wished to look at the country thoroughly. On 13 February his mother wrote to him again:

I suppose you cannot understand the pleasure with which we peruse your letters. Your father was more particularly interested in the last because you are on ground where the sympathies of his early manhood were formed and where his thoughts revert with more interest than even the place of his birth and childhood. The Southern States exercise over him a magnetic influence which he does not attempt to explain or perhaps understand, but his queer feelings and sayings during the war seemed to me to come from the struggle between the difficulty of forgetting the alluring attractions of the past and the desire to hold a principle in view and abide by it. So he was swinging between the North and the South and has hardly got steady yet . . . I shall have a map to follow your steps.

She followed them south, but at some point Harry turned north-west, back to Washington, where we find him still on 4 March, witnessing the inauguration of President Grant. Then he proceeded south again and on 8 March his mother wrote to him as follows:

Your letter relating to your adventures with the bear has reached us, but not the propounded newspaper containing the whole detailed report of the trip. I hope you will not lose the good health now obtained in a wild goose chase after buffaloes.

What his adventure with bears could have been, which was reported in a newspaper, we are left to guess, but it is perhaps worth noting that it was in Charleston, where Harry arrived soon after, that his father had been issued with an official testimonial by the State of South Carolina on 23 June 1833:

We, the undersigned, do hereby certify and declare to *all whom it may concern* that the Bearer of these presents, Mr Christopher Starr Brewster, has been long and favourably known to us as a practitioner of Dental Surgery. He has had the management of a very large number of cases throughout the United States and especially in this State and City, in all which he has exhibited a skill and judgment not to be excelled.

Christopher Starr may still have had friends in Charleston to whom, no doubt, his son would have been furnished with letters of introduction. From Charleston Harry travelled to Savannah and on to Jacksonville and Key West off the southern tip of Florida, but never got to Cuba. Cotton and tobacco had been given up in favour of sugar which was now coming into serious consideration. It had attracted him from the start for some reason which remains unclear.

From Florida he turned westward to New Orleans and as far as Galveston in Texas. Then at some stage he travelled up the St John river full of alligators. Is his hair turning 'nigger-like', Anna wondered? Thereafter he may have gone northward to St Louis – or so one might infer from the letter she wrote, with a touch of motherly anxiety, on 15 April:

Perhaps by this date you are at St Louis. I feel still as if you were *getatable*, but the journey from there to California fills me with dread. It is described in New America by Dixon and I inwardly hoped you would not be tempted across those endless plains and breathless heat of the sun, dust or sand in your eyes, and to suffer from thirst and every kind of hardship *sans compter* the red skins that may long for your fair undulating locks.

I think you might have left California for your next trip, there is so much yet to see in the Northern States; you will not find other places like New York fortunately.

By the end of that month her worries had become painfully intense:

When I think of you in the increasing heat on rough roads, alone on horseback, then that frightful ride to San Francisco, I come to the conclusion that till I hear of your return from there and arrival at Chicago or some other place within reach and where I can find you if ill, I must be resigned to having an aching heart as well as head and wait in patience till you speak of return.

Apparently it had been Harry's plan to ride westward as far as San

[73]

Francisco from St Louis across the prairies of the Mid West, over the Rocky Mountains to Salt Lake City and on to the Pacific coast. Anna was reading William Dixon's *New America*, which had just been published by Lippincott. In this book travelling on horseback across the prairies of Kansas and Colorado, beset by perils and hardships in the 1860s, is most graphically described. No wonder she felt anxious for her son amongst rattlesnakes and redskins. But in any case Harry had changed his plans. He had turned south again from St Louis or had simply never gone there, for we find him back – or still – in Texas, making his way westward across the vast stretches of that state. The only surviving account by his pen of his impressions in the course of his long ride to the west relates to this part of the United States and emerges in a section of a letter of many pages which he wrote to Julia nine months later, after his return to Versailles. Its purpose was less to describe a particular stretch of his journey than to illustrate an argument on aesthetics.

You ask me about Texas. Nothing is so crushing as those endless prairies where the skyline seems no further than twenty steps from you. The sensation of solitude far from being restful becomes a burden. One day I had been travelling nine hours on that petrified sea without seeing trace of man but the ruts of wagon wheels; the sky looked like a dome of lead; a cold rain was coming down. Never had I felt so discouraged. At last, as the day declined, I penetrated one of those magnificent forests which from time to time interrupt the monotony of the scenery – immense trees bound to each other in festoons of lianas, a Mexican vegetation, brilliantly coloured flowers shining through innumerable shades of foliage. At the same time the sky lighted up and the last rays of the sun came plunging into my forest. As much as the sensation of infinity had crushed me, this spectacle now filled me with enthusiasm. 'From this you reach a conclusion,' you will say. Well, I conclude from it that it is not an apprehension of eternity which is around me in the presence of grandeur in nature and which kindles that feeling of 'ennoblement' to which you refer, for otherwise I would experience this on the high seas, or in a desert, and always at the sight of mountains. But the ocean and the desert oppress me and mountains feel like falling on top of me sometimes. On the other hand I

[74]

become aware of a sensation of intimate joy, peace and often pride wherever the landscape has some points of comparison. It is easier to have an idea of the size of things, it is a geometric pleasure so to speak. The intimate joy consists in the pleasure derived from the beauty created by the contrast of lights and colours; the feeling of peace comes partly from the silence which usually reigns in such places, and partly from the meditation which accompanies the enjoyment of beauty; finally the feeling of pride comes from the awareness of a difficulty overcome.

When Harry's mother wrote to him thinking he was still at St Louis and expressed all her worries, she went on to say that she was not over-anxious he should decide too soon on a sugar plantation. She ended with the following sentence: 'Louis's visit to Key West and yours in Texas may be over about the same time and as in novels the two brothers may unexpectedly meet at the corner of a street in New Orleans.'

But before this was to happen – more or less – Harry was continuing to ride from Texas into New Mexico, where he received a letter from his mother in which she said:

I am glad that you have 'sworn off' the sugar question, for at present at least. It would not be wise, I think, to decide anything to bind your future career. We must talk this important subject over, on your return home, and you must give yourself time to digest all the things you've seen and heard. From your present plan it strikes me that you are leaving out the New England states, New Hampshire, Vermont, Rhode Island and Norwich, your father's birthplace. If you go there do not forget to visit the Churchyard to see the grave of the old man with his three wives by his side.

What Harry was interested in, however, was not his grandfather Seabury, the minute man,* buried with his three wives – three wives in succession leaving their husband a respectable widower every time – but the polygamy of the Mormons. 'I cannot help being amused,' Anna had written to him while he was in New Mexico,

at the faces and exclamations people make when I tell them

* 'Minute men' or the militia in the American Revolutionary War. Seabury served as one, was captured by the Royal Navy and tortured.

[75]

the answer to their enquiries, that you are probably with the Mormons. 'Heavens, I hope they won't kidnap him and make him take six wives to begin with! Grand Dieu, madame, et vous n'avez pas peur!' But I should like to have a peep at them myself. I am not surprised that you have been tempted to go and judge for yourself.

Harry had indeed planned to visit Salt Lake City before going on to California. He also had very likely read Dixon's *New America*, a book that was most informative on the Mormons and their customs. Brigham Young, their able leader, and his twenty wives were still very much alive. Thousands of other men with him were leading blissful polygamous lives. This strange community was then at the apogee of its local success, enjoying virtual independence from interference by the federal government, whose laws against polygamy it was still in a position to defy. Their way of life as well as their peculiar religious ardour must have tickled the curiosity of the sceptical agnostic Harry already was at the age of eighteen. But at some point in New Mexico he changed his plans, for what motive we know not, and turned back. His interest in the Mormons and their polygamy was left to be reawakened: several years later, for specific reasons, he did indeed manage to visit Salt Lake City. On 16 May his mother wrote to him:

> Your letter with 'News! News!' I need not tell you was met with a hearty reception. I am indeed glad this long separation is drawing to a close and that you have left something in America for your next visit. I had been trying hard to persuade myself that I did not at all mind your immense journey to California, but from the relief I experienced upon knowing that you leave it for a future period, I discovered that my persuasive powers had only very partially succeeded.

By the time Harry turned back he had given up the sugar plantation plan, so one gathers from his mother's letters. His parents, in fact, had never been excessively enthusiastic about it. Already at the outset of his journey to the South, when there was much enthusiasm on his part, they were considering the whole question with some degree of caution. Anna wrote as early as the middle of February:

> Your account of sugar plantations made me fly off with kith and

[76]

kin, and thinking of turning one and all into the sugar trade, but your father upset my sweet castles by saying that it is as easy to lose one's life as to fill one's purse – away with sugar, cotton, rice and too great a crop of dollars.

At New Orleans Harry met Louis about the middle of May and hurried back to New York with him. By this time a revulsion against the American way of life had come over him. The distaste increased during the remaining weeks he spent in the metropolis and then crystallized in the expatriate attitude he adopted and retained throughout his life. The first extant written expression of it is to be found in a letter he wrote to Julia as soon as he got back to New York after a silence of more than eight months. Had he been trying to forget her?

You might be able to make yourself a faint idea of the pleasure I shall have in returning to Europe and on your being informed of what is the only subject of conversation in the United States: business – in other words two things, my money and the money of others. . . To tell you the truth I don't think life is endurable here for a European if he has any other aim in this world than dollars.

America was eminently, at that time, the continent where you went to start a new life and make money.

It is worth noting at this point a trait in Harry's nature which was about to develop – namely an interest in Oriental thought and a consequent attitude to life he was already then beginning to adopt. In a letter he was to write to Julia soon after his return to Versailles there is a passage which gives expression to this side of his nature for the first time. In a way it accounts for his negative reaction to America.

Mieux vaut le repos que la marche, mieux vaut le sommeil que le repos, mieux vaut la mort que le sommeil – c'est le dernier mot d'une philosophie qui compte des millions de sectateurs. En Europe on invertie l'ordre des termes et en Amérique on ajoute 'Mieux vaut le pas de gymnastique que la marche.'

In a later section of the same letter he says:

En Amérique tout le monde affecte le dehors de la réligion, ou la

[77]

moindre légèreté de conversation est un crime, et ou en réalité la morale et la religion sont des mots vides de sens.

Evidently he was beginning to regard America as the extreme Occidental opposite of the Oriental way of conceiving life to which he felt inwardly drawn, though he never cared to assume an 'Orientalizing' style of living. This trait was only one side of his nature, for there was another, a Latin, European, Continental side he frequently like to stress – the Gallo-American man as Henry James would call him – and yet a third side, the inevitable Anglo-Saxon, American-English facet. He went on regarding himself as a citizen of the United States and travelled about with an American passport as his father had done. He preferred to do his prose writing in English and his verse writing in French.

After a few weeks in New York Harry hurried back to Versailles leaving his brother behind and probably omitting to visit New England. Shortly after his return he took his *bachot* examination again and this time sailed through.

9
Metaphysical Courtship

By the time Harry was back in Europe to carry on a life congenial to his temperament, most of the attitudes that progressively characterized his personality and found expression in his writings were already recognizable. In his correspondence with Julia, which he resumed with regularity on his return, he argues dialectically in favour of materialistic rationalism and a pagan interpretation of life, as against Julia's agnostic but transcendental idealism. Equally significant, in the forum of his arguments opposing Julia's belief in the immortality of the soul is the influence of the Oriental literature he was reading with increasing interest.

At Versailles there was a young student of medicine by the name of Henri Cazalis whom Harry had already met and who was to become a lifelong friend. Cazalis was a few years older and extremely well-read in Oriental literature. He introduced Harry to Hindu, Buddhist and Taoist writings as well as to the Persian language. It was thanks to Cazalis that Harry set about learning Persian, studying Oriental poetry, mythology and thought, and collecting Oriental books. It may have remained a background pursuit, but it had its share of influence on his way of thinking and, later on, his writings.

The two women with whom he became closely involved were believers in personal survival after death. One was a child of German philosophic idealism, the other an Anglican believer with a Hebraic notion of God and a Christian conception of after-life. Harry was to carry on a voluminous correspondence first with one and then with the other, in which he repeatedly expresses his aversion to the idea of a personal god and to the possibility of personal survival after death, although not rejecting the entire concept of spiritual continuity. It is a stance that recurs continually in his four-year correspondence courtship of Julia.

Apart from all this epistolary activity and a considerable amount of reading, not only of Oriental literature but also of European

[79]

philosophers and sociologists up to Herbert Spencer, he spent these years visiting Spain, North Africa, Italy and Scandinavia, although home remained the family house at Versailles. He was away in March 1870, touring Spain, when his brother came over to Europe on a visit. Louis was already speaking with an American accent and displaying American ways and attitudes which amused his mother. She records in a letter to Harry that almost at once Louis cleared the drawing-room of his brother's 'objectionable books' such as *La Revue des Deux Mondes* and Darwin's *Philosophical Ideas on Transubstantiation*. She adds: 'I had a good laugh and put the albums on the table while the ugly books were carried in a haste to your room.' Evidently Anna, who no matter how pious had always had a sense of humour, was more broad-minded than her elder son.

Shortly after his return from Spain Harry set out again, this time for Sweden and Norway. It was from here that he hurried back to France at the outbreak of the Franco-Prussian War in order to join his father at Versailles. Though sympathizing with the French to the extent of feeling an urge to join the *francs-tireurs*, he had little use for the passions of nationalism displayed on both sides of the Rhine. Writing to Julia, he commented on the stupidity of the war, and the hopeless concatenation of one act of revenge upon another. His mother, on the other hand, seems to have followed the conflict with a greater feeling of anguish: a letter from England laments the help-lessness of France in 'the struggle of a giant against a child'. She also sounds somewhat resigned about Harry's reluctance to complete a proper course of studies for a specific career: 'By the time you attain the age when you men are generally considered to have brought their studies to a close, I trust so kind a fairy will have touched you with her wand and made you look upon the future as I do.'

After Christopher Starr Brewster's death, 'The Hole' at Versailles still remained the family house for some years, though Louis was by then back in America and Harry kept travelling. His correspondence with Julia went on uninterrupted, but it dealt almost exclusively with metaphysics and aesthetics and therefore provides scarcely any biographical information. However, new impressions and ex-periences transpire from time to time. In February 1871 he wrote to Julia with enthusiasm about his new discovery, Ernest Renan, and commented on *La Vie de Jésus* as 'le plus délicieux poème qu'on ait écrit depuis longtemps'. His finding that the hero of the book, Jesus,

[80]

was treated – though with veneration – as a man and not as God struck a responsive chord. No doubt this accounts for the works of Renan among Harry's books, although Harry will surely have had some reservations about someone whose views were so highly controversial. When Renan died twenty years later Harry wrote to Ethel Smyth:

> Renan's death is the loss of a friend to me. I rejoiced to see him honoured. I think he is the only man to whom I owe the debt of intellectual gratitude one owes to one's master. 'Le monde tel qu'il nous apparaît n'est ni clair ni simple et vouloir le représenter comme tel c'est se mettre à un point de vue arbitraire, choisi en dehors de la réalité.' Simple words but they came to me as the message of freedom in days when I was groaning under the load of abortive systems.

As soon as he had read the *The Life of Christ* Harry sent the book to Julia for her comments, which turned out to be critical. In a letter that followed he took up the challenge and discussed the book, admitting that Renan had 'felt the ground sink under his feet' at a certain point. Then, in reaction to a remark Julia had made about the Christian idea of human solidarity through humility and recognition of one's common weaknesses, Harry bursts out in protest: 'Amis comme cochons, dit une expression vulgaire mais pour laquelle je vous demande pardon. Frères en humilité, me paraît juste aussi grand et noble.' He goes on to say:

> For the majority of men the great thing is to drink, eat and make money. Let them drink, eat and make money to their hearts' content, but let them not come and tap on my belly in the name of our common weaknesses. Furthermore this idea of innate sin and corruption of the flesh seems to me a monstrosity. How beautiful were the Greek goddesses, laughing all naked in the sun without being aware of their nudity! If it was Jesus who made the concept of evil triumph I curse the memory, for my poor goddesses are now hiding in shame behind the doors of taverns and hovels or do not let themselves be adored except by self-denial – and laughter then, and the sun, where are they?

At the very time he was writing the above lines he lay basking in the sun with no clothes on near Terni in Umbria. He had given up his plan of travelling to the Far East with Julia's brother, at least for the time being, and was spending the spring of 1871 in Italy with his old friend Georges du Buisson. In writing to Julia he cannot help plunging into pages of metaphysics, followed by copious comments on Goethe, Heine and Swinburne, the new English poet who had greatly impressed him in spite of certain features which seemed to him of questionable taste. Verlaine, too, was another discovery. Many years later he wrote to Maurice Baring:

In 1870 or 1871 I found in the galleries of the Odéon a poor little *plaquette* – a few rough pages of verse. Nobody that I knew had ever heard of the author, and it was years before I saw his name mentioned in the press or heard him talked of; but I had stored the name in my memory as that of a great poet. It was Verlaine.[1]

In addition to du Buisson and Cazalis, a third man came into Harry's life during those years who might have became a close friend, the painter Henri Regnault. It was on Cazalis's recommendation that Harry was persuaded, early in 1870, to go to meet him at his home in Tangier. After a somewhat tentative start, the friendship matured within a few weeks, and it was with Regnault that Harry was touring in Spain when Louis returned from America. Regnault fell on the battlefield in 1871. To Julia Harry wrote about him after his death:

In spite of the veil behind which we nearly always kept each other and perhaps even because of this reserve, without which there is no lasting charm, intimacy grew between us unawares. We had very seriously planned to travel to the East together and to share the task of learning the two most important languages, he Hindustani and I Persian. Until last February I thought I was well on my way towards complying with my part of the agreement by learning Persian; now I am carrying on learning it because I have done the most difficult side, and if necessary I shall go alone. He had a very manly nature.

It was about that time, September 1871, that Julia asked him what sort of a life he was leading at Versailles and whether he had many friends. He wrote back, probably to her satisfaction:

I am living quite alone and know absolutely nobody except my

[82]

old friend du Buisson and Cazalis who has succeeded in forcing his way through my barred door. As he leads a worldly life he sometimes drags me to Paris into very agreeable company, but I am not proposing to look for friends there, for if I fancied doing so I alone would be the loser.

Even during the most sociable periods of his life there was always a tendency to withdraw. The misanthropic mood was probably not entirely in deference to Julia.

They exchanged poems, they discussed the possibility of revolution. Harry was convinced that the time had not yet come, that they were only witnessing the prelude to something, that nothing much could change for a while, but that profound alterations to society – for better or worse – were bound to come before too long.

For all his avowed loneliness he kept frequenting Cazalis's group of friends; he even suggested introducing Julia's brother-in-law to them, the musician Heinrich von Herzogenberg. They consisted, he wrote, of musicians who worshipped Wagner (this would have hardly pleased Herzogenberg who hated Wagner), of painters to whom Regnault had been their 'star', of poets to whom Baudelaire and Edgar Allan Poe were gods, of philosophers who kept talking about Buddha and Schopenhauer. Among them were a Russian nihilist prince, a female sculptor, and Theophile Gauthier's daughter by his mistress Giulia Grisi, the Italian opera singer.

Harry returned to Italy every year for several months. He was there again in 1872 from April to September, and again in 1873 from March to May. There is no evidence that he and Julia saw each other during these years – a curious state of affairs, for Harry was a young man very much on the move. It may be partly accounted for by Anna's attitude to Julia, which was scarcely favourable, perhaps because of the seven years' difference in age. Perhaps she feared the almost certain conclusion, and already in 1870 made in this connection a significant though obscure remark in a letter to her son: 'If my last letter does not settle the whole affair it will prove that Julia is stronger even than I supposed.'

The correspondence between Harry and Julia proceeded month after month in the same high tone of intellectual eagerness, mutual appreciation and criticism, but always in the name of friendship as a matter of course, in a tone of cordiality and even warmth, but with

[83]

few personal remarks except on an intellectual plane and always with that touch of reserve of which Harry was so fond. His letters begin with 'Chère Godsister' and usually end: 'Croyez à mon amitié dévoué, H. Brewster'; sometimes with 'Your Godbrother, Henry Brewster'. And yet they were coming closer and closer together, and marriage may have been, though evidently unmentionable, already a probable conclusion by 1871.

Harry was spending more and more of his time, when not in Italy, in Paris itself, where he took a flat early in 1873 – 138 rue Bonaparte – leaving his mother and sister at 'The Hole'. Probably his mother's depressed mood and her aversion to Julia made the Versailles house progressively less welcoming.

In March of that year Harry's friend Georges died in his mother's house at Claix of galloping consumption. With repressed grief Harry mentions his death laconically in a letter to Julia from Naples. 'The illness', he writes, 'broke out during a short visit I paid him last August on my way to the spa of Allevard. When shortly afterwards I returned to see him I was alarmed at the progress of the disease. I urged him to leave for Naples and in the end succeeded in persuading him to do so in the hope that the climate there might save him.' He goes on to reproach himself for not having accompanied Georges, but he had scarcely realized the end was so near. In November Madame du Buisson had gone to Naples to fetch her son back at his own request. On receiving an urgent telegram Harry hurried to Claix, but it was too late. Georges was dead. 'There is something odious', he concludes, 'about the human course of daily life where nothing changes except the passing away of someone you love. On the other hand when you suddenly change occupation and interests a new centre shapes itself where the sad thought takes its proper place almost as a friend.'

Harry was still at an early stage of a long trip to Sicily and Greece. From Naples he travelled to Palermo, and from there went on to Athens where he had arranged to meet his mother. In the same letter to Julia he had expressed hopes of meeting her in Vienna on their return from Greece in the summer, when the family planned a long sojourn in Austria. On her way to Greece Anna succumbed to an epidemic of cholera which had broken out in Vienna. She died there while her son was waiting for her in Athens.

On 21 August Harry wrote, on his return to Paris:

Dear Godsister – it is the last time I am addressing you as such. Either I shall call you differently or it will be the end. We shall have met and quitted, we shall have travelled together for a short while, I shall stay where I am, you will proceed on your way and everything will have been said. It is all very simple. What is extremely simple for me is that I don't care for life without you and everything I love and admire is attached to your name – your Christian name. May I call you by it? I don't want to try to persuade you. Apart from secondary considerations you must pronounce yourself either for or against.

This I must tell you however: whether you answer for or against, you have had, for the time I have known you, and will continue to have, until I have joined the dead of yesterday, my first, my last and unswerving love.

Your Godbrother,

HENRY BREWSTER

The answer was yes. They were married three months later and soon after settled in Florence where a new life for them began.

In one of the letters immediately following their decision to get married there is a request from Harry that Julia should promise not to admire him too much. It seems an amazingly presumptuous request but he had already detected a tendency on her part to set him on a pedestal – which persisted into the years of their marriage. Such had been the emotional reserve of their 'courtship by correspondence' that when now Julia could express surprise at his having failed to detect her feelings for him from between the lines of her letters, he admits that he had more or less missed the point.

I only saw abstractions which had nothing to do with me. But why did you, one fine day, burn in your heart the words I had said: 'I can predict to you with certainty that the nature of my feelings for you will never change – the name of friendship will always suit them.' I never overstepped that line and I have floated between the hope of being able to forget you and the desire of being at least your friend. If the latter prevailed it was because I realized time and again that to part with you amounted to condemning myself to indifference, torpor and even degradation, and that without you the world was for me without sun.

10

The Sunflower at San Francesco

In the long dark dining-room overlooking the back garden, where the sixteenth-century furniture seems to have grown from out of the floor and walls, there is a large portrait on the wall over the dresser of a dark-eyed, attractive-looking young girl in a crinoline. This is Irene Schäuffelen, Hildebrand's wife-to-be, and the room is still saturated with her presence, perhaps more so than any other room in the house. It is a good portrait, dating from the early 1860s; the artist is not known – it is not by Marées, for at that time they had not yet met.

Irene belonged to a rich Swabian family of industrialists and came from a cultivated background. Her diary and memoirs show that at the age of fifteen she was already a mature young girl, pretty, very feminine, romantic and intelligent, keenly fond of riding and dancing, with a sense of humour and wide interests, especially in the field of literature. It was she who introduced the world of books to San Francesco long before other sources contributed, and she was far better read than her husband, Hildebrand. And yet there was nothing of the bluestocking about her. No doubt her children, as they grew up, owed much to her for the importance she attached to the cornerstones of European literature – Homer, Shakespeare, Goethe and Cervantes.

In the winter of 1862 she undertook a journey to Italy with her mother which proved her most thrilling experience so far. The Roman Carnival, as it still was in those days, offered a fascinating picture of costumes, colours, life and fun, and the beauty of the Roman architecture and the Italian landscape in general remained so deeply impressed upon her that she kept conjuring it up throughout her long and roundabout return journey through Austria and Bavaria to her home town of Heilbronn. She had a moonlight flirtation with a young Austrian officer on the way, and indeed serious doubts crept into her mind about her feelings for Franz

Koppel, the young student from Tübingen University to whom she was engaged. But she felt sorry for him, he had gambled all his money away, and she had given him her word. She felt she could not withdraw.

On returning to Germany she and her mother settled in Dresden and shortly afterwards she was married. Because of her youth, the marriage contract was subject to a signed agreement that if either partner wished later to be released from the bond, no difficulties would be made or objections raised to a divorce.

From Irene's point of view Franz Koppel proved a hopeless husband – without character or initiative, content to do nothing and live comfortably on his wife's money. Worst of all, he had a habit of making silly jokes. Years later, after many efforts and strings pulled, she succeeded in obtaining for him a lectureship in history at the Dresden Polytechnicum. But her diary covering these years shows her often in a depressed, almost desperate state of mind. The entries abound in introspective analyses and outbreaks into poetry.

It was in Dresden that she met Marées. There developed a friendship between them which proved of great comfort to her: she tells how she went for walks with him and learnt to appreciate his humour and wit, the poetry of his nature and the value of his work. But how impossible it was, she adds, to fall in love with him. There was something absurd, ridiculous about his presence and his person, which hopelessly interfered with the process of romance. From the extant records we may deduce, however, that Marées's own feelings for her were not limited to friendship. Platonically, certainly, her appreciation of him was unstinted. She records: 'The soul of art is poetry. Marées's soul communicates with me through the poetry I find in his work.' Then she adds a reflection on poetry in relation to art in general:

> Without poetry no art can be conceived as genuine, whether eye-poetry, ear-poetry or word-poetry. Poetry is the mysterious, ungraspable means of communication between things in time and space and things beyond time and space. It is the light which shines down from God into the darkness of life upon earth, limited by time and space, as the means of communication with eternity.

Irene returned several times to Italy in the 1860s, sometimes for

[87]

prolonged sojourns. With her husband she spent part of the winter of 1867 in Rome where their circle included Fiedler, Marées, Feuerbach, the Koppels, Böcklin and Hildebrand as well (though there was nothing between them at this stage – they met in Naples when Hildebrand and Marées were working at the newly founded aquarium in the summer of 1873). There is an entry in Fiedler's diary dated 25 December 1867 which reads as follows:

> Koppel dominates the conversation, not always in a pleasant manner. He talks too much in order to talk brilliantly; admittedly he is able to introduce into the conversation a string of excellent jokes and observations which are often very true – you cannot help liking him, but his wife even more so. Without any doubt they constitute an exceptionally original couple and my relationship with them is indeed pleasant.

The real drama started in Florence towards the close of 1873. It was a strange, subtle drama which was to unfold itself over the next two years, shaking the lives of the four main characters involved down to the very roots of their existence.

The Koppels had returned to Dresden in the autumn. Irene was finding life with her husband more intolerable than ever. His superficial nature and coarse sensuality had tried her to breaking point, so she had made up her mind to return to Italy almost at once without him. As it was she who had the money, she could exert a certain pressure on her husband and achieve some degree of independence. She left with her mother and little son, a child aged three.

Fiedler was worried. Like Marées he was an old admirer of Irene. He had taken an active interest in her life and for years kept up a constant exchange of letters wherein his feelings of friendship for her find expression in a manner which discloses repressed passion. He realized that Irene, now twenty-seven, in the full bloom of womanhood, was extremely attractive to men. He knew that her marriage was unhappy and that however hard she tried to keep it going, she instinctively longed for an escape from what she felt to be slavery. She yearned after a great mutual love she had not yet found. Fiedler knew her well; he knew that this was a dangerous state of mind to be in. He was a friend of her husband. Admittedly, he did not think very highly of him; he found him amusing and entertaining, but disapproved of his amateurish, student-like and somewhat irresponsible approach to life. He could well understand Irene's difficulties with him, but Koppel was a friend: the thought of injuring him in any way was abhorrent to him. Although he must have been tempted to take advantage of their matrimonial disquiet his moral principles forbade him. He repressed his emotions, continued to be a friend to both and in fact behaved as a perfect gentleman. His attitude to Irene and Adolf throughout the crisis may not have been entirely free from bias, but such detachment could hardly be expected in the circumstances.

Fiedler's principles led him to pursue a policy of admonition. The contents and tone of his letters to Irene were, and remained, highly intellectual and yet full of sensitive thoughts, sympathy and consideration. Psychologically there was a strong affinity between Fiedler and Irene; both had a deep moral introspective side to their natures. Their interest in art was extensive, though Fiedler was far more of a connoisseur than she herself cared to be, as well as a remarkable thinker. But what they particularly had in common was an interest in the workings of the psyche and in moral values which require such interest if they are to be taken seriously.

Fiedler was determined to remain cautious and recommend caution. He advised Irene to hold fast to Franz and endeavour to develop their relationship along lines of mutual respect and affection. He shrank from the idea of a separation, with which Irene had been toying and had already ventured to suggest as a possibility. He feared that if let loose from the bonds of marriage her temperament might lead her into serious difficulties. Fiedler either believed it or persuaded himself to believe it.

When Koppel wrote that his wife had left for Florence without him to spend the winter there, Fiedler was full of apprehensions. Yet the thought of Hildebrand as a source of possible complications did not enter his head. His anxiety was more about Marées, who was then with Hildebrand in Florence. Irene and Marées were old friends. The precise nature of their friendship Fiedler found hard to determine, not without reason. Besides, the vision of Irene at large in Florence, anxious to get away from her husband and still hoping to make her life worth living according to her way of thinking, kept worrying Fiedler, the meticulous friend who recoiled from the thought of family disruption or breach of respectability.

Irene, it was true, always travelled with her mother, child and

[89]

luggage, but these impedimenta, as he knew, would not interfere with her freedom of movement and mind. When he heard that what he feared – her escape – had actually taken place, the news came like a clap of thunder. It was Koppel himself who gave the alarm. He wrote to Fiedler, who was at his country house in Saxony, entreating him to come straight to Dresden. Fiedler went without delay and Koppel showed him two letters he had just received from his wife in which she claimed divorce, mentioning the right she had to it according to the agreement signed by them on the day of their marriage.

Neither of the two men knew what exactly had happened. It was decided that Koppel should immediately join his wife in Florence to put things straight. On his arrival there, what had happened became clear to him and soon after to Fiedler. The cause of the trouble turned out to be not Marées, as originally feared, but the innocent-looking, naive nature-child Hildebrand, 'der kleine Hildebrand' as they called him. For all his talent, energy, dynamic personality and indubitable intelligence – for which he had become the apple of Fiedler's patron-eye – he had seemed so inoffensive and unthreatening. It was most unexpected.

But it should not have been unexpected, for Hildebrand had neither Marées's hesitation, lack of self-confidence, ambivalence and self-preoccupation nor Fiedler's moral scruples, loyalty and fastidiousness. He liked the opposite sex, was wholesomely sensual and had often made love to, and slept with, the more easygoing women he had come across in Italy.

He was not superficial, however; the deeper experiences of love were not beyond his range, but he was young, healthy, attractive to women and not too particular about sexual morality. When Irene came to stay in Florence for that winter he kept seeing her without being bothered by any feeling of loyalty to Franz Koppel, whom he hardly knew.

This was the situation at the outset of that winter 1873-74, when San Francesco was about to be bought. Irene, having arrived with mother, child and baggage, had put up at a hotel in the building where she and Hildebrand were soon to meet the Brewsters. Whether she had decided to come and stay in Florence instead of Rome because she was already interested in the young sculptor – she had seen him again in Naples the summer before – is a question which the records do not clarify. But there is a hint in her diary

[90]

where she confesses that the idea of closer acquaintance with the 'young gifted Hildebrand' attracted her, though owing to his extreme youth, she adds, he could never be more than a harmless friend. Maybe; but he was not as young as all that. He was twenty-six, though he looked younger, and she twenty-seven.

Her diary covering the following months is a remarkably vivid record of her love affair with Hildebrand which was to lead to marriage two and a half years later. It is written in a fresh, graphic style full of humour, passion, psychological insight and without any trace of prudery. Already at the beginning of her journey she confirms in writing what was being suspected, that the real motive was to prepare the way for separation if not divorce. The vulgarity of her husband's nature, she stresses in her diary, jars upon her more and more, 'his noisy cheerfulness, his superficial, fluent, facile dialectics in dealing with serious matters has made the rift between us more discordant than ever'. She was looking, she frankly admits, for a man she could love and admire at the same time.

When she came to Florence she brought with her, being well off, a Swiss governess for the child and a Swiss maid for her mother. A few weeks after her arrival she rented a roomy flat on the riverside, at 16 Lungarno Acciaioli, and engaged a manservant to run the household and do the shopping since their maid knew not a word of Italian. But when he was discovered to be cheating he was replaced by Bartolo, a trustworthy old butler whose wife undertook the cooking.

Hildebrand was still in Naples when she arrived, but he turned up in Florence almost at once with Marées. Looking back to the ensuing days Irene wrote the following passage in her diary many years later:

Let me plunge into the recollection of the golden hours spent in those happy days, days of intensest pleasure and suffering, days in which there began for me the great love that was to dominate my whole life and that was to give me that wealth, that plenitude of feeling for which my entire being was yearning. In Adolf I found the sun, the light round which like a sunflower I turned, *I had to turn*, since he was the fulfilment of all the longing of my past life. The love I felt for him was to pour into my life the brightest radiance and the purest light. The boundless joy I experienced in Nature having brought about the existence of such a man, such a complete, pure natural creature as I found in Adolf,

[91]

was something I had only imagined and longed for in my wildest dreams. There he was before me, an image straight from the hands of Nature, great, pure, holy, and we were bound in a love full of joy. Without interruption my entire self was plunged deep into him; past and future were dispersed into a cloud, and only the present was alive, the glad, joyful, rich present, filled with his wonderful personality. His spiritual and physical presence irradiated a perfect unity.

The modern reader may smile at these rapturous terms of expression, but it surely says something that a woman at the age of seventy-three, looking back over all the years of her life after her husband's death and shortly before her own, should be able to express herself about him in such a way and recall with such vivid intensity a past of total fulfilment. Here she was in a situation which enabled her to project her subconscious image of longed-for manhood, her *animus* as Jung would say, upon a particular man who could take it, who could embody it. Luckily she was intelligent enough to make the necessary psychological adjustments as time went by. Although later in life she was to discover that her idol, Adolf, had his limitations, and although the mirage of absolute love was to be clouded in the end, her projection remained by and large a happy and successful one. What an intelligent nineteenth-century *feminine* woman sought in a man was precisely a unity of presence, a pleasant wholeness of intellectual and physical elements, a harmony in which the physical and spiritual were balanced and merged. Evidently Hildebrand provided this, as not only Irene recorded in her journal but as indeed countless others testified – including Ethel Smyth, Lisl von Herzogenberg, Clara Schumann, Cosima Wagner and Franz Liszt.

Moreover Hildebrand was gifted with a remarkable ability to live the present to the full and to make others live it with him. He could squeeze the juice of life out of every moment, so that full significance of the present could relegate the past and future to their proper places. It is the good lover's knack.

As soon as Hildebrand was settled in Florence his attention, apart from the distractions of San Francesco, became centred on Irene. Not only had she all the charm of a young and physically attractive woman but also an unusual maturity of mind, of experience, of *savoir vivre*, which he as yet lacked. Hers was a natural sensibility of temperament feeding an interest in art and literature which was seldom found in a woman of those days.

As soon as she arrived in Florence, Irene hired a horse and carriage for her entire stay. Frequently she and Hildebrand drove out into the country for the day, sometimes taking Marées with them, more often leaving him behind. Often Hildebrand took her to the theatre or showed her the city from different viewpoints: he was a master at communicating the beauties of Florence and the famous hills which encircle it. They would laugh and joke, even indulge in childish pranks; then their talk would turn to more serious questions of poetry, sculpture and aesthetics, or to practical issues such as the problems affecting their friend Marées. Often, too, Hildebrand would visit Irene and her mother at their flat in Lungarno Acciaioli. He would bring his viola and she would accompany him; or she would play the piano and sing.

In addition to the Brewsters, they made the acquaintance during these months of a young Englishwoman who was destined to play a great part in their lives as an intimate friend. Jessy Taylor, who lived with her mother in Florence, had been married to a Frenchman, Laussot by name, from whom she was separated. Later on she was to marry a German economist, Karl Hillebrand, and became an outstanding personality in nineteenth-century Florence, with a well-known salon frequented by the most prominent composers, musicians and men of letters.

Before settling at San Francesco, Hildebrand had rented a studio in Via San Leonardo where he persuaded Irene to visit him and let him finish the bust of her he had started shortly after her arrival. So she came for the sittings and the hours there were prolonged with talking and passionate love-making. She lived entirely in the happy present: as she says in her diary, because of his youth the idea of marrying Hildebrand had not yet entered her mind.

Then Koppel turned up in Florence, the picture of affability, understanding and apparent grief – justified grief no doubt, but Irene had suspicions about how genuine it was. He played his part with consummate skill; possibly thought out and prepared under Fiedler's influence or even direction.

After lecturing his wife for several days without success, the frustrated husband decided to take the bull by the horns. He invited

Irene and his young rival on an outing to Fiesole and the neighbouring hills. As they drove away in a hired cab Koppel and Irene sat facing Hildebrand who occupied the less comfortable seat in front of them. He could see Irene's pale face and dark worried eyes as she leaned back almost hidden in the corner. Koppel, on the other hand, red in the face, sat up and a little forward, his body swaying with every jerk of the cab as it squeaked uphill along the stony road. Hildebrand felt physically as well as mentally more uncomfortable than he could blame on the shortcomings of his seat. The conversation, which had started stiffly and disjointedly, relapsed into virtual silence in spite of his efforts to keep it going by pointing out the landmarks and the beauty of the hills. The tone of his own voice struck him as quite unnatural. He had not the vaguest idea what the other man was up to, apart from having been told by Koppel that he wanted to have a word with him alone. Koppel could scarcely be intending to challenge him to a duel, for there was no sign of firearms and besides no witnesses were present, apart from Irene and the cabman who were hardly suitable candidates. He had a feeling there might be something more sinister to it all. Irene for her part was in a state of even greater anxiety since she had been given no clue as to the purpose of their outing and the atmosphere in the cab was such as to make her fear the worst.

About halfway up the hill the cab stopped. Koppel, now almost purple in the face, gave Hildebrand a wink. The younger man was as pale as death. They left Irene alone in the carriage and strode off rather solemnly along a lonely path. When they came to a flat clearing, Koppel stopped. The setting was perfect for a duel. But no, a duel would have conferred additional romance on the situation and that would not have suited Koppel. He was thinking about money. He behaved as a man of experience, or was it Fiedler's brand of wisdom coming through? Instead of drawing pistols they stood in front of the view and had a talk. Koppel reminded Hildebrand of his youth and his career.

Of course, he said, he was perfectly prepared to grant his wife a divorce, but on one condition which Hildebrand would well understand as a gentleman. He would have to marry her. It would be irresponsible on Koppel's part to let Irene loose in the world just to facilitate her becoming Hildebrand's mistress for as long as Hildebrand found it convenient. 'Think the matter over, young man.'

[94]

If Hildebrand were unable to give the necessary undertaking that he would marry her, Koppel could only insist on his immediately breaking off all connections with his wife and refraining from seeing her in the future. This was only fair and right, for her own sake. Did Hildebrand agree?

Dumbfounded, Hildebrand was unable to answer, unable to give the undertaking requested. It was all too unexpected. Was it not Fiedler who had always stressed that his first and foremost duty was to his art, that no other commitment should stand in its way? Koppel had done well to consult with Fiedler before coming to Florence. Hildebrand could only reflect on the bitter irony of it all. For no matter how deeply in love he was with Irene, he was not prepared to plunge into marriage at this stage of his life. Crushed, he returned to the carriage. The triumphant Koppel, almost jovial now, sat beside him and there in front of them, as they drove back to Florence, was Irene, alone, leaning back, her dark eyes fastened on Hildebrand. But he avoided them; she understood and drew back further still into the corner of her seat under the blow of despair. As the cab rattled briskly downhill, Koppel grew talkative and facetious, while Hildebrand from time to time managed a lame remark about the view which was by now receding into the darkness. Irene was silent. As Hildebrand parted company with them on the doorstep of their Lungarno house he gave her an icy cold hand and said: 'We must separate for ever.'

The next act of the drama, which lasted eighteen months, was one of resignation and inner struggle. Both Hidebrand and Irene were under the influence of Fiedler who did his level best to bring her back to reason, to the path of duty, to what he considered best for her. She was a remarkable woman, yes, but according to his way of thinking dangerously prone to the sway of passion. So Irene, shifting from despair to resignation, made an effort to live with her exasperating husband again, while Hildebrand's inclination to shrink from marriage received every encouragement from Fiedler, who kept reminding him of his prime duty to his art. Meanwhile Marées, for obvious reasons, was annoyed and hurt. He had, in all innocence, introduced Adolf to Irene: that Hildebrand should now become his landlord was the last straw.

The months dragged on. Irene and her husband settled in Germany and at first both she and Hildebrand made strenuous efforts to keep the tone of their letters on a level-headed basis of pure friendship. In Dresden, where the Koppels now lived, Irene's life became worldly again and she mixed with the city's most intellectual circle in an effort to forget the pangs of love. In the meantime Hildebrand had settled at San Francesco and was immersed in his own work. But the image of Irene was never far away, a disturbing spirit. Little by little his letters to her became loving again and then more and more passionate; she could but respond in the same fashion.

At last they met at Bex in Switzerland. It was early in the autumn of 1875 and what followed is vividly described by Irene in her journal. Their efforts at restraint were powerless against the reawakening of passionate love which invaded every instant spent together. Not a word is spared in describing the fullness and completeness of their love, physical and emotional. Without a trace of prudery she gives an account of every detail. And they lived the present in its full intensity.

They chose for these late summer days of love a small hotel on the Lake of Geneva near Lausanne, called Beaurivage. It was, she relates,

A little house overgrown with roses. I wove myself a wreath and on the first night I received Hildebrand with roses in my hair, naked on the bed. He almost fainted with joy and we sank into blissful love. In the daytime we would sit in the park, in the cool shade of the bushes, and listen to the soft waters splashing on the wall below. We felt as if there was for us neither past nor future. We felt as if we could and did absorb through all our pores this beauty, this happiness of the present, giving ourselves to it and intensely living it.

They parted only to meet almost immediately again in Venice, where Irene rented an apartment on the Canal Grande. As the weeks of love continued in that wonderful setting, Irene, as a sideline, indulged in buying pictures – some of which are still hanging on the walls of San Francesco – and lace. Throughout her life she collected rare lace for which she had an extravagant passion.

Irene was a woman who in the end would not shrink from the fullness of a great love affair, whether acceptable to conventional society or not, whether legalized by marriage or not, provided such love was serious. Once she knew that it was, once she realized that for both of them it meant a new life, she plunged into it headlong

[96]

without hesitation and so did he. The Rubicon was crossed. They were married only late in 1876 and long before the wedding she was expecting a child.

Until the end of her days the love she had sought and found remained the dominating factor of her life. If in the course of time some doubt came to trouble her as to whether this mutual love had been entered into with equal commitment, the fact remained that it did endure throughout their lives, strong enough to weather the occasional storm. If by the end their marriage fell short of perfection, perhaps, in the spirit of the times, she would have agreed with Milton:

> Man's love is of man's life a thing apart,
> 'Tis woman's whole existence.

As for Hildebrand, the experience of that autumn of 1875 was decisive; for him the matter was settled. If there had been hesitation in the past, if the idea of marriage had been impossible to accept when suddenly thrust upon him, everything had now changed. The career of a sculptor no longer seemed to him incompatible with marriage. Indeed the full possession of a beloved woman could hardly be conceived of, in that form of permanence he desired, without marriage. So there remained only practical obstacles to be overcome; and these involved problems which only Irene could solve.

It was not easy for her. Her husband, when he married her, had signed that agreement which was deliberately intended to leave the door open. But that was many years ago; though he reluctantly acknowledged the agreement, he prevaricated skilfully. In the end Irene put her case in the hands of lawyers at Dresden and succeeded in obtaining her husband's cooperation for the divorce proceedings – but at a price. She had to grant him half her fortune in order to avoid delays which might have gone on for years.

Fiedler was annoyed that Koppel should have let himself be bought off in a manner scarcely becoming a gentleman. Koppel thought otherwise and Fiedler in a spirit of extra-scrupulous impartiality found arguments in the end to excuse the wronged husband's interest in money. Koppel's moods of black despair, which had been greatly troubling Irene's conscience, changed into cheerful cooperation almost overnight. She obtained not only her divorce but also the custody of her child.

As soon as it was legally possible, the two lovers got married. Fiedler did likewise. He married that same year Mary Meyer, an ambitious, rather commonplace some people thought, but extremely pretty young girl. While Marées withdrew permanently to Rome to brood over his soul, Fiedler remained a close friend of the Hildebrands.

Irene's entry into San Francesco as mistress of the house, which had not yet experienced a feminine touch, opened up a new era of happy family life. To Hildebrand Irene was the ideal wife: not only did she give him love and bear him six children, but she also brought him the wherewithal to lead a life dedicated to his work without financial worries.

She took over the management of the household and the entire property, as well as the education and upbringing of the children. It was she who saw that the frequent visitors and guests were properly received. As Hildebrand became progressively better known as a sculptor, the social side of their life broadened but at the same time involved them in irksome duties that kept increasing. Irene shouldered the entire practical burden of San Francesco with such skill that everything ran smoothly and neither her husband nor anybody else was aware of how it was done.

She also played a prevalent part in the arrangement of the house, not least in procuring and arranging the books; indeed the general atmosphere of San Francesco at that period owed as much to her as to her husband, who – though painting several murals in the house – was left to apply himself with intense energy to his studio work.

In her political views Irene was outspokenly democratic, but privately she was more conservative. She had a love of luxury, enjoying both the fine things of life and the pleasant ones, and surrounding herself with good furniture and Oriental carpets as well as books. She also went on collecting lace. Her attitude towards peasants, subordinates and servants was patriarchal.

Perhaps the greatest passion of her life, apart from what she felt for her husband, was her love for the beauties of nature. It was she who took an active interest in the farm, the fields, the laying out of the garden and park of San Francesco, she who planted most of the trees. Her response to the elements and qualities of nature, of scenery, of the Tuscan landscape, became highly developed, more so than Hildebrand's. Certainly he always stood for the beauty and

[98]

mystery of nature, for its importance to art, but as a sculptor his principal involvement with it was through the human body. Irene on the other hand drew relief and happiness from contact with the things of nature. She belonged far more than Hildebrand to the old romantic world of Germany; indeed she was a product of it.

To her son by her first marriage she wrote in 1887:

Today 28th December I am writing to you from the terrace bathed in sun which warms the heart. The books have just arrived and at once I wanted to quench my thirst by opening them and plunging in – but I haven't the necessary quietness of mind, for high up on an olive tree a peasant is picking olives and singing. The church-bells are ringing: the olives glisten and the beauty around is overwhelming. If only you could cast a glance on this landscape with its slight morning haze resting upon the earth, binding everything into softness and letting the far-off landmarks emerge in a dream-like manner; and then the cypresses standing in the foreground and the children shouting with joy as they romp about on the Paretaio* in their red clothes looking like large flowers – it's too lovely. Ah poor me, helpless and awkward as I am at expressing myself; I must weep for not being capable of writing verse, for not being able to grasp all this beauty, all this joy!

To Adolf's sister Sofie she wrote six months later:

How long it is since I wrote to you! In springtime it is the restlessness of life that prevents one from writing, then comes the lovely quiet time of heat and Adolf and I enjoy each other and pay each other an indemnity for the previous restlessness. I turn round him like a sunflower, we drive out to town and do shopping together, then I sit for hours in his studio and watch him work or, in order to keep her still, I read out loud to Nini [Eva] who is at present sitting for a relief he is making of her. In the evening we dine on the terrace and rejoice over the children and the wonderful natural setting in which fortune has placed us.

Her diary and countless letters to relations and friends, to her

*The name by which the hill of San Donato a Scopeto was locally known since the sixteenth century.

[99]

sister-in-law Sofie, to her husband, to Fiedler and Marées, to Hermann Levi the orchestra conductor, to the Herzogenbergs, Julia Brewster, Cosima Wagner and many others, reveal an impulsive woman, active, passionate, full of interests, always in love with her husband, uncompromisingly loyal and intensely jealous. To Ethel, whose judgement was admittedly not unbiased and who appeared not to mind Lisl's German gush, Irene too much epitomized the German housewife; but by those who knew her better, such as Julia, her great friend, who though likewise German by birth was anything but the housewife type, she was cherished for her intellectual qualities. In particular she had the gift of feeling and expressing things poetically, of thinking and being able to convey her thoughts clearly, always disclosing a strong personality of her own, which was not just a reflection of the man she adored. She possessed, too, an outstanding degree of human insight, a capacity for constructive criticism and balanced judgement. Above all she was a woman made to love, who loved a man with her entire heart and body, a sunflower to his light.

11

The Ivory Tower

Harry and Julia spent the first ten years of their marriage in solitude, wrapped in each other and away from the bustle of metropolitan life. They chose to live in Florence which had ceased to be the capital of the newly formed nation of Italy three years before their arrival. Here was a medieval-Renaissance city that looked inward to a glorious past, but scarcely outward to the contemporary world. It was what they wanted; in their private quest of discovery, learning from each other, modernity was an intrusion.

At first they rented a flat in an old palace in Via dei Serragli, which from the left bank of the River Arno runs southward to the city gate, Porta Romana. Subsequently they moved to a more permanent and much finer building in Via de' Bardi. For the first two years neither was ever absent for any length of time and so we can glean little information about this early period of their life together beyond the fact that it was happy and harmonious – though, so it sometimes seemed to Harry, 'like a dream'.

Thereafter he began occasionally to travel, making short trips to France and Germany, partly on business but chiefly to re-establish contact or smooth out frictions with family relations and friends. The first extant letter from him to Julia was written in 1875, about a year after their first child, Clotilde, had been born. The letter, in French (as were all their letters to each other), shows that their relationship was not entirely free from problems. It is written from Dresden, where Harry had gone to see his parents-in-law.

I have your bedroom, which is well worth the journey. It is the first time I have been away from you for any length of time and what I wish to tell you at once is how happy I am to have you and how unhappy not to be more worthy of you, but I am confident that I shall become so. I keep pondering over the two years that have gone by and fail to understand how it is that I have been

[101]

slumbering for so long. You have left your spirit behind in this room and I ask myself whether I dare face it, whether it hasn't much to reproach me with, whether it would have received you with joy had you come with me as the woman whose present is the continuation of her past, whether it wouldn't say to you: 'Have you chosen your mate well?' There comes then to my mind the picture of those many days of ours so colourless, so inert, and I then grow aware of the time that passes by as it did over the house of the sleeping beauty in the wood. I feel so guilty towards you that tears come to my eyes in thinking of the days that are no more. I have not done what I hoped to do. I have been cowardly, stupid, I have acted as I used to do when I was in the habit of spending my nights in public houses, roaming in the dwellings of the dying, with Rudra* in the graveyards. For all this I ask forgiveness of you, of your spirit that dwells with me in this room.

But also I look out of your window and see the road along which I used to go in a blissful turmoil of the mind, drunk with love for you; and now I feel nearer to the inebriation of the Sufi. The love I used to dream of was less wonderful than the love I am now experiencing. Humanly we have not grown as we should have – notice that I say *we*, though I attribute the fault to myself entirely. But as eternal beings we have come closer to each other, and we do not want happiness.

Now if we wish human development to take place in us, it will not do so unless it contributes to the peace that unites us. If it comes about in this way all is well, if not it is better it should not come at all, better not at all than if it came only such as we understood it in the past.

Though somewhat cryptic, this deeply introspective letter, questioning and searching, throws light on the nature of their relationship and on much that followed. It raises a crucial problem of marriage: whether both partners will mature together, at the same pace and in the same direction; and the inherent dangers if they do not. In the event, the Brewsters' closeness and unity endured for several years to come. Then the problem of development became acute and there was trouble.

*In Hindu mythology

On the subsequent absences from home Harry's letters reveal a remarkable degree of intimate tenderness without passion. They are totally lacking in the usual terms of endearment; the protestations of love are indirect and subtle, you read them between the lines, and yet strangely enough these letters, in contrast to those before their marriage which were scarcely personal, show exceptional warmth and affection. They are intimately personal within the established limits of propriety. The metaphysics recede, making way here and there for the practical matters of life – without, of course, disappearing from the agenda. But at least they usually come in as a passage without dominating the whole letter.

From what Harry writes to Julia about the books he keeps buying and reading, we gather that they are both steeped in Oriental literature. Persian is the language Harry goes on studying under the encouragement of Cazalis in Paris, but now there is also Sanskrit on the programme with which they are struggling. Apart from the Vedas and the Upanishads, they discuss the Vishnu Purana, the Bhagavata Purana, the works of Kalidasa and those of other Indian authors including books on Buddhism. As for Chinese literature, Lao Tse's *Tao-te-king* predominates and is often quoted. Their whole relationship, indeed, is coloured by the literature, mythology and philosophy of the East, which they digest with considerable intellectual thoroughness.

From time to time a few old friends are mentioned, including of course the unfailing Cazalis. Harry also refers frequently to his sister Kate. She had married a Frenchman, the Baron de Terouenne, and was living with him at their château in the country. On one occasion she joined Harry in Florence while Julia was away on a visit to her parents at Dresden. Harry writes to Julia: 'Kate and I spend our time discussing politics and civilization, not too badly either. Yesterday the Hildebrands came to ask us to tea on their terrace. We went and stayed on for dinner.' Then he is off again on another trip to France and Julia writes to him on 12 October 1879: 'Hildebrand came to see us. He looks very well. He has been working a great deal and says he has made considerable progress. Until now his serenity has not faded: it is the sun itself at noon.'

Writing from France Harry says, referring to Kate again:

This evening I went for a walk with her in the beautifully

[103]

moon-lit valley. I tried to make her understand what I mean by 'religion', or rather the difference one should make between dogma and sensation. She has no idea of this. Evidently such distinction presupposes a rhythm. You prove it only by engendering this rhythm, by arousing it in the other party and it is exactly this I am always unable to bring about . . . Perhaps it is very unwise to want to awaken in someone who is not of your stamp the rhythms which in your own kind are the best.

Kate was on the eve of conversion to Catholicism, hence Harry's reference to dogma. Little did she know, poor girl, that her brother did not regard her as of his 'stamp'. However, throughout his life Harry remained persistently gentle and lovingly kind to her – and she accordingly flooded him with usually colourless letters.

After telling Julia about his talk with Kate, Harry goes on in the same letter to quote passages from Lao Tse, followed by extracts from the timetable of trains he has to catch, details of business and references to the investments, shares and dividends to which he has to attend. One gathers from these letters that the practical side of everyday life is not neglected, even when metaphysics swing forward again with long, subtle arguments too abstract to be cited. But the tender passages never fail to infiltrate, redeemingly and harmoniously. In reading these letters one feels that everything centres on their own private ivory tower, in relation to which the world outside is but a shadow.

For six years this conjugal life goes on in the same strain, then there is a change of rhythm. At some stage – it is impossible to tell exactly when – they both began to crave for an estate of their own, not in Italy where they were living, but in France, as an investment as well as for pleasure. They were not in the least hard up, what with the investments Harry had inherited from his father and the shares Julia had received as dowry from her parents; so they could easily afford it. Harry's idea of running a plantation had perhaps never quite died, for it re-emerged ten years later, adapted to a European context: they would buy forest land, attached, if possible, to an old château in the south of France. Harry dreamt of becoming a forester. The plan, one suspects, must have stemmed from a psychological need – at least on Harry's part – for a joint enterprise at this stage of their marriage, without breaking the magic circle. They must have

[104]

discussed the plan in detail day after day and they made preliminary inquiries, with encouraging results, before the actual quest started in 1879. The initial, unsuccessful, steps were rather impractical. We find Harry travelling in Corsica at the beginning of that year, assessing various forests that were for sale. He writes to Julia describing the mountainous character of the place and says he was tempted at first by one or two pine forests, but was soon discouraged by reports of the fires that kept breaking out and causing irreparable damage. It was apparently impossible, too, to keep away the trespassing shepherds and their destructive goats. So he gave up the idea of finding a suitable estate in Corsica and turned his attention to the south of France. Here the quest, which lasted almost two years, though naturally with some interruptions, started in earnest.

Harry's letters during this period consist of a series of reports on the various wooded estates he visited, including country houses and medieval châteaux for sale. The letters are forthright in tone and full of facts, details and figures. He visited one estate after the other: some were too big, some too expensive, others had delightful châteaux that were too dilapidated or else the forests attached were too recently planted to be profitable in the short term. Often he was on the verge of clinching the deal, but snags suddenly cropped up which made him change his mind. It seems that if he were to find the right property they intended to divide their time between there and Florence.

Towards the end of 1880 the ideal property was found near Grenoble. It was called Avignonet and contained a charming medieval château which could be restored without unreasonable expense. From a letter to Julia which Harry wrote from Grenoble and in which he said he was occupying the same hotel room they had shared when Christopher was ill (their second son, born to them the year before), one gathers that they were together when Avignonet was found. This accounts for there being no detailed description of it in any of his letters.

They still had a house at Claix, not far from Grenoble, which they had rented on a long lease from Mme du Buisson and to which Harry was very attached. But Mme du Buisson herself, who lived on the premises or in the immediate neighbourhood, was troublesome, so Harry preferred to put up at a hotel in Grenoble while his

[105]

presence was required in the area in connection with the purchase and restoration of the château.

The letters he wrote at that time to Julia in Florence deal mostly with the legal aspects of the purchase and with the restoration work to be organized. He says he hopes they will be spending Christmas of that year at their château. He seems extremely happy; his letters are full of warmth and affection but always couched in a language of restraint. Time goes by. He is reading the Persian epic of Firdousi. The property is finally bought, but there are still complications ahead. There follows a lull of six months. Christmas is not spent at Avignonet.

Early in February 1882, when Harry was back in France, Julia wrote to him as follows:

I notice something worth noticing, which is that when you are absent I become more natural; but this naturalness vanishes as soon as you are here again. It is my fault. I am like the courtesans of Louis XIV, like Frederick's grenadiers.

Yesterday I was with the Hildebrands and we talked about guess whom? Goethe. But this time it was worth it. Goethe was only a symbol for Hildebrand. [There follows a summary of the discussion they had as to whether Goethe was guilty of pastiche or not, with implied reference to Hildebrand's own work].

Oddly enough M. and Mme Hildebrand gave me the impression of being somewhat repressed in relation to each other. I silently sang the praises of a regency marriage such as ours. . .

Harry answered this letter at once, reacting to Julia's remark about her naturalness:

I feel that what you say is sometimes true, but I explain it differently. It seems to me that I am not at all Louis XIV freezing the world around me, but rather a poor ambulating actor who seduced you having dressed himself up in a velvet doublet and with whom you are ashamed to live when he fails to play his part properly. I have often told you so. My impression is that it is not you but I who becomes unnatural in daily life. Perhaps I am unable to be natural on that stage. If the same applied to you it would explain why each of us feels he is being swallowed up by the other.

[106]

The letter then plunges deeper into the problem of marriage in general and of their own marriage in particular, but with tact, delicacy and affection. This is the first time a certain degree of strain becomes apparent in their relationship and is dealt with openly in their correspondence. That they were able to write to each other about it was to their credit. Evidently Harry was beginning to feel restive in the role he was expected to play or thought he had to play.

Meanwhile the work of restoration at Avignonet proceeded, but more slowly than expected. Difficulties arose over the new village school for which a building was needed. Although the village was a couple of miles away, the mayor wanted to use one of Avignonet's farm buildings and Harry and Julia found themselves threatened with partial expropriation. This became an issue, with lawyers intervening on either side. Harry was deeply involved, and the only relaxation he admits to in a hectic life is occasionally playing his 'cello. There then follows another interruption of seven months, with Harry back in Florence.

The correspondence starts again on 18 September 1882. Avignonet is almost ready for them to move in, but not quite. The work of restoration has been slowed down because of labour problems and the school question is not yet solved. However, they are evidently expecting to settle down on their property very soon. They are looking forward to it, they seem happy. In the meantime Harry returns to Florence. Then suddenly, less than three months later, we find him in Sardinia on his way to North Africa in search of lions to shoot. Avignonet is no longer a subject of correspondence. Letters follow, but it is never mentioned.

[107]

12

The Breach

Harry and Julia approached marriage with diffidence. Fully aware of the precariousness of the marital bond, they pledged themselves to part amicably should either of them one day wish to go his or her own way. They therefore kept referring to their marriage as a 'regency', a period of office which might or might not be renewed. But at the same time they were consolidating their friendship with mutual understanding, the tie of metaphysical concepts and delicate sensations deeply shared. They felt confident of the resilience of their relationship based on a constant questioning dialogue. When this faltered as the result of living under the same roof, it was resumed at a distance through the medium of letter writing. So they genuinely believed that they were far more dependent on each other, far more interlocked and self-sufficient than if they had ever let themselves go to the vulgar euphoria of passion. They would talk about their 'friendship', seldom their 'love', and they went on calling each other 'my friend'. They were convinced that like this their union would stand the test of time, which indeed it did in a strange way – not only in the field of metaphysics which they went on cultivating all their lives. Their relationship represented the acme of sophisticated experiment, as well as the antithesis of modern 'togetherness' or wallowing in communal relationships. But human nature had not been fully taken into account. When Eros intruded it played unexpected tricks.

In the tenth year of their marriage their relationship had reached a dangerous degree of saturation. They were still wrapped up in each other, but Henry was beginning to feel uncomfortable and slightly claustrophobic. He gently complained that they were eating each other up. It was a delicate situation to be in.

There was no actual fracas when things went wrong; their defensive network was too carefully prepared for that. But it did give rise to a most extraordinary triangular relationship drama, which lasted

[108]

many years and was perhaps no less painful than the most conventional breakdown.

Recorded in her memoirs we have Ethel Smyth's own impressions of Harry and Julia as she formulated them over the years following the first encounter. She writes:

> ... Face to face with them I soon found out that the real hermit was Julia, her husband being a rather embryonic lover of humanity, hitherto accustomed, owing to circumstances, to pay exclusive attention to abstractions. As I learned many years afterwards Julia was just then beginning to notice in him a new and strange impulse to extend a furtive hand to his fellow creatures and thought it wisest to offer no opposition. Thus it came to pass that instead of being politely warned off the premises as I had half expected, I was warmly welcomed in Via de' Bardi.

At the end of a long description of the Brewsters Ethel concludes: 'A few weeks after my arrival, and not to my great regret (for as usual it was the woman who at first absorbed all my attention), H.B. suddenly decided to go off lion-hunting in Algeria.' Dynamic, extroverted, socially-minded Ethel had unwittingly struck deep into the defences of their inner world. But the citadel was still far from being captured. All Harry wished to do at that juncture was to get away from both women by plunging into a life of physical action and adventure at a good distance. Even Avignonet was swept from his thoughts. But the psychological side of the programme was more easily planned than carried out, for he felt duty bound to keep in touch with his family.

His first letter to Julia was from Sardinia early in January 1883 – just a few words: 'I have my American passport; it cost me twenty-six francs and a terrible oath to serve and cherish the Constitution.' But a few days later, from Cagliari, he writes to her a long letter on mysticism.' At Tunis he receives a short letter from Julia; 'cold and cruel,' he says in his reply. He adds a paragraph full of veiled and double-edged apologies, concluding: 'I am very sorry about the misunderstanding; have you now grasped that I wanted the whole matter snuffed out?'

The letters that follow are more objective, dealing with the programme of his travels in the wild North African country, the possibility of shooting game, his preparations for it and so forth.

They are not lacking in the usual reticent tone of affection, but there is a melancholy touch from time to time, such as in the following: 'I don't know what sort of pain I feel in me, like void. It makes me love the shapes of box bushes I see here which have an expression of impersonal ancient pain.'

He rents a Moorish house at Tunis and there establishes his head-quarters; then off he goes into the interior of the country with a flannel shirt, a gun and a horse. The trousers are not mentioned. He has already learnt Arabic and consorts with the natives. He goes on writing to Julia about his experiences, his adventures, graphically describing the forests and *maquis* through which he rides, interspersing his account with philosophical reflections and never failing to ask about the children. Not a word about Ethel, not a word about Avignonet.

The lions are not easy to come by; after several weeks he has shot only a quail. Although in his letters Harry could scarcely refrain from abstractions, his reflections have now a poetic as well as a meditative quality. The narrative and descriptive passages dealing with the life he leads, with the scenery, the people in general and with individuals in particular, are excellent, often because they are concise. He meets, for instance, a young man who 'for three weeks has been spending his nights lying in wait for a leopard. He is alone; very well bred, almost like a girl, good-looking and rich, and he lives on milk and eggs, which does not prevent him from being as strong as a giant and shooting a panther once a year.'

Some of the letters from Africa are full of gloom, but always with a poetic flavour. In reading through them it becomes progressively clear that he cannot get away from himself. The metaphysical dialogue with Julia continues, though in a more personal tone than before, with indirect references to their problem. He spends much of his time cleaning his gun, making his own cartridges and scouring the scrub and forest on horseback, but without any luck apart from a few wildfowl he manages to shoot. He says he likes the life he is leading, but the cold and the vermin bother him. On one occasion he says he is glad to learn that Julia has a new dress, but why doesn't she tell him more about it? 'I should have loved to lay a leopard skin at your feet for your birthday, but all I should have been able to do would have been to place my own cloak spotted in black and gold.' Another time he remarks: 'You don't give me much confidence in my relation to others, we differ in this, and the difference is not to my advantage; but in solitude you give me a great deal. Send me a photograph of Hildebrand's statue.' And then: 'I am glad you are learning Arabic; I shall send you a list of mnemonics if you don't despise them.'

'I left Batha early in the morning', he writes in another letter, 'with horses, mules and donkeys; the same had happened to me there as at Ain Mokra; the lion I was hunting was shot by an Arab. I received Clotilde's poem and I will answer her. Here is a sheet of paper for you, which I have scribbled over in pencil as I lay on the ground in my tent.' Remarks follow about the ease and intimacy of Julia's letter which he appreciates and on which he then proceeds to make philosophical reflections.

In the same letter he describes his life with the Arabs and the sheik with whom he is staying, as well as the hunting expeditions, following tracks and trails and lying in wait for lions in the rain and snow. He accepts it all with equanimity.

In the middle of one night I woke up and looked around. You must know that the Arabian tent is entirely open on one side to enable a fire to be lit on the threshold and moreover, virtually right round, it leaves a gap from the ground of nearly three feet. Ventilation therefore is complete. The tent in actual fact is no more than a roof. The moon had come through the clouds and before me I could see the forest of cork trees, their dark leaves powdered white, at my feet a great carpet of snow and beside me lying on their rugs my Arabs and Sidi Abdallah sleeping wrapped in his cloak.

Although the elusive lion persists in being cleverer than its pursuers, Harry enjoys riding out in the forests with 'his' Arabs, as he calls them, climbing trees in the icy wind, hiding among the leaves with his gun, peering into the dark. Once he discovers that the growling noise he has been hearing does not come from a leopard, as he thought, but from a wretched jackal tearing to pieces the carcase of a wild boar in the bush. Beyond their reach the lion roars out a laugh at them.

He cultivates a tender relationship with the poor little ass the Arabs are going to use, in accordance with their traditional method of hunting, as a decoy for the lion. The unsuspecting creature gets

[111]

pushed into the middle of a glade to browse on the grass while the hunters lie in wait, well concealed in the bush.

At last on 13 March, two months after his departure from Florence, he mentions Avignonet in a letter – the only time it is referred to throughout the four months of his travels in North Africa. He says he is glad to be informed that work has been resumed there since 1 February. The only direct reference to Ethel appears casually in a letter to Julia dated 26 March. He says:

> Give my best greetings to the Hildebrands and to Miss Smyth of whom I am not jealous. It is a good sign when you attract very lively human beings whatever their own ways of life, one of which being certainly to their favour, namely not the way of life of those living on unearned incomes.

This touch of self-criticism is not amplified or pursued beyond the limits of a short paragraph.

As time goes by and spring sets in, his letters become more cheerful. He looks back on the winter as a period in which he was seriously ill, like a man about to die, and he says he keeps touching himself to make sure he is alive. The colourful descriptions of his rides into the wild country of North Africa in pursuit of the ever-evasive lion – whose roar is heard from time to time – are as vivid as usual, and always followed by, or interspersed with, philosophical meditations, sometimes closely pertinent, sometimes more general, perfectly formulated in exquisite French.

Finally, at the beginning of May, after four months in North Africa, he quits Tunisia for Sicily and Italy. He is full of yearnings for family and home. So the series of letters from Africa comes to an end. It is a quite remarkable collection.

A month after his return to Florence he was at Grenoble again, to see about Avignonet – but Avignonet was no more. They had received news in Italy that the château was at last ready for them to move in, the final touches had been completed. Fittings, furniture and books – nothing was missing, everything was perfect. This would be their new ivory tower, where life could recommence under hopeful auspices in a new setting. Then a telegram came with the news that the château had caught fire and burnt down. It was a total loss. Their dream was symbolically consumed.

[112]

13
The Trio

After surveying the disaster at Avignonet and endeavouring to obtain payment from the insurance company involved, which was being held up by various bureaucratic complications, Harry came back to his family in Florence to find that Ethel had just left for Germany and England. He had only seen her for a few days on his return from North Africa before hurrying on to Grenoble. In her memoirs she says:

> Just before I left Florence news came that the Brewsters' château near Grenoble, a grand old pile made habitable by them at great expense, had burnt to the ground. Julia, the superwoman, was overwhelmed and remained invisible for two or three days, but the bearing of H.B. was a revelation to me; he took it as one might take the loss of an old cigarette-holder.

In fact Harry was far more upset than he chose to show, as later records disclose. But he was trying to live up to his creed, never to be emotionally enslaved by the things of this world.

He now settled down again until the end of 1884 to a family life of superficial harmony, only leaving for a short break in France at the end of December in connection with the Avignonet affair. His letters to Julia are friendly and warm, in much the same tone as his letters from France of old. He tells her that he is hoping to get 40,000 francs from the insurance company out of the 60,000 they would need for the reconstruction of the château. For that amount, he adds, they could look elsewhere if necessary to build the delicious castle he had in mind.

Meanwhile Ethel in England was receiving effusive letters about the Brewsters from Lisl, who had been spending some time in Florence. Amid the usual enthusiasm there is a dissonant note about her sister's lack of sympathy for her own feelings of frustrated motherhood:

[113]

Julia's children are charming; they give me joy mingled with a little pain. At times I delight in them, freed from all thoughts of self, but there were weaker moments in which my own needs came between us and clouded my vision. When others are happy with their children, each laying a protecting hand on some little head, it hurts me that no one seems to think of me, and sometimes it is hard to fight down one's tears. One word would be enough to banish the mood, but no one says it. . . Whether all this doesn't occur to Julia, or whether she merely cannot find the word, I don't know.

In another letter she writes:

I have grown fonder of Harry than ever before, and though his views are not mine I respect the iron consistency with which he carries them out and accepts the consequences. I have met no one who is such a perfect, harmonious result of culture in the best sense of the word. Compared to him we are all peasants . . . but once in an unguarded moment Julia confessed to me that it was a strain being his wife . . . this in spite of the deep love and intimacy between them!

At first sight certain passages of the correspondence between Harry and Julia suggest they were playing a part for each other's benefit. More likely, however, they were striving to live up to those intellectual and spiritual standards they mutually expected or demanded of each other: there was nothing sham about the rising and falling tide of metaphysical dialectic that flowed between them.

Between Lisl and Harry, on the other hand, literature was the issue. He loved everything French and nothing for him could match French literature, to which he was about to introduce Ethel and little by little convert her to writers such as Flaubert, Baudelaire and Verlaine. She in turn tried to convert Lisl, but – unlike her sister – Lisl was *bouchée* to everything French, even though her early childhood had been spent in Paris. She wrote to Ethel:

I will gladly read the article on Flaubert and Baudelaire, but I believe more and more in the limitations of taste set by nationality. I am too German by instinct and education ever to feel more than respect for an 'artist' like Flaubert. For me, the manure heap on which his flowers bloom never loses its stench –

[114]

San Francesco di Paola, with (below) the view of Florence from the house.

The loggia, San Francesco di Paola.

Irene with children: relief portrait by Hildebrand.

Hildebrand as a young man; portrait by Marées.

Marées, *self-portrait*.

Drawing of H. B. by Elizabeth Brewster.

Frédéric Chopin, 1847.

Conrad Fiedler

Jessie Taylor

Christopher Starr Brewster

Bodo von Stockhausen

Hildebrand marble bust of Julia

Anna Bennet Brewster

Clothilde von Stockhausen

Ethel Smyth

Maurice Baring

Portrait of Henry James by Philip Burne-Jones at Lamb House, Rye.

Julia Brewster

Portrait of Julia as a child

H.B.

Julia in later life

Ethel Smyth by Sargent

Hildebrand marble bust of Clothilde von Stockhausen

Hildebrand portrait relief of Gerald Balfour

ABOVE, LEFT *Hildebrand relief of Lisl playing the organ* RIGHT *Hildebrand relief portrait of Lisl* BELOW *Hildebrand bust of H.B.*

a feeling every Frenchman would jeer at. The French indifference to subject-matter, whether in literature or in painting, is too foreign to our nature and notions; to us it is important what an artist uses his powers on, not only how he uses them – such is the tradition we have inherited from Schiller and Goethe – and a puddle in which the sun reflects itself remains a puddle. But these gentlemen fancy that everything their magical pen touches is thereby lifted into the region of Art, and demand of their readers an indifference on this point that none but such as possess French culture can achieve. The consequence of that principle is that a dying frog may inspire as fine a work of art as the Virgin Mary – a statement I myself was once obliged to sit and listen to!

Fiedler, German though he was, would have certainly not agreed with her standpoint.

Towards the end of December 1883 Ethel joined the Brewsters in Florence, spending the next seven months there with only a short break in the spring during which she travelled in various parts of central Italy.

'Before this trip,' she says, 'Julia having now ceased to ration my visits, I saw the Brewsters constantly, and found them more and more delightful.'

She then quotes a passage from a letter she had written to a friend from Florence some time in April 1884:

Her great idea is that he is to be a sort of Prophet, for which reason she encourages him in a bad habit of stooping from the neck, declaring it makes him look scholarly and unsmart! On the same lines she, the diplomat's daughter, is fond of assuring him that he hasn't the knack of associating with his fellow creatures, but this I think is partly because she herself loathes the world and wants his company in dual solitude. Last year I once said to her that I thought his manners, though not traditional, were absolute perfection, and felt certain that if he chose he would have a great success in the world; and I saw at once how she shied away from the idea . . . No one ever fascinated me more utterly than Julia does, though perhaps a good deal of it is the charm of things mysterious and unfathomable; one can't help hoping she may turn out to be human after all. . . They are the deepest of friends and I imagine were once passionately devoted to each other; but even if that part died down, as I suppose it always does, it wouldn't matter, for he is the sort of man it is impossible, besides all the rest, not to be fond of in a most comfortable way. Speaking of myself, what with comparing notes about mankind, morals, art, literature, anything and everything, what with laughter and fighting and utter good comradeship, I have never had such a delightful relation with any man in my life. . .

Small wonder that it developed – not into sexual intercourse but something far more binding, a mutual love declaration. Recalling the events of those days, Ethel says in her memoirs:

Harry Brewster and I, two natures diametrically opposed, had gradually come to realize that our roots were in the same soil – and this I think is the real meaning of the phrase 'to complete one another' – that there was between us one of those links that are part of Eternity which lies beyond and before Time. A chance wind having fanned and revealed at the last moment, as so often happens, what had long been smouldering in either heart, unsuspected by the other, the situation had been frankly faced and discussed by all three of us; and I then learned, to my astonishment, that this feeling for me was of long standing, and that the present eventuality had not only been foreseen by Julia from the first, but frequently discussed between them. To sum up the position as baldly as possible, Julia, who believed the whole thing to be imaginary on both sides, maintained it was incumbent on us to establish, in the course of further intercourse, whether realities or illusions were in question. After that – and surely there was no hurry – the next step could be decided on. My position, however, was, that there could be no next step, inasmuch as it was my obvious duty to break off intercourse with him at once and for ever. And when I left Italy that chapter was closed as far as I was concerned.

But it was not. The atmosphere had become tense during the last weeks of spring. Then, after Ethel's departure, a three-way correspondence began. The situation was far from simple for, no matter how deeply Harry was by then in love with Ethel, he could not, or would not, detach himself from Julia. The psychological links held out. He wrote to Ethel in terms which declare his predicament:

[116]

My love I will never harm you. How can I marry you unless she joins us hand in hand – how can I give you that outward sign of respect if it were at the same time an outrage to her? The curse would be on us. . . I don't want to love you unless I love nobly. . . She says I am deceiving myself and that a new love however excellent is not the reality I need, but general interests and the fight with men. I admit the second part but think that reality presents itself in a complex shape and that as I loved when I entered into solitary thought and found my mate, so must it be when I begin to set my thought in contact with those of others and gather strength in human atmosphere. . . Are you so tender-hearted my sweet Ethel that you needs must be married before the altar or cry your eyes out? I can admit it if you were to jump out of all social connections into nothing but one feeling – however strong; it is not your nature and I quite feel that. Do you think I would spoil the generous delicate machine?

Ethel would be shocked by the idea of becoming someone's mistress. Worse, being by temperament impetuous, she was evidently in a hurry. She wanted to see things simple and clear-cut. But the bond between Harry and Julia, given its nature and the manner in which it had been interwoven, was complex and could not be easily undone. It certainly was not a conventional world-weary relationship between husband and wife which might be expected to succumb to the serious amatory intervention of a third party. So we find Harry at pains to explain the situation:

Consider this: how could I have found the courage to confess to Julia that I long for you, and to meet her look then and ever since then with a quiet confident look, if I were not deeply persuaded that you have for me a double value, not that of an allegory or symbol mind you, where the same words convey two meanings – they might convey a dozen without ceasing to be tedious – but that of the concrete individual and that of the abstract part. And not only that, but I feel sure that the group in which you take that part comprises us three inseparably though we might have momentarily to fight. Do you recollect my telling you some months ago that no amount of desire legitimated action but that perception must come? I will explain all that to you later but I felt that we formed together a drama such that one is always

[117]

working for the others and cannot go astray. Or fancy a song which must not be interrupted and which two persons sing. All of a sudden the song cannot go on – there lacks a third voice and if it come not the song dies and with it the singers; better one should have to keep silent for a little while until the burden has changed. Well all this supposes much seriousness and is equivalent to the difference between a work of art and a sensational novel. How can it grow into a complete and delicious reality if we rush directly and blindly to the grand effect? My darling, I want you not to stifle your love but to manage it.

What in fact Harry was trying to achieve was a trio, or in other words a quasi-bigamous arrangement whereby Ethel and Julia would each play a complementary role reflecting two different sides of his personality and fulfilling the psychological needs of all three. He genuinely believed that exceptional human beings in an exceptional situation could successfully bring off this kind of triangular relationship. The task was far from easy, but he worked hard at it. Early in June 1884, while trying to bring Ethel round to see the feasibility of the scheme, he was at the same time writing to Julia, who had gone to Germany on a short visit to see her sister:

> *Mon amie*, have confidence in me. I will do nothing to demean us. I know that we hold a treasure in common which without you I should be unable to keep in its entirety and without it I am nothing. . . Believe me that I shall be such as you would wish me to be if you could understand the necessity of the way I am following.

He invokes dialectics and Buddha in his effort to convert her to his point of view:

> It seems to me we are caught up in a drama where everyone changes place. Now it is you who are Buddha and I am the beggar, the one who accepts the sacrifice. I am not ashamed because I feel I have thereby saved the progress and the unity of the drama and because in the new part you are playing you have recovered in my eyes the interest you used to arouse as part of my life and have made possible that beauty towards which I can strive with you. . . The security to which you refer lies in your affection for Ethel and in the joy it gives me to feel much closer

to you, to feel the need for you not as a thing of luxury but as part of the tissue of my life, to feel that we have entered the drama again with dignity. If it were not for all this I wouldn't be loving this new friend of ours who belongs to us both.

While, before any practical stage, he was pleading in principle for the advantages of a trinity rather than a *ménage à trois*, Harry had also to think of his children, of whom he was very fond and from whom he would not contemplate being separated.

The two women remained unconvinced by Harry's contention that they could only be happy if all three held together, each dependent on the other for something essential. Ethel moreover, impulsive as she was, found it hard if not impossible to accept Harry's argument that if she were patient enough all would be well in the end. Given her Anglican and Victorian upbringing the idea of becoming Harry's unofficial second wife was anything but appealing. Julia meanwhile, fighting a desperate battle to retain her husband, went on maintaining that Harry's love for Ethel was imaginary, a temporary infatuation which had blossomed out of all proportion. There was no hurry, wait to see what time made of it all. If it turned out that he was really in love with Ethel, he would have to make a choice: either give up Ethel and never see her again, or face a total break with his wife and children. The situation had the makings of a full-scale drama.

Early in August Harry left Florence for France, ostensibly to see about the rebuilding of Avignonet but in fact to get away from the tense atmosphere of Via de' Bardi. He had pledged himself, however, not to meet or see Ethel during his absence. It was nonetheless his intention to keep up a correspondence with both women from a distance, for he would not give up the battle.

To Ethel he wrote from Paris:

My position towards you and Julia is this. I can say to both of you the same thing: I do not believe that Ethel can give me up and do not accept my dismissal; of course I cannot write to her since she declines corresponding, but I am convinced that she will not manage to free herself and will be mine in the long run and when the proper hour has arrived. I look upon the whole affair as a work we have to undertake in common in which we have all three toil and trouble before us. First I think your love

[119]

and mine, darling, must chime in to the trio, and secondly that this itself is part of something larger. You say you are not cast for tragedy pure and simple; that is very true, nor for comedy either, so that the trio may possibly be unattainable directly. But of all this I intend to be judge and will fight against both of you if necessary; against you to tempt you into 'sin and folly', against Julia if it should turn out that there must be a tragical episode.

To Julia he wrote about the same time:

Ethel declares she is unable to cope with the situation and whilst assuring me that she has not changed she refuses to remain in contact with me whatever the media or envisage resuming contact with me in the future. I think she is right and acts in the right way. The fact that I haven't thrown myself headlong into a mad adventure without issue means that it represents a new development which encompasses all three of us.

A few days later again to Ethel, who remained stubbornly silent:

Ethel I cannot bear this. You will drive me to something desperate and thus do wrong indeed. If I have to give you up I give her up also. What will you have gained then? You will have made us all three miserable and brought everything to a complete smash. Pray do me the honour of believing that I am honest when I tell you that I will not and cannot love either of you alone and against the other. The only difference is that if I turn away from you I shall turn away from her for good and all. Let me tell you this: she would never forgive a stumbler and I could swear that at the present moment she hopes in secret that I am right and trusts that I shall succeed. Don't fancy that being hurt will injure her health or in any way pull her down. It does not hurt her at all to be hurt. She is just like the full-blooded horse who says according to the Arabs: 'Feed me like a brother and ride me like a foe.' What would kill her would be to lose the poetry of her life and that would be the case either if we had run away together like the fools out of a French novel, or if she found that she had loved a man who could 'make a mess' of it and come home asking pardon and promising to behave better . . . Time and again in our best hours Julia and I have assured one another that what bound us together was not we ourselves but

[120]

the remoter interest, and that anything which would vivify it could only knit us together more closely. Passion we looked upon as accidental therein; also even death. She would never attempt to save my life if she thought the right moment had come for me to fall; and if at the first attempt she may look on my love for you as harder to bear than that, it is simply because she is afraid of my going astray – the contrary of which I must prove and that is why we have to be patient.

In some letters to Julia he tries to make her understand his need to venture out of the ivory tower and mix a little more with the world.

I don't like you to say that the multitude doesn't interest you; it must interest you and if you don't understand it in one way you must try to understand it in another. One does not have to succeed at once. But it does not prevent me from loving events and people who push me towards this attempt, even if it is doomed to fail, and from finding that they belong, or she belongs, to us in common. . . You may both of you kick the dust off your sandals; I shall throw it over my shoulder like those handfuls of earth from which the race of men did spring.

From Paris Harry withdrew to Buchetin near the Loire in the neighbourhood of his sister's property, where he settled in a lonely hunting lodge, catching wild rabbits with dachshunds and carrying on his two-pronged correspondence. Ethel stubbornly refused to answer at first, but her determination to enforce a total rupture weakened in the end. She resumed writing to him, but without showing any signs of conversion to his vision of a viable trio. Undaunted, Harry went on battling away, employing as usual his metaphysical dialectics as his weapon of onslaught against Julia's obduracy. But these letters, written as always in delightful French, are also full of vivid metaphors, affection and warmth. In tackling Ethel's opposition he uses more passionate and less abstract language.

At the same time we find Harry hoping to arrange for his little daughter aged ten to visit him for a while, a plan to which Julia was reluctant to agree. Clotilde's pony is ready for her, he writes; he pleads and pleads, but Julia still hesitates.

In September news reached him that the lawsuit for the recovery of some of the money owed for Avignonet by the insurance company had been lost. He wrote to Julia that he could lodge an appeal, but before doing so he wanted to be surer about their future. Even so, he still wished, he says, to rebuild Avignonet, in fact he would like to offer it to her as a gift. Would she join him in Paris where he was planning to spend the winter? If not what would she do if, as expected, there were an outbreak of cholera in Florence? Would she go to Dresden?

> Did you find out anything about Hildebrand's statues? [he asks in a letter], I must write to him and tell him that in Paris there are no small shows of sculpture as there are of paintings. Tell me if you are reading anything interesting. I have been engrossed in Weber. I see my sister once or twice a week. The rest of my time I spend with my dogs and horses in the heather.

Passages such as this come at the end of long letters full of abstract philosophical disquisitions, though with a bearing on their own problem.

At last, towards the end of September, Julia agreed to let Clotilde join him with her governess, Miss Gardiner. There would be a stop at Salzburg – twenty-five hours from there to Paris where he would meet them. Not too long for Clotilde, he writes, for she would sleep in the train most of the time. The north of France, he adds, is free from the cholera raging in southern Europe. He has bought himself a new horse; Clotilde's pony is excellent and waiting for her. But no, at the last minute Julia still hesitates, driving Harry frantic. In the end Clotilde is not allowed to come. Exasperated, he writes to Julia:

> Do not retain my daughter in a spirit of hostility. I am already scarcely human. I shall tell my children: It's good for a husband not always to be at home – this is a woman's place. In the good old days he went fighting on a crusade in the Holy Land or joined the Vikings in piracy. C'est ainsi qu'on aime et qu'on pense.

The reason, whatever it was, remains obscure. Perhaps Julia got wind of Harry's secret but rash escapade in October when he jumped on a train and joined Ethel in Leipzig, where she had gone to attend the performance of some chamber music she had recently composed. The meeting lasted only a few days and after he had left she wrote to him at once:

[122]

Harry, it is all wrong – I am all wrong... You know I cannot care for or marry anyone else, that though you may never claim me I belong to you and to no one else. But otherwise what have I to wait for since I know the world will go the other way round before I could be yours with joy... And so for the sake of my work which is drowned in longing for you – for the sake of everything and because you love me, give me no further sign of your existence... When your work comes out Julia will, I know, tell me and see to my getting it and reading it will be in a way to speak to you – otherwise let there be *utter* silence.

Ethel was referring to a manuscript he was working on, based on their triangular drama.

Harry keeps on writing to Julia in a friendly warm tone, arguing his case with her in metaphysical terms and here and there putting in a few words about the country life he is leading – stag hunting, for instance, with the Terouennes. He is reading Tolstoy and Dostoyevsky with enthusiasm. To Ethel there are now references to the possibility of a formal separation from Julia, for he finds it increasingly hard to put his trio proposition across convincingly. Ignoring Ethel's plea for silence he goes on writing to her; at last she yields and answers his letters.

From Paris, where he would go from time to time on short business visits, he writes to her in November:

I have been working very hard at the theory of our history and think I have got it clearer than ever from a new point of view. This is my only chance with Julia; it is very strange that I happen to be able to fight for you with my own weapons on my own field; you are in a position to determine.

The manuscript, already mentioned by Ethel, was in French at this early stage. Later, in America, Harry elaborated and completed it in English – the first book of his literary career. The psychological strain under which he was then living provided the stimulus he needed.

The months dragged on into 1885. The situation continued undecided and painful for all three. Harry was beginning to lose heart. In February he wrote to Ethel:

My darling, even if I should not succeed I hope I shall not have done wrong by you. Perhaps I ought not to call you my darling as things now stand for there is something of triumph and mirth in the word and we have to be earnest and enduring.

The correspondence that followed during the next few months shows a steady decline in Harry's hopes for the realization of his ideal trio. In the end he gives up, albeit slowly and reluctantly, primarily on account of Julia's opposition even to the idea of a Platonic trio. At this stage, during the first half of 1885, it looks as if Julia were winning the battle, though Harry's letters to Ethel still talk about love – though sometimes with a touch of sadness. They write to each other about books, especially Russian novels.

In April he made up his mind to go to England to see Ethel, though she made it quite clear that because of Julia's opposition she preferred him not to come. She reiterated her feelings of admiration and affection for Julia and her reluctance to act in any way that might hurt her. But Harry insisted on coming. He arrived in London about 10 April, and went down twice from there to Frimhurst, her house in the country. The visits were unsuccessful from the point of view of romance, for Ethel adamantly refused to step beyond the limits of propriety. On his return to Buchetin he wrote to her at once:

> I did not want to agitate you; I was glad and still am so and thoughtlessly told you so. You know what we said and thought from the very beginning – that for our work to be good there must be gain for all three, which means that each of us must, in the new era, make a step forward towards realizing his scheme of life. Hitherto I have been bent on showing clearly that I have not given up and do not intend to give up 'playing the game of life' with Julia, but on the contrary am striving to carry on according to the true spirit of the contract* which merely free it from the corruptibility of the flesh. . .

He says 'hitherto' because he now felt the time had come for him 'to strike out some new path'. He had, however, not only Julia's but Ethel's opposition to reckon with, for she was unwilling to tread an unorthodox path; with the result that he found himself having to drop the 'darling' and 'my love' endearments from his letters. From April onward he addressed her simply as 'Ethel'. On 3 June he wrote to her:

*The marriage agreement between H.B. and Julia.

[124]

I had a letter from Julia desiring that I should state to you just all that I did state during our conversation at Leipzig about the nature of her and my contract; all we know, you and I, and feel. No use talking about it any more.

I have replied that the request has been fulfilled before being made and have told her that I went to see you against your will and that you wished her to be acquainted with the fact. Also that I did right in going, insomuch that instead of stifled regrets and nipped hopes we are now in possession of a high and blameless friendship. Our work reminds me of ceiling painters who have to work over their heads.

I am going to Geneva this evening (poste restante) and have asked Julia to meet me there with the children. I shall try to make my MS a little more intelligible and then have it printed. After that I know not.

Up to now Julia had been slowly gaining ground. A trio on the basis of friendship might have been possible given the esteem, if not full understanding, between the parties. Meanwhile, Lisl's attitude to Ethel's affair with Harry, as her letters disclose, had been at first to ignore the whole business; she felt or liked to feel it was unimportant. When the situation grew more acute she would make veiled references to it in grief rather than annoyance or anger, finding it all somewhat of a nuisance and eventually embarrassing. She adored Ethel but loved her sister too, and she was beginning to feel upset about the havoc which was being caused in Julia's life. Mary and Conrad Fiedler intervened on Ethel's behalf to explain to Lisl that there was nothing glaringly improper in the relationship between Harry and her dear friend. She went on writing affectionate letters to her, though the 'innocence' of the two lovers scarcely made the situation any better. From her point of view Julia's married life was wrecked.

About the middle of June, however, something happened which upset the whole situation. Looking back to this event, Ethel wrote in her memoirs:

Suddenly her letters ceased altogether. As I afterwards learned a new figure now came on the scene, a woman whose chronic jealousy was legend, and who during my long spell of delightful intercourse with her and her husband had had cause in early days – perhaps during a week – for jealousy. It had happened long ago; the whole thing was utterly harmless, born of spirits and vanity, indeed more jocular on both sides than anything else; still it was the only time in my life I had done anything distantly approaching to what Lady Ponsonby called 'prigging hairpins' and no doubt I deserved the drubbing administered by Lisl after confession. Since this peccadillo jealousy had died down – as well it might – and all three of us had been the best of friends and comrades ever afterwards.

It is only fair to say that this lady was much attached to Julia Brewster, and rather late in the day had developed into a strong upholder of the domestic hearth – as beseems a convert, a jealous woman and a mother; all the same I sometimes wonder whether in that summer of 1885 some real cause of complaint against her husband accounted for the zeal with which they both joined in the hue and cry led by my old enemy. Men and women are mean on different lines, and there is a particular sort of male meanness inherent in the relation of the sexes which permits erring husbands to go to great lengths in the way of propitiation; otherwise I cannot account for this belated double-barrelled zeal against me. But the effect was deadly, for it appears to have been a necessity of Lisl's nature to harden her heart against me before she could summon up courage to break our bond; and just because these two were by way of being my friends, their influence told where ancient animosity such as that of her relations would probably have achieved nothing. . .

At length in August came a letter in which only the exquisite handwriting . . . reminded me of Lisl. As I said before there were no fresh accusations to bring, but everything I was and ever had been was drawn by the hand of a stranger – almost an enemy. It appears I was a Juggernaut car driven by a *Lebensteufel,* or rather by a wild horsewoman blinded by self-love, galloping rough-shod over all I met. It was conceded that I was innocent of desire to wreck any fellow mortal's happiness, least of all of a woman I dearly loved, but of what avail, asks the writer, are innocent and excellent intentions if nonetheless devastation marks the path? . . . Re-living this shock, as I did the other day thirty-three years afterwards, it seems to me strange that I did not go mad . . . for life was inconceivable to me without Lisl. . . I wrote to her, bewildered, appealingly, in despair, and received on or two letters in reply, each colder than the last; finally, on September 3rd, in the very words I should use today, I bade her farewell till better days should dawn, and silence fell between us.

It can be easily guessed who the wicked woman was 'whose chronic jealousy was legend' and whom Ethel does not mention by name but refers to with such venom. She does, however, mention for the first time her flirtation with Hildebrand, something that Clotilde Brewster witnessed as a little girl and described most vividly many years later. That it may have been nothing more than a 'peccadillo' was almost certainly thanks to Irene's prompt intervention. She was indeed jealous by nature – and not alone in that – and besides she knew that her husband was a man not excessively particular about the borderlines of a peccadillo. Whether a stricken conscience induced this volte-face to self-righteous morality, such as Ethel infers, is more than unlikely at that still early stage of his marriage, which continued to be harmonious for many years. The trouble which did eventually arise, though without disastrous consequences, came much later.

The simple fact was that Ethel never got on with Irene, though she did manage, for the sake of Irene's delightful husband, to establish very cordial relations with both of them – as she states herself. Beneath the surface, however, her aversion to Irene remained unchanged and when rumours reached her that she had had a hand in Lisl's making up her mind to break with her, her feelings turned to rage. Which is why she probably exaggerated her influence or participation in the matter. The naked truth of it we do not know, but Irene was a close friend of both Julia and Lisl; therefore it is more than likely that the three women should have sometimes got together and talked about Julia's marital troubles. Harry had been absent for more than a year, for which Ethel was naturally held responsible. In the general climate of nineteenth-century morality it was not surprising that Irene, without being the fiend that Ethel made her out to be, should have suggested to Lisl that her close friendship with the young English girl was scarcely in keeping with her loyalty to her sister, and that perhaps a break with this Juggernaut of a friend might help to bring Harry back to the family hearth. Although Lisl had been convinced by the Fiedlers that there was nothing adulterous in the relationship between Harry and Ethel, what was the use, she thought, of no 'sin' being committed if the result was the same and the family unit broken up?

Reluctantly, therefore, Lisl took the fatal step. As a tactical move, however, it was disastrous since it had the opposite effect to the one aimed at or expected. Julia had almost won the battle, for Harry could not bring himself to break with her and his family. He felt that if the bigamous relationship could not be achieved, at least a platonic arrangement among the three of them, as a second-best solution, might be agreed upon, whereby he would be able to consort with them intellectually and spiritually. This, he felt, was better than having to choose one of the two women to the exclusion of the other.

Now, however, Ethel was mortified. She was particularly incensed by the fact that she had not been presented with an ultimatum: either Lisl or Harry – choose. From the remarks she makes in her memoirs it would seem she might have chosen Lisl. Be that as it may, her fury at the interference of the Hildebrands was such as to trouble Harry deeply, even though he had never had much enthusiasm for the Lisl-Ethel infatuation. He took up the cudgels in Ethel's defence, his feelings hardening against Julia.

After not having seen each other for nearly a year and a half, Harry and Julia agreed to meet at Milan early in November. This meeting proved inconclusive. They met again in Florence on 22 November. Harry presented his wife with an ultimatum. Either she gave up the Hildebrands and the Fiedlers, who were now regarded as the arch-intriguers, and undertook never to see them again, in which case he, in return, would limit his relations with Ethel to a line of pure friendship, or, if Julia did not accept the requested condition, he insisted on a definite separation.

Just as Lisl's move in breaking with Ethel was a psychological boomerang, Harry's ultimatum was also to prove a mistake. He should have known that Julia's self-respect, dignity and sense of justice would never have permitted her to give up her closest friends because of their well-meant intervention, however ill-advised it may have been. Her negative answer to his request led to a 'treaty' agreed between them which they formulated in French. It is entitled 'Traité de Florence, 22 Novembre 1885' and is in duplicate, each copy being in their respective handwriting and signed by them both. The agreement reads as follows:

Having accepted all the conditions imposed upon him, Harry for his part demands that Julia should give up certain friendships (outside her family) and should come to live with him in Paris.

Julia having been unable to accept the first of these two conditions agrees to the following stipulation made jointly between them:

1. Each of the two shall be free and independent to act as he or she chooses.

2. Julia shall have the custody (personal and untransferable) of the children.

3. Harry shall have the right to invite them and have them with him during three months of the year, separately or together.

The meeting must have been painful or to say the least unpleasant, though it was no doubt held in an atmosphere of exemplary affability – both protagonists were the embodiment of civilized behaviour.

Harry returned to Paris. He could not have been happy at heart but he triumphantly paraded the agreement in his next letter to Ethel:

Julia is not coming to Paris; we separated outwardly and as far as inwardly is concerned I consider myself, and am recognized by the treaty we have drawn up and signed, as free to follow without any restriction the course I judge best. I make over to her the guardianship of the children and retain the right of having them with me three months of the year. In short my position is not that of a husband but of a brother who is not to be called to account. I am *unmarried* or *dis-married*, as far as I can without a divorce. I am looking for an apartment in Paris and am starting a new life. . .

You told me that the result of my interview with Julia would in no manner change your attitude. I will talk of this presently but I wish you to observe that the separation has taken place on grounds to me personal, to wit that Julia refused to give up the Hildebrands and the Fiedlers, at my demand; it was on this point that two things clearly appeared warranting an entire change in our connection; firstly a practical incompatibility (is that English?) in our feelings, and secondly a lack of influence of the husband on the wife. I sincerely did all I could and offered

[129]

every sacrifice, that could be asked. I am perfectly quiet about the result, for that reason. Also because I really believe it is the truth of the situation.

But was it really the truth of the situation? Why did he not ask for a divorce? In any case Ethel was far from persuaded by the arguments that followed in the same letter that the treaty provided them much greater freedom. In spite of her warning Harry evidently did not foresee the violence of her reaction. It was peremptory and crushing. A few days after the dispatch of his letter he received, on 5 December, the following reply:

No – it cannot be – can never be. I have been too mistaken – have sinned too deeply.

By all you feel for me I entreat you not to answer this – never write to me again – nor try to see me. . . Try to understand each other – to get nearer to each other than you are now – you cannot do that merely by offering sacrifices.

And do this for me – the one thing I may ask and do ask you to do – cut off your life for ever from mine.

ETHEL

So now, after a year and seven months of struggle to keep both women, then, when this became impossible, to hold on to the one with whom he was in love, Harry suddenly found himself with neither. Ethel not only had a bad conscience for having been instrumental in the break-up of a family, but she also shrank from becoming somebody's mistress. And Harry probably knew that even if he were to obtain a legal divorce, a step he was anyway not prepared to take, Ethel would never marry him: she would not accept what she knew would have meant an even greater sacrifice for him than separation. So a silence fell between them that lasted a couple of years, although this extraordinary Jamesian drama was destined to go on for another decade.

Harry, in Paris, was indeed alone. He was genuinely fond of his sister but she did not and could not fill this new spiritual void. He was only thirty-five years old, still a young man. Feeling in need of fresh air, he turned to America, the land of his forebears. His uncle, Seabury, had recently died in New York leaving a considerable fortune. His will, however, was ambiguous. Harry knew that a large proportion of it should come to him and his sister, as Seabury's closest heirs, their brother Louis having died some years previously. But unless the issue was contested by means of a lawsuit most of the money would go to various of Harry's relations. So the lawsuit had duly started and his presence in New York was advisable. This provided a good excuse for leaving Europe. On 6 January he wrote to Julia informing her of the lawsuit and his consequent journey, adding that he would be travelling with Kate and concluding: 'Il faut que j'oublie mes idées pour apprendre ce que savent les plus ig-norants. Il est bon que j'aille en Amérique.'

14

House and Friends

The essence of San Francesco consists in its strong walls, its space and proportions and its close harmony with those who have determined its life. But much has been added by its friends. Some came and stayed, some were constant visitors, returning again and again, some just stepped in with a curious eye like the tourists of today.

Hildebrand's friends were not only numerous but varied and interesting. First and foremost comes Conrad Fiedler, a friendship which, having started on the basis of patronage, soon developed into a close dialogue of mind and heart. From the earliest days of Hildebrand's life at San Francesco Fiedler was a constant, faithful visitor, a real family friend as well as an intellectual companion. His aesthetic views and criticism remained always of integral importance to Hildebrand, both as sculptor and thinker.

When Fiedler married in 1876 he rented a small house within the grounds of the San Francesco property and spent much of his time there when he was not staying at Crostowitz, his home in Germany. During his absences from Florence the two friends constantly exchanged letters, which have been published and bear witness to the intellectual liveliness of the relationship.[1]

Mary Meyer, Fiedler's wife, became a close friend of Cosima Wagner and an enthusiastic supporter of the Wagnerian group at Wahnfried. Her appearance on the San Francesco scene came rather as a shock. She was a Bavarian girl, remarkably pretty, with a forceful personality and with much sex appeal. But she was hopelessly commonplace, '*derb*' as the Germans say – or at least some of her husband's friends thought so. There were also doubts about the quality of her intellect, suggestions that at times she seemed 'silly', and at San Francesco this was a serious charge. How was it possible that Fiedler, the picture of refinement and sensibility, should have chosen her? Yet because he had, she had to be accepted. Irene made great efforts to establish a sound basis of friendship with her, which

[132]

endured the test of time as well as of Irene's patience. But one suspects she was not nearly as stupid or shallow *au fond* as she was made out to be at San Francesco. Ethel made much of her for several years and only cooled off when she suspected the Fiedlers had abetted Lisl's estrangement.

In fact Mary Fiedler was both formidable and ambitious; a creature of common sense and social direction and probably utterly ruthless. She had always been in love with Hermann Levi, the famous Wagner orchestra conductor of the times, whom she appears at first to have failed to ignite. She married Fiedler for money, position and social advantage; she scarcely appreciated or understood him. He doted on her and spoilt her to the point of absurdity.

She persuaded him little by little to spend most of the year in Germany, away from Florence and his friends at San Francesco, because in Germany she could be within reach of Bayreuth and Levi whom she seduced in the end. After Fiedler's death she married him, but by then he was old and ailing. He died and she married again, another musician and conductor, Michael Balling. She got on well with personalities. Her staunch support of Wahnfried and Bayreuth sharpened the friction and coloured the drama between the Wagnerites and the Brahmsians which throughout the second half of the last century in Germany so divided the musical world. Nothing was more topical, more modern or more burning than the debate on the stature of these two composers; nothing in the musical world could give rise to greater animosity. There were moments when the members of the opposite camps were scarcely on speaking terms.

Hildebrand, as a sculptor, could hope to keep out of the fray. If he was unwillingly roped in from time to time, he would claim that contemporary music lay beyond him – which perhaps in a way it did. Two of his best friends, the Herzogenbergs, and later Clara Schumann herself, together the spearhead of the Brahms faction, were pulling in one direction, while good friends such as Jessie Taylor, Mary Fiedler, Hermann Levi and in due course Cosima herself, kept pulling in the other. Besides, the pose of musical innocence must have been awkward for Hildebrand who played the viola and organized informal concerts at San Francesco. Conrad Fiedler, who tried to act as a mediator between the two factions, being able to appreciate both composers though with some

[133]

reservations about each, did not make the situation any easier for Hildebrand by his constant efforts to convert his friend to a more acceptable frame of mind towards Wagner. The fact of the matter was that Hildebrand had little enough enthusiasm for Brahms, though he sculpted his memorial, and even less, to put it mildly, for Wagner whose bust he stubbornly refused to make in spite of Cosima's blandishments. Extremely musical himself, as Ethel remarks in her memoirs, and always eager to get his musical friends together to play trios and quartets with him, his taste was conservative, though perhaps not to the extent Ethel made it out to be. In any case it was a convenient conservatism, for it enabled him to keep out of the hottest hostilities and retain friends in both camps.

Fiedler's efforts to soften his feelings towards Wagner were of no avail. At the beginning of their respective marriages and at the time of Fiedler's initiation to Bayreuth, there began a lively exchange of letters on the subject between the two friends. In the end Fiedler succeeded in leading the discussion at least to a point where both agreed to leave the matter open until they should hear Wagner again and together. Hildebrand closed the argument as follows:

> Opera as a composite form of art presents two sequences instead of one and therefore is not a pure form of art; not art given by nature, but a fabrication by man. Wagner wants to make it art of a single 'sequence'. Therefore the result of what he creates is not a new form, as Rembrandt created, but an entire new art sequence which has not existed hitherto. Herein he stands alone and cannot be compared with any other artist. . . Whether there is a clear, unifying imagination which holds together this sequence is, I believe, the kernel of the issue. We must, of course, leave the matter open till we both know Wagner's works more thoroughly. That we should agree up to this point is important to me, for it is evident that this new imagination divides itself into drama and music as soon as it becomes clear, and this has been the case in opera so far. It seems to me that this coming together of the two into one (as in Wagner) can only occur as long as it is nebulous and therefore non-artistic, for it falls apart as soon as the fusion clears itself. You believe in the possibility of a further coming together through clarity. *Vedremo*.[2]

Fiedler agreed to drop the argument until they were better prepared

[134]

to resume it, but insisted in the meantime that the advent of Wagner was far more important than he had hitherto suspected.

The friendship between Fiedler and Hildebrand continued through the years on this high intellectual plane, and both as a close neighbour and as a regular visitor Fiedler contributed greatly to the world of San Francesco. Tragedy came of a sudden, the news of it like a clap of thunder. On 3 June 1895, while opening the window of his room in Munich, Fiedler fainted and fell to his death on the pavement below. There were rumours that his married life had been unhappy; indeed there are letters which disclose that Mary did not love her husband at all. For his part he must have been unhappy about her closeness to Levi, with whom she may already have been on sexually intimate terms. Fiedler's death may have been suicide, though in the Hildebrand family circle it has always been held that it was an accident, the result of ill-health from which he had been suffering for some time. There is no evidence, except circumstantial, to the contrary.

Fiedler's philosophical works have been translated into English only in part. Much remains to be done to make him better known outside Germany. Herbert Read held him in high esteem as a thinker in the field of aesthetics. His importance in relation to modern art and to new ways of conceiving art is not insignificant. From a book of his published in 1876 one can gauge the perspicacity of Fiedler's mind as it scoured a horizon of thought until then totally unexplored. The Impressionist school of painting in France had only just started and was hardly known. Fiedler says, on the subject of realistic and idealistic art, that 'the works of the realists and idealists are artistically unimportant'. The realists 'descend to low levels of undeveloped perception of nature', while the idealists

> by neither feeling satisfied with nature such as they perceive it nor being able to develop their perception of nature to higher levels, try to remedy their artistic insufficiency of their own creations by giving them a non-artistic content. . . Art can have but one task. It is a task which art has solved in every one of its genuine works. This task will again and again await new solutions so long as men are born with the desire to bring the world into their consciousness in artistic forms. Art is always realistic because it tries to create for men that which is foremost in it, its

[135]

reality. Art is always idealistic, because all reality that art can create is a product of the mind.'[3]

Even more interesting, perhaps, and well ahead of his time, were Fiedler's ideas on the artist's alienation from nature in so far as he stands outside, facing it as a separate entity. He gave expression to these thoughts in a letter to Hildebrand dated 17 May 1877, which was published first in Germany with a selection of other letters of his and then translated into English and published in the United States in 1951. The following passage from that book is worth quoting here:

Before perceiving anything recognizable and in need of being recognized, man already feels the need to overcome the isolation in which he finds himself as an individualized component part of nature. It seems to me that the consciousness of loneliness, of foreignness (which necessarily must arise in a being who finds himself suddenly in opposition to the whole context of unconscious nature to which he belongs, almost expelled from it on account of what we call his human consciousness of himself) is the first element on which we can lay our finger when we talk of human intellectual activity. The urge to escape from this isolation is the really productive urge in man. His need for scientific cognition which seemed to us founded directly on the spiritual nature of man and in no need of further explanation, is now revealed as stemming from the desire of the individual to eliminate the dividing wall erected between him and nature. It is one of the means whereby man believes he is able to make his own again what he lost the moment he became an independent being. . . All true artistic activity springs from the need to overcome the distance between the individual and nature, to bring nature close and ever closer, until it can be grasped and held. Art then is not simply a sort of cognition, but rather one of the means by which man tries to extricate himself from his isolated position and tries to regain contact with nature. . . I would like to know whether you agree with me on the fact of the isolation of man and his urge, often passionate, to overcome this isolation by every means.

From this interesting and convincing vantage point Fiedler

proceeded, elsewhere, to explore the participation of the receptive mind in the aesthetic value of the work of art it is contemplating or reacting to, and hence the interdependence between the work of art and the mind that understands and enjoys it.

There was another man, a Scotsman, who ranked among Hildebrand's oldest acquaintances and remained until his death a close family friend. Charles Grant, son of a tradesman who spent much of his life in West Africa, was born in 1841. His mother, a forceful woman, had been previously married to a Methodist missionary in Africa and brought up her son in an atmosphere of strict Methodist piety. In the sixties of the last century we find him at Jena as a lecturer and teacher of English, and for some years as Hildebrand's tutor. It was thanks to Grant that Hildebrand spoke English fluently throughout his life. At Jena they both became friends of the biologist Anton Dohrn and were later together in Naples where Dohrn had founded the aquarium and where Grant was destined to spend much of his life, when not at San Francesco with the Hildebrands. On one of the aquarium frescoes at Naples painted by Marées, Grant, Hildebrand, Dohrn and Marées himself are portrayed.

Fiedler's relationship with Hildebrand was always on a high intellectual level. There was a place for affection and intimacy that stopped short of the frivolous and unrestrained. On the other hand between Hildebrand and Grant there was an undemanding fellowship which dated back to early youth. They could relax together. Grant was a man of sensibility, open-minded and witty, with a keen sense of humour and great charm of manner. Fiedler was the embodiment of nineteenth-century respectability; Grant was not, though he tried hard to conform to convention, which weighed upon him heavily. He pulled himself together only by the most strenuous efforts of self-control. This ultimately broke him. Although he fell deeply in love with a girl who died of consumption, one suspects that this was a spiritual love and that his sexual tendencies were homosexual; and that in an age of Victorian respectability the inevitable repression brought on one of the main problems of his life, excessive drink. He died a dipsomaniac, but until the end Hildebrand remained intensely attached to him.

Italy had loosened the Methodist stiffness of his background. He shared with Hildebrand a fondness, if not for women, for wine, for fun and frivolity. A typical letter of Grant's is the following:

[137]

My dear Adolf, it was rather inconsiderate of you, not to say malevolent, to go home and fall ill just as we were hoping to spend a happy winter together. You were, if you allow me to use a rather commonplace expression, the olive oil in our salad. What Marées is I don't quite know. His talk is as sharp as mustard, but then again it is as nourishing as an egg. His brother is without any doubt the sugar. As for me, well, I'm the vinegar and just now very acid. We are all of us excellent each in our own way, but you were the binding element and without you we can neither really unite nor each of us alone bring out his proper flavour.[4]

After settling at San Francesco and getting respectably married at last, Hildebrand could not help looking back with nostalgia to the merry days in Naples. Now he had to behave; but he encouraged his old friend to come to stay as often as possible.

Grant had given up teaching and taken to writing. He was gifted. He wrote poems, some rather beautiful, and produced a plethora of articles and essays on literary and political topics for both English and Continental newspapers. But as a writer he will be remembered especially for a collection of delightful stories about life in the streets of Naples.[5] The slums and the poorest people of the city fascinated him. He devoted years of study to them, resulting in a book remarkable not only for its observation but also for its sympathetic understanding of the Neapolitans, good and bad.

Grant was a cultivated man with a wide knowledge of German as well as English literature. He was interested also in art and religion, especially Roman Catholicism towards which he felt a strong affinity, perhaps in reaction to his Methodist background but perhaps too because he thought he might find in the faith emotional relief from his psychological troubles. Much as he wanted to become a convert, out of consideration for his sister's Protestant piety he never actually took the step. It was later discovered that already before his death she had become a Catholic herself, but had never told him for the same reason.

A large proportion of Grant's correspondence with Hildebrand is of a dialectical character, but now and then there are some letters which show the lighter-hearted, and perhaps truer, nature of their relationship. This is Hildebrand writing to Grant in December 1877.

[138]

Dear Grant, I don't know why, but today I love you quite particularly and would like to indulge with you in nonsense. If only you were here we would have a wonderful breakfast tomorrow. I have seen some delicious things in town; smoked salmon, goose liver pâté, brain sausages I have just received from home and also Rhine wine. Grant, we would eat and drink well and the world would become to us a large, stupendous pâté; human beings would become sausages from which we would cut slices, the slices that taste nice; and the ends we would throw away. Woe to all human ends; the best part is sliced off in between, and yet they, the extremities, regard themselves as the beginning and the end of everything. Grant, I believe there is more in woman than in man – men are after all superfluous. In course of time they will let themselves be replaced by machines, but women never. After all men belong to the outer world; it is women who are human. The human in us is feminine. Men are the reasonable side of nature, therefore of the outer world. What is truly human is the sensitive unreasonable, dream-world; this is feminine, and we men are only there as cement to hold it all together. This is our task. Listen old boy, the wine is good here and proof of it is that I'm not in the least moody. Moreover I have only been drinking coffee now and I have been all fantasy with you. What is your opinion of the Holy Ghost? I believe in it, or him. If you know him well you can do without God the Father and Son, but if you disown the Holy Ghost you are immoral. Only in him full consciousness is to be achieved as holy I, true human consciousness, namely of feminine nature. So it is that we love a woman as our holy ghost; through womanhood we develop our most human element into full sensibility; the rest of our being belongs therefore to the outer world. Give yourself a woman, Grant – you won't be able to keep up otherwise – we have an endless supply of wine here and when you are prepared to turn morality into love and love into morality, it is impossible to be either sober or insipid.

Not long before this letter was written a tragic event had taken place in Grant's life. Helen Baronowska, sister of Mary Baronowska who was married to Dohrn, had died. Grant had loved her and her death came as a blow from which he recovered with difficulty.

[139]

There were, however, cheerful moments. Hildebrand describes one of them. 'Today Liszt visited us, extremely old. Last night we were all at a party given by Jessie Hillebrand and Liszt was playing the usual rubbish, virtuoso trills. But Grant was in high spirits, a little tipsy, and expressing himself in every imaginable language didn't hesitate to tell everybody his mind.'

To Hildebrand Grant could write in the following strain with a touch of good native sense of humour. It was on 1 August 1883 from Trinity College, Cambridge:

Everybody here – Mr Dew most of all – wishes you would come to England again. The other day he showed me an old book of his in which you had drawn a number of nude figures.

The very undressed character of your pictures reminds me of the following advertisement which appeared the other day I think in *The Times*: 'Mrs Sylvester having left off wearing apparel of every kind invites a personal inspection.'

But Grant had also his darker moods, his phases of inner suffering. It is unlikely that Hildebrand could be of much comfort to him then. For Hildebrand was a man so taken up with his work and the pleasant and happy things of life that he would turn a deaf ear to the woeful disclosures of his friends. This trait is stressed by the poetess Isolde Kurz, an admirer of Hildebrand, in a passage quoted below from her book *The Master of San Francesco*:

I was enchanted and carried away by his gay self-assurance, as much as I was pained by the total indifference with which he would isolate and push aside a sad event from its living surroundings. It was as if a lid had clapped down. I was not the only one to suffer dismay when confronted with the artists's merciless eyes full of light.

Indelibly impressed upon my mind have remained the words of his oldest friend and most enthusiastic admirer, who though not a Christian believer himself – who was in those days? – had grown up in a deep religious atmosphere as a son of a missionary. Constantly a guest at San Francesco he would often escape from that dwelling of happiness to throw himself upon his knees in one of the churches of Florence, and once I overheard him exclaim with an anguished heart: 'O rather the nails! The nails!'

Isolde Kurz's experience throws an interesting sidelight on Hildebrand's character. He was not heartless as one might infer; on the contrary, he was known to his friends as kindly, benevolent, cheerful and in certain respects helpful; and for both Grant and Fiedler he certainly had genuine affection. But he also had a ruthless, even callous, quality which showed itself in a kind of impatience about other people's problems. He felt he had not the time for them a friend might expect. If he saw he could do something he would do it straightaway, but if he realized he could do nothing he would push the matter aside.

Her statement that Grant was not a Christian believer is probably inaccurate, though he may have had periods of difficulty with his faith. For his Methodist upbringing he had only regret. This is from a letter he wrote from Jena to Hildebrand, at that time only twenty:

Most people are so thoroughly one-sided that they have only one range of interest and look at the whole world from one point of view alone. They have no tolerance for differences of character and seldom even for differences of opinion. All the summer through I was a political bigot which was the more inexcusable in me because I have always considered tolerance as the highest result and end of culture, that is the highest tolerance which is based on comprehension of, and sympathy with, all parties and modes of thought. I was educated among narrow interests and in a bigoted religious sect. I have had to cut myself free from a thousand bonds which were made of my own flesh and blood, but the struggle has dwarfed me and weakened my powers and cast a shade of sorrow over my life. I shall never be what I might have been had I grown up in the heathen atmosphere and wide intellectual range of a home like yours.

From about the middle of the 1880s we find references in Hildebrand's letters to Grant's growing addiction to drink. Friends were worried. Hildebrand dismissed the matter, however, as not being very serious. Irene wrote to her sister-in-law in February 1896:

Grant has now left for Naples. We have had some very pleasant days with him. As Adolf has not been very well recently and therefore not in a mood to work, Grant's company proved particularly agreeable, stimulating and cheerful. . . As regards Grant himself our worries are of a different kind. He has come back from England having caught there the habit of drinking spirits, a complaint which might prove difficult to heal. Jessie says he is suffering already from incipient *delirium tremens*, but we see his condition as not nearly so serious. In other respects England has done him a lot of good; he has become more cheerful and more sociable and doesn't plunge with passion into love and hatred as he used to do. The eternal puffing locomotive has somewhat calmed down allowing into the foreground the humorous grandpapa. He has grown all grey and has developed a little paunch like that of Dr Luther.

Reluctant though the Hildebrands may have been to attach too much importance to Grant's drinking, it proved a fatal weakness. As years went by he spent much of his time in Carinthia, a province of Austria where he was making a study of the country and people. He had said he wanted to live in a German-speaking country, but not a Protestant one. Hildebrand's brother was professor at the University of Graz. The news that came was always more alarming. In 1889 he died in *delirium tremens* after suffering from almost complete paralysis. Hildebrand wrote to Fiedler:

Yesterday I got a telegram from Richard that Grant had died. I don't know yet the details. It all went so quickly. Since I was fourteen he and I have been together time and again. Never was there a period of more than three years in between. When those die with whom you have shared the past it is hard to believe in death which becomes more and more shadowy.

The full story of Charles Grant remains to be told. The following passage from a letter of his to Marées, written in 1872 when he first came to Italy, shows the modesty, refinement and sensibility of his mind:

You will not I am sure, like some people, expect me to tell you what I think of Italy. It is a new world to me and I feel like a child who has not yet acquired even the rudimentary knowledge which would enable him to form an opinion on the simplest facts. The seeds that are sown must have time to take root and ripen and I have no wish to dig them up in order to see if they are growing. I was perhaps ill-prepared for my journey for I find that

[142]

the new truths do not at once enter into harmonious relations with the old ones. They alter and modify them, sometimes they appear even to contradict them. Nor is this all. A new intellectual sense seems to be awakening within me though as yet it only enables me 'to see men as trees walking'. Hitherto the impressions made upon me by natural scenery have been vague though vivid. They have awakened long trains of thought and feeling and these have remained impressed upon my mind rather than the scene itself. If I went further I endeavoured only to analyse my own impressions. But this is here impossible. The old wall with its clump of cypresses and evergreen oaks may suggest a thousand thoughts or feelings but it is also something in itself. I cannot get rid of it as I did of our northern rocks and trees by placing a group of children or lovers beneath them and then dwelling rather on my own creation than on that of nature. The thing itself haunts and confuses me. It has an eerie unreal existence. I find that the most important words are wanting in my vocabulary, the words which like those of Dante are things.

I need not say that this is even more true of art. The terse concise expression of the great masters, which gives all and nothing more than all that is required, is new to my uneducated eyes. One cannot think a number of pretty things about their pictures, one can only see them. I hope the light which began to dawn upon me in the Berlin gallery will gradually become clear and full, but I shall have to spell my way through many passages of the great book of nature first.

It was Grant's influence that lay at the heart of Hildebrand's knowledge of English and his liking for English people. Early in the 1880s Grant shared a villa in Florence with a close friend and fellow Scotsman, Gerald Balfour, a younger brother of Arthur James Balfour, later Prime Minister, whose peerage Gerald inherited. He himself went into politics and became a member of Parliament after spending a number of years settled in Florence with Grant – where, like Grant, he became a close friend of the Hildebrands. It was a long-lasting friendship. When Hildebrand visited England for the second time in 1911 it was largely due to Gerald Balfour that his impression of London was more favourable than it had been in 1877. On that occasion he had been commissioned to make a bust of

Prince Leopold at Windsor Castle. In London he put up at the Grosvenor Hotel. The weather was foul; he was short of friends; Windsor Castle, to which he repaired regularly for the sittings, did not impress him apart from the paintings and Holbein's drawings. In his letters he complained of having to dine with frightfully boring gentlemen at Windsor Castle. 'When my friend Dew is here life is not so boring,' he writes, 'but unhappily he is most of his time at Cambridge. He takes me to his club where you eat well and are not swept away with the dishes and plates as in the restaurants.'

Dew-Smith was one of the Englishmen Hildebrand had met in Italy, probably through Grant and Balfour. Dew-Smith asked him down to Cambridge again, but as soon as the bust (which is still at Windsor Castle) was finished, Hildebrand left England without a second visit to his friend at Trinity College. Perhaps he was disgusted because, on a wave of Victorian respectability, the drawings he had made and donated to the college laboratory had been wiped out. On 9 September 1877 Dew had written to him with healing levity informing him of this puritanical act of vandalism.

I so much want you to come over to see us again, because Michael Foster has built himself a new house with a porch, and I have induced him to leave the stucco plain and smooth in order that you might make drawings on it. I am sorry to tell you that your drawings in our old Laboratory have been obliterated. The Vice-Chancellor of the University went down to see them and thought them indecent and had them all rubbed out, and yet he did not know that the Adam and Eve were intended to be illustrative of the Dawn of Physiology. That little fellow in short pantaloons that you called David I never much liked, but I liked him still less when one of your countrymen came over and asked me if I served as a model to the dreadful-looking creature whose head David had just taken liberties with.

Grant is still in England. He is not very happy I am afraid. He is longing to return to Italy again. His mother is still lying ill and I am afraid will never recover. Please come over and see us some day. If you do not I shall never see you because I have determined never to leave my native land again.

Gerald Balfour had bought the villa in Florence in the days when, it seems, philosophy was his principal interest, although he maintained a vicarious involvement in politics because of his brother.

In 1888 Hildebrand wrote to Fiedler: 'We never see any newspapers. I am kept informed, however, by Grant and Balfour of the Liberals, the election, and the situation in Ireland' (Arthur Balfour had been appointed Chief Secretary for Ireland the previous year). But then Gerald decided to be actively involved himself. 'Just think,' Hildebrand says in one of his letters to Fiedler, 'Balfour is selling his villa and wants to throw himself into politics and enter Parliament. We see him every week.' And in another letter adds: 'The Sudan stinks and Balfour thinks very badly of it.' From Balfour himself he hears, after his departure from Florence: 'On my arrival in England I found that as far as politics were concerned I had not returned a moment too soon, if I meant to stand for Parliament. What constituency I am to stand for is not yet settled however.'

Events pleasant and unpleasant followed each other in quick succession in Gerald's political life. A year and a half later we find Hildebrand writing to Fiedler: 'I have news of Balfour. He has got himself engaged, but is quite broken under the stress and strain of parliamentary activities and he must now undergo a milk cure for a month. He is quite worn out. His letter sounds so soft.' Balfour, however, was perhaps not as soft as all that, even though his health was delicate, for he wrote to Hildebrand at about that time:

> Democracy is on trial just now in England, and it must be confessed that in many respects it is showing the seamy side outwards. But if the upper classes are not prepared to stick to public life notwithstanding all the *désagréments*, we are done. So all that remains is to wrap oneself in one's own virtue and face the inclement weather as best one may. You will probably have seen in the papers my brother's appointment to the Chief Secretaryship of Ireland. It is a fearful responsibility and I wish him well through it.

This wrapping oneself up in upper-class virtue sounds rather priggish, but Gerald Balfour was appreciated by the Hildebrands who were anything but priggish. Over the years the friendship endured. In 1906 Gerald wrote to his friend in Florence:

> I believe it is eighteen years ago this month since we met and

[145]

since I was last in Florence. At that time I was so ill that it seemed doubtful whether I should ever be strong again. However, thanks chiefly to my wife, I have pulled through and have been able to stand the ten years of hard work in political office. Now that the whirligig of time has brought about his revenges and has made me a comparatively free man again, I should dearly love to revisit old haunts and renew old friendships.

Perhaps that may come about sometime. Meanwhile we are doing the next best thing by sending our eldest daughter, Ruth, who is with her grandmother Lady Lytton, to spend a month in Florence. I am sure you and Mrs Hildebrand will be glad to see them if only for the sake of old recollections and therefore I have not hesitated to tell them to call at San Francesco. I was glad to hear from my friend Donald Tovey that you are both well. I hope you liked him. Of all our young musicians in England I think he has the most talent and he is a great favourite with Dr Joachim.

It was indeed at San Francesco, the cradle of their friendship, that Hildebrand made the relief of Gerald in 1882 (see p. 23, and note). It ranks among Hildebrand's finest works.

Gladstone himself came to San Francesco in 1887 with his youngest daughter Helen, who was Vice-Principal of Newnham College. Two years later she started a correspondence with Hildebrand about a bronze bust he had made of Francis Balfour for Trinity College, Cambridge. Francis, a younger brother of Gerald and a distinguished biologist, had met Hildebrand in Naples through Anton Dohrn at the Stazione Zoologica in the early 1870s. Unhappily he fell to his death at the age of thirty in attempting to climb Mont Blanc. A laboratory was established at Newnham College and named after him. Helen Gladstone took all the necessary steps to procure from Hildebrand a marble copy of the bust at Trinity for the new laboratory. As he had retained the original plaster of Paris he could make the marble copy in Florence; and from there, on completion, it was shipped to England. When it arrived safely at Cambridge Helen wrote to Hildebrand thanking him and expressing much appreciation on behalf of Newnham College and herself.

Among Hildebrand's artist friends who were closely connected with San Francesco or left some imprint upon it was a painter, John Sattler, who frequently came to stay and painted murals in the library – scenes of Holland, Flanders, Spain and Italy. Years later his son married Hildebrand's eldest daughter.

Sattler had a kind of peasant-like simplicity which endeared him to his friends and to Hildebrand in particular. The following story about him was handed down to subsequent generations:

> He was a little man interested in food as well as painting and had three daughters, big, somewhat buxom, handsome girls endowed rather in the Brünhild mould. He was so worried about the degree of attention they kept drawing from the opposite sex that he would change residence from country to country. Their ways were notoriously free for the times. When at one period they were living in Saxony the neighbourhood was intrigued. Out of curiosity someone questioned the maid of the household.
>
> 'Do tell me, what sort of people are these Sattlers?'
>
> 'Well, sir, he stands in the kitchen all day long and cooks; she, sir, is always lying on a sofa reading the Bible, and they, the daughters, sir, they leap about the house in the nude all day, playing the guitar.'

A talented painter, too modest to make much of his paintings which were full of poetry and charm and too unobtrusive to take steps to exhibit them as he should have done, Sattler's claims to fame were his daughters, his gifts as a raconteur, his sense of humour and his remarkable arsenal of swear words. There was reputedly a wineshop he frequented in Florence where his acquaintances would go to hear him swear. With his closer friends, such as Hildebrand, he did not have to rely exclusively on such idiosyncratic appeal.

Then there was Hans Thoma, certainly one of the better painters Germany produced at that time. He appeared on the scene in the eighties and soon became an enthusiastic admirer both of San Francesco and of Hildebrand himself. He left a considerable number of letters which testify to his appreciation. He spent the whole spring and summer of 1887 at San Francesco and painted an attractive picture of the ground floor loggia, now in the Bonn Museum. As he says in his letters, the atmosphere of San Francesco was congenial to his work. To his own family he wrote on Easter Sunday of that year:

[147]

Mrs Hildebrand is a wonderful woman. She farms with her peasants. They have excellent wine; which she makes so good and lasting by exposing it in bottles for weeks throughout the summer on the terrace in the broiling sun. In this way it becomes something quite superb. Today the sun is out again and I delight in warming myself in it. I sit by the open window and the bells of Florence are ringing and the finches are singing in the garden. It is so lovely. . . . My paintings are much more at home here than at the Frankfurt Union. There are big fine rooms in Hildebrand's house, my own room is at least twenty-four feet by twenty-four. . . . Mrs Hildebrand, her son and I are dining with Mrs Brewster this evening.

A couple of months later he wrote to a friend:

I feel happy to be able to swim again in elements so different from those familiar to me and then there is Hildebrand who takes me away with him with his fiery youthful stride. His recent output is of a very high quality and with it he leaps so far beyond all modern sculptors in that he has succeeded in preserving his naive contact with nature. He is more than a sculptor – he is a seer in art. The eternal youthful present of all art is alive in him, and totally absent from him are those archaeological ghosts which are liable to haunt the Renaissance as the vaults of the dead.

I have quoted this passage, coming as it does from the pen of a prominent German artist of the time, because it throws light on how Hildebrand's work was looked at and understood. It is interesting because though Thoma's appraisal is without any doubt true and applicable to much of his sculpture, one would scarcely say today that his entire output is free from 'archaeological ghosts'.

To San Francesco there came, of course, Böcklin, who lived on the other side of Florence, and Hildebrand made a very fine bust of him which is now in Switzerland in the Basel Museum. But he was never closely associated with San Francesco. His form of late German romanticism was too remote from Hildebrand's world.

It was at the end of the seventies that Henry James came to know the Hildebrands. At that time he was a frequent house guest of the Huntingtons on the top of the hill overlooking San Francesco. Again

[148]

in 1887 he was to see a great deal of the sculptor whom he liked and appreciated. 'He had the feeling', he said, 'of the Greeks and the early Tuscans too, by a strange combination.' When James was working on *The Portrait of a Lady*, it would have been possible for him to have met Henry Brewster through the Hildebrands. Indeed a Connecticut University professor has propounded a theory that Henry James based his character of Osmond on Brewster, but this seems far-fetched since the first encounter between Henry James and Brewster and the friendship that followed did not take place until a few years later.

There were also a number of local Italian friends who were constant visitors and guests to San Francesco – among others, the Cinis, Giuseppe Rasponi, in particular the remarkable Angelica Rasponi, Carlo Guerrieri Gonzaga, active in the political world of Italy, and Carlo Placci, a cosmopolitan *homme du monde*.

San Francesco's *raison d'être* has depended on the interplay of its cosmopolitan tradition with the physical and cultural influences of Florence. As soon as Hildebrand settled there, its development owed much, during those initial twenty years, to the very cosmopolitan Jessie Laussot and Karl Hillebrand, who as friends were nearly as close to the Hildebrands as Fiedler, Grant, Julia Brewster or Lisl Herzogenberg.

Jessie Taylor, or rather Jessie Laussot as she was known to the Hildebrands when they first met her in the early 1870s, stands out as one of the most remarkable women in Florence of those days. Born in 1826, into an older generation than the Hildebrands, she inherited from her father a large library and a considerable fortune. He was a distinguished London barrister and the first person to translate Grimm's fairy tales into English. His contacts with the Continent enabled his daughter to travel a great deal from her earliest youth. She visited Germany, France and Italy and became an excellent linguist. Socially-minded, charming and versatile as she was, her interests and talents, though extending to literature and philosophy (she translated Schopenhauer into English), centred on music. At Dresden she took piano lessons from Hans von Bülow and at Leipzig she was on friendly terms with Mendelssohn-Bartholdy. But most important for her was her meeting with Wagner at Dresden in 1847. It was the beginning of a lifelong friendship.

After her father's premature death Jessie and her mother went to live at Bordeaux where in those days there was a considerable English colony connected with the claret business. A local wine merchant, Eugène Laussot, wooed her and for some inexplicable reason she accepted him although his life and activities lay utterly outside her own world. The marriage was a failure from the start and she soon loathed him. When for political reasons Wagner fled to Paris from Dresden in 1848, Jessie was able to induce her mother to assist him financially and they invited him to Bordeaux. There Wagner fell in love with the intelligent, musical and charming Jessie and she, still with her husband, responded with equal enthusiasm. They planned to elope, but her mother intervened and the *aventure d'amour* came to an end. Wagner went his own way; Jessie after a while left her husband, but was never able to obtain his agreement to a divorce.

In 1850 Karl Hillebrand came into her life. He was a young man as polyglot and cosmopolitan as herself, and yet as German as she was truly English. He became her friend and love for more than thirty years. Only in 1880 were they able to marry, Laussot having died the year before, but throughout the sixties and seventies they were well-known in Florence for having the most brilliant musical salon. For the sake of respectability, which the conventions of those days demanded, they lived in two adjoining but separate flats on one of the *lungarni*. There was, however, a secret connecting door.

Karl Hillebrand was an economist, sociologist and *littérateur* who was equally at ease in German, French, English and Italian. He had been Heine's secretary in Paris in the days of Chopin and George Sand, correspondent for *The Times* in various countries and half a dozen other things as well. He had acquired French nationality after having repeated his studies and taken his doctorate degree in Paris. In the fifties and sixties he was in touch with most of the French literary world. The Franco-Prussian War made him feel so ill at ease in France, his country of adoption, that he decided to retire to Florence, where Jessie had already settled several years previously. He became actively interested in Italian politics and economics, and while Jessie set about organizing the Cherubini Society, of which she was one of the founders and which for many years provided Florence with excellent concerts, he established close relations with several prominent politicians, economists and writers – among them Gino

Capponi, Pasquale Villari, Mario Pratesi, Giosuè Carducci, Sidney Sonnino and Quintino Sella. He was also an active member of the Circolo Filosofico of Florence.

When in Florence the most outstanding musicians and composers of those days frequented the Hillebrand-Laussot salon. Jessie adored Wagner, but consoled and looked after her old piano teacher and friend, Hans von Bülow, when he came to Florence after his wife Cosima had deserted him for Wagner. She would take him with her to the restoringly convivial and cultured milieu of San Francesco. She virtually launched Bülow's favourite Italian pupil, Buonamici, who was to become Italy's foremost pianist. Liszt was an admirer of hers and visited her often. Karl Hillebrand himself had known Comtesse d'Agoult in Paris, Liszt's famous mistress in his earlier days and Cosima's mother.

When Hildebrand first came to Florence, Jessie Laussot and Karl Hillebrand were already middle-aged but still prodigiously active. Jessie was loved by her friends for her simplicity and directness. They took immediate interest in the young artist and in Irene as well. The liaison between the young couple was for a while as unorthodox and romantic as their own long-standing relationship. There was much mutual approbation; Jessie's feelings towards the young man were full of motherly affection, while Karl, the intellectual man of the world, was keenly appreciative of him as an artist. No doubt he influenced Hildebrand and widened his field of interests.

San Francesco, which inherited a large part of Jessie's library, benefited much from this friendship. Some of the most outstanding personalities of the age, especially in the world of music, came as visitors and subsequently as friends though the Laussot-Hillebrands.

When Liszt first came in 1876 he referred to Hillebrand and 'son quasi homonyme Hildebrand' in his letters to his great friend Princess Caroline Wittgenstein. Nine years later his reference to Hildebrand, when again writing from Florence to Caroline Wittgenstein, was to be much more detailed and appreciative, and for his old friend Jessie he had many affectionate words of esteem. One gathers, however, that Hildebrand was struck by Liszt's extraordinary looks far more than by his performance at the piano. The composer's display of virtuosity got on his nerves. Good old Grant, who happened to be present, was also unimpressed.

In December 1876 Hildebrand wrote to Fiedler:

[151]

Just imagine what sort of visitors we had yesterday: Richard Wagner with wife, governess and four children came with Madame Laussot and Hillebrand. Cosima is a clever, distinguished woman and he was introduced by Madame Laussot as 'The Master'. Unfortunately the limited time in which the acquaintance was made did not enable me to have any impression of him, particularly since his features are not alive externally. They had a good look at my Adam, but afterwards hardly visited the house.

This visit was made almost immediately after that animated discussion by correspondence between the two friends on the merits of Wagner, when they had finally agreed to leave the issue open until they knew the music better.

A few weeks after Wagner had come to San Francesco Hildebrand repaid his visit. Wagner and Cosima were staying on in Florence. Hildebrand wrote to Fiedler:

You would like to hear more about Wagner. Well, I called on him and throughout my visit I felt like a fellow who had been enticed into a gambling house. Extremely friendly – in fact I was received with quite remarkable affability by him egging me on, like a sharper, to play cards with him as it were. He was in the best of spirits, very natural, talkative, but I couldn't find any breadth of views in all the things he said. They were commonplace and in no way did I find any distinguished keynote in them. He seemed to me very modern in the interpretation of the world. At the same time it struck me that he regarded people exclusively according to their reputation, otherwise he would say nothing about them. Somewhat of a theatre man, always looking at the effects rather than at the source. Of course he has always been busy with the theatre and this must have had its influence. I had the impression that his approach to the world was academic and not one of direct perception. Very one-sided, without any spontaneous sense of art. As a man I wouldn't trust him, there is no clarity in his eyes.

Obviously there was immediate aversion on Hildebrand's part which prevented him from understanding Wagner's genius – which Fiedler, on the other hand, was beginning to recognize.

[152]

Wagner came to San Francesco again. Hildebrand, however, never took to him, whether as a man or a composer, nor would he let himself be persuaded to make a bust of him. The efforts later on to establish terms of friendship between the Wagner and the Hildebrand children ended in failure. The Hildebrand girls found Siegfried too undiscriminating in his appreciation of Italian art and ridiculous as a young man; he, for his part, resented their collective intolerance. For Cosima, however, both Hildebrand and his wife developed considerable respect and affection and after Wagner's death they became real friends.

No sooner had Karl Hillebrand at last married Jessie than his health began to fail. The form of consumption from which he must have already been suffering took a turn for the worse. They went to Switzerland and then to England where they stayed for some time; but Karl's health deteriorated further and he died at Florence in 1883. The passing away of the man who had been the centre of her life for over thirty years was, naturally, a terrible loss to Jessie; and it was deeply felt and regretted, too, by the Hildebrands. With energy and devotion Jessie set about editing several of her husband's manuscripts and these were posthumously published. She also kept her salon in Florence going for a while. But soon old age began to intervene: her hearing became defective and in the end she was virtually deaf. It was a sad misfortune for someone of such musical talent, as it was to be for Ethel Smyth almost half a century later. Jessie died in 1905.

It is strange that these two remarkable English women, cosmopolitan and steeped as they were in the world of nineteenth-century music, should never have met. There is no reference to Jessie in Ethel's memoirs, nor have I found any in the letters I have scrutinized. Yet though their respective lives had in common nearly fifty contemporaneous years they were each the product of two different ages, they were in rival camps over the Wagner/Brahms issue; and Jessie was first and foremost a woman and then musical and intelligent, whereas Ethel was first intelligent, musical and in a certain sense intellectual and thereafter feminine. Both had enthusiasm and warmth of heart, but each in a different way.

Besides Jessie herself, the Fiedlers, the Brewsters and the Herzogenbergs remained always the closest friends of the Hildebrands as well as the most frequent guests at San Francesco, in particular Conrad, Julia and Lisl.

[153]

It may be wondered how it was that Irene, though she got on well with Lisl, was on so much closer terms with Julia. Lisl was by nature and temperament much more of a kindred spirit, for both women were feminine, passionate and motherly, both very much creatures of instinct. Julia, though capable of vibrating intensity of feeling, was aloof, rational and highly self-controlled. The two sisters were indeed extremely different. Yet it was with Julia that Irene felt the stronger affinity; and it was because of this deeply felt friendship, as well as of a reaction based on a matter of principle, that Julia, at the cost of a greater rift with her beloved Harry, refused to give in to his demands and break with Irene.

In 1889 Irene wrote to her sister-in-law these revealing lines, in which she refers to Lisl's love for her husband Heini and also for Hildebrand and his brother Richard:

> The Herzogenbergs have been here a long time and I have got on very intimate terms with Lisl – she undoubtedly has a wonderful nature and presence. But in spite of all our intimacy Lisl's love for Heini remains a riddle to me and I find it hard to understand her measureless enthusiasm for both Richard and Adolf. I cannot deny also that the way in which she gives expression to her love for Adolf is sometimes unpleasant to me. But still, I like her so much that I take it all as an effusive form of self-expression and once you realize that she displays this kind of enthusiasm for several people you need not attach too much importance to it.

Irene's quite natural feelings of jealousy are here mixed with a kind of irritation that Lisl should show equal enthusiasm for the two brothers. Richard was the black sheep of the family. He was regarded as unprincipled and immoral, but though a much lesser man than Adolf he was amusing and particularly successful with the fair sex. Irene disapproved of him – indeed she could barely stand the sight of him – but she had to put up with him because Adolf liked his brother. So Richard came to San Francesco as a regular guest and member of the family. Though her own earlier life had been far from orthodox, as years went by she became more and more principled, particularly about matters of sexual morality.

Eighteen months after the situation described in the letter quoted above, the situation seemed not much changed. She wrote to her sister-in-law:

[154]

Richard seems to have been quite happy in Berlin. Lisl has looked after him with tenderness. She keeps writing such love letters to Adolf that it is clear she knows not which of the two brothers she loves most. In certain respects she remains a riddle to me, and yet one must admire and like her. Still Julia is much dearer to me, and stands also much closer.

Extremely attractive to men, Lisl could no doubt be innocently demonstrative – just as she could be equally enthusiastic about women. In any case Irene, who was jealous by nature, was apt to misunderstand her.

As the years went by and Hildebrand's reputation as a sculptor spread, the age of royalty on visits to San Francesco set in, mainly but not exclusively German. It was still the Germany of dukedoms and princedoms, many of them patrons of the arts in the old Weimar tradition. But it was not until after 1895 that they started playing a preponderant part in Hildebrand's life. They belonged to the silver age of San Francesco, which superseded the first golden years of closely knit friends and hard work.

[155]

15

In America Again

On 14 January 1886 Harry embarked for America, where he remained and travelled until the end of the year. He then returned to Europe and went back to the United States for three months in the following year, and again for a few months in the spring of 1889. On the first and longest of these three trips his sister Kate went with him to New York, but three months later returned to France while Harry travelled westward, eventually to California where he spent the summer and early autumn, returning to New York in October.

There were no letters to Ethel, since silence had been imposed upon him. The letters of that period that have survived are to Julia and to his children, with whom he kept up a regular correspondence – particularly Christopher, his little son. To Julia he went on sending metaphysical disquisitions in the usual style, bearing more or less directly on their own problem and referring in detail, almost as a running commentary, to the book he was re-writing in English. There are only occasional references to the outside world. But from reading Kate's letters to him after her return to France, many of which have been preserved, and especially his letters to Christopher, one soon realizes how many sides there were to his nature and what an open eye he had to the world around him.

Kate was a tall, blonde, blue-eyed woman of twenty-eight, who was not only warmly devoted to her brother but also got on well with her cousins in New York – at least until they fell out over money. She was as socially minded as Harry, it had seemed, was not. But a jealous husband in France and a passion for hunting, a preoccupation of the French rural upper class, soon drew her back to her château near the Loire. Most of her letters to her brother in the United States deal with hounds, horses and the hunting she and her husband were enjoying day after day. Her descriptions are sometimes extremely graphic and one gathers that Harry must have responded with some degree of interest – he had, after all, enjoyed

[156]

the same sport the year before, when he was living at Buchetin close to his sister's estate. Otherwise Kate's letters dwell on the lawsuit and their 'beastly cousins', as they had now become, in particular the Elisha Brewsters who were enjoying more than their fair share of the Seabury fortune. Metaphysics do not feature.

You have missed two fine hunts. It was raining cats and dogs, nevertheless we start a deer and go round and round for about two hours ... but the animal was not inclined to leave the woods. At last it goes off towards Château Bruel (de Murat's), swims across the huge lake and goes on to a little island where it lies down by a bed of geraniums. The inhabitants of the château were unfortunately not there and the house was shut up and empty. So we had to go to the farms all around to get men to help, haul the boat out of the water where it was quite sunk and empty it, which lost lots of precious time. Then René* got in with two hounds and was rowed over to the island. The deer nearly knocked him over twice, rushed from one side to the other and finally leaped into the water with the two hounds after him. They swam for at least ten minutes, all the others yelling at them and going in all directions in the water to meet them. It was great fun. But the deer managed to get to land, jumped over the hounds and everything and went off at a wild speed towards Orléans. We galloped after, and on and on, till night came and the rain was so thick that we could not see our horses' ears! A farmer told us that the deer had frightened him, had lain down by his side on a heap of dung. And yet we had to go home without him. The next day he was seen lying by a haystack. I suppose I hardly had an inch of anything dry on me and was almost as tired as the deer.

Yesterday we lunched at Perceval's and he hoped to have a stag, but there was no stag and no deer, only a huge boar! So we got friends who live near there to come along with guns, and René put two hounds in a spinney, very thick. They were sent away by the boar who knew he was too fat to run. So then René put in about a dozen hounds. I had a little gun, and Pichelin and I stood behind, me holding up my riding habit. I even pinned it up very cleverly while I was all emotion waiting for my prey. At

*Her husband

[157]

least an hour went by to get him out of the wood, the huntsman was constantly calling out, he was on horseback and fortunately the beast did not try to gore the horse. At last off he went and all the hounds and people after him, men running just as fast as they could, a great excitement. He had received two bullets but they had not gone into his body, only into his skin. I got on horseback and gave my gun to Pichelin, who galloped off with it. We then, after about a quarter of an hour, got to an enormous pool – the guns had not yet arrived. Pichelin had tied his horse and was on foot on the edge of the water with the little gun. The boar looked at him, saw he was alone, and charged straight at him. Pichelin, with great calm, waited until he was within five metres and sent a bullet between his eyes which brought the boar dead at his feet. Only two hounds were hurt and will probably not die. Then we got a cart and brought the animal to the château of the d'Etriés where he was weighed – 235 pounds!

This is the brute, physical obsession with the chase, beloved of the French aristocracy of that time. Sometimes, too, she would write to Harry about dinner parties and household activities, descriptions in which she would ramble on, though with a certain verve:

Oh so hot! And notwithstanding I am a marvel of activity. Every morning I am in my bath at six thirty and busy from that moment until half past nine at night. I teach the cook how to cook, the man servant how to do everything, a girl (quite unsophisticated, she had never left her village or seen a railway) how to become a housemaid and clean a little of everything. I do without another man as I haven't found one yet. I teach the *piqueur*'s wife how to iron like in America. I make chairs and stools new from old ones that were at Orléans, part of our share of the furniture. I make the most delicious cheeses, like *petit suisse*, I gild old frames of inherited pictures, I paint doors and in a general way make myself useful.

It is a contrast to the letters between Julia and Harry, a contrast, too, to the more charged correspondence between him and Ethel. But these down-to-earth accounts were not entirely outside Harry's ken, or even range of interest. One detects this in some of his letters to his little son.

[158]

Kate's role in this great crisis of her brother's life was as go-between. Ethel would come to see her from time to time or write letters to her seeking information about Harry. Her letters, she would say, were to remain confidential and on no account to be forwarded. But Kate, reading between the lines, suspected that Ethel wished her to use her discretion. Occasionally, therefore, she felt at liberty to quote passages from Ethel's letters when she wrote to Harry. Not that this affected the status of their relationship. Ethel remained determined to keep away, at any rate for the time being.

On the whole Kate's letters tell us little about Harry's life in America. There are the odd shafts, but they are not that illuminating.

Your long letter from San Francisco telling me about your trip to Mexico is very interesting and I enjoy your wanderings over the great big world. San Diego must be very amusing from what you say, and I intend to keep your letters to see if your prognostics turn out correct.

In a subsequent letter she says she is sorry he missed voting for the new president, their lawyer friend Baldwin being responsible for his getting back to New York too late.

'As to William,' she says elsewhere, referring to their cousin, 'you will perhaps finish by finding out some good quality in him and get more chummy than curious.'

Another letter, written to him on his subsequent trip to the United States, descends into a tirade against her cousins:

I now hate those Elishas with a deadly hatred and wish more than ever to get them into a bad bargain and laugh at them. If they had been sweet and nice, taken their $15,000 each and said 'Thank you, my good unlooked-for uncle,' we might not have felt so wretchedly towards them, but now I hate them wanting to get Uncle's money and our own besides, which has come away from us by his wily ways and dogmatic proceedings.

No doubt when not travelling in the Far West Harry was busy in New York trying to settle the complicated affair of Uncle Seabury's inheritance. He had written to Julia on leaving Europe, 'It is certainly not money I am after in going to America; I have not the knack of amusing myself with it. It is activity and self-oblivion.' One suspects, however, that he was not uninterested in the matter.

[159]

The only graphic glimpses we are able to get of his travels are to be found in the letters he wrote to his son and daughter, several of which have survived. The picture he gives is naturally in a tone and within a frame appropriate to his juvenile audience, but these were remarkable children well in advance of their years; so that we learn more from the letters than we might have expected. Harry's relationship with his children was one that even modern educationalists would regard as exemplary. It was almost unique for the Victorian age. It is almost as if he is writing, simply and easily, to friends. In a letter to Christopher he describes a dog show he went to in New York with his sister:

Many of the ladies who have sent their dogs to the show in hopes of getting a prize feel either so unhappy without their pets or so afraid of their pets being unhappy without them that they sit by the side of them to keep them company and comb and brush them and talk baby talk to them, in the 'did the windy pindy' and 'cher petit frère' style. Sometimes one hardly knows which is the other's toy and whether the dog belongs to the lady or the lady to the dog. It is rather amusing; you can get two exhibitions instead of one.

I have seen some nice pictures but I dare say you prefer dogs. I prefer them both – some days the pictures, some days the dogs.

The Italian comedy the little Hildebrands played must have been quite pretty. . .

Tomorrow I am dining out and going to the theatre with Baldwin my lawyer, but I don't know yet what we shall see. The other evening I saw Mrs Langtry, who is a celebrated beauty, play Rosalind in *As You Like It*, but not very well. Does Granny* still read Molière to you in the evening? I think it is a very good idea. Then there is Gil Blas which you might propose to her. As Mother has never read it, it would also improve her education. Talking about education your letter was very well written. Who gives you your English lessons? . . . Yes, I heard all about Archduke Rudolph's death and Boulanger's election. I read the newspapers at dinner.

This letter was written on the last of the three consecutive visits to America Harry made in the 1880s. Christopher was now nine years old. The extract quoted is typical of the whole correspondence.

*Clothilde von Stockhausen.

[160]

Harry had been asked by Christopher to bring him back a monster from his first visit to America.

I shall try to bring back a monster if I can find one, but I am not sure that I know the sort you would like. Would a sheep with five legs or a calf with two heads suit you? That would be hideous enough I should think.

I am sending you a newspaper today in which you will see an account of the wreck of the *Oregon*. It was one of the finest steamers and had almost reached New York when the accident happened. Today they say that the ship was not run into by another one but blown up on purpose by the firemen (the men who work at the machines) so that they might plunder the passengers and get off in the boats. Is not that horrid? Perhaps it is not true. We shall know in a few days as they are sending divers to examine the ship under water. It seems the masts stand out fifteen feet above the sea which is quite shallow in that place. The officers refuse to speak until they are tried by a court, which seems very strange. Nearly all the letters were lost and all the goods on board and all the passengers' baggage. I hope they had none of their manuscripts with them. And think of the poor emigrants, several hundreds of them, who arrive having lost all their clothes and little parcels and have no banker they can go to. Aunt Kate is very frightened to go back because if the firemen are set on blowing up the ships there is danger around and danger within.

You ask who obeys, Aunt Kate or I. Well sometimes one, sometimes the other, but we don't give each other many orders. . . . I have been to Boston for four or five days paying a visit to Mr Abbot who is one of my lawyers and a sort of friend. It is a very large town of about 500,000 inhabitants and much prettier than New York, but colder and if possible windier. It takes six hours by train to get there. The trains would amuse you here. One can walk from one end to the other, so you could eat all the time – chestnuts for instance. And there are little tables for those who want to write. . .

The trains in Europe in those days had no through corridor and you could not pass from one carriage to another.

When Harry first arrived in New York he put up with Kate at the

[161]

Victoria Hotel, but they soon moved to 138 Madison Avenue. He wrote from there: 'We have taken a little apartment where we are much more comfortable. We have two bedrooms and two sitting rooms and a bathroom and our meals are served in our rooms.'

Scraps about his daily life appear here and there in the letters to Christopher. On one occasion he describes a club he has joined, the Central Club at 109 East 15th Street.

I am writing to you from a place I like very much, an old-fashioned club chiefly for artists and authors; it has a splendid library and there is no ceremony about it; you can smoke every-where and throw your ashes on the floor – which is delightful. If you are hungry or thirsty you ring the bell and a nigger brings you what you want where you are; you need not leave your book. There are pictures too and engravings to look at.

Do you know they have made a play out of Little Lord Fauntleroy and are playing it at one of the theatres. I can hardly fancy it interesting on the stage, yet I am told it is charming. A little girl eleven years old plays Cedric. Perhaps some evening I shall go to see it. Goodbye dear Christopher.

Occasionally, when he touches on household problems, one cannot help feeling that the information was possibly also meant for Julia, to whom he would not write directly about such things.

I must tell you about a manservant we had here in the house a few days ago. There are two maids and a manservant. Well, it is very difficult to get a manservant so one has to get foreigners, mostly Swedes; sometimes Germans or English. And they don't seem to be good for much, for we are constantly changing. On an average they remain a week. The last one we had went off without saying anything, and took a pocket book from the room of a gentleman upstairs, with ten dollars in it. And what was worse he took all the money of one of the maids – 20 dollars. It was her little fortune. And he has not been heard of since.

One of my Western cousins is here – we are talking over our business. Another one, a judge, will be here in a few days and then I hope we shall settle everything pretty quickly.

Also the circus had to be described, a rather special one for a child accustomed to the European variety:

[162]

I wish you could see the circus they have here just now. There is a performance called 'The Far West' where one sees buffaloes, deer, bears, Indians, Mexicans, miners, cowboys, and all sorts of fine things, even a prairie on fire. There are about a hundred real Indians who dance their war dance; and there are battles between Indians and white men; and Mexicans throw the lasso and catch horses and bulls with it, and guns are fired till the whole circus is full of smoke. I can tell you it is quite a fine thing. I would go there every evening were I not busy at home.

At home he was busy writing, but there was plenty of time for distractions:

Today I have seen a Japanese village; that is to say a lot of Japanese in a large exhibition room; they have made many little shops and go with their work there. They look so funny! Quite little and gentle and cunning and patient.

At another circus he goes to with Kate, who seems to like them, he sees a hideous monkey which he describes to Christopher in some detail. He is tempted to bring it back as a suitable monster, but concludes that it is too fierce to travel with. Kate wanted a little bear.

I tried to get her one, but could not find any young enough. In California one meets families of them, babies, nurses and parents walking about in the hills, especially in raspberry groves. They are not savage unless attacked; but the grizzly bear is.

After Kate's departure in May he writes:

It is getting quite warm and pleasant and I want to go off into the Rocky Mountains and try to shoot a bear. Would you not like to come with me? We would camp and have a nigger to cook for us. But stupid lawyers keep me here. Don't you become a lawyer – gamekeeper is much better.

At last he is off to the Far West and his next letter is from Chicago dated 5 June 1886:

This is just to say how do you do from Chicago. Do you know what Chicago is? Well fifty years ago all this part of the country was full of Indians, and there were no towns, no roads, nothing. Some white men came (one of them is still living here) and built a

[163]

log hut to trade with the Indians and sell them powder and blankets and whisky. That was the beginning of Chicago. Today there are six hundred thousand inhabitants most of whom are very busy salting pigs or passing them through the machine. You put a live pig in at one end and he comes out at the other in the shape of sausages all ready prepared. It is a wonderful machine. They have also tried to make it work the other way, that is to say to put the sausages in and get out the live pig, but somehow it does not work well that way. There is always a piece of the pig missing or he has got put together all wrong. Anyhow the town is very large and grand-looking after a fashion and is by the side of a lake as big as a sea.

Tonight I am off to Omaha in the state of Nebraska. There begins what one calls the West, the new country. Anybody can go and take as much land there as he wants and only pay a few cents for it; only he must put a fence round it; then it is called a ranch. And one begins rearing cows or horses or sheep. Would you like a little ranch? Aunt Kate wants one. We might go there and build a loghouse and ride about all day. I shall look round and see if I find a nice place. Goodbye dear Killy.

From Omaha he travelled on to Salt Lake City, his Mecca, and after some days there he went to San Francisco from where he wrote to Christopher again:

I was very glad to get a letter of yours at Salt Lake City and, as I guessed, I have found one here from Clotilde. But is not that Salt Lake a fine thing, and would you not like to swim in water in which you could not sink?

There were other things to fascinate him at Salt Lake City, perhaps the main objective of his travels. Ever since 1868, when he had planned, but failed, to get there from New Mexico, he had been interested in the polygamous practices of the Mormons. Now that his own experiences had brought the question into such compelling relevance, a visit to their stronghold had become imperative. Unfortunately no letters giving an account of his impressions have survived except one which he wrote to his daughter from Salt Lake City and of which I have translated the relevant passage. She was five years older than her brother and therefore a marginally better

[164]

target for Harry's views on polygamy – at least her father obviously thought so. To Clotilde he would always write in French, as he did to Julia, whereas his letters to Christopher were in English.

I have arrived here with a letter of introduction to one of their elders, but on the very morning of my arrival the police arrested him on the charge of polygamy, for he would not desist. He then asked permission to say goodbye to his wife (or to one of his wives) who was sick, and he never came back. The police searched his house but it was too late. They only found an open window and a ladder outside leading down to the garden, and another ladder in the garden by which they had got over the wall. Vanished! It is said that they are off to Mexico over the mountains and that they want to establish another state where they will be left in peace. Others let themselves be put in jail. The women are more exalted than the men. Not one of them in twelve years has voted against polygamy, which shows that every one has his own ideas and that it is no use forcing others to think as one does oneself.

Or was this letter really meant for Julia via their daughter who would presumably show it to her?

After this letter to Clotilde he resumes his descriptive ones to Christopher. In one of them he gives a very detailed account of a descent he made into a gold mine, adding at the end some of his impressions of California and San Franscisco. In another he reports the acquisition of a snake:

I have got a King Serpent for you; perhaps you will accept him instead of the monster you asked for. Do you know what a King Serpent is? It is a little red snake, quite harmless to men but goes about killing other snakes which are six or seven times as big as himself. No matter how big or strong they are he kills them all; he is stronger than all of them. He catches them by the neck and shakes them to death. They say that if a man were as strong, proportionately to his size, as a King Serpent, he would be stronger than sixty horses. Is not that a fine little fellow? I think one ought to make houses for them, and rear them, and let them loose in places where there are lots of rattlesnakes or vipers.

He does not restrict himself to writing only about things he sees in

[165]

America. Often he picks up something prompted by a letter from Christopher:

As I owe you an answer already I will write to you today, but only just a little 'how do you do' as I have nothing interesting to relate, like your visit to the Duke of Meiningen. Was he dressed in armour? Or had he a sword? What does a duke look like? Has he a pigtail like a Chinaman? Had he his troupe of actors with him, and did he play for you like in Hamlet? It must have been charming. Do you know the story of the man who was going to be introduced to a duke? The friend who was going to introduce him told him: 'Be sure you will always say your grace when you speak to the duke.' So the first time he was spoken to by the duke, he began his answer by saying: 'For what we are about to receive the Lord make us truly thankful.' The duke thought he was mad and walked away without listening for any more. Did you say your grace to the duke? . . .

In July Harry wrote from San Francisco about his lawsuit in New York, no doubt intending the relevant part of the letter for Julia's information.

My lawyer writes to me from New York that I have won my lawsuit, so that whatever may become of Uncle Seabury's fortune I shall lose none of my own. That ends the first part of my business and the most important. There remains the division of Uncle Seabury's property to be attended to. Aunt Kate and I can keep the other heirs out as long as we choose and prevent a settlement if we are not satisfied; and we want to recover a lot of money which our uncle made us lose by bad administration. After a while the other heirs will get tired of waiting and have to compromise with us. We hope this will take place in the course of the summer, though whether at the beginning or at the end no one knows. For that reason I am waiting quietly here. This is a beautiful country and New York is horrible. I will get you and Clotilde each a little ranch. Aunt Kate is going to buy one too. The land costs very little and increases steadily in value as the country becomes more populous.

So one gathers that the assets which had belonged to Christopher Starr had been, after his death, incorporated by Uncle Seabury into

[166]

his own property for reasons of administration and not merely kept under trusteeship as his brother, in the interests of his children, had perhaps intended. These assets, which Harry and Kate were in danger of losing after their uncle's death, had now been secured as the result of the successful lawsuit. What remained to be settled by the lawyers was the share of Uncle Seabury's fortune to which each of his heirs was entitled, an issue on which there was as yet no agreement, though Harry and Kate were the only nephew and niece. The other claimants were cousins.

Now that the first part of the struggle was satisfactorily over and the next stage a question of waiting, Harry felt he could stay on in California working at his book and travelling. He wandered further south to San Diego and northern Mexico, and back to California. In October he turned eastward into Arizona on a leisurely journey back to New York. One of the most detailed descriptions of nature that he made in his letters to Christopher comes from a scribble in pencil after visiting the Grand Canyon.

I am writing to you in the train, so I dare say you will have some trouble to read my letter as the car shakes. Do you know where Arizona is? It is just north of Mexico, between California and New Mexico, and I am passing through it now. It is a big country and an interesting one. I got off the train at a place called Peach Spring, yesterday, and went to visit one of the wonders of the world, the great Canyon of the Colorado. .. As you drive there the road goes gradually down and down and you descend a long gully whose walls are naturally higher and higher as you advance. They look exactly like walls of red brick so that one can hardly believe that they have not been built by giants, especially as they have quite the shape of fortress walls, with bastions and turrets. At last they get to be over six thousand feet and then you come to the Colorado that flows for three hundred miles through a canyon or ravine like the one you have gone down to meet it. Sometimes its walls are quite perpendicular, and sometimes they slope backwards or form terraces. In one place they are in white marble, but generally in layers of red sandstone that look like brick. There is no path by the side of the river and no place to make one except by cutting it out of the stone. And only one expedition has gone all through the canyon, in boats of course. Two of the boats were dashed to pieces. But though you cannot go down the main canyon and can only catch a glimpse up and down it, you can form a good idea of it by going up the smaller canyons which join it and through which little streams flow into the big river. These little canyons are beautiful. I went up one whose walls are only two thousand and six hundred feet high but as they rise perfectly straight and the canyon is very narrow they look an incredible height. It is shady and cool in there with a clear stream to bathe in. And there smaller canyons join it and still smaller ones join them like the veins of a leaf, and finally you get to places where the wall between the two little canyons is not more than six feet thick and looks like a thin slab of stone. These little canyons get so narrow that they are only just wide enough to walk in. When a shower comes they fill with water a hundred feet deep in a few moments and dry again just as quickly. Only the longer ones keep their stream of water, where antelopes and wild mountain sheep come to drink. I think you would like the canyons. And then they are full of beautiful stones and there is gold in the sand. Only it is fearfully hot in the summer down there, except where the canyons are too narrow for the sun to shine in them. The rocks get so hot that the snakes cannot live there; and snakes will stand a good deal of warmth.

Now you know all about one of the greatest curiosities of Arizona, and indeed of the world, as it is said that there is nowhere anything like it, and geologists come from all countries to see it and puzzle their brains about it.

He goes on telling his son about less pleasant things in Arizona – the poisonous centipedes, scorpions and tarantulas, the 'slow and stupid' snakes whose bite can paralyze the heart. They can be avoided unless you sit on them by accident. Finally he mentions in the same long letter the interesting villages he has not yet visited and will describe another time.

Back in New York Harry went on writing to his children and receiving letters from them until he left the United States at the end of 1886 ('waiting' had led to no results in the legal arena and it had become evident that the inheritance question would drag on for a long time). His letters are sometimes rather didactic but the tone is always friendly, with no 'talking down'. The following, written on one of his subsequent business trips to the United States when Christopher was two years older, reveals Harry's characteristic spirit of tolerance:

I have received your letter with an account of the terrible animosity between Herr Lange and Monsieur Oberlé. I hope they will not come to blows. If they do I hope they will both win. But it seems to me that both the French and the Germans are very silly; as though the world were not big enough for both and as though both had not charming qualities. The French are better writers and the Germans better musicians. The French grow better wine, the Germans brew better beer. France has a better climate and Germany prettier towns. I am thankful to them both and don't see why one need swallow up the other. If they want to kill someone, why don't they unite and kill the Chinese who wear pigtails? There would be some sense in that; pigtails would explain the quarrel; but unless there is some important reason like that, better be friends.

The pigtail as a reason for quarrel is of course introduced to show the absurdity, in Harry's eyes, of all quarrels. He takes it for granted that Christopher is clever enough to see the point. At the end of the letter he adds:

Last night I went to an auction sale of pictures, some of which were very fine. One of them *Joan of Arc* by Bastien Lepage (whom Mother perhaps recollects), sold for $24,000. The painter when he sold it got 4,000 dollars for it. So goes the world.

Elsewhere there is a dramatic picture of shipwreck, with an account of the hazards at sea in the days when there was neither wireless nor radar, ending on a moral note. Harry's sense of justice and fairplay is outraged by the greed of colonialism. After giving a graphic account of the destruction of three German and three American men of war in a storm at Samoa, about which the newspapers were full, he describes the behaviour of the local inhabitants:

The shore was covered with natives watching the scene and trying to help; they were very brave; they formed long chains of men holding each other by cords and went out into the waves where white men could not have gone, and nearly all the lives

[169]

that were saved were saved by them. Now I think it is touching. The Germans go there to steal their country; the Americans run after the Germans to say 'No, you must not take it', not because they care for the Samoans but because there are some American commercial firms doing business there who don't want German competition. They snarl and point their guns at each other. Then comes a storm that wrecks Germans and Americans alike, and the poor heathens rush into the waves to save the soldiers of these nations who only want to get rich at their expense. Now I suppose we shall be sending missionaries to convert them to Christianity. We ought to be ashamed of ourselves.

16
'Anarchy and Law'

In between the calls of the lawyers, the diversions of city life, and then the actual business of travelling across the country, observing and no doubt storing up impressions, Harry remained hard at work on his book. It was a tormented period. He felt tied to his wife by the threads of their long and intricate relationship, yet he was desperately in love with another woman at the same time. The darker, more anguished side of his soul, seeking a solution on the edge of reason, is reflected in a 'scribble book' of his, in which he expresses himself at Philadelphia towards the end of May 1886 'as a man brooding on the borderland where civilization ends and the unknown woods stretch away in the fog full of the monstrous fauns of our dreams'.

From the stress he was undergoing came the incentive he needed to complete his first book, redrafting and elaborating in English the basic ideas he had thrashed out in French the year before. Hoping to make his point of view intelligible to Julia 'in the only language she understood, that of metaphysics', as Ethel put it years later, he had been developing his themes and restating them in terms which he hoped would be more convincing. Already on 16 March 1886 he had written to Julia on the subject from New York: 'I have thrown my French book into the fire. . . I am re-writing it in English in biblical style and in the form of a dialogue between four characters with whom I live day and night. I have put into it greater goodness or rather warmth of feeling and less logic.' He completed it before leaving America at the close of that year. *The Theories of Anarchy and Law* was published in London the year after.

Throughout 1886 Harry's letters to Julia, when not directly referring to their triangular problem, are full of disquisitions of religious dogmatism and a special brand of scepticism. The book mirrors the arguments: two of the four characters in its dialogue form take up one of these positions. Harry tells Julia what he believes has

[171]

happened, namely that she has been for a long time inclining towards religious dogmatism and he towards a kind of scepticism wherein the idea of authority is substituted by that of sympathy. This outlook constitutes one of the most important themes of the dialogue. Julia points out that his position is that of an inconsistent dualist pantheism. He protests, maintaining that what he believes in is *complémentarisme* or the harmonious coexistence of many disparate but complementary attitudes in a single uncommitted sensibility. The only creed with which this position is in permanent conflict is dogmatism.

> You know the position I have chosen [he writes to her] and I shouldn't be surprised if you have chosen the other one, which would account for much in the history of our relationship. You see, there are only two thoroughbred human beings: the pope and myself. The others are afraid. And if you are afraid of me you must not be afraid of him. Needless to say the 'pope' is a figure of speech.'

And so with her moving further to the right, he says, her belief in monogamy becomes an article of faith, while his shifting to the left enables him to accept polygamy not only as practicable but also as just.

The argument between them must have at this point triggered off an impassioned proclamation of faith by Wilfrid in *Theories of Anarchy and Law*. He is the protagonist closest to Harry's innermost feelings. Both the content and the tone of the outburst sum up much that is typical of Harry's stance throughout the later part of his life whenever he was pushed into a bellicose mood:

> Whoever believes in philosophical truth, is in search, or fancies himself in possession, of some autocratic principle, some one great law – as, for instance, evolution; some great force – such as *Der Wille*; some one conception – such as Substance; some supreme being in whom all things are summed up: he believes that all knowledge and all thought converge toward one formula, he believes that all he can lay hold of with his mind, the physical, the intellectual, the social, the moral worlds, the universal growth follows one direction – which he can name. This is what I protest against; this work of connection of ideas is

[172]

valueless and this supreme principle, whatever it may be, cannot stand in its isolated grandeur. I want a confederacy of equal states, an Olympus without a ruler. I look upon abstract opinions and profound views as personages who step to the front of the stage, say what they have to say, and disappear, to return again according to the working of the plot; the entire drama is none of them, they come and go, and struggle, and rejoice, and behind them all, or between them, unspoken, unseizable, the drama unfolds itself. I hate the very idea of a truth that would sum them all up in one lesson, the more of which we had learned the higher we should rank in class. It is a schoolmaster's idea.

Yet in spite of this apparent irreconcilable opposition between the two attitudes of dogmatism and *complémentarisme*, Harry wrote to Julia most warmly before embarking for Europe, telling her he very much wished to see her again and hoped she would not refuse. By then the book, where the argument is carried on more flexibly, was finished and ready for publication.

Harry's anarchy, which interested, in particular, Herbert Read, was in a general sense part of his cosmopolitan culture and in a more restricted philosophical sense part of the spirit of detachment he strove to cultivate. This stemmed from his reaction to the materialism of America a hundred years ago. So also is his spirit of toleration, intimately linked to the anarchy he propounded, when looked at against the prevailing tendency of the anarchists of our own times, whose impatience, prejudices and intolerance are more evident than the genuineness of their anarchy.

The spirit of toleration Harry acquired was not merely the outcome of revolt against the religious and moral conformity of his rigid puritanical upbringing, which had shaped his childhood and broke up during his later boyhood in the urbane ambience of Paris. This rebellion could have led to some other form of intolerance, as rebellions often do. More likely it was his intellectual training that held in check his anarchical bent, blending it with a respect for other people's views and with a spirit of tolerance against which a more modern thinker such as Marcuse would have cast anathemas.

Of course his civilized life as the intellectually active gentleman of leisure made assumptions of an unequal society which had not then undergone the social upheavals of two world wars. The anarchist of

[173]

today, the protester against the so-called 'system', is *engagé* or at least mentally committed to the task of improving or erasing what rightly or wrongly he feels to be a rotten society. Brewster accepted the conventions of society without ostensible protest, without outright revolt, but with a deliberately cultivated inner aloofness and mental independence. His disapproval took the form of a tolerant, intellectual anarchism.

The Theories of Anarchy and Law is not a treatise on the subject of polygamy versus monogamy as one might perhaps have expected. That particular issue remains entirely in the background, and is dealt with only by inference within a much wider framework of expositions that communicate Harry's attitude to monotheism, polytheism, positivism and moral progress, law, anarchy and deliverance from selfhood. The range is wide enough and yet the complex subject matter is concisely held together by the close interplay and encompassing influence upon each other of the four voices. They reflect extremely original as well as generally established views; and the author shapes each protagonist to an individual stance. There is something, but only something, of H.B.'s self in each of the voices.

The style, not in the least biblical, is colourful and vigorous, with a touch of Gallic measure and clarity. The method by which the debate is conducted and by which the different views are brought out to confront each other is the opposite of that used by Plato in his dialogues, where the main character little by little crushes his opponents by superior reasoning and logic. Brewster's four mutually opposing voices, Ralph, Harold, Lothaire and Wilfrid – the *progressiste*, the nihilist, the mystic and the sceptic – keep a fair balance between their positions, a balance which in the end slightly inclines towards the positions held by Lothaire and Wilfrid. These two are closer in stance to Harry himself, though he declared to Julia, 'Don't ask which I am; I am all four.'

The setting, where the characters meet, is an old inn. Harold describes it in an introductory speech that opens the debate:

Gentlemen! this, as you well know, is the inn of the Moorish King. There he stands on the signboard in front of our window, wrapped in moonlight, brooding on his old dream of unheard of, impossible conquests, and mistaking, I have no doubt, each time the wind stirs, the creaking of his rusty hinges for the groan of dying infidels, or the rustling of the wild vine and honeysuckle for the murmur of enamoured slaves. Nor for hundreds of years has he heeded aught of the living, neither the busy noise of the street below him nor the hum of voices in this room, once his, where doubtless every act and scene of the human comedy has been played since then, until at last we came, and chose it as a midnight resort for music, wine and words.

'A Midnight Debate' is indeed the subtitle of the dialogue and after the setting has been given by Harold and the discussion started with his challenging 'What is the use of living', we hear practically nothing more about the background of the inn. The voices are too closely wrapped up in each other's arguments to notice the immediate scene of the world outside. The four positions face one another and yet slightly move with the interplay of the voices as the debate proceeds: the pragmatist believer in progress and law who is not a dogmatist and shows practical wisdom; the nihilist or iconoclast who initially tends to side with the legalistic approach, if only because he has to have something to rebel against, at the same time defending moral relativism, but eventually inclining toward the sceptic's attitude; the monistic interpreter of the universe, believer in individual personality and the survival of the self after death, in religious dogmatism and monotheism, a position which shifts under the influence of the other arguments, especially those of the sceptic Wilfrid. In the end he adopts both dogma and doubt, both the position of the man who is obedient to Jehovah and that of the man who does not take thoughts, feelings and facts at face value because the reality he recognizes lies in the relation between them; and finally the position of the sceptic. In the first part of the dialogue he proclaims his position clearly enough, his belief in *complémentarisme*. At the end of the debate, however, where he is the last speaker, Wilfrid's attitude has softened:

You seem to me to cling to your theories because each of you, through his own particular one, has worked his way up to a point where a force may be found that we cannot discover within ourselves. And one of you finds it in the creed of an after-life, and the other in that reciprocal pressure of one individual on another whence our social fabric results; and the third in an uncompromising negation of the boundary lines of the self. If I say that

[175]

to me there is something incomplete in these and any teachings, if I refuse to choose between them because I hold that their value lies less in their tenure than in the previous unconscious work that they complete in you – all you can rightly demand of me is that my denial should furnish me with the same outlet as your assent. Whether it be, as with you, by means of belief and theories, or, as with me, by ascribing them all to the same plastic power we see manifested in the invisible world, that we issue forth from ourselves – it matters little. We have ceased to look inwards, we have caught sight of an outward fire; and the clamorous love of our own ways is silenced, hushed in the solemnity of a deep-fathomed space. Yes! the light has come from without.

But the last word is with Harold who simply echoes Wilfrid's final statement for his closing dismissal.

'Enough, friends! The sun is rising.'

Herbert Read regarded *Anarchy and Law* as Brewster's most profound work as well as the most pertinent to our times, which from a certain point of view is a correct assessment, though *The Prison*, his next book, has other qualities and drew somewhat greater attention.

On the importance of *Anarchy and Law* as a philosophical work and on its originality in relation to future thinkers, Martin Halpern, in his study of Brewster's writings,[1] has aptly stated that 'the specific linguistic turn' Wilfrid gives to his views 'points ahead to the uniquely twentieth century philosophical emphasis on the science of semantics' and that his 'recognition of the large role played by the unconscious in formulating our ideas and attitudes anticipates one of Bergson's major preoccupations and the whole of science of modern psychology'; that 'Harold's and Lothaire's views on pagan polytheism and Hebraic monotheism anticipate Santayana's', and that Lothaire's pronouncements also bear 'ideological resemblances to modern existentialist thought, especially as represented by Martin Buber'.

It is worth noting that William James had in his possession a copy of the dialogue given to him by his brother Henry, which is personally annotated by him and which he must have read before he wrote the main body of his work. Several of his most striking strains,

Halpern points out, to be found in publications of his that appeared decades later, such as *Pragmatism* and *A Pluralistic Universe*, are clearly traceable to the ideas voiced in *Anarchy and Law*.

Harry returned to Europe with a prospect of painful uncertainty in his private life. However, his book was completed, and if it met with little response on publication from the general public, it was to be appreciated by a select number of readers. This encouraged him to continue along similar lines. At last his thoughts and views had found a wider form of expression than the limitedly personal medium of letter-writing.

17
A New Life

There sometimes comes a turning point in life whereby a new or even different man emerges from the old. Often it involves a break with the past. Something of the kind happened to Henry Bennet Brewster. (I shall refer to him from now on as H.B., for he was known to his circle – including Ethel – by these initials throughout the later part of his life.) For him the past was embodied in Julia and symbolized by metaphysics; and both were still intrinsic to the present. But after his eleven-month visit to the United States in 1886 the tenor of his life took on a new direction. He became socially more active as well as intellectually more productive; he moved about with almost nomadic impulse – from London to Paris, from the countryside in France to Geneva and to the countryside in Bavaria, from Florence to Munich and Dresden. The winter months were spent in London where he took a flat, the spring in Paris and in the country with his sister. This peripatetic phase lasted about six years and importantly broadened his acquaintance.

In a way Julia had won her battle, inexpensively yet inconclusively: H.B.'s opinions on marriage remained unchanged and so did his feelings for Ethel. He had pledged himself neither to see nor to communicate with her, but made no secret of his feelings in discussion with Julia, though he would never refer to Ethel personally and would take tactful care to couch the subject in terms of abstract dialectics. At the same time he went on loving Julia in his own oblique way; his letters are usually full of affection and concern for her well-being, even if the reassurances are formulated in philosophical terms. As philosophical sparring partners they are combative yet oddly at ease: paradoxically the clash seemed to create the bond. The pluralist would attack the monist, the sceptic would set himself against the dogmatist, yet always allowing the possibility of reconciling differences metaphysically, as Lothaire and Wilfrid had virtually done. However, H.B. began to tire of this

[178]

kind of intercourse – it was too exclusively abstract; and there were practical difficulties, too, in the offing. Julia was attached to Florence. She loved their flat in Via de' Bardi, was devoted to her few friends, the Hildebrands in particular, and fond of the secluded life. H.B. on the other hand was thinking of living elsewhere. Florence was too closely mixed up with the Hildebrands and he had irredeemably broken with them for Ethel's sake. Besides, it was time to turn his back on that kind of life.

What H.B. wanted now was something new, and yet by reacting against the past he did not reject Julia. It was their practice of communicating in the language of metaphysics that began to seem so needlessly complex.

> I wish we could both decide to write to each other in such a simple and clear style that our letters would be intelligible to the first comer who may never have heard of metaphysics. This is more than a literary scruple, it is an exercise in piety. Ideas become less absolute and the mood less egotistic when one talks everybody's language. It is a step on the way towards sympathizing with others if we express ourselves like them. Having myself offended a great deal in this respect, let's imitate the language of human beings in order to learn how they think.

Probably the metaphysical had too strong a hold to be abandoned altogether and perhaps ultimately he would not have wished it anyway, but for a time he made a genuine effort to curtail the abstractions and dialectics in his intercourse with Julia. Sympathy, understanding, peace, connection – life in fact was what he wanted. Writing to Julia from Paris, where he was feeling lonely at the end of March, he expresses himself almost harshly. His first visit to Florence on his return from America had not gone as smoothly as he had hoped:

> I don't wish to live with you – *chez toi*. Since you are independent of me with regard to religion, choice of human relations, locality of residence and finances, it is clear I cannot accept – save as a visitor passing through – hospitality in a house where I would in the long run have the moral position of what is called in Berlin *ein Louis* and in Paris *un Alphonse* – he has not yet been thought of as a character for the stage. I am called, or at least I

[179]

have called myself 'Henry' for a long time – *noblesse oblige*, and I shall put up at the hotel.

He goes on to express himself against a life of seclusion, a 'claustral' life, for the children: 'I shall travel with them because I love travelling and because I think it is good they should travel.' He also wants them to see more of his sister and brother-in-law, the Terouennes.

Meanwhile he feels the need to be more assertive:

I am prepared to give up both the theory and the practice of anything which conflicts with your ideas of marriage. But I cannot on top of that obliterate my real self: that way lies self-debasement. You cannot force me to think as a dogmatist. As for what I really wish, must I repeat it? It is a deep constant wish to succeed with you, to reach complete achievement with you. We must therefore stop discussing and summing each other up. Busy yourself with your children, your friends, with everything that is outside yourself. Put aside your book for the time being. Be frugal with the introspection. As for mine, I shall publish it because it is written and because it is a book without doctrine and without advice. I will endeavour to keep a clear and balanced view, to be reasonable, active and intellectually sober, and to take interest in things without prejudice to other people. After a few months of this kind of gymnastics it will be easier to come together again and to draw up and accept another treaty.

The 'gymnastics' were evidently undertaken with some degree of success for they agreed to meet and live together, not in Florence of course, but in Bavaria or Switzerland, from April to October every year.

One would have expected some bitterness toward Julia. Here was a wife who frustrated him sexually and even obliged him to ration his direct communion with his family. She would not transfer herself to Paris, as H.B. wished, and insisted on retaining Florence as the base for herself and the children. The arrangement they reached, however, may in a way have suited him. Leaving aside that rather acid letter he had written to Julia from Paris, the correspondence he kept up with her when away from his family was one of exemplary warmth; their *modus vivendi* proved harmonious

[180]

as well as workable. There were none of the usual animosities of an ailing marriage, more an atmosphere of civilized conflict in which mutual respect and even genuine affection could still find a place. Conflict there certainly was, but they agreed to disagree on certain points and maintained an alliance on others. It was an extraordinary relationship. She was an impossible monist from his point of view, as well as a dogmatist, but at least any subject could be discussed with her at any length without the risk of being bored, the great killer even of friendship. There were other things to talk about, besides the theory of marriage – what they saw and read and how they reacted to such things, and then of course the children. He remained an impenitent sceptic, with a deep, and for Julia, redeeming religious streak. Their ties of conflict remind one of the sixth-century Byzantines who from the palace down to the fish-mongers in the market were passionately divided over the procession of the Holy Ghost, a populace held together by the opposition of the Blues and Greens.

H.B.'s new attitude to metaphysics and his efforts to banish them from their correspondence proved impermanent. But though they crept back, it was never again to the exclusion of all else. Physics, mathematics and jurisprudence, into which he delved from time to time, as well as literature and music, took their place with the events of everyday life. Biographically, the letters to Julia become far more informative than they had ever been.

In the month of April 1887 he wrote from London, where he had taken rooms at 11 St James's Place. Julia and the children were spending the spring with the Herzogenbergs at Berchtesgarden in the Bavarian Alps, where he would join them later in the season.

> We should court the external side of life which smiles only on those who take the trouble to please it. And since we have to struggle to get out of our old weakness for introspection, we should not neglect any little help we might get towards leading the kind of life that would draw us outward by involving us in some activity – as far as I am concerned, physical activity.

He then suggests that they should rent, or perhaps even buy, a country house in the neighbourhood of Salzburg, with land to farm. He wants contact with the earth; it would suit the children too, far more invigorating than just a *villégiature*. The cry reminds one of the

[181]

old days when the search for Avignonet was on, but now it assumes a different symbolical meaning, an anti-metaphysical significance as it were. Money would be no obstacle if they bought a house, he adds, he would see to it and she could contribute to the scheme whatever she liked at a later stage.

But if the Salzburg plan proved impossible, Berchtesgarden would do for that summer. Only he would have to have a horse, and Julia too if she didn't despise the idea, and for the children they would hire a pony carriage. In fact they would need two horses, a pony, a groom and a trap as well as a roomy country house.

He goes on to say that he is planning to rent a little flat near the British Museum as a permanent *pied-à-terre*. The windows give on to a nice garden.

> I have another book in mind [he adds], 'un livre très tranquille et très positif'. It wants far more research and reading than thinking. The philosophy of the book is already there and I can find nowhere better than the British Museum for the records I need and nowhere better than London for a conducive atmosphere.
>
> I should certainly like to see Fiedler's book. I am continuing to read Don Quixote in Spanish. What an excellent book! A real antidote to the gospel. Have you read Wilfrid?

A few days later he writes that his book *Anarchy and Law* is being published by Williams & Norgate at his own expense, which he does not mind, he adds, since there is no public for so abstract a subject. He has already sent Julia a typed copy. A fortnight later he writes again but from his new address, 7 Bloomsbury Square. This flat was to remain his London base for the next two and a half years during those weeks in the winter months and early spring when he was in England. His book has left Julia somewhat perplexed, he observes, and he proceeds to defend Wilfrid's position. England, he thinks, is the country best suited to his book since

> Nobody cares whether the author belongs to the academic world or not, in other words to a body of scholars and teachers. As long as he has something to say and says it intelligibly, people will listen to him. If nobody reads my book, it is the fault of my style and myself.

[182]

Do you think we shall ever find anything better than Avignonet? Unless it be in England, in Devon or Cornwall.

He reads Henry Maine and seriously considers studying law in England. Enough of abstract metaphysics, he wishes to understand what governs human relations:

I want to be able to move among people with ease. This objective may seem humble enough but it is a question of knowing where to start. I am convinced England is the country where I am most likely to achieve it. Ask yourself now whether it might not be extremely advantageous to us both and to the children if our *industrie commune* were based in the country in which I am striving to take root. It would not prevent you from keeping your winter quarters in Florence as long as you liked.

H.B. frequently refers to their relationship as an 'industrie commune'. But that their life in common could be transferred to England was to remain a fond hope. Two weeks later he writes on the subject of deliverance from the self by rejoicing in the life around one and on the dissolution of the self in the immensity of life. 'Je suis fier de ce qui est en dehors de moi.' He says he has now a tutor to whom he goes three times a week for lessons in law. He is going to take his law books with him to Berchtesgaden for the summer.

The correspondence then ceases, the summer months being spent together in Bavaria. The autumn takes him back to New York for the same old purpose, but before embarking he writes to Julia optimistically about their relationship. They have made a step forward, he thinks.

Shun whatever isolates is the motto we can boldly inscribe at the head of our new book of maxims and we can add *cultivate externalization*. We should read a great deal, for we don't see many people, and we must read not only for our own pleasure but because every book represents different ways of feeling and judging, different interests, and by associating ourselves with them for a few hours a day we are able to achieve a degree of sympathy with the world.

From New York he writes to her one of his rare letters in which depression gets the upper hand. By nature H.B. had a serene mind

[183]

seldom clouded by complex psychological problems, no matter how much they could make him suffer. Perhaps it was the long-drawn-out haggling with his cousins and co-heirs to the Seabury estate that got him down so that he now looked at himself and life in New York with a jaundiced eye. He refers to a book he wanted to write, *Le point d'appui*, but has cut himself off from it, he says, at a moment of doubt about his ability to write. Perhaps he is a solitary man after all, notwithstanding his efforts at 'externalization'?

In his next letter from New York he says:

> More or less all of us are psychopathic nowadays, we people of leisure and culture. A total change in the way of living is needed amongst the leisured classes. Kropotkin says, in his *The Coming of Anarchy*, that there should be four hours of manual work a day in the life of every one of us. Tolstoy says more or less the same thing. These are the men that interest me.

In another letter he says that he was tempted to undertake a stage adaptation of *The Brothers Karamazov*, but has given up the idea. He is working on something more serious because it involves not only literary effort. Then he remarks that there is a good chance of an amicable agreement being reached with his cousins Brewster Cook and Judge Wheaton, and at the same time refers to Julia's own problems of inheritance with her brother, their father having died not long before.

No amicable agreement with his cousins is reached. Negotiations break down with the result that a lawsuit is likely to follow and drag on for ages. So H.B. leaves his affairs in the hands of his lawyer Baldwin and decides to go back to Europe by the end of the year. Before departing he writes:

> It is nice of Fiedler to have read my book. If he cannot grasp its unity it is because inwardly he builds on the model of a monarchy and not a confederacy. This is not a criticism of his method that I am making. To have it translated into German? Well this surprises me. I thought one had to be a professor or a least a doctor of philosophy to expect the slightest attention to be given to one. Or would it be accepted in the *Bellettristik* category? For this it would seem to me too exotic, too Anglo-Saxon and, what is worse, too heavy. I fear that this suggestion comes simply as

the result of a benevolent attitude and it would have to be confirmed by some other literary-minded and impartial German. As for the English lady who recognized the *American* in the author of my book, I attribute this perspicacity, as you do, to the natural, relaxed style. The English who think think unfortunately in Greek or Latin half their time and translate into English more or less well. Do you remember Pater? True, there is Herbert Spencer, but as you say he works with the fury of a machine always along the same lines. I should prefer to ask Maine to dinner, as you would. As for Gobineau's remark, it is that of a man who by temperament can only see the other side of the medal in a democratic country. What he says is to some extent right, but there are other things he has missed, like Taine who is unable to take in the French Revolution. They are people who see clearly, but what they see is very small. I am reading *Ancient Society* by Morgan, a sort of work on early institutions – most interesting. I shall bring you the volume.

I have been somewhat sad, somewhat lonely and not very well (but this is over now). Your letter gave me pleasure.

But in Washington, a few days before embarking, he goes out for walks, he scribbles a bit and goes to the theatre to see *Fedora* by Sardou. 'It doesn't translate well,' he says, 'but I have my doubts as to the quality of the original. Last night I heard Handel's Messiah, which I enjoyed.'

On his return from America early in 1888 he is much on the move in Europe, first repairing to London, where he spends a few months, then proceeding to Munich and Geneva where he looks for a house to rent for the summer, then on to Paris and Villiers to be with his sister, and after a short visit to Florence back to Geneva in April where at last he finds a suitable house in the neighbouring countryside to spend the summer months with his family. He waits there for their arrival after a rush back to London for his summer clothes and a visit to his old friend Cazalis in Paris on his way through. His letters to Julia continue without a word about Ethel or the Hildebrands, but in a friendly, warm tone, arguing without animosity, discussing books and marriage as usual. He agrees on the need for an 'area in common', of close and intimate association, but with no shackles, so that both partners should be free to commune

[185]

as they wish with their fellow beings. In Geneva he resumes the study of physics, finds a 'cello and enthusiastically looks around for a violinist to be ready to play trios when Julia has joined them to play the piano. He also sees much of his American banker in Geneva, Bates, who was to become a good friend. Not only do they study the Stock Exchange together but they also engage in wide-ranging discussion. H.B. was lucky on the Stock Exchange and Bates was evidently a good adviser.

The correspondence ceases again for several months, the summer having come and his family life in Switzerland having started. At the end of October Julia and the children return to Florence and he goes back to London, stopping in France on the way to see his sister and brother-in-law at Villiers where he spends some days of perfect weather.

> They seem happy [he writes to Julia] and I was glad to see to what extent agreement between the two on religious and politi-cal questions can contribute to the enjoyment of life. I get on well with Kate, the individual, but her social relations and her world bore me stiff. It is always easy to reach that point where one is no longer in agreement with the others, for there is in every one of us a certain substance which cannot be assimilated with the substance of others. It is the crypt. The great mistake is to want complete agreement.

He goes on to write about human relations and the gift of being able to listen to, and hear, several voices at the same time without becoming infatuated with any single one.

Back in Bloomsbury Square he waxes enthusiastic over London, notwithstanding the November fog.

> Every time I am back here I experience the same sensation of well-being which derives perhaps from the fact that there are so many reasonable people in this city. I get on with my work because I am drawn to it, not like in New York where it only constitutes a refuge, of the two evils the lesser. Baldwin and my cousin William are urging me to go back there. But I am afraid William's principal motive is to have me there in order to play billiards with him, and Baldwin's motive is his great appreciation of the charm of my conversation, since no solicitor with any

self-esteem can converse with his customer without charging at least six dollars the talk.

About London he says again in another letter to Julia:

I don't know whether it is the air of London or this extraordinary crowd which soothes me as the sea used to soothe the romantics, but there is something here which is immensely appeasing. You can hear the grass grow under the din of the omnibuses, and I can tell you straight away that this grass comes from the seeds of wisdom.

A year later he was to complain bitterly about the fog and climate, but still his love for London remained unabated:

You ask which do I prefer, Paris or London. The answer is London, save during those three or four months of fog which unfortunately constitute the greater part of my stay here. Je me suis brouillé avec le brouillard. It is a sin against the beloved sun to breathe this filth when you are not obliged to do so. So I like Paris better from November to February. But apart from the climate I prefer London because here, after all, religious and moral questions are far more alive and more boldly discussed than anywhere else. Maybe Berlin is also a centre of this kind, but I am too old to become a German.

It was at this time, the end of the 1880s, that H.B. was tentatively emerging from his cocoon and beginning to meet more people in London and elsewhere. The arrangements he made for his intermittent family life meanwhile seemed to work out fairly well. At the age of thirty-nine he was taking the first steps, at the rate of two forward and one back, towards a more sociable way of living which in later years was to earn him the reputation of *un homme du monde*, although it was an epithet that applied only superficially to his many-sided self. The leopard spots of the introspective metaphysician could never be entirely rubbed away.

On his third crossing to the United States in connection with the Seabury affair he met extremely pleasant fellow passengers whom he described with humour and wit in his first letter to Julia from America early that winter of 1889. Some of them he met again in London and they became friends.

[187]

Metaphysics were not forsaken even in New York, however, but only in the context of their own lives and his problems in general.

With regard to those idols, namely those illusions and errors that are due to our individual passions, yes, I shall strive to beware of them for I recognize that I have a tendency to take my own emotions as the norm — a sign of immaturity. 'Those prejudices which bear the effigy of our present century' which you mention, well, here we have to be careful. Of course it is all wrong and quite ridiculous to prostrate ourselves in worship before all modern ideas because they look new and, as Turgenev points out, to swear by the last issue of the *Asiatic Journal*. On the other hand one should be able to sympathize with the ideas of our times and it should be possible to translate into the language understood by one's contemporaries those thoughts which might come to one more naturally in a more archaic form. Likewise a great effort was needed at the time of the Renaissance to stop thinking out poems in Latin. If we fail to translate into the language of evolution and socialism those problems which in the past were discussed in the language of Aristotle and the Church, we shall remain old babies tugging in vain at the breasts of the muses, old pupils struggling with Latin verses. Let us look at the idols of the street from closer range and several times before making fun of them.

In another letter he says he would like to write a book entitled 'Animal Religion'.

I have a grudge against all religions since the days of paganism because they glorify a single ideal. They extract and isolate one part of our nature which is upheld as the only legitimate factor in civilization where the other factors expressing the other sides of our nature are placed in opposition and declared impious. . . For the pagans everything was religious. . . We should 'numinify' the entire animal that we are with all its faculties and discover everywhere the gods that preside. . . I am not trying to destroy Christianity but complete it.

This is a crucial strand in H.B.'s thinking. It inspires all his writings and the whole of his 'metaphysics' as expressed in his numerous letters. It reflects a deep-seated sentiment which often comes to the surface in bantering *boutades*, thereby constituting a stumbling block for those who, though they knew him well, could still mistake him for a pagan in the conventional sense of the term.

From New York he goes on writing to Julia a great deal about Tolstoy, towards whom Julia is unsympathetic. He defends Tolstoy's view of life: it is his comprehensive picture of life, such as he provides in *War and Peace*, that delights H.B. – the fullness of life in all its aspects. It ties up with his own ideas for 'Animal Religion'. He feels in need of *joie de vivre*, but is lonely, sees only Baldwin and sometimes his cousin William. He engages a physicist who comes to his flat in New York three times a week to give him lessons. Having failed to find a 'cello, he hires a piano instead on which he practises. He also goes to auction sales, at one of which he buys a very large painting for Julia.

He maintains a surprising degree of solitude for someone in a great city who has both money and connections. He was good-looking and still young, with a manner and a way of speech that enchanted all those he came in touch with; and this at a time of his life when he professed the importance of contact with the outside world. It is strange, too, that he should never have become involved with other women at that period, at least as far as one can tell. Probably, as well as being still deeply engrossed in the personality of Julia, he was pining away for Ethel.

At this time also we find him enthusiastic about a book he was reading, *Concepts and Theories of Modern Physics*, by an American of German extraction called Stallo who had had an extraordinary life and was the United States ambassador in Rome. But besides physics and reading generally, 'I am having a good time', he says, 'working at my own book' – presumably 'Animal Religion'. He plunges also into trigonometry and on the subject of Tolstoy he returns to the charge.

On 1 May he quits America, the Seabury affair having been finally settled by compromise – not entirely to H.B.'s advantage. The next letter to Julia is again from Bloomsbury Square, but soon he has to hurry to Geneva to find another house for the summer, as the old one is no longer available.

[189]

18
Real Friends

The year 1889 was to prove important in H.B.'s life. Among his many new acquaintances and friends, two turned out to be of enduring significance, each in a different way: the Swiss writer Edouard Rod and Henry James. With both he was to have an interesting exchange of letters. Moreover in that year he started work on his next published book, *The Prison*. 'Animal Religion' was never finished. There are only fragments among his extant manuscripts which may belong to the work he had in mind but never completed and which may have served for a much later book he wrote and published in French, *L'âme païenne*.

Geneva, the capital of French-speaking Switzerland and the cradle of that rather dour breed of Protestants, the Calvinists, had in the literary world of the last century produced a school of reaction to its stern, middle-class and somewhat provincial spirit of respectability. Men of letters, from Rousseau onwards, had gravitated away from their canton to the culturally and physically broader plains of France. But for all their agnosticism and Gallicized ideas, these French-speaking Swiss remained Calvinists at heart; they never entirely broke away from their roots.

In the second half of the nineteenth century there emerged a group of Genevan novelists who under Parisian influence could be classified as 'naturalists'. Zola was their model and they stood in opposition to the conservatives who dominated Geneva – including the university. These conservatives looked askance at the French idea, prevalent since Balzac, but particularly since Flaubert, that the novelist's duty lay in describing life as it was, not as it should be. Perhaps the most outstanding exponent of this Swiss school of naturalists was Edouard Rod, a friend and admirer of Zola and also of Bourget. He poured out novel after earnest novel, purportedly true to life and yet according to some of his critics not true enough. Virtually no one reads them now, although Swiss scholars have recently been trying

[190]

to revive an interest in them. Such *romans de moeurs* need an exceptional literary ingredient to hold the attention of subsequent generations attuned to different customs and conventions; and Rod was no Henry James. The trouble was that he wrote too easily, too prolifically and with too facile a success. Being a Calvinist at heart, though intellectually an agnostic and sceptic, he retained a social and moral conscience which kept giving a tormented twist to the insoluble situations into which he would plunge his highly respectable characters. The married country parson falls in love with the chaste and romantic parishioner; the staunch, highly placed, bourgeois university professor (such as Rod himself was), more or less happily married, falls in love with the ravishing, highly intelligent young female student under his care. Nothing original about such situations, but the resulting tormented conscience expressed through sacrifice was typically Calvinistic. No French 'naturalist' would have had any use for such sacrifice; on the contrary, he would have thrown himself delightedly into all the aspects of disintegration. Both were true to life, but life in different social surroundings, with a different background and from a different angle. But how it was that two men such as H.B. and Edouard Rod, so disparate in temperament, taste and habit, should have got together and struck up a lifelong friendship has always been something of a puzzle.

Le Sens de la Vie was a novel Rod published in 1889 and which H.B. came across in Geneva. He briefly commented on it in a letter to Julia: 'Beaucoup de critique, mais extrêmement bien écrit.' On the whole H.B. never held Rod's literary output in very high esteem. It was something about the man himself that attracted him when they eventually met. It centred on Rod's scepticism as a reaction against the stern, humourless, conventional atmosphere of his upbringing and surroundings, for like H.B. he regarded himself as a pagan of sorts in protest against the prevailing Calvinistic background to which he belonged. New England Puritanism on the one hand and straightforward Genevan Protestantism on the other were the influences to which they both reacted with revulsion; yet for all their pagan scepticism, both retained a moral conscience and an impeccable code of behaviour, both being committed to their respective wives and children, and yet in love with another woman at the same time.

Rod was evidently a pleasant man, but there was nothing

[191]

glamorous about him. He on the other hand saw his new friend in a dazzling light, for by that time H.B. had virtually cast off his protective shell and was emerging from meditative solitude into the sociable, affable, ingratiating personality he little by little became – the guise in which his numerous later friends recalled him. Rod's biographer, Cécile Delhorbe, on the basis of extant letters and other records, relates how the Swiss novelist saw H.B. at the outset of their acquaintance and how he felt about him. The picture, however, is not only slightly flawed but varnished with misleading glamour, although the superficial elements of his first impression must have lingered with him and even coloured the obituary he wrote of H.B. nearly twenty years later.

> He saw him as a friend free from every kind of prejudice, to whom he could say whatever he liked without fear of being misunderstood. He did not give up any of his friends but at the same time strongly attached himself to Henry Brewster, the Englishman [*sic*] educated in France, well off and perfectly cosmopolitan, whose sister had married a French count and who had himself married the daughter of a German diplomat, who was bringing up his children *à l'americaine* and who would end by spending his days in Italy. At that time he was constantly coming to Geneva with his family, on account of his wife's health, and rented a house near Nyon every summer. Rod was overwhelmed with admiration for Brewster's horsemanship as well as for the general ease with which he could pass from the language of Racine to that of Dante, from Shakespeare's to Goethe's, being amazed at the same time by the eclecticism of his views concerning the arts and every imaginable system of philosophy. Without any doubt the little bourgeois of Nyon was dazzled by the dashing unconcern of this worldly exponent of Cosmopolis.[1]

Worldly at this stage H.B. certainly was not; but to be on horse-back was a most natural part of life. 'Le cheval et la métaphysique', Rod observes, struck by the unusual combination, 'sont les distractions favorites de Brewster.' Indeed H.B. succeeded in getting Rod himself on horseback for the first time in his life, and having him follow through the countryside in a painful and precarious canter. They would stop by the way for Rod to recover his poise, only to have H.B. unbalance him in quite a different way with an outpouring of paradoxes and provocative statements on anarchism, stoicism and Buddhism mixed with a display of worldly wisdom.

This glimpse from Rod's biography illustrates the sort of impression H.B. could increasingly create as time went by and he became superficially more outgoing. But it was in direct contrast to his inner self, meditative, introspective, a solitary thinker until the end of his life.

The relationship between the two men was soon firmly cemented. There exist today in the state library of Lausanne 200 sparkling letters which H.B. wrote to Rod — though that adjective is scarcely descriptive of the replies. The fact that H.B. was not merely interested in the 'little bourgeois of Nyon', the realist provincial writer, but contracted a warm and lasting friendship with him, brings to light another, important, side of his nature. He was definitely not a snob. Both his writings and his letters show that his political views were democratic, radical, inclining to anarchism; he had no use for royalty which he regarded as dead wood involving outdated, useless ceremony; he was intensely anti-colonial in outlook and disliked every form of nationalism that smacked of jingoism.

In a long criticism of Taine, made in a letter to Julia, he says:

> And what a perculiar theory he has that the more you are able to pay in the way of taxes the greater is your right to wield power. Indeed power becomes the dividend of wealth which in turn is the profit derived from the work of others. You already benefit from it and are privileged by virtue of your wealth. Well it is only right then, so he holds, that in addition to all this you should be rewarded with power! In my opinion you have a right to power in proportion to the services you render, to the hardest and most essential services such as those of the farmer and the factory worker. We can't do without them; at a pinch it is possible to do without civil servants, artists, bankers, lawyers and even physicians. But it is essential to eat and have shelter against the cold. Power belongs to the lower classes; not exclusively but mainly. It is up to the others to achieve agreement with them and keep themselves going on the strength of persuasion and charm, just as women are able, by such means, to guide men.

This is a typical Brewster stance, ideal for arguing with Julia and bewildering Rod. Nevertheless it discloses where his political sympathies lay, although he was not the type of man to extend his sympathies into political action.

H.B. was beginning to feel he could wear his cosmopolitan cloak with ease and elegance. He was perhaps accordingly tempted to play the part suggested by his presence, looks, manners and qualifications. Was this a form of self-protection? For the crypt, and his solitude in the crypt, remained. It was just about then, the end of 1889 and beginning of 1890, that he had started work on his book *The Prison*, in which full expression is given to the anguish of an imprisoned soul.

He was back in Bloomsbury Square at the end of November 1889, after a short halt in Paris and a short visit to Villiers where Kate was expecting a child. We find him plunged in work but also availing himself of the letters of introduction from his learned and well-connected friend Cazalis – one of them to Henry James.

To his son Christopher, at that time aged ten, he wrote on 20 December 1889:

> I have begun making some calls so as not to turn into a savage by sitting too much alone, and today I have made the acquaintance of Henry James, the author of *Daisy Miller*, your friend. I was very much surprised as he is not at all like what I fancied. Instead of that I found a man who looks like a hard worker and is rather embarrassed and nervous and very kindly, intelligent and shy. I like him much better than I thought I should; and as he asked me to lunch with him in a few days I shall have an opportunity of making his acquaintance a little better.

Writing to Julia a week later, he refers at length to *The Prison*, the first draft of which he has sent her, and adds:

> I have seen Henry James again who invited me to luncheon the other day and whom I like very much. I don't know whether it is an affinity of race or education but we talked to each other with the ease of two old friends. He is very talkative, but he knows how to listen as well. We would eat in turn; when one of us had finished the other began. He is a hard-working man, takes his art in earnest, believes in the novel as the highest form, is not satisfied with anything he has done so far and aspires to the

supreme work of art. He says a great deal of witty and gay things as he goes along, at which he laughs heartily. His brother is a professor of psychology at the University of Harvard, if I remember rightly. But he is himself a psychologist as M. Jourdain was a prose writer, which is far nicer.

In another letter to Julia at the beginning of February he says:

Henry James has paid me great compliments, extremely detailed and evidently quite sincere, on *Anarchy and Law*. He is bewildered by it, but seduced. For me this suffices. He gave me a book by his brother William James about their father Henry James senior. He had a twisted but extremely original mind; he was an unusual character and a mystic, a man out of place in his century and for whom the philosophic problem was as follows. Given the existence of God, build up man by deduction. His deductions are maddening as a method, but the results are extremely curious, for as soon as he forgets about the metaphysical apparel you come up against a vibrating soul and a great prose writer. His sons have evidently a touching cult for his memory. William James's account is a work of admirable cleverness and piety, the *tour de force* of an advocate.

Between Henry James and H.B. a rhythm of friendship was established whereby for the next two years they would ask each other to luncheon, tea or dinner at regular intervals or meet to pay calls on friends. It was largely thanks to Henry James, who introduced him to many of his friends, that H.B. was able to extend his circle of acquaintance in London society. Their correspondence at that time was accordingly limited to short missives extending invitations or making appointments for joint calls on friends. Some of these short letters from Henry James are typical of his fussiness about the details of such arrangements. Here is one, written from his flat at 34 De Vere Gardens on 3 February 1891:[2]

My dear Brewster,
I have an engagement tomorrow Thursday, at 4.15, and shall therefore (as my engagement is near, comparatively, the Victoria big station) ask you to await me – *de vous trouver* – say at the big book stall of the said Victoria station at 5.30 sharp, where I will find you so that we may go easily to Mrs Humphry Ward's

[195]

which is 25 Grosvenor Place, *à deux pas de là. Je ne vous ferai pas poser*. I shall be punctual – I mean the big bookstall, not the Chatham and Dover, in other words the far away part, but the part near the entrance from Grosvenor Gardens and called, I think, the Brighton and South Coast part, where you go to the Crystal Palace.

Yours (in frantic haste)

HENRY JAMES

In the meantime H.B. had written to Julia:

I have sent a copy of *The Prison* to Mrs Humphry Ward, the author of *Robert Ellesmere*. It seems she was enchanted with it and circulated the volume amongst her friends and having found out that Henry James knows me has asked him to introduce me to her, which he is going to do next week. I forget whether I told you that he has obtained for me an honorary membership at the intellectual and literary club of London, The Athenaeum, to which he belongs himself, and also an introduction to Mrs Humphry Ward, so that I am now a presentable gentleman at Mrs Ward's where without this social guarantee (what an astonishing country!) she would have read my book with some pleasure but without acknowledging receipt. The mysteries of London!

A few days later, in a long letter to Julia, H.B. described in detail Mrs Humphry Ward's party to which Henry James had taken him:

I must describe to you my visit to Mrs Humphry Ward or at least tell you about the impression she made upon me. First of all I must say – it couldn't have been otherwise – she resembles *him*. He is that mysterious ancestor of most great men, the unknown Aryan Abraham from whom Richelieu and Schiller are descended and I don't know how many others. One of these days I shall make a collection of portraits of famous people who are variations of that theme; it interests me not without reason. I have found several samples of which I had no knowledge, at the National Gallery here. But it is a bore I have found none that resemble me. I must confess, however, to console myself, that I am a sort of Abraham myself and that my posterity one day will be legion like the stars.

To return to Mrs Ward, she is a lady of uncertain age, let

[196]

us say about forty, with a very pleasant manner. She is the fashionable woman at the moment, so it appears, at least I should say in this 'world' exclusively English where literature and religion are appropriate to the highest social circles. There is perhaps in all this a feeling, quite felicitous, of fraternity or confraternity for the enrichment of life with fictions – social fictions, religious fictions, artistic fictions, everything that is the product of the imagination in opposition to science. It is, I believe, a little select world where it is necessary to be cultivated, rich, loving the poor, and to be a lord if possible, but this is not absolutely indispensable. I am probably expressing my views much too soon, my impressions being still superficial. But I cannot help thinking of Paris in the eighteenth century where you could be de Voltaire, de Rivaral, de Chamfort merely on the strength of being able to write well and where when you happened to be called Jean Jacques you lived with la Maréchale de Luxembourg. I don't quite know what I think of it all; there is something of the bohemian and anarchist in me, and it all irritates me and bores me. But there is also something of the dilettante in my nature whereby I get on better with this 'worldliness' than with the austere smartness of Desjardins or Vernon Lee – at least as far as I can tell from some of her short stories – according to whom a salon is a frivolous resort of perdition unless at least the ladies sit darning some old socks and the gentlemen display their fingernails in mourning.

Well, there is a smartly dressed crowd at Mrs Ward's and before I had understood anything about the situation I found myself engaged in a conversation with a titled old spinster on the subject of stuffed birds, a collection of which she insisted I should visit at the museum, and also of butterflies from Java and Sumatra. I kept racking my brains to find stories about butterflies and birds to tell her about, but as my stock was rather limited I managed to substitute the butterflies with ghosts and everything was running smoothly like on skates when, I don't know how, the old lady was replaced by an ex-governor of Ceylon who kept explaining to me a detailed plan for cheap housing which a philanthropic society was in the course of putting into effect for the benefit of workmen. At least I was given a chance to sponge my forehead and I was getting on

[197]

splendidly with the ex-governor when Mrs Ward called me aside to thank me for having sent her my book. I asked her whether she hadn't found it obscure. She answered yes, or rather what seemed to her obscure as far as the conclusion one was to draw, but that the separate handling of the themes had charmed her and especially 'the separate handling of the English'. Curious that it should have been necessary for me to be French by education and a metaphysician by birth to obtain agreement from everybody on one thing only, the quality of my English prose! Shot a pigeon and killed a crow. Better than nothing. Perhaps in the end a pigeon will fall as well, either because he has already been wounded but is hidden by the crow, or because I shall have to aim at him again more accurately. Perhaps also there is no pigeon and that one never shoots anything but crows. However one must not say so, even if one believes it. Il faut croire au pigeon pour être grand chasseur. . . But to go back to Mrs Ward, little by little the crowd thinned and we had a chat between the three of us, herself, Henry James and myself on the subject of Mary Bashkirtseva, which she wants to read again — not a dazzling conversation but one of those nice little talks where each says something sufficiently subtle to be happy about his neighbour, and in this spirit our talk came to an end with an invitation extended to me for every Thursday when Mrs Ward is at home. Of course it is clear it won't always be amusing, on those days for instance when there will be only stuffed birds and sanitary housing schemes to talk about, but it is worth while trying it out, and the hostess is without any doubt a distinguished lady. Her husband less so. C'est le mari de madame. He seems younger and writes articles on art.

The letter expatiates on the subject of the advantages and drawbacks of worldliness and then discusses various writers of the day, among them Oscar Wilde and Anatole France.

Mrs Humphry Ward, as well as being a fashionable lady in the literary world of the 1880s and 1890s, was turning out one novel after the other. Her friendship with Henry James, who would occasionally give them polite praise, was of long standing. She knew everybody worth knowing. At one of her parties H.B. met Edmund Gosse, with whom he got on well and made friends, and Thomas

[198]

Hardy, whom he found unlikeable, although he had considerable admiration for his writings (this in spite of Henry James's reservations, who regarded *Tess of the D'Urbervilles* as 'vile').

At about this time H.B. moved into a flat at 12 Cork Street, Burlington Gardens, from where he went on enlarging his circle of friends, Whistler and John Singer Sargent among them. Even so his inborn aloofness made him critical and selective. Henry James remained throughout a good friend, appreciated especially because of his wide culture and profound knowledge of the French language and literature. This meant a great deal to H.B., for it was extremely rare, so he found, to come across such qualities in an American or an Englishman. James's New England background was an additional bond. To James H.B. stood as a unique specimen of the accomplished, civilized and polished international gentleman, 'such a strange handsome cosmopolite ghost', as he saw him. But there was a touch of something else as well which Henry James valued and yet could not grasp, as the later correspondence between them discloses. H.B. remained 'the inscrutable Brewster'.

Throughout the winter of 1891 they went on seeing each other very frequently. In many of his letters to Julia H.B. says at the end: 'Henry James m'attend à déjeuner.'

When *The Prison* came out early in 1891, published like *Anarchy and Law* by Williams and Norgate, it had, predictably, a limited circulation and drew the attention of a very small public, though the few that did take notice of it were warmly appreciative. Henry James's response to it is recorded in a letter from H.B. to Julia shortly after its publication: 'Henry James came to see me the other morning to tell me how much he liked my *Koran* and so forth, adding however, "I don't understand it." Of course he doesn't feel the need to understand it. Provided it is distinguished and suggestive, it is enough for him and as a literary whole he thinks it is a success.'

Before leaving England in April to join his family for the other half of the year, he received a letter from Mrs Benson, the Archbishop of Canterbury's wife, to whom, after having met her, he had sent a copy of *The Prison*.

I feel almost too much ashamed of my delay in thanking you for *The Prison* to dare to do so now. Still I must – for not only was the style and the expression a most intense enjoyment to me, but

[199]

the thoughts and the whole set of the view of life it put forth, coming to me at a time when from various causes the problem of life pressed with peculiar persistence,* came to me as a power in a way too complicated and too fine to put into words. But I was and am deeply grateful. It had the effect of water to the thirsty.

To Julia H.B. comments:

The formulation of the praise is a bit contorted but it has deeply touched me as coming from someone who suffers. It is odd, however, that the first person to tell me that my book has been a help in finding a solution to the problem of consolation should be the wife of a prelate who receives several thousand pounds a year from the state to lavish the balms of official religion.

In Paris he saw his old friend Cazalis again, and also Mallarmé and Maupassant whom he had already met on a previous occasion. Then he went on to Geneva and rented another house near Nyon, a villa by the lakeside called La Colline with a garden down to the shore and a magnificent view of Mont Blanc across the stretch of water. This house, which he took on a long lease, became a permanent summer residence where for reasons of health Julia would spend much of her time in the forthcoming years.

The end of 1891 and the beginning of 1892 marked the beginning of a new era. The ruins of Avignonet were finally sold, the reconstruction plans having been definitely given up – much to young Clotilde's regret who had done her best to persuade her parents to retain the property. Lisl died at San Remo a fortnight before her mother's death in Florence; both she and the old baroness had been ailing for some time. The Brewsters gave up their flat in Via de' Bardi and transferred their permanent winter quarters to Rome where they rented a large apartment in an old palace. Arrangements were made for Clotilde to go to Newnham College, Cambridge, to study architecture, and for Christopher to go to boarding school. H.B. resumed contact with Ethel Smyth. The drama of life was touched by the gentler hand of maturity, soothing but never healing.

*Mrs Benson's daughter had just died of diphtheria, aged twenty-five.

19
'The Prison'

The Christian approach to the problem of death is familiar enough, centring as it does in the belief in a supreme god, in the survival of the personal self, in sin and salvation. But ever since Buddha there has been another approach, often misunderstood, which strives after freedom from the shackles of the self, which excludes the survival of the soul as personality and also the concept of a personal god. This is not atheistic in the materialist's sense, for it does not reject survival but sees it in a different form; nor does it shrink from the concept of the divine. Whatever may have been the Oriental element at the origin of this approach, H.B. expounds his views with a distinct Western flavour of his own in dialectical form interspersed with lyrical passages. The cultural tradition is European, not atheistic but pagan in the ancient classical sense.

The publication of *The Prison* in 1891 rounds off the second period of H.B.'s life. The book is to be appraised both for psychological insights into the author's mind, and for its qualities as a philosophical and literary work. It introduces no fresh elements of thought that are not discussed or adumbrated in *The Theories of Anarchy and Law* – which is for that reason adjudged the superior work in terms of philosophical originality. But as a literary work *The Prison* is not only satisfactory, as Henry James pointed out, but more successful and more compelling than *Anarchy and Law*. Attention is focused on a central theme, sustained to the end in an increasingly lyrical tone. Its form is more integrated and assimilable, though Mrs Humphry Ward, Ethel Smyth and even Henry James had initial difficulties in following the theme and grasping the message. In *Anarchy and Law* the characters shift position; in *The Prison*, which also has four characters or voices, the characters' positions are more rigid. The unpredictability which is part of the charm of *Anarchy and Law* is missing from *The Prison*. But in *The Prison* there is a fifth and dominating voice of a different kind which is

[201]

anything but rigid, heard through a dead man's journal. He has been condemned to death, though innocent, and during solitary confinement preceding his execution goes through various stages of inner torment, meditation, introspection and finally spiritual deliverance.

The dialogue takes the form of discussion around this central text. There is no scene-setting, the four protagonists who take part in the debate – Clive, a super-naturalist, Beryl, a neo-Christian maiden, Croy, a positivist, and Gerald, a wise man – take the reader straight to the central subject matter without a setting being provided. There is no inn by the wayside as in *Anarchy and Law*; only at the end of the dialogue one gathers that the debate has taken place somewhere on the border of a lake. The prisoner, on the other hand, whose voice is heard through Clive reading out loud those passages of the surviving journal that seem to him best suited for discussion, briefly but graphically describes his own surroundings, which play a significant part in his more Kafkaesque moods.

They treat me kindly after all, as far as kindness goes with gaolers. This is neither a dismal dungeon nor an attic under the leads. I have a few books, and I am allowed to write. There are things to grow fond of in the room; an old spinet, voiceless, or worse than that, but dear to look at; a crucifix on the wall (we have met again!) and the portrait of an unknown girl. Also a quaint table and an oaken armchair. These are my friends and my treasures.

Their friendliness however comes to him only after an inner struggle verging on despair. It is heralded by a key passage:

I was born with my prison within me; I have secreted it unconsciously during the years, and there it stands now, suddenly visible to all, a hard massive shell with something small that stirs in it and that I call myself.

There follows a cry of pain straight from the heart, which subsides in a mood of resignation, a stage in the struggle for inner deliverance:

They have thrown me in this tower and barred the windows and bolted the doors; they have taken my liberty from me, and my good name and the faces of those I loved and the sound of human voices, everything in the world except the sunlight and

[202]

the sky and the footfall of the sentinel on the battlements; they have utterly bereaved me – or think they have; and I thought so too at first. I have lain face downward with my hands clenched till it hurt me to open them again; I have lain for hours unable to move as one who is bleeding to death, inwardly repeating the bitterest of all cries: 'Unjust, unjust!' It is over now. I have more than forgiven – I have understood.

From this premise the prisoner is able to proceed upon his meditations. The course is devious; there has to be a search for identity, or for a principle of selfhood, before the ego and its burden can be shaken off.

I cannot get over the thought; it haunts me; if there is no future life our notion of self is false. It is a survival empty and meaningless, without the belief which it survives.

This thought leads him to consider the problem of identity. It is his books, their company, the part they play, that focuses his mind on the question:

My books bear me scant company; they seem to have faded. Some of them which I read with great pleasure in former days sound very strange in here; meagre and forlorn as the voice of the chorister quavering alone in a deserted choir. They used to sound otherwise. Books are written for classes of people; some for lovers and some for scholars; some for the active and some for the pious. No books are written for men; nobody has time to be a man. As long as we mingle with others we are unconscious choristers; a division of labour which we do not suspect forces us into certain moral and intellectual attitudes. We have a character as we have a station or calling, because other people have another one. What we term our individuality is just that share of the task which nobody else was there to undertake; 'I' means 'NOT YOU', and what you are makes what I am.

Having ceased to be of significance and comfort, the shadowy company of books now leave him in solitude:

In solitude the great difficulty is to recollect who one is, to be anyone in particular. The pressure from without is gone and as the blood streams out in too rarefied an atmosphere, so a solitary

[203]

consciousness diffuses itself through space till it seems to belong indifferently to every form of thought. I have ceased to belong to any class of men. Whatsoever lives I yearn towards, and all is equally fair to me that lies beyond these moats, that which I used to call good and that which I used to call evil. Whatever lives is sacred. *Homo sum.*

In fact it is now life rather than the ego or the question of selfhood that matters. But also the problem of continuity worries him.

Of all the troubles of men this is the chief: nothing remains of yesterday. We somehow get through some sixteen hours; then we sleep. And tomorrow we must begin again, and the day after once more. The same moods that swept over us will return and chase each other as before. It is an endless drifting of clouds over a barren moor. Only the endless clouds which once were white and fanciful lose their outline and their brightness till they melt into gloom.

Then we are dead. Someone gives the machinery a push, and a day breaks over another waste; our place is filled. It was so with our fathers and will be so with those that come after us. Nothing remains; nothing grows.

This mood of pessimism is followed by the hope that continuity might be secured through the survival of man's works:

I remember the saying of Buddha: works alone are imperishable. It is a modern view, too; we are supposed to live for our fellow creatures and for posterity as our ancestors lived for us. Shall we not be grateful to the dead? The world is very beautiful; and if they have not made all its beauty, at least they have enabled us to feel it; without their inheritance we might at the present moment be gnawing bones in a cave. Many things remain: the statues and books and cathedrals and songs; wisdom and good manners, kind deeds, even a kind look. Effects survive. Many things grow; empires grow, even wealth can grow; all is not ephemeral.

This solution is rejected at once:

And yet I am not satisfied with this doctrine of eternal works. It is the evangel of the happy few whose works are masterpieces, but it will not apply to our dealings with those around us nor to

[204]

the bulk of the legacy of centuries. If our forefathers have made the world beautiful or made us keen to its beauty, so too have they made it ugly or made us keen to its ugliness. And the gain and the loss are equal. If our good deeds last, so too must our bad ones. We do our neighbours as much harm as good, even as they do to us; and perhaps most harm when we strive to do most good. It is a poor consolation for our brevity that our mistakes will continue to work hot mischief long after we are cold and stark; that our blunders innumerable, our weakness which we took for kindness, our cruelty which we took for justice, our fanaticism which we took for earnestness, our levity which we took for tolerance – that all this or its effects will survive us no less surely than our wisest deeds, some of which have perhaps cost us remorse.

Perhaps in the magic of thought there is consolation – H.B., after all, is not going to abandon his beloved metaphysics so easily.

Today this seems to me the most wonderful thing in the world: the healing power of thought. No matter what our trouble is, and however wretched we may be, even to the hunger fever of utter solitude or the wracking of bodily pain (so at least the story of the martyrs proclaim), there is some thought somewhere which, if we could only lay hold of it, would instantly lull us to rest or revive us out of prostration. What is this mysterious virtue? Is there a miracle greater than this; just a few words murmured from I know not where, and the troubled waters are calmed, the blind see, the lame take up their bed and walk, and the dead arise from the grave. Who speaks these words?

Beryl, the neo-Christian, gets excited when she hears this. The prisoner, however, swerves off in his journal, perturbed again by the problem of continuity:

There is this inexplicable character of the days of our lifetime, that taken separately they may be such common ware as glass beads; threaded together they turn into precious pearls. But how shall I thread them together?

Close on the heels of this problem of continuity recurs the question of the survival of the soul, or in other words survival of the self.

[205]

I have taken to thinking once more over old questions which I had put aside long since as settled. What about the soul? Like most men of these times I have crossed it out of the list of my beliefs on the strength of this argument: we have no knowledge of minds without bodies, of thoughts without brains behind them; then by what right can we assume that when the material organization is destroyed the spiritual organization persists?

Perhaps some one knows a good answer to this argument. I have not found it. All I can feebly say is that the limit of our knowledge is not the limit of reality, and what we have no right to assume may yet perchance be. A weak reply. It may prove that the soul cannot be disproved; it does not justify a faith nor change the balance of probabilities.

Then a further step in his meditations leads him to a sensation of stretching out in an area beyond the limits of his own self which is at the same time included.

Slowly and silently the hours have passed, first the hours in whose aching emptiness the same heavy word swings as a pendulum ceaselessly to and fro; nothing, nothing, nothing; then the hours of foolish, tender self-pity that must be a remainder of childhood, and that, like sorrowful children, find comfort in the excess of their grief. The light has changed on the wall, mellowed and glowed and faded; the silence is deeper than ever; it is dusk, almost night. I know not what delicate air floats in and out of the window, and seems to bear me away and yet leaves me greater than before. And now, clearer than I have ever felt it, a strange feeling comes over me; I am not alone. It is as though the very core of me had been missing and now I have found it; and at the same time as though this deepest and most intimate ME stood outside me so that I would fling my arms round him as a lover. Also he seems to me quite above my troubles, unaffected by my individual lot, impersonal, the same in all men and yet ME.

As he goes on meditating, the debaters break in intermittently with their own comments and theories which, it must be remembered, are also part of H.B.'s thinking. The prisoner returns to consider the question of selfhood. In the following passage, as elsewhere in the meditations, the reader might feel tempted to draw autobiographical inferences. This is dangerous – there are too many facets to H.B.'s debate. Certainly the prisoner's voice echoes what is perhaps deepest in H.B., but if one tried to abstract from it the author's mental history one would get a picture that was incomplete.

I was a stranger in the land even as a child. I think I lived for years as one who is dreaming and who knows that he is dreaming, and yet cannot wake up. Around me were men who had no such feeling. They were wonderfully awake. They had their joys and their sorrows which they referred unhesitatingly to given circumstances and tangible causes. No question as to the reality of the whole scene crossed their minds; no dull sense of its incompleteness numbed their faculties as mine were numbed; nor did they know anything of a delight apparently without cause, to bathe in which I courted solitude. Quick as true metal they responded directly to every touch from without. But with me, the sound turned inwards and awakened echoes that would not cease; as soon as one had subsided it was taken up farther back as a cry wandering through corridors, and raising whispers ever more remote from the immediate world, ever of more general and abstract import. I was an instrument so made that in its response to the world, the world counted for very little and the structure of the instrument for nearly all. And as it was then so it is now; a tyrannical consciousness of my own structure rebels against everything that is around me and makes it all seem as a vain show. And such it must remain unless the core of ME, the innermost self of myself, is also the core of everything, the self of everyone else, so that seeking inward I may grasp the essence of that which is without. I am cut off of all contact unless I am the image of god. I am cut off from the universe unless the universe is the image of ME. I stretch out my hungry arms and they enfold but shadows, if in what they clasp there is no answer to the great cry of love in which I recognize myself, and in which I melt away. What furious and divine selfishness is this, that asserts and sacrifices itself at the same moment; that refuses to hear of aught but itself and resolves itself in allhood? And why do my lips taste to me of infinite space and time?

Identity is finally detached from selfhood. Breaking through the bonds that enthral the self and communion with life as a whole

[207]

do not necessarily imply disintegration of personality. The original quest for identity becomes a quest for freedom from the shackles of the ego.

> That whereby I AM, that which outlives the fleeting hours and gathers their scattered flock is also that whereby men are brothers; my life is continuous and I am myself instead of a succession of disconnected events, only through that in me which is universal, the same in others as in myself; and the stronger it is in me the closer knit I am; and the closer knit the closer bound to my fellow creatures.

Through this paradox the notion is drawn of the difference between self and ego which later psychologists accentuated.

The prisoner proceeds along a fluctuating course of meditation which touches upon the concept of God as a warrant for the reality we apprehend.

> Must there not also be a warrant for this broader reality which vouches for the immediate one; and, again, a warrant behind a warrant? If men can agree at all, must there not be a grand warrant the same in all and the framework of each of them?
>
> What if it be this that they call God?
>
> Then, properly speaking, he is the condition of all reality, and as there is nothing by reference to which we can perceive him as real in the same manner as we perceive other things by ultimate reference to him, his existence must both escape the tests which apply to all other forms of existence and yet be the object of our highest certitude.

But Clive, who is the prisoner's nearest exponent in the debate, is sceptical of this line of approach. He expresses the prisoner's own scepticism. Referring to him, he says:

> Though he starts from the good remark that nothing can be a reality to us without a broader and familiar reality around it, I don't like the way in which he proceeds to dispose realities like the successive layers of a Chinese ball, till at last we reach, or rather cannot reach, but are forced to assume an exterior, all-comprising sphere whence reality filters into the included ones.
>
> Abstractions may enfold one another in that regular way, but

[208]

realities do not, they soon dovetail, and so do our apprehensions of them.

Croy and even Gerald express views, in the course of the debate, which are virtually at the antipodes of the prisoner's position, without necessarily reflecting the author's own position.

In due course the prisoner reverts to a lyrical mood of reflection:

I am one dying of inanition. I can live no longer on these thoughts. If they are the truth, the truth cannot feed man. It is a momentary stimulant, it is another kind of brandy; it is not bread. I was like a man who, having climbed a solitary peak, sees nothing around him but icy blue air, and above a dreadful splendour of fire that rushes straight down on him through millions of silent miles and burns into his brain.

Come to me from all quarters of the heavens, thoughts that bear company and console; pipe to me once more, dear flock of garrulous birds; bring me a distant murmur of life!

It is early summer out of doors. I get its warm gusts of air and its rustling of unseen leaves. I have crept nearer to the living again and can almost hear their voices. Nearer through vain regret and fruitless desire and pity through the thought of perfect unity. Of this pity I hardly know whether it is for myself or for them; it is to me as though I were at the same time their father and their child –their child, because the weakest and poorest of them is richer than I; their father, because I look back upon the joys that have not yet departed from them.

I lean my forehead against the bars of the window and there is a languor of music abroad, and I remember a song they used to sing in France four centuries ago: 'I saw a fair one, my darling – imprisoned in a tower. Would the Virgin Mary – that I were lord thereof – and that the sun were set – and morning not yet near – and that I clasp you, dear one – flesh to flesh in my arms! – Heart, my heart, what wilt thou do? Thy joy is lost – thy pleasure and thy toy. Thou canst not live without her.'

The note of hopelessness with which this outburst ends leads him back to scepticism, to doubting any principle of unity and the consolation it might give.

I said to myself: 'There is one state of mind of much higher value than any other; although through the imperfection of my humanity my thoughts will frequently be called in other directions. They must return to that point as the needle to the pole, and the less they swerve the truer my path. Or, granting that I am on this earth to develop all my faculties and not to confine myself to this one endeavour, yet must it everywhere accompany me as a subdued light underlying and gently shining through all my moods and actions.'

Ah, me! I lie to myself when I profess to carry about with me any such vestal lamp. I lie to myself when I try to believe that if my faith were stronger it would be adequate to my needs. It cannot suffice because there are other truths which it ignores. However hard you may thump a note it will never sound as the full blast of a symphony.

Today all this inner life with its joys of companionship in a cherished ideal, its sense of the presence of God within us, its pride in a secretly tended flame destined gradually to illuminate the surrounding darkness, seems to me the futile effort to collect into one hour of consciousness the infinite and conflicting aspects of reality; an effort born of a feeling of helplessness and forlornness; even as a child suddenly thrown among strangers might clasp desperately in his hand some little familiar object, precious simply because familiar, with a vague sense that he could not quite lose his identity as long as he clasped his toy.

Neither the personal God without nor the mystical God within can suffice when you are confronted with the infinity and conflicting aspects of reality.

What have I been doing here these many weeks; whither have I wandered? I see it now; the hour is still and lucid. I have been seeing the thing that enchants, the cloak whose wearer may pass the door behind which on floors of diamond the king's daughters nightly dance – the talisman that all men covet. Who has not a prison to forget? I stand muffled in the cloak that carried me through not long ago, but the doors remain obstinately shut; and the wind blows the vain folds about, speaks to me words of doubt and hope: 'It is not true that alone gain admittance who come clad in this garment; seek again, you whom it helps no longer.'

[210]

From this turning point a further step is made:

My eyes are foolish and my ears forgetful. There is nothing of me and there never was anything – only this great longing, this passionate desire that refuses to descend into nothingness, that clings to the skirt of the hours as they glide by and cries to them: 'Abide! Abide or take me with you into the time that does not pass.' Yet, foolish as they are, my ears and eyes are almost able to take me there. The forms I have looked at a thousand times are strange and new to me today, and sounds as familiar as the sighing of the wind, or the never-ceasing footfall beneath my window, are full of beautiful wonder.

I am beginning to think that the perfection of any sense introduces us into the company of the gods. It may be that as soon as any one of them attains a certain degree of intensity and fineness it reveals to us something that stands apart from and above the ordinary everyday world, and in presence of which our narrower self dissolves...

What else have they ever striven for, the teachers and the saints? Is it possible that these scorners of the flesh have been lovers of the same beauty, under another garb, as those whom they sought to reclaim? Is it possible that the thirst of immortality should be merely the perfection of a faculty more developed in them than eyesight and hearing?

In the pursuit of this line of reflection the prisoner is led to a concept of the divine which is certainly not the orthodox one:

It is a flower of the senses awaking while the rest is asleep in the city of the brain. Surely this is the stuff whereof the gods are made; for what is the core of religion but a sense of the grand unfamiliarity of life? And if beauty is a powerful abstraction of lines and colours and sounds from the tangle of our everyday brain industry, what is holiness but the same abstraction at work in men whose aptitude for reflective thought is more developed than their sensuous organs? They deal not in colours and in sounds. There is no appeal to them in lines and rhythms. Having eyes they see not, and ears they hear not. But the inner world is full of mystery to them. Their moral consciousness is the only spot in their mind capable of that total intoxication, that concentrated activity in the midst of surrounding sleep, which is the first touch of the wing of genius; and as soon as that touch is given, the scene that lights up before them in sudden solemn beauty is their destiny; the room in which an atmosphere of fiction has floated is their life lifted from the dust of the road into the everlasting freshness of poetry and the superior reality of which they have become aware, is what they call God. Let them call it so. It is right that this form of enchantment should have a distinct name as it has virtues of its own. But let it be clear that God is only a form of the divine, the God of certain memories; that which makes him divine is the enchantment of which he arises, the chariot on which he takes his turn.

Unorthodox as this approach may be to the usual concept of godhead, Clive, the prisoner's frequent though not invariable advocate, follows a parallel line.

They say [Clive argues] that doubt desecrates — meaning, I suppose, that from each successive basis proposed for belief it withdraws absolute worth and supreme authority; there is nothing that it does not condition. But a thorough doubt conditions itself; it conditions the desecrator and measures its tether. Who, then, is left to say of the range beyond that it is not sacred? The faith which shall stand must be dragged from its vital doubt. It must be the disenthronement of the great doubter: Reason.

When the prisoner resumes his meditation he arrives at a concept which a Christian, which he is not, might call 'grace'.

Oh, yes! There is another wine. But it cannot be asked for, for it has no name; it cannot be offered, for no vessel will hold it; it runs through the crystal of thought as brandy through ice. No one knows whence it comes; Ponce de Leon is sailing still in search of its enchanted vineyard. No one knows why or by whom or at what moment it will be tendered to his lips. No one knows why this hour or second was perfect, imperishable, evidently superhuman, and not so the one before it or the one after. There are men who for years have prayed daily in hopes of meeting once again the flash which is never forgotten; others who pursue woman after woman as though they were lifting up masks in quest of a face once seen; and some who work furiously, and some who cross their arms and wait. But neither

[212]

prayer nor pleasure nor work nor patience can summon the silent and certain message that something of us has been tossed aloft and garnered in for ever.

He still toys with the mirage of after-life:

I awoke in the middle of the night and heard the sighing of the wind. Even so, I thought, my life is passing away. A little rustling in the dark; a little traceless rustling. Then a great yearning pained me as when I used to think of those by whom I am forgotten; the pain of one lying in his blood and who dares not stir but waits and listens if perchance someone is coming who will bear his farewell message. But there was nothing save silence and gloom and the passing of the wind.

Thus minutes and hours went by, and all the time the yearning grew wilder, till it grew so wild that at last it tore itself away from me. It rose and soared off, and its place was filled with peace. The room was not cheerless any more, but companionable, as with the haze of morning and the twitter of swallows.

Then I said to myself: 'These many years I have longed to master a secret so precious that its possession should grace life and make death worth dying. Now behold! In this very moment I am outliving death. Give me this thrill of eternity and I quit you of the rest.'

But what sort of eternity? He leads us on along avenues of reflection where the idea of after-life is very different from the usual concept of enduring identity.

We are full of immortality. But it dwells not in the beauty of our moral person; it stirs and glitters in us under the crust of self, like a gleam of sirens under the ice, and any blow which breaks this crust brings us into the company of eternal ones whom to feel is to be they. That blow you will surely strike somehow, you will live and die. The film you have spread you will likewise rend; surely, surely, you must slip into heaven. There is no rule of divine conduct, no text book of enchantments. Say if you will, that they are always the same, one under many forms. Call them disguisers of the emancipator. This you may do, but you cannot prescribe to him the method of your emancipation. He tears the veil as he chooses, with dawn rose fingers of adoration and fiery

[213]

fingers of enthusiasm, but also with the scarlet hand of passion and the livid hand of death.

The method of emancipation is certainly not the ordinary way of Christian salvation:

I would proclaim unconditioned salvation to man. Others have stood forth and said: 'Believe this or that and your faith will save you; it will show you the meaning and the reward of life; but without this faith there is neither meaning nor reward.' I say that your beliefs and your disbeliefs matter no more than your nationality or the colour of your hair.

A far cry from the beliefs of H.B.'s own Puritan forefathers! Subsequently the prisoner closes this stage of meditation in a fluctuating mood of despondency where the self reappears only to suffer for its pride:

Then in the faint grey morning I heard a sound as of distant surf, I breathed a breath of the ocean, and it seemed to me that I was a doomed ship whose crew – a motley crew of hopes and thoughts and passions – had suddenly recollected that they could not drown, but would surely reappear and, drenched with the brine of oblivion, man some new craft, putting their pride again in some gallant ship of self till its sails, too, hang in rotten shreds and pitiful timbers give way once more.

The debaters go on discussing the text. In the end Clive reads the closing meditation where the prisoner begins to break from the bonds of the self to the edge of freedom.

We are not made only to master death but also to tame wild life and caress it into beauty. We were made for the plenitude of our form in which beat many hearts. Not I, but the pure elements liberated by rapture from the tangle of me, this is what will last. What then? Then I am a fragment and the entirety is the many. Then, too, I am made for a work of love that shall constitute outside and around me the unity which I renounce within. In the same measure in which I crumble into indestructible atoms, I must grow in the human communion. If not, I may have outlasted death, I have not learned how to live.

I would like to go out once more among the living, if only to know how it feels. Should I seek them as one who comes to join hands in a ring, as one whose eyes inquire and all his frame wants to understand? Would they seek me as singers seek a noble room in which their own voices sound new to them? If so, 'tis well; 'tis the plenitude. If not, I have too soon escaped destruction and am as he who cruises for ever round Cape Horn, listening to the songs of a phantom crew.

Deliverance comes with the last meditation:

Now my struggle is over; the time has come and my choice is made. I abandon to destruction the unity of which I am conscious; I take refuge in the lastingness of its elements. I bid farewell for ever to the transient meeting of eternal guests who had gathered here for an hour; they are taking leave of one another and never perhaps throughout the course of ages will they meet again, all of them and none but they, under the same roof. I hear them overhead moving to depart, and the sound of their several footfalls quiver through me in sweet bitter shudders. I hear the flight of the divine vultures that bear away my substance shred by shred; the wind of their wings is as ice on my forehead and from I know not where wells into my eyes the tranquil glory of a boundless sunset.

What are they waiting for, the departing guests? Only a word that shall set them free. Go, then; pass on, immortal ones. And, behold, I burst the bonds that pent you up within me, I disband myself and travel on for ever in your scattered paths. Wheresoever you are, there I shall be. I survive in you. I set my ineffaceable stamp upon the womb of time. I am whatever I have felt, and what I have felt is what some must ever feel. For years I have been conning my lesson, learning to say: 'Not mine, not mine'; ashamed of both sorrow and of joy till they were slowly lifted from within me and stretched overhead, endless and unchangeable as the Milky Way whose soft light descends indifferently on all men from generation to generation. My hopes have become an heirloom of the centuries which it is my turn to take care of; my thoughts are here on deposit for a little while; they have been passed round since the dawn of time and someone else will have charge of them tomorrow; the laughter I have laughed rose in the bulrushes of yore and mingled with the sound of the syrinx; the

[215]

kisses that have wandered to my lips will never grow cold; no heart but mine shall ever ache and leap. My passions are the tingling blood of mankind. Now someone says to me: 'It is well so far; taste also the death.' Then let there be banners and music; this is my leave-taking; I am not even going home. I thank you, days of hope and pride; I thank you, lamentable solitude, and you, shades of those that loved me. I sorrow with you, grieving ones, and melt with you, O fond ones. I triumph with those who vanquish and I rest with those who are dead. I descend to my fathers and return again for ever. I have nothing that is mine but a name, and I bow down in my dream of a day to the life eternal. I am the joy and the sorrow, the mirth and the pride; the love, the silence, and the song. I am the thought. I am the soul. I am the home.

After these last words of the prisoner the debate comes abruptly to an end. 'Oh, shut the manuscript. I think Beryl is overtired,' says Gerald. 'Look what a lovely evening it is! Let us row across the lake,' exclaims Croy. 'Yes, come,' joins in Clive, 'and Beryl shall hum to us, as she did the other evening, the song of some old Flemish master. Orlando . . . something.' 'Orlando Lassus,' says Beryl. 'Just so,' Clive concludes.

Before the book draws to an end the reader will have become progressively aware that the prisoner is seeking and eventually finding salvation neither in the Christian doctrine of matter and spirit, nor in the monism of philosophical idealism, nor in orthodox Buddhist nirvana, nor in the usual forms of pantheism where everything is resolved again in monism.

The prisoner remains faithful, as indeed H.B. did himself, to the idea of plurality wherein the ego must be dismantled if freedom is to be achieved.

Life everlasting is not of the self but of the cosmos, both in a physical and a spiritual sense, in which personality participates by bursting the bonds individuality has formed. The salvation sought is not through divine immanence but through *émanence* into the divine, a stretching out, as it were, to life, to death and beyond into endless multiplicity, rather than through an inward search for a unifying principle. Here lies the originality of the author's metaphysical approach. It stands a pole apart from Ethel Smyth's orthodox theism and at a good distance from Julia's monism, though her mystical bent and metaphysical introspection place her much closer.

In this chapter I have limited myself to following the prisoner's line of thoughts with quotations from those passages of the journal that seemed to me most significant. The other voices, however, those that discuss the journal whether by differing or agreeing are almost of equal importance in the evaluation of the author's own stance. In this dialogue H.B. again lays emphasis on his undogmatic, decentralized view of life and of religion in general, a view which already dominated *Anarchy and Law*. Through Clive he declares that belief in divinity does not necessarily mean belief in 'supremacy' and that the error of all European philosophy lies in the assumption that the only alternative to atheistic materialism is either Christian duality or a type of monism which would confine man's apprehension of the divine within a single governing principle.

H.B.'s most daring views enter the debate, such as his theory on the participation of the subject in the creation of the reality of the object and the significance of self-projection evinced by Jung decades later. But it is only by reading the book[1] that one gets a rounded picture of his different trends of thought, opposing and completing the main theme.

What H.B. himself felt about the form in which he had chosen to write is expressed in a letter to Ethel shortly after the publication of *The Prison*.

> Dialogues, autobiographies and letters are the only pure true sincere forms. What business have we to peep first over one person's shoulder and then over another's as the novelist does? Fancy a painter always shifting his stool about and getting up and turning round between time to explain how one bit of landscape hangs on to another bit! Above all what business have we to start with a thesis and demonstrate it point by point? Nobody thinks like that; it is a preposterous convention. The real thing is a seething mass of thoughts and impressions; our thinking so far as it is alive and genuine is a conversation between our different selves, aye and a fight. The rest is a professor's work; second-hand goods even if extracted originally from our own brain. C'est du réchauffé.

Among the various tributes paid to *The Prison* there was one in

[217]

more recent times from an eminent Jesuit philosopher who as a Christian held opposite views. In his *Mirage and Truth*, M. C. D'Arcy referred to it as 'a remarkable but too little known book' in which the prisoner formulates through his meditations 'almost all that can be said on the side of those who look for an ideal beyond that of orthodox theism'.

20

Ethel Resurgent

Five years had gone by since the break between Ethel and H.B., during which time they neither saw nor wrote to each other. As time went on it looked as though H.B. had accommodated himself to his compromised mode of family life. For six months of the year he lived with his wife and children, most of the time in Switzerland; the remaining six months he lived alone in London and in France, seeing old friends, meeting new ones, occupied with his own work and yet feeling lonely, perhaps indeed wanting to feel lonely. Real contact with his fellow beings, to which he attached an ever-increasing importance, he still found difficult. 'I was born with a prison within me,' says the prisoner, and it was during those couple of years which preceded 1890 that H.B. worked at and wrote *The Prison*. During the six-month absences from Julia there would be much of the old introspection and self-questioning in his letters but at the same time they were becoming more entertaining, more informative, more open to the world around, and always full of genuine affection. Of course neither of them was happy *au fond*. H.B. could not help feeling that the harmony between them had been achieved at the cost of sacrificing Ethel, and for Julia it must have been a painful concession to allow him his freedom without her breaking away.

In the end, as the result of his spending so much time in London, the inevitable happened. Early in December 1890 H.B. saw Ethel at a concert of hers in London and afterwards met her for tea.

'You looked very well on the stage the other evening,' he wrote to her a few days later, 'handsome and "sympathetic".' He also said in that letter:

I don't ask you to take upon yourself the burden of duplicity – hiding what you do from your friends and being neither one thing nor another. It is too heavy a load; I doubt if anything be worth it in the long run. But I shall ask you not to go into

[219]

heroics. For my part I should have no difficulty in saying to my friends, to Kate for instance, or to Cazalis, or to a man I know in Geneva who has the cleverness of a very clever woman and something of the same charm (his name is Rod) – I should have no difficulty in saying: we keep apart but not as though we were likely to give one another the plague; on some rare occasions we meet, when there is any particular reason, a business reason so to speak, for there is business too in the world of thought and sentiment; and when we meet nobody need look away ashamed. We are not ashamed and if the Lord's voice were heard suddenly in the garden calling us we should not feel flurried. . .

This is a line of conduct which possibly I may some day free from concealment towards Julia herself, but only on condition that she finds herself *en présence d'un fait accompli* and that I can say to her: 'This has been going on for ever so long; judge it by the results; the proof that it was the right thing is that I am still for you the right man and have been so all along.' She will never give her consent beforehand because she is timorous in the highest degree.

In her memoirs Ethel recalls this meeting of theirs as follows:

Still the same pale clean-cut face, the dreamy far-apart eyes, the abundance of soft, fluffy fair hair; still the striking-looking man he had always been. The only shock was that he had grown a beard. In the course of our long discussion over the tea-table about our future, I implored him to get rid of that disfigurement, though I admitted it might be very effective in preventing our intercourse from becoming too personal, which we decided should be our object for the present.

Further meetings were excluded, however, at least for the time being. Ethel was going through an intensely religious period. She had become a close friend of Mrs Benson, the Archbishop of Canterbury's wife. But there followed an exchange of letters, brave, cheerful, forthright in tone and denuded of terms of endearment. Most were on the subject of religion and written in an affectionately combative spirit, with both H.B. and Ethel striving to convert each other to their respective positions, he the pagan pluralist on one side, and she the Episcopalian Anglican on the other. Neither could find common ground though their mood was of mutual tolerance and sympathy. At least they both enjoyed arguing, or so one has the impression. Religion was a favourite subject with H.B., both for argument and for meditation. The years of arguing with Julia were over, arguing that had been on a metaphysical rather than a religious, denominational plane. By this time H.B. and Julia knew each other's positions well enough, and though both positions were unorthodox, they commanded respect from the other party. There was even an area of understanding, the mystical field. From time to time they would exchange views and explain them further without getting into an argument – at least not on the subject of religion. But between Ethel and H.B. religion became the main issue.

H.B. sent her first *Theories of Anarchy and Law*, then *The Prison* to read, and was hoping for greater understanding than he seemed to be getting. She, for her part, sent him *The Imitation of Christ*. From their mutually dubious reaction the argument starts:

That is the worst of your little book [H.B. complains], the imitation. He is all the time asking himself if he is doing right or wrong and how his soul is getting on. He is perpetually saying to God: 'Do you love me dearest?' He ought not even to think about it; the certitude ought to be in him unconsciously and only manifest itself by his joyful free and bold activity. The passage you point out is certainly very pretty (though much too self-conscious). There are lots of pretty passages. But what a dangerous emollient book! About the passage alluded to, listen to Marcus Aurelius: 'O Cosmos! Whatever suits thee, suits me.' That is the same thing and better said to my mind; without the anthropomorphic imagery and the tenderness that will grow later into pious pictures, flaming hearts with daggers in them and tearful faces with crowns and thorns.

But she keeps harping on the importance of the Church, to which he reacts strongly. He writes from 12 Cork Street:

If there is one thing in the world I have dread of, it is the Church. I should think generations of obscure ancestors of mine must have wept and gnashed their teeth and gnawed their hands in silent rage under the Blue Laws of New England; and all their compressed rebellion has burst forth in me. Figuratively I can feel my bristles rising when there is a priest or a clergyman in the room before I have caught sight of him. If I had not intellectual training I should probably be a revolutionary of the rankest dye. . . . Now you have bishops in your pedigree – horrible to think of! – and heredity, which always comes out stronger as we advance in life, is pushing you in the contrary direction to mine.

On the other hand, far from being averse to I am extremely fond of religion. You say you don't understand it. Allow me to point out that this is a question of definition and that if what I care for so deeply – the eternal, the transcendent part of life, the part of it which passes reason – is not religion it is at least something of which I understand, in the measure of my strength, the whereabouts and the importance, which is all that anyone can profess to understand of something that passes reason. If you like I will put the word, not being able to think of another, between inverted commas so that you should know what I am alluding to and not get puzzled. This 'religion' then I hold to be an interior, an individual affair, the greatest of affairs for every man no matter where and when he was born – and consequently having nothing to do with the Church.

Now here is where the strange twist comes in. I can agree with you perfectly about the Church and feel that you have got hold of something real; but I have not at all the feeling that we understand one another or could understand one another without months of conversation about 'religion'.

My standing out of the Church, arrayed against it, does not in the least prevent me from recognizing something very true and genial and persuasive in what you say about it. I like Cardinal Newman and feel in charming company with him – at least as far as all I have read of his goes. He is a mystic and I can always get on with them. If you come to me with 'visions' I will forgive almost anything. . .

It occurs to me that you may be puzzled at my talking with so much animosity and so much friendship of the Church. That is on account of a confusion that has crept into the Church and thanks to which it may with equal justice be looked upon as a world-embracing institution uniting men in a bond of love, or as a little party of bumptious people assembled and reviling nine tenths of their own nature. The two judgements can be passed with equal firmness and facts without end produced to support either view.

Sometimes H.B. feels that he may have gone too far and hurt her feelings:

Don't imagine for a moment that I would like you out of the Church, since you feel its love. But what I do is this: I think of the double aspect of the Church and sincerely, violently hope that you will not take to looking at your tongue and feeling your pulse. I persist in thinking that *The Imitation* is an unhealthy dangerous book. But at present you are gulping the whole Church down – both of them at once. Perhaps it must be so at first.

But in a later letter he lashes out once more:

You come to plead for the spirit against the letter and you enshrine your teaching in a crumb of belief, the nearest crumb – 'Love Me, I am the son of God'. That crumb has become the inquisition and Calvinism before you have time to say Jack Robinson. The English Church which you are fond of citing may possibly avoid this danger better than others on account of the intensely practical reasonable moderate character of the English. But look at the Scotchmen and the Spaniards.

Then the subject of Julia intervenes.

I found a letter from Julia when I came home from dinner but I have quietly gone on with mine before telling you about it. It is just as I had anticipated at first; she does object, at least to our meeting. She says nothing about writing, and considering how very much more eloquent personal contact is than pen and ink there is a certain fine instinct in this. Now unless you again insist, which I hope you won't, I shall not broach the subject of our correspondence and take silence for consent. I think it is a point where the side lights ought to come in. It will be a great loss to me not to see you again. And yet I don't know if it is not better. I saw quite enough the other day for what we want, and so long as we merely exchange notes now and then we can stay there in peace. I shan't say such pretty things to you again so you needn't be afraid of that.

[223]

Pretty things? Intimate things? No record has survived. A subsequent letter touches a note of melancholy.

There is something rather sad in all this because I can't help feeling that I am often, very often, in the same boat as those whom you profess to loathe and despise. There is nothing particularly cheerful in this.

And yet they loved each other, although the correspondence goes on for months in the same tone of mutual aggression on the all-pervading subject of religion. In the end H.B. does say, however:

I don't mind your being a Christian if you remain a good girl besides, and you don't grow benumbed or despondent or peevish, or (I must add that for it is in reality my only fear) intolerant. You call me a ghost on account of certain superficial traits, but at heart I am a child of Apollo and what I love is the sun that shines on all, and the minds and hearts that reflect it and beam – as 'tis your nature too.

I should like to wrap you up in some cloak that would prevent you from feeling alone. And I should like you to love me according to the manner we defined when discussing the difference between letters of love and love letters.

Their letters had been neither, more round after round of religious pugilism. But gradually the subject wore thin, other topics eventually took over in a more personal, tender tone. But the style still remained, deliberately, not the style of love letters.

In May both of them were travelling independently on the Continent. Ethel had in the meantime become a close friend of the ex-Empress Eugénie, the widow of Napoleon III. H.B. nourished an aversion to royalty:

I was in the sitting-reading-smoking room of the Hotel de Milan the other evening with a vague idea that you had left Mentone for Venice, and Milan was on the way; I might see a welcome face. There was an English girl in shirt sleeves evidently writing an elaborate description of the cathedral to her friends at home, but that was not what I was looking for. So I took up a local newspaper. The first thing I saw was that the ex-Empress Eugénie had left that morning the Hotel de Milan on her way to

Venice. This took me immediately to the office of the hotel where I learned that Her Majesty had indeed honoured the house (occupying Verdi's favourite rooms) and that she had departed in the company of a young lady generally believed to know quite as much about music as Verdi. Thereupon I returned to the smoking room and collapsed in a cup of coffee. I felt like the detective or the avenger in a novel when he arrives just five minutes too late.

I think it is an expression you made use of, about 'being on good terms with several royalties' that roused me in the religious spirit of Jeremiah or whoever the dismal old fellow was who used to go about in sackcloth and ashes shouting 'Woe! Woe!' Of course I dislike royalties. Of course they strike me as instances of the same petrification as dogmas and ceremonies, the same degenerescence of symbolism.

In spite of the little stabs there are signs of a deepening mutual affection. They went on being forthright in expressing their differing points of view, but at the same time began to show more concern for each other's feelings. Both Ethel and H.B. were easily hurt. More than once he referred to this problem.

We rarely understand how the natural and agreeable expansion of our own plumage can break other people's tender feathers, particularly those very people out of gladness at whose sight we ruffle up in instinctive pleasure.

In all these letters they wrote to each other throughout that year of 1891, hers being always addressed Poste Restante so that he could collect them without Julia's knowledge, not a single word is to be found about the Hildebrands with whose children H.B.'s own children went on happily consorting in Florence. The Fiedlers, however, were not beyond the pale. In December we find H.B. writing to Ethel about them and about Henry James as well:

So you are going to Bayreuth? I suppose the Fiedlers will be there. We dined with them the other day at Munich. She has a very pretty expression of countenance, something brave and nice in the eyes that is quite an invention. He seemed to me to be looking younger than in former days. Perhaps that is because he is not writing anything just now. I told him that his book on the

[225]

artistic Tätigkeit ought to be translated into English to counteract some of Ruskin's poison. But would the English read it? I wish you could have heard Henry James's lamentations over the British brain, the other day at the Dresden gallery. Of course only as concerns things intellectual, otherwise it is a powerful instrument. So don't be offended. What made it so very comic is that he doesn't like the Germans — is affronted at their meals and the hours of their meals, their beds and their bed clothes and their stoves and sausages and their faces and their beer; so their power of following ideas — which he was comparing with amazement to English incapacity — seemed to come in as an extravagance against them, a way of adding insult to injury.

I am glad you have a Latin friend at last. It is an utterly unknown race in Gothdom, whether English or German, as I am sure you will find out in a few years if your friendship prospers; as known as the Chinese and as remote. I am never weary of watching them and always discovering things I had not suspected, especially in the French who are the strangest of the lot and the hardest to read. Your friend seems an interesting person and from what you say I think I should like her. Thank goodness she is not a pretender to the throne. . .

Who the 'Latin friend' was is not clear. Ethel was busy at this time cultivating Lady Ponsonby. H.B. goes on writing about music in Germany — Mozart's operas, nearly all of which he had been to again, an excellent performance of *Lohengrin*; he had heard, too, the famous Hermann Levi conduct a performance of Mascagni's *Cavalleria Rusticana*, with its admirable libretto; and so on.

Ethel, for her part, was carrying on an active correspondence with her brother Bob Smyth who was in the Army overseas. This exchange of letters went on for decades, until the end of her life. A passage where Bob describes Winston Churchill is worth quoting. They were on the march to Khartoum with Kitchener.

I find I have got an addition to my troop, Winston Churchill of the 4th Hussars. He is Lord Randolph's son, and has been fighting in Cuba; . . . He arrived the night before we started and taught us a new game called Bridge which comes from Constantinople and is like whist, but more of a gamble. At present he is attached to my troop, but when we arrive at the place of concentration and form a fourth squadron he will be given a troop in that. He rides with me sometimes on the march and is such good company. Keeps one awake, which is a great thing, for starting so early and going to bed so late one is apt to sleep in the saddle. . . He is only twenty-three and frightfully keen. He started by telling me he was more interested in men than in horses, so I asked him to look after the men's rations, and I said I would do the horses. He asked to see the men, and spoke to them (very well too) and had a great success; in fact they liked him. He said it surprised him that I, at thirty years of age, was content to be only a troop leader of cavalry! That amused me. Anyhow I *do* know how to do it.

I shall be very sorry when Winston Churchill leaves my troop. He is aggressively clever and bumptious, but you can't help liking him in spite of his very apparent but superficial faults. If ever you come across him, get to know him. I know you'd delight in him. . . He said too that he did not mean, or wish, to stay in the Army, not caring to spend his life 'in the company of intelligent animals'! Of course he's very young and knows it. But if he lives, he'll be a big man some day.

Ethel always kept in close touch with the many members of her family, to whom she felt closely bound. It was out of consideration for them as much as out of religious scruples that she refrained from overstepping the border of propriety in her relationship with H.B. – even if he had been willing to take that step with her. But it does not seem at all certain that he was, as long as Julia was averse to such a situation.

In December 1891 we find H.B. in Rome looking for an apartment. Julia's increasingly delicate health had now come to the assistance of his long-cherished plan to transfer the family home away from Florence, where he could no longer share it, to some other more congenial city. Ethel had exchanged views with him on the possibility of a reconciliation with the Hildebrands, but H.B. remained reluctant, for the time being at any rate, mainly for tactical reasons. He felt that the relationship between Ethel and himself, however harmless, was less likely to be interfered with as things stood.

Julia was suffering from recurrent bronchitis and spells of faintness. She was finally persuaded that the winters in Florence were pernicious for such ailments. So she reluctantly came to the conclusion that a move to Rome, where the climate was milder, was both advisable and reasonable.

> I am alone in Rome [H.B. wrote to Ethel at Christmas], the others are in Florence till I have chosen a dwelling, and I spend my time in an imbecile sort of way which has always a great charm for me, strolling about in the streets and hunting for apartments. Nothing disorganizes the brain more effectually. I have a new idea for a book, and walk about with it, but I don't know whether I shall carry it out; not unless I acutely enjoy the writing of it.

The sun was shining in Rome, the weather was lovely. In Florence it was colder and cloudy. Clothilde, the old Baroness von Stockhausen, was staying with her daughter but lying in bed, nearing her end. H.B. wrote to Julia to get bottles of champagne for her at Christmas. He could not come as he was in the middle of negotiations for the lease of a new apartment. Then Clothilde died before the year had come to a close and H.B. had to rush to Florence. To Ethel he wrote again on 4 January 1892:

> I was called suddenly to Florence on account of my mother-in-law's death. I think I told you that she was with Julia in Via de' Bardi. Not knowing how long I might have to remain in Florence and fearing complications if Maquay, H. & Co. forwarded letters to me there, I wanted to warn you against writing to their care. . . It is extraordinary how many things there are to be done when a relative dies, especially when the coffin is taken to a foreign land. Did you get my letter telling you that I give up going to Paris and London this month in favour of April? . . .
>
> You don't expect an *oraison funèbre* from me. Peace to the dead. I never could give her my sincere affection; but I honestly gave some admiration and a great deal of kindness which I hope will be counted to my credit in some future life.

Perhaps H.B. was forgetting the remoter past when there had been real affection between him and his godmother. Subsequently they had always been on affable terms, but a relationship between mother-in-law and son-in-law can have its pitfalls. In more recent years old Clothilde's support for her daughter Julia in the struggle with Ethel, and her own – in the circumstances quite natural – dislike of Ethel,

[228]

had brought about a certain degree of estrangement between her and H.B. But to his credit he behaved towards her with the utmost consideration and kindness until the end. She was indeed a remarkable woman, as her letters and extant writings show, and her son-in-law was too fair and objectively minded not to recognize it.

The apartment H.B. had found is described in a letter to Ethel which he wrote a few weeks later:

> Here it is lovely. I wonder if you know Rome well enough to recollect Piazza Colonna? Quite close to it, in the direction of the Pantheon, there is a small piazza with eleven old columns (belonging formerly to a temple of Neptune) and called Piazza di Pietra. One side of this small square is formed by an old-fashioned Italian house called Palazzo Cini, of which I occupy the second floor. From my window I see the Pantheon and the statue on the top of the column of Marcus Aurelius in Piazza Colonna. The weather is delightful and I have taken a sudden interest in the old Romans and am working them up with the help of Mommsen and others. As regards living people it so happens that I have made lots of acquaintances and have the key to all that I wish to make. Now tell me about yourself.

To Julia he had written some weeks previously about the various aspects of the apartment he was about to take. Whatever could be said against it, it was the best he could find and had positive qualities. It was not banal, *il est très quelqu'un*. There follows a detailed description of it – on the second floor of the palace, high up, with a fine view 'on the ruins of the temple of Neptune', as he reported to Ethel, with many rooms facing south and so enjoying the full benefit of the sun. Clotilde and Christopher would each have their own room. He felt she would approve of the flat, he urged her to come to look at it at once. But she had an attack of 'flu. He then wrote:

> I don't know which is the cosmopolitan's most noble mania. Sometimes I say it is life and sometimes the wish to die; there is a word missing to express the two together, but both are equally dear and desirable. Sometimes I say, so long as one 'understands' what matters the rest? To understand is a perfect pleasure, imperishable and more than consoling. At other moments it seems

[229]

to me that the intellect by itself is something fragmentary which demands to be embodied in a whole work of prose or of conduct. Rome pleases me. I want it to please me and it does.

Between these two letters and shortly after the death of Clothilde von Stockhausen a far more shattering event took place. Her daughter Lisl died suddenly at San Remo on the Italian Riviera where she had been advised by her doctors to spend the winter. She had been ailing for some time but nobody expected this; she was still relatively young, barely forty-five and in the full bloom of her intellectual and social activities. Her death desolated her many friends, men and women, who delighted in her company. First and foremost were Brahms himself, Clara Schumann, the whole Brahmsian coterie, the Fiedlers and of course the Hildebrands. On her tomb at San Remo there is a relief portrait of her playing the organ which Hildebrand specially sculpted in remembrance of her. But no one was quite so overcome by the event as Ethel, who had not been in touch with Lisl for nearly seven years. She refers to it in a few words at the beginning of the second instalment of her autobiography, *As Time Went On*. 'The bottom fell out of my world.' She was always hoping for a coming together again. Now it was too late.

H.B. wrote to her at length on the subject as soon as her initial violent reaction, verging on despair, had subsided slightly.

I am glad to hear you speak of Lisl as you do. Very glad. With your Celtic exuberance of expression you once spoke, or rather wrote, about her in a way that grieved me and shut me up on that subject, though I hoped, as it turned out, that sometimes you felt otherwise. It was about your having wasted your time and your treasures on her. No, you certainly did not waste your time as your sorrow for her now proves. You really did love her, and that in itself is enough. Perhaps she returned less than you gave; if so the loss was chiefly hers; but *as far as I know* I don't think the word traitor applies to her. It may be that I don't have all the facts (you speak sometimes as though I had not) but I doubt if you have them either or have ever quite realized the cruel position she was in. Yes, we were on quite friendly terms, she and I; never intimate of course, first because there was a great silence between us about you and the Hildebrands, and because of something so German about her that all my Latin colours glowered at once with redoubled fury as soon as we met. But she had a wonderful grace of mood which I could not look at without admiration and I suppose she had the penetration of her sex in finding this out, and so she liked me well enough, as an unclassable curiosity of a brother-in-law. Julia was fond of her in the usual proper, sisterly fashion but nothing out of the way, whereas she worshipped her mother, to whose shortcomings her eyes were lovingly blind; and the minor loss has been swamped by the greater one. Love is good, no matter whom it goes to; and if perchance to one's mother, who would protest or breathe a word?

I am glad you grieve over Lisl, because a great affection ending in total indifference is inexpressibly sad to me. Why go on with one's self, with the same body and the same name, why not blow one's brains out and make a fresh start if such things could be forgotten? Times may change and trouble may come, even strife and separation; but something must surely remain as long as those who have loved one another remain alive — respect for the feelings they wrought together, and gratitude therefore to one another. You cannot at all be sure, I should fancy, that because Lisl turned away from you and held aloof, or was hard and unjust on some point or other, she had forgotten. I imagine not. She was too musical to forget, and her eyes were too deep and pure. The strife and separation were necessities of the foreground, one of the tragedies we are all called upon to play without knowing why. I wish you could have been sure of this, and, as you say, joined hands for a minute; but unless you have very strong facts to the contrary — something of which I am quite ignorant — judge by yourself, and what she felt by what you feel.

'Understand, understand' was H.B.'s recurrent motto, a principle which ruled his approach to life. But what rankled most with Ethel was that Lisl should have been allowed to die without her knowing that she was seriously ill, without there having been a possibility of their coming together again, forgiving past differences, forgetting sore points and saying goodbye to each other lovingly. For this calamity, as she saw it, there had to be a scapegoat, just as there had to be one, or rather two, when the break between her and Lisl occurred in 1885 – the Hildebrands. Now it was Julia herself whom Ethel picked upon. In her memoirs she says:

[231]

One thing was now certain; from this hour a new course should be steered. I forthwith wrote a letter to Julia that must have astonished her a great deal, so new was its tone. I told her that for years I had striven to repair as well as I could the harm I had unwittingly done her; while she on her side had told me that my fate was none of her business. And now, thanks to her implacability, the thing of which I had ever lived in dread had happened – Lisl had died without even sending me a word of farewell. 'From henceforth', I wrote, 'I mean to fashion my life as I choose, not giving you a thought.'

In practice, this refashioning of her life meant that instead of merely writing to each other from time to time she and H.B. would meet and see each other whenever the occasion arose. But the extraordinary thing about the whole matter was that although they met from time to time in London or Paris more or less secretly, they always put up at separate hotels. There was no question, as yet, of their becoming real lovers. Evidently psychological obstacles, or religious principles on Ethel's side, stood in the way – in spite of the 'dethronement of Julia', as Ethel put it. In her memoirs she says:

Anyone who should have known how, when, and where we met would doubtless have concluded we were lovers; and if Julia knew anything about it, probably she held that belief. There is a story by Anatole France which begins with a paragraph about the Senator and the Marquise who for years had been in the habit of meeting daily. 'Le monde selon son habitude soupçonna le pire. C'était exact.' But in our case 'le monde' would have been wrong. From the very first our relation had followed lines of its own. And just as I had understood four or five years ago when he paid no attention to my S.O.S., so he understood that this time it was I whose 'No' could not be circumvented, that people must move forward on their own lines and at their own pace.

Occasionally H.B. grumbled, feeling like St Joseph in relation to the Virgin Mary – 'plus le gardien de sa virginité que son époux'. But probably H.B. was not pressing that hard for a sexual relationship with Ethel. He was still attached to Julia and there may have been other psychological factors as well.

[232]

Predictably, the ones who were most distressed about the new situation were Mrs Benson, to whom Ethel would always tell everything, and her husband the Archbishop. They objected to 'the dethronement of Julia'. 'Mrs Benson', Ethel says, 'at last felt the hopelessness of converting me to her point of view, and as there seemed no likelihood of the Archbishop getting over his aversion, we agreed that both visits and correspondence had better be discontinued for the present.'

So the iron curtain descended between Ethel and her great friends and when later relations were resumed they were never quite the same, in spite of *The Prison* continuing to be appreciated by Mrs Benson and Ethel's Mass by the Primate. But she kept in touch with Arthur Benson, their son, who was a house master at Eton. They wrote to each other frequently and she was happy to receive the following letter from him one summer day in 1892, most of which was about H.B.

Well, you must know it was a very literary party – Pater and Hardy and Gosse and Austin Dobson, and many others; some borrowed names, and some who like myself had written a book of which no one else could see the point.

And – I am not being insincere, because I have said this several times already – the most agreeable and delightful person there was Mr B. I must except Gosse perhaps (tho' he was rather cumbered like Martha with much flurry and shuffling a party of hot guests who had lunched well) – for he, Gosse, has a most singular knack, to me at least, of fascinating talk. But I suppose all the others were saving their epigrams for their books and trying to get hold of other people's good things. Whereas Mr B., not writing for bread, could afford to be generous.

His looks interested me: in the first place he was what I call a fine gentleman in the best sense – except Lord de Tabley, and dear Gosse again, the other had not the happy flexibility of good breeding. It is a curious face. He looks as if he had seen and hoped and thought much, and was a little weary of things in general – of the stupidities and banalities at all events; he came and sat next to me and I had an indefinable wish of wanting to interest him, which is a hopeful sign I think. We talked about many things, his books, and I told him frankly – was he vexed? –

[233]

that I was not, I thought, interested in philosophy as a subject at all, but that I recognized the charm of his writing; in fact his books are almost the only ones I have lately seen that I can read on such subjects. He talked about my book, and of course we talked about you: I said frankly again what I have said about you, that I do not know anyone whose personality is so potent, whom I would rather see in a room that I entered than yourself, and I think to be candid we went on talking about you till he went: and I recognized with sorrow that here was another of the persons going up and down the world that I should have wished to see more often, and to find out what he thought and what he had gathered and unlearnt, but that time and space would probably effectually bar the wish.

By that time H.B. had secured his apartment in Rome and established his main residence there, though the Via de' Bardi apartment in Florence had not yet been given up. Everything was ready at the Palazzo Cini but for some furniture which was still expected from Florence and, from France, the pieces that had not been destroyed by fire at Avignonet. Julia was awaited; but although she had agreed to come, she prevaricated. It was hard for her to tear herself away from the home she loved and had lived in for over seventeen years and from her dearest friends, the Hildebrands. In his letters to her H.B. keeps describing the charms of the new apartment, the beauty of Rome, his wanderings and discoveries in the old streets; he goes to Florence to facilitate the move, but there are always little problems cropping up to delay it.

Ethel wrote to him urging him to make the acquaintance in Rome of a friend of hers, the Italian politician Count Primoli. He answered negatively:

I am not of the world. I have managed to learn with infinite expenditure of divination, attention and thought how to pay a visit to a lady without feeling like a fool, but with creatures of my own sex I am not capable of the effort. The last time I tried I failed miserably. They must be highly cultivated writers like Henry James and Rod or businessmen for me not to feel distressed like a fish out of water in their company. I never find anything to say and labour under the painful impression (probably an illusion) that they are eyeing me with hostile curiosity.

[234]

The man of the world is a terror to me and the higher his spirits the lower mine sink.

Spring came and it was time to go to Nyon where Rod and Bates were awaiting them. Then H.B. wandered off to London again from where he wrote to Julia about the importance of having roots. 'Façonner son milieu', as he puts it. He tells her about a performance of *Hamlet* he has been to, 'mal joué mais enfin supportable', and an excellent performance of Ibsen's *Doll's House*. He adds:

This is an example of the necessity I mentioned above to make constant new efforts to understand the language of today; c'est l'étude des classiques qui nous perd. Je te quitte sur cette bonne pensée pour aller déjeuner avec Henry James.

Meanwhile arrangements were being made for Clotilde, now eighteen years old, to go to Newnham College at Cambridge and study architecture. 'Yesterday I went to Cambridge,' he writes to Julia in May, 'it was delightful. A wonderful ensemble of natural beauty, architecture, perfume of the past and beautiful youth – never have I had a more ravishing impression. Tell Clotilde I am bringing her photographs of Newnham College.'

In October 1892 arrangements were made for Christopher's further education. He was thirteen at that time and H.B. went to Zurich to interview a tutor by the name of Kagi, who ran a small boarding school in his own house. Why it was thought a good idea to send Christopher to such an institution rather than a proper school remains unclear. But Julia had ideas of her own on education and besides in international circles the system of education provided by a tutor with a few boys under his care in his own household was not uncommon in the nineteenth century. In any case H.B., reporting back to Julia, was on the whole impressed. He objected to Professor Kagi's Swiss accent and found German grammatical mistakes in his letters, but these were minor shortcomings, he pointed out, when his profound knowledge of Greek and Sanskrit was taken into account. In addition he knew how to keep discipline; the boys were under proper control. In the event Christopher did not stay long and new arrangements had to be made for his education elsewhere.

The question of education was constantly discussed between the parents. H.B.'s viewpoint at that time is worth noting, as expounded

[235]

in a letter some months later when they were both settled in Rome but she was temporarily away visiting her son – and evidently finding the separation trying:

No, Rome is not at all paling away. I give it my preference out of natural inclination and for reasons politic. It is our best residence, the dwelling in common which we both like; we have our books here, our desks, some friends, all things which agreeably furnish the ambience of life, the town which we love, tastes we share, our own private life. From the point of view of policy I would regard it as deplorable if we turned ourselves into satellites of our children. You know that I have the utmost respect for the young generation but I don't think it is good if they imagine that they are the centre of gravity in their family. It is perhaps regrettable that we may not keep Christopher with us, as it might have been possible if we were living in the north – but I am not even convinced about this. From a certain point of view it would have been an advantage for both of us and him. I think it is very good for a boy to regard his parental home as a world superior to the one in which he is living, both as far as culture and scenario prestige are concerned. Especially in the case of our children with whom aesthetic sensibility and sense of criticism are more developed than the Swiss-moral sense (of which I don't wish to say ill)... Doubtless there are children who in the present and later on, recalling everything, will above all be grateful for your daily company, guidance and encouragement. This is not the case of our children. They will be grateful to us for the wideness of our outlook and for everything that might stimulate in them the idea of a *maestria* of some kind. Nothing else. One should therefore leave the little task of daily discipline to others. The general, chief of staff, should not play the part of the corporal.

In the same letter H.B. goes on to write about her work and his own:

All you tell me about the book you want to write seems to me excellent and I entirely approve of its philosophy; you will write the book and I will not smile. It must well up of its own accord. As a matter of fact I don't know whether something might not surge within me, but I often think of a sort of Gargantua, more sublime. It seems to me that as long as you think, you are not living the life of a parasite. Only you should think as one thinks in this century and not like Parmenides. I am bringing you a volume by Pater on Plato. Parmenides is in it. And we shall read the old English dramatists from beginning to end; there are seventeen volumes (selected works).

Unfortunately it is impossible to tell from any subsequent letter or extant record whether the book Julia had in mind was in fact the book of reflections she began to write at about that time and was years later published posthumously – *Via Lucis*. There is no Parmenides in it.

21

Henry James and H.B.

The move came as a wrench to Julia when finally the Via de' Bardi apartment was given up. H.B. played on the allurements of Rome and the charms of their new apartment at the heart of the city. But when, in addition to the antique furniture they had collected in Florence, eighty-one crates arrived from Geneva containing the unburnt Avignonet furniture and books, as well as all the things they had in their now relinquished Nyon house, H.B. was quite overwhelmed. 'It looks as though the pieces of furniture were breeding like rabbits.'

By the time all this was over it was the end of 1892, and at last they were both settled in the Palazzo Cini. But H.B. kept wandering off; he liked travelling, there were business trips to be made and old friends to be seen again, particularly Rod and Cazalis – not to mention Ethel. So we find him soon at Geneva, Dresden, Paris and London once more. From London he says in one of his letters to Julia:

> Rod had again one of those miserable fits of sentimentality, *un rhume d'âme*, so that one was afraid of breathing the same air and inhaling moral *tisanes*. . . Of course I know at other times he is delightful and that I shall sometimes miss him terribly, like the tune of a flute in the mountains when one is drowned by the noise of machines and factories. But at the moment my mood is one of reaction to Rod, to neo-Catholics, neo-Romanticism and neo-Gothicism under all their aspects. Here in London it is like bathing in the cold sea, it tightens up your pores and you feel like hitting hard. . . With Henry James I get on splendidly.

This intercourse between the two friends was to lead, not long after, to a lively exchange of letters. But in London H.B. was still retained by cultural attractions which only a great city could provide. To Julia he writes again after his departure:

[238]

In London I saw some fine paintings, amongst others the retrospective show and all inclusive work of a painter I have always disliked because of his 'poetic' rather than truly artistic leaning, but I was compelled to recognize the strength of this work; his name is Burne-Jones. Here I have tried to go hunting again but must confess I'm hopeless at it.

Then he and Julia are in Rome again for the rest of the winter and early spring, thereafter in Switzerland until July, when H.B. gets restless and travels backwards and forwards between Switzerland, France and England, keeping in touch with Henry James wherever he goes.

He may have had difficulties with men of a certain category – 'men of the world' as he called them in his letter to Ethel, though later on he was himself to be regarded as such by those who did not fully know him. But with women, whatever the initial effort may have been, matters were different. He was liked, he was sought after. In Rome he made the acquaintance of a distinguished young lady, American by birth, who had married a Roman nobleman – Marchesa Lily Theodoli. She had begun to write plays and was later to write novels. H.B. wanted to help her and sent the manuscript of a play she had written to Henry James for advice and, if possible, for assistance. In July 1893 James wrote back to him from 34 De Vere Gardens, where he lived in London, while H.B. was with Julia at Constanz in the Grand Duchy of Baden-Baden:

My dear Brewster,

I am very glad to hear from you, even though a painful duty devolves upon me in consequence. At the words 'painful duty' I see you *me voir venir*, and as you are thus prepared let me briefly and quickly dispose of the subject. Your sending me the Marchesa Theodoli's little proverb, and your earnest and temperate plea for it, do a real honour to the high principle of sympathy within you: all the greater pity therefore that the case should not be intrinsically a happy one. Even your kind intellect confounds perhaps the bearings of virtue and *la portée toute autre* of the art of deserving or of holding attention. Virtue never deserves attention, it only deserves paradise. Madame Theodoli may perhaps get a good share of the latter for her little play, but she would be ill advised for the former. Crudely, brutally, from every

[239]

practical point of view, *ça ne vaut pas le diable*. I am better placed than you for saying it − out of the lady's radius: therefore I say it for you − as well as for myself. The little art is much more difficult and special than she can suspect, naturally − and there would not be the faintest ghost of a chance that this little piece, or anything like it, should reach the footlights or should 'cross them' as the phrase is, if it did. The after is as the before − no woman can write a play. At any rate even if Madame Theodoli's attempt were more successful there is no chance here whatsoever for one-act things and the curtain-raiser has practically ceased to exist. The only thing that here and there lingers is the gross, agile, obvious old English farce. For even 'skilled' *marivaudage*, a dialogue, which is more conversation of nuances and delicate points, there is neither a public nor interpreters, nor a taste, nor a want, nor any sort of even the most remotely preliminary possibility. *Ecco*. Excuse my bald veracity. You ask me and I tell you − but I hate having to say such things. As dialogue in a slight story Mme Theodoli's dialogue would be well enough in its place, but it hasn't the individual scenic quality. If it had, moreover, it wouldn't help it, for dialogue is flesh, and the Briton, carnivorous as he is elsewhere, will at the play look at nothing but bones − a rattling skeleton, kicking up his legs and arms in obedience to the *ficelle*.

I am full of admiration for the Zurich telegraphist and satisfaction at your confirmatory allusion to your reappearance here in a couple of months. You will find me then on this spot. I came back from the seaside 48 hours ago. Yes, the Swiss are very decent folk, just as the French are *à peine* one. I find myself − I found myself in the early summer at Lucerne − was it the effect of the early summer or of my own vital winter liking them in a kind of desperation. One must believe in something, at last. I return the typed dramaticule. I should like to be on mountains and by lakes.

Yours ever,

HENRY JAMES

P.S. Paul Bourget and his wife are in London on their way (on the 5th) to the U.S.A. to write a book about it. A most strange to my sense incident.

The interest of this very Jamesian letter principally lies in the

[240]

writer's own relation to the stage at that time. For it was just about then that he was himself struggling with the problem of writing plays, a period which began with the moderate success of *The American*, produced in 1891, and ended with the stage disaster of *Guy Domville*, produced in London in 1895, when he was booed off the stage when he ventured to take a curtain call. James then realized with reluctance that the chances of his ever being a successful playwright were remote. Thus, although this letter of 3 July is written with wit and good humour, the breathless intensity and uncompromising virulence of his criticism of Lily Theodoli's 'dramaticule' undoubtedly reflect his own difficulties with the London stage. Hence his scathing remarks about flesh and bones.

A few days later Henry James wrote again to H.B., who was then in Zurich, without emotion of the ill-fated 'dramaticule'. The letter is from Ramsgate.

You are indeed a Gallo-American, in all the force of the term; for you combine the grand idiosyncrasies of both types – the inveterate failure to give an address (the giving one seems a purely British eccentricity. The Gaul localises his letter by 'jeudi' or 'ce 13'; the American, it is true, sometimes goes as far as 'London', 'Rome'). So I launch these few whimsical words simply into the 'Zurich' towards which you seem gracefully to wave your hand. I shall not make them many lest, though I have a substantial faith in the Swiss post, they should vainly seek you. Let them however be sufficient to re-express to you that I am very sorry you should have come and gone without my seeing you. I have stuck fast to this rather squalid shore – protected by its squalor and refreshed by its climate. I am very glad to know that you are likely to return in October. I think there is little doubt that I shall be in London then, so you must give me an early sign. May Zurich meanwhile not dry you up and still less the flow of your prose. I am delighted to hear of the book. I watch for it. *Stia bene.* May the young Lady's cigarette not set fire to Girton! Have you read *Le Docteur Pascal*, which I just lay down? *Quelle bouffonnerie!* 34 De Vere Gardens always finds me after a moment.

The lady's cigarette was Clotilde's, who had taken to smoking with zest. But when H.B. turned up in England on a short visit at the

[241]

end of July, in order to take Clotilde to Cambridge, James was not in London. He wrote to explain:

I am, alas, utterly and hopelessly out of town and very sorry to miss you thereby. London is just now, with its absolutely ferocious complications, as impossible to me as Rome in the spring turned out to be. I never got to Italy at all and though I spent three months abroad I have returned to the metropolis (the British) only to take to my heels – *et je cours encore* – astride of my pen as a witch on a broom stick. I regret as much not making the acquaintance of your daughter. But as you are placing her in England I think this but a pleasure postponed. I can't flatter myself, I fear, that you will be led to direct your steps to this seaside. But I hope good things from your daughter's being in this land, i.e. your speedy return at a calm hour. Please believe that I deplore the loss of the great pleasure of seeing you.

One sees how Henry James kept interspersing his letters to H.B. with French and sometimes Italian words, like grains of pepper. It was H.B.'s cosmopolitan world, and particularly his French culture, that fascinated the expatriate James.

More than a year previously H.B. had started work on a new book, 'The Statuette' – he had announced the event to Ethel in a letter of 2 June 1892. Subsequently he kept briefly referring to it, but only towards the end of the following year did he feel it was ready for publication. He had drastically cut the text by forty pages and reduced the manuscript to two-thirds of its original length in order to make, as he told Ethel, 'the main points and the thought sequence come out much more clearly'. Then he revised the whole text and sent it to Henry James who, approving of it, sent it to Heinemann.

It was in the autumn of that year that H.B. got to know Edmund Gosse more closely. In October he wrote to Julia: 'The other day I had tea with Edmund Gosse, a rather distinguished man of letters who introduced Ibsen into England. It was through him that I made the acquaintance of Pater.'

There follows an account of a talk they had had on the subject of Newnham College where Gosse was planning to send his daughters. His views were critical for he felt that the college produced only bluestockings who knew nothing. H.B. on the other hand was more lenient, perhaps because his own daughter was already there. Then in the same letter he adds:

'The Statuette' is with a publisher who has not yet given his verdict. He publishes only at his own expense and risk. I wanted to try my luck with him since he is a publisher who draws the attention of the public, whereas no one ever knows what goes on with Williams & Norgate. Henry James, to whom I have shown the manuscript, assures me that no literary review would accept it without cutting it down considerably and he feels very strongly that I should not let it be mutilated. He dines with me tomorrow.

But to place a philosophical work a hundred years ago was as hard as it is today without the backing of an institution. On 27 October Henry James wrote:

My dear Brewster,
The enclosed has come from the heartless tradesman, accompanying your MS. I opened it as I thought I might save you some trouble here by doing so. I keep the MS and that is I seek the earliest opportunity of showing it (as I understand you authorized me to do so) either directly to Heinemann or to him through Gosse. This I shall do in a day or two. Let me add that, again confronted with your beautiful copy, I don't, however, frankly see how the question of length, that is of shortness, can be got over. It is terribly between two stools – the book and the magazine.

Yours ever,
HENRY JAMES
M.P. Forgive my summary treatment of the question and you. I happen to be much pressed. But I send *bien des choses à la France.*
[Added on the envelope] I send you another little story book.

'The Statuette' is not a dialogue like H.B.'s former writings but an exchange of letters between three friends enabling them to express their respective views: Rhoda, Humphry and Walter. Rhoda is again a version of the theist much closer to Ethel's position than to Julia's, Humphry is a sort of aesthetic positivist and Walter another Wilfrid or Clive. Though the opening of the epistolary discussion suggests that a dissertation is going to take shape, particulary on the 'art-for-

[243]

art's-sake' theme so dear to the 1890s, the argument soon pushes deeper into territory covered by the former dialogues. The question of the self becomes uppermost; the pluralist's view predominates, with abundance of imagery and striking metaphors. In a remarkably concise form the whole gamut of H.R.'s philosophy, including his aesthetics, is harmoniously expressed. There is no mention of a setting save the 'snowy mountains' where Walter is roving, mountains in the Alps where H.B. himself had been climbing.

This very conciseness, however, created a major obstacle to 'The Statuette's' publication, of which Henry James had to inform his friend again, this time in unequivocal terms. The letter was written on 3 November, only a week after the somewhat hurried note quoted above, and was addressed to Champandry, where H.B. had gone to stay with his sister Kate before returning to Rome:

Alas, I have no good news for you. Gosse assures me, *de science certaine*, that there is absolutely no use of offering him, or offering any publisher, for a *book*, a MS of less than fifty thousand words. That is the least number they will almost ever consent to – and even that makes a very small volume. Your MS, my practised eye judges, contains at the most 15,000. The usual English magazine adores 6 or 7 thousand – a dozen pages of their usual size. Believe me, as regards the publishers it is a question of 'trade'. The trade – i.e. the British bookseller – won't take a thin book – he says he gets nothing for his money; and you know the fatness of his customary wares. I honestly think the slender physique of your little offshoot is a grave obstacle to placing him. Why not, as you say, marry him, even polygamously? Give him a pair of concubines if you can't manage a legitimate union – give him a sultanesque girth. With another beautiful dialogue or two let me return to the charge. *C'est le vrai moyen.* And you are so young, the *time* is at your service. I hold the MS at your disposal – but hope awfully to have time to read it before parting with it again. Many thanks for your letter. Nothing would induce me to shoot with you save the reflection that I should probably kill you first. Charming of you to see something in 'The Lesson of the Master', a tour de force of which few have been capable. I found Gosse much pleased with a charming article about him by Augustine Filow in *les Débats* (roses). Your slow journey to

[244]

Rome suggests pleasure by the way – which I wish you much of – with much to follow. Excuse this jaded, faded *griffonnage*.

H.B. followed Henry James's advice and set about working on something that could be added to increase the girth of the book. The union was closer to legitimate marriage than concubinage. Little by little *The Background* emerged, to reach completion and publication with its spouse three years later.

Meanwhile life in Rome was on the whole proving a success, though prejudiced by the fact that Julia remained by inclination a recluse, while H.B. had grown much more social. The letter he wrote to her from France in November 1893 reflects this problem:

> As regards our way of living in Rome I agree with you that the ideal of pure worldliness is both insufficient and out of keeping with our own natures. But I don't think we are running any serious risk of being swallowed up by it. Amiable intercourse with our fellow beings, especially in Italy where everybody is so natural, seems less superficial than in the North. This is one of the good aspects Rome presents and is not to be despised by persons like ourselves who have abused of solitude. To rid ourselves of the bloatedness of those in the North and of the recluse, to find again simplicity, to become like children as the gospel says, this is the way to be pursued in Rome. I know very well that an inner effort is needed... It may be that I don't do it enough as the result of a reaction. But to get out of the apocalyptic, what a rebirth! I am in love with ease of mind, with clarity, benevolence and the smile of discretion. I am weary of Scythians and Barbarians.

Whether social life in Italy, pleasant as it may be, is less superficial than in the North is extremely doubtful. The reverse is more likely to be true. But there was in those days something quite enchanting in the air of Rome which came from the people as a whole, from the architecture, the light, the colours, the rhythm of life. To all this H.B. succumbed. There was a danger in succumbing, as Julia kept reminding him. The side of his nature turned outward to the world, which he felt had been repressed and which Ethel was striving to liberate, could dominate the inner, more creative self – as indeed it did years later, when Julia's influence could no longer be felt. At this stage, however, he was endeavouring to establish a harmonious balance acceptable to Julia.

There was, too, a major practical problem. H.B.'s landlords in Rome, the Cini, were reluctant to renew the lease of his apartment. Although he had an option and the right to renew, he amiably backed out after having discussed the matter with Julia. The Cini, who were in serious financial difficulties, wanted to sell the palace or lease the whole building to an institution – the records are not clear on this point. As they were good friends and in financial straits, both H.B. and Julia felt they did not want to ruffle the relationship. So they decided to look for another flat and to quit the Palazzo Cini. They found what they wanted in the Palazzo Marignoli, off the Corso. On the floor below theirs, lived an old lady of the best society but with a dubious past – Contessa Papadopoli. The huge palace, which belonged to Marchesa Marignoli, sister of Prince Torlonia, the old lady's lover, was a nest of gossip. But H.B. and Julia, undisturbed, cheerfully settled there in the spring of 1894.

Henry James was then in Venice and H.B., faced with having to leave shortly for England to see to various problems affecting his daughter's studies, was urging him to come to Rome. It was from Venice that Henry James wrote to him on 16 April:

What on earth do you think of me? I am a relaxed, a flaccid, faithless Venetian, and you a corrupt father, a high-toned Roman. Therefore you will judge me severely. I ought, doubtless, to have returned to you 'ere this your beautiful and eloquent manuscript; and yet I wasn't sure of this, not sure that – in the absence of a direct behest from you – you didn't want me to (as they say at Cleveland, Ohio) 'hold' it. I have held it, and hold it at this moment – having put it down (for spending my time hanging over it) only long enough to write to you these feverish words. I hope to be in Rome for a few days towards the end of next month. Would it suit you that I should wait and bring it to you then? Otherwise I shall be for ten days before Rome in Florence – and the rest of the time till I leave Italy, *here*. I took this little *quartiere* a fortnight ago for three or four months. Do you ever come here? I long to go to Rome, later. *Troppa gente – troppa gente*! I mean here. I try for quiet conditions of work; but the great Cook has willed otherwise. Do you leave Rome early? I

[246]

much desire to see you. I will send you the divine dialogue the moment you ask for it. I have had, and still have worries. Therefore write to me kindly – not in the Catonic or proconsular mood.

P.S. Moreover I was 51 yesterday.

One cannot help wondering what H.B. might have been like in 'Catonic or proconsular mood' – scarcely in keeping with his nature. But perhaps Henry James was simply pulling his leg. Much as he wanted to go to Rome he was plunged in his own work and not in a hurry to leave Venice.

Although he must already have started on *The Background*, H.B. went on working on 'The Statuette', tightening and improving it and consulting Henry James all along. He pressed him, too, to come to Rome, wanting to enjoy the city with him. A week later from Venice came another letter:

I wish I could definitely say that I mean by the end of May, the middle or thereabouts. But I left England for the express purpose of escaping from dates and pledges – the death-scourge of appointments – which end by bringing on brain fever, especially *là bas*, where they are demanded without having been offered. I am in the situation of not being able to stir till I have finished a piece of work, promised for a date (1st June) which I shall forfeit money (that I cannot afford – in honour – *pas davantage*) by not finishing. If I get on with it or within sight of port, as I fondly bravely hope, I will try to reach Rome by the 10th. But for this I must lose no day and no hour; and these Italian cities, confound them, have now practically resolved themselves into dense Anglo-American watering places – stuffed with the utterly unoccupied – who cut one out an amount of work in the way of dodging, escaping, lifesaving, which is so much *off* one's regular fruition. One would rather exercise the wisdom of the serpent more monumentally.

However, I try to believe I am through the worst here; and will write you more clearly later. I wish we could meet even in Florence. But I respond to you that I should like Rome better. Will you kindly *mention* to no one that I may possibly be there? I shall return you your correspondence by post tomorrow or next day at furtherst. I postpone so scandalously further simply

[247]

because I have had a big packet to send to London today – and I shrink selfishly from the effort of braving the Italian post-office with a double job – or rather, more correctly, from a double envelope question on the same day; the more that I happen to be dolorously afflicted with indigestive pangs. 'The Statuette' is full of beauty and interest, perception, suggestion, expression.

April 24th. I am sorry to say that I had to tumble into bed yesterday instead of finishing my letter. But I am better today – though rather battered with the fray. 'The Statuette' shall go back to you with this – in a different cover, letter postage and *raccomandata. Buon viaggio*. I won't profess that I find your solution, if solution or *dénouement* it be (i.e. your Walter), absolutely free from obscurity – just as I rarely find joy in any discussion of the question more or less at issue in your pages – conduct versus art, aesthetics versus morality. I am in all this region of a primitive simplicity, ignorance, naiveté. Art, for me, is conduct and conduct art – aren't they, *che vuole*? I imagine that almost any *praticant* artist is necessarily *out* of almost any discussion of these mysteries and subtleties. At any rate they only make me cuddle closer to my little, vulgar, personal special empirical industry. *Tout est là*. Yours – your art, and your industry – is to have admirable perceptions, illustrations, facilities, and to be wiser than the likes of me can measure. But I mustn't write letters!

At that time Henry James was busy thinking out and writing 'The Coxon Fund' which was published in the second issue of the *Yellow Book* in July 1894. He was longing to visit Rome again but, in his need for 'quiet conditions', he shrank from having to meet too many people. The morning of 18 April, as his Notebook shows, was spent in starting 'The Coxon Fund'. The 'worries' referred to in his letter of the 16th were probably about whether the theme he had in mind could be compressed into 20,000 words. These letters from Venice are full of Jamesian charm, stimulated by H.B.'s letters – none of which, unhappily, has survived. It is tantalizing that the numerous letters 'the last of the epistolarians' wrote to Henry James, who greatly appreciated them, are either untraceable or, more likely, were destroyed.

By the time Henry James arrived in Rome H.B. could only enjoy his company very briefly, as he had to hurry to London. James himself went back to Venice soon after, from where he wrote on 24 June:

> I returned yesterday to find your letter. I think the reason why I hadn't sent you the note to Warren has simply been that I have done nothing but write letters – even at Naples – since I parted from you some time ago. Therefore this *petit mot* is brief. So go to see him about 2.30 or 3 p.m.; but write him an accompanying note on sending him my letter, to say that you will do so. He is a thoroughly good fellow and lives in a funny provincial purlieu of Westminster – in a pleasant old house. He is just frantically *fiancé* but I don't know that that will render him *d'un abord difficile*. On the contrary. I stayed and stayed in Rome – that is a fortnight: so great was the charm to me. I took three days in Naples and two or three more in Rome. Giuseppe Primoli, after you left, threw me into the arms of Mathilde Serao etc. etc. – and Madame Gabriele D'Annunzio! In Florence I had influenza – a horrid little fever, but Baldwin broke it up with a magic wand. I stay here till the first days of July. 34 De Vere Gardens always reaches me. Venice, after dustier elsewhere, seems deliciously watery and breezy. I have come back to a terrible pile of letters. Do let me know if you arrange or settle anything.
>
> Tout à vous,
> HENRY JAMES

On his way to London H.B. stopped in Paris to see Bates, his banker and friend. To Julia he wrote: 'The immortality of the soul – a good dinner followed by a good cigar, he simply can't get away from them.' Then, in the same letter, he briefly brings the Hildebrands back into the picture – a subject he had been eschewing: 'There is apparently a row going on between our daughter and Eva, nicknamed Nini, the heated argument springing at any rate from Eva who has written four pages of insults and outrages to Clotilde because she does not take Emanuel and Ferravilla seriously.'*

Both Clotilde and Christopher had always remained on the closest terms with the Hildebrand daughters of their own age. They had played together as children and now they exchanged thoughts and ideas. H.B. had never raised any objection to this, but for several

---

*Two popular Italian actors of the day, for whom the Hildebrand girls had developed a passionate admiration.

[249]

years had simply avoided the subject in his letters to Julia – perhaps even in his conversation with her.

Although Ethel was also in the reckoning, H.B.'s trip to London this time was mainly connected with his daughter's leaving Newnham College. In those days it was considered unnecessary and a waste of time for a student of architecture to stay on at Cambridge for the full term of three years in order to obtain a degree; a mere diploma would do. What was really needed was apprenticeship in the office of a good architect where the practical side could be learnt. This was the prevailing custom. H.B.'s task now was to find the architect.

In the meantime, while the search was being made, father and daughter set about leading an agreeable life together. They went to the theatre, to the opera, to concerts and exhibitions and saw performances and people – Sarah Bernhardt in *Phèdre*, Duse in *La dame aux camélias*, Ibsen, Henry James, Oscar Wilde, Sargent, Gosse, Pater, Maeterlink and others. Clotilde was now an attractive fair-haired girl of twenty, with eyes set far apart like her father's and a rather long, curved, teasing mouth – a girl bursting with life, humour and talent to whom Henry James took a special liking.

In a letter to her mother she described the women's club she had joined:

> I have been to see the club – there are some curious creatures there! Above all correspondents of inferior newspapers, their hats pulled down over one ear and a briefcase under the arm; then there are poetesses with pendulant ear-rings over their backs wearing dressing-gowns embroidered in sunflowers. Also old spinsters who call themselves 'antivivisectionists', and others who are champions for the emancipation of women etc. etc., *enfin* a whole lot of enchantresses. Never mind, the club is two steps from my office and I can conveniently have my meals there.

The difficulties in finding a suitable architect for Clotilde were finally overcome. Mr Blomfield appeared to be not only a competent architect but also easy to get on with. In his spare time he would go out riding in the country with H.B.

In the end, after a performance of *Tristan* which both father and daughter attended – 'Dieu que c'est long!' H.B. wrote to Julia; 'Cependent il faut être juste, il y a de beaux moments' – they quit

London. Clotilde went on her holiday to join Julia at Freiburg in Germany where Christopher had been put in a proper school. Meanwhile, H.B. fetched Christopher to go mountaineering in the Alps during the boy's holidays, for he did not want him to feel, as he informed Julia from Chamonix, that he had been neglecting his son in favour of his daughter. Christopher, or 'Killy' as he was called in the family, was now fifteen.

Yes, the scenery here pleases me immensely, perhaps because I always absorb it with a good dose of physical fatigue which replaces the need of bicarbonate of soda. It smoothes away any wave of emotion that might engulf the soul, the romanticism that always alarms me when I enjoy the contemplation of nature. The air is delicious, you inhale light like a delightful smell through the nose. There are bells of little innocent creatures such as sheep and cows and at the same time you develop the hunger of an ogre which rescues you from any sloppy emotion. You feel your muscles tense without collar and cuff-links, you forget the time of day and the date, you are five thousand years younger and the great lines of abstract thought rise like tranquil walls of granite. But you, Julia, talk to me with great ease about my catechism; do you really think it can be written in twenty minutes? It is a question of choosing the right ridge, of dividing the waters and losing yourself along lateral crests. You have to give up the same course twenty times.

Killy will write to you. We talk to each other a bit. It is curious how he reminds me of your father. We walk side by side very courteously.

They climbed Mont Blanc or part of it. But Christopher did not seem to enjoy mountaineering as much as his father did, to judge from a letter H.B. wrote to Julia in August 1894.

We spent a day swimming and rowing at Lago Maggiore. Killy was delighted. Funny little man he is. He has admitted to me that mountains fill him with horror – they are too wild, too silent, too remote from humans and he then sees black. As soon as he moves away from the railway lines he is overcome with melancholy. Also he has a passion for timetables. From Chamonix we went for a wonderful climb up Mont Blanc, as far

[251]

as Les Grands Mulets, but he confessed that when we started off he was literally terrified. A steamship, a train, a stage-coach, Italy, a smiling landscape, a little boat, a swim in a lake Clotilde has not yet seen – that is his great pleasure. And as I do care to make him enjoy things I associate myself to his programme with zest.

Clotilde returned to her architectural studies in London, Christopher to his school at Freiburg, and H.B. and Julia back to Rome for another winter.

Ethel and H.B., in their letters, gave up discussing religion specifically; evidently the ditch between them was too wide to span. But there were other fields, and they were coming closer to each other both in their emotions and in their concern for each other's work. Ethel was composing her opera *Fantasio* and H.B. set about criticizing the libretto constructively if not actually contributing to it. He was at pains to explain to Ethel his approach to his own work. Julia had no difficulty in grasping it, being, like him, mystically minded, but it was difficult for Ethel to have the slightest idea of what H.B. was writing or, for that matter, thinking, when he strayed outside the boundaries of clear-cut empirical response.

What do you mean by saying that you have no idea what I am writing about? Don't you know that I always write in praise of the Holy Ghost? But oh! do you think he will understand it? I hope so fervently he will. Look here: underneath all our precise, clearly defined thoughts and desires there is an indeterminate thought and desire which we every now and then slip back into, more or less completely, but always with the impression that we have got back into heaven for a moment. This is what I mean by the Holy Ghost – though I don't speak of him by name in my book lest someone should be scandalized and others bored. Now as his essential characteristic is the state of indeterminateness it is no use trying to *focus* him either in thought or desire. We can neither define him nor pursue him directly – which is what religion and morality undertake to do. He is quite outside the domains of truth and imitation which are focused efforts. If what we seek is veracity and accuracy we must restrict ourselves to the scientific and business sides of life. But it isn't. We are above all constructive animals, architecture in various kinds of

[252]

materials even unto clouds. Our religion and moral beliefs are architectural performances, valueless as images of any reality just because they are realities themselves. To enquire if they are true is about as reasonable as to ask if a house or a horse or a pile of clouds is true. They can neither be true nor false; they can only be real or hallucinatory and this is a question of consensus of opinion in a given group of men – a question of local catholicity. And I try to show what kind of value these beliefs (which I call myths) have, neither as truths nor as symbols of truths but as backgrounds without which there is no 'relief' – in both senses of the word. This is the main theme crossed by several others and I dare say it is all very obscure because it is not a lecture, not the exposition of a theory but a thicket of thoughts just as they grow, or at least intend to produce that effect – something like landscape gardening, which many consider an abomination and perhaps they are right as regards gardens; but there is this difference to be considered: the eye is an instantaneous organ; the play of memory a book appears to develop itself in time. This is a great difficulty I struggle with and that makes me so slow a writer: thoughts must form theories or they remain so chaotic, and on the other hand once reduced to theories they have lost their life. The theory must be in them dimly visible, an extractable but not extracted quantity. I want each chapter to sound as an independent impromptu, and the connexion of them all to be felt without being said. I may or may not succeed but some day people will not tolerate books otherwise written, any more than they will tolerate nowadays scholastic demonstration. Spencer and Co. will take their place on the shelf by the side of Duns Scotus.

In the spring of 1895 Julia as well as H.B. started to get restless. She was in poor health and anxious to be near her son, so she went to Freiburg. H.B. meanwhile was longing to be with his daughter in London again – and also planning to see Ethel, whom he arranged to meet in Paris. On his way there he wrote from Mentone to ask: 'Shall I take a room for you Hotel Castille and one for me Hotel Metropolitain like last time?'

No. This time they shared the same room. What happened then in Paris could have occurred ten years previously and it is amazing that

[253]

it took place only now. Ethel lost her virginity at the age of thirty-seven. One might have expected it, certainly, three years before when, on hearing of Lisl's death, she wrote that enraged letter to Julia: from now on she would follow her own course in life regardless of her rival's feelings. But not until April 1895 was H.B. able to seduce Ethel physically, and then only because she was determined to get rid of her virginity. It was about time, she felt, and also an act of kindness she owed him – a reward for his patience. In her memoirs she explains her attitude:

> When I was settling in at One Oak, M . . . , a very amusing friend of mine, whose husband was stationed at Aldershot and who had met Harry, remarked one day, 'But you can't ask H.B. to *stay* here, can you?' I replied, 'Certainly I shall! I shall ask him, or Sargent, or Rikano, or Maurice Baring or anyone I choose, to come for week-ends, and to establish the fact that I am Caesar's wife.' 'O Elly,' she exclaimed (that being her name for me), 'what *does* that mean? I suppose *past fructification*.' (I was then thirty-six.) In fact, but for a vague wish not to end my life as what she called a 'Stonehenge Virgin', I had no immediate intention of changing my estate.
>
> But now the time to change had come. 'Why now?' is the unanswerable question. On Tuesday you look at a certain corner of the lawn . . . nothing! On Wednesday you look again; still nothing. But by Thursday even the crocuses have 'crept alight'. For one thing this jaunt would be the first deliberate break in my life of work for two years, and perhaps now I had leisure to reflect how generously and patiently he had borne with me for ten; how his time and thoughts had been devoted to my affairs without ever an attempt to overcome my reluctance to cross the boundary between friendship and love – a matter that means so much more to men, I think, than to women. Anyhow it seemed to me negligible compared to what I already possessed in him and set chief store by.

This last sentence is significant. Whatever the fun of taking Ethel to bed may have been, it was not the sort of seduction Irene had enjoyed when, naked and covered with roses, she received Hildebrand on the shores of a lake. H.B. was not undersexed and his Latin upbringing most probably allowed him other outlets in this direction, without qualms of conscience, behind the customary screen of discretion; but for Ethel the simple fact of the matter was that the performance was both physically and psychologically almost superfluous. It was a cerebral step. It had to be taken for the relationship to be complete and mainly out of consideration for him. She does refer, however, to her *vita nuova*; their letters, too, become slightly more like letters between lovers. Yet one may suspect that the performance was repeated only occasionally. Indeed, writing to her friend Lady Ponsonby three years later, Ethel defended her position morally, apparently referring to the Paris episode as if intercourse had taken place only once, though the text is somewhat ambiguous.

The year 1895 proved a sad one for both the Brewsters and the Hildebrands. In June Conrad Fiedler fell to his death in Munich. In a letter to a friend, Hildebrand expressed his deep grief:

> Where is one more alive, enveloped in one's own skin or in the consciousness of a friend? Which of the two is it that firmly holds the continuity of your 'I', yourself or the other one, your friend who never misunderstood you even when you wandered in the dark, bewildered and lost? It is as though I had to start from scratch building up a consciousness which was until now secure.

Fiedler's death came as a blow to Ethel too. In spite of her initial misgivings about his negative influence on Lisl when the break took place, he had always remained an appreciative and understanding friend to her. H.B. on the other hand had been on cooler terms with him in recent years, although continuing to hold him in high esteem. As Julia, on hearing of Fiedler's death, wrote to H.B.: 'One feels one has lost a friend not so much because of the nature of the personal relationship between us which was not ardent, but because he who has just died was *un homme de bien*.'

H.B.'s reaction, replying to Julia, is more measured:

> It has given me a feeling of vague regret, but what I am able to say more precisely is that I can well imagine a sensation of much intenser regret had I seen him more often. Without any doubt he was a man of great distinction. In general I envy sudden deaths, but it is a bit of a bore to fall out of a window. Thereafter between being alive and dead there is perhaps not such a

difference to which one may attach excessive importance. He who is directly affected by the loss, whose tissues of daily life and habits of thought are torn, for him grief is only natural and right. Not to feel it would be an infirmity, like partial anaesthesia of the skin. But for the spectator, or even a good friend? One doesn't try to experience in common a violent toothache out of sympathy, does one? Pourquoi un deuil?

His words had a particular irony when in September there was indeed a bereavement in the Brewster family – the death of Julia herself. Her health had always been delicate; in the last two years she had fainted a few times and fallen, luckily without injuring herself, but perhaps her general condition had not been taken seriously enough. According to the available records her health gave no cause for serious alarm until she had a serious heart attack at Freiburg in July. H.B. was with her. He wrote to Ethel:

She knows her state perfectly, is fantastic, obstinate beyond words, cheerful, affectionate, witty, quite unmanageable and to me very touching. I am not at all muddled morally. The gist of my meditations is simply that our monogamic system is not suited to all natures. If we were Mahomedans, nobody and none of us, the concerned ones, would find it at all strange that I should take tender care of one wife and sit soothingly at her bedside all night as I have just done, and at the same time love another one. Yet because of our marriage laws and the artificial psychology in vogue, I must be supposed to wish evil to one woman and forget a past for which I am deeply grateful, because I wish well to another woman and the present is richer with her. All I can say is that the lie is not in me but in the system.

For fully twelve years, since the triangular drama had started, H.B. had been consistent both in his philosophy regarding marriage as well as in his emotions and attachment to two women at the same time. He remained deeply attached to his wife until the very end – when Julia died following a second heart attack. He wrote to Ethel:

Everything is finished here; even the speech of the odious little clergyman whom I wished to knock down. The graveyard is pretty; the mountains and the forest look on it in gentle silence. Like you I hate the Jewish positivism and believe in – that is to

[256]

say 'love' – a kind of immortality that would not satisfy most people but that satisfies me and was all she herself cared for. I want to tell you, this once, how I feel towards her now that she has gone. Think of a beautiful villa with a garden of unsurpassed dignity in malarious, desolate country. It is ague and almost death to linger there, and yet almost impossible to tear oneself away. I have loved her and hated deeply, not successively – simultaneously.

Against this love-hatred image given to Ethel, beautiful and uncannily morbid at the same time, is to be set the somewhat different picture that emerges from the copious letters exchanged between H.B. and Julia over a period of nearly thirty years, from their early youth to her death. Whatever moments of hatred he may have had there are no overt traces of it in his letters. When not discussing and arguing in terms of metaphysics, sometimes on the verge of exasperation, he expresses feelings of concern and affection. Characteristic of the letters, all written in French, is their high intellectual standard and the need they disclose to be kept at that level. If H.B. found it strenuous at times, the tone never became artificial or *voulu*. It sprang, whatever Ethel may have thought, from mutual need. It is also worth bearing in mind that H.B.'s best philosophical and literary production belongs to the period when this relationship, though under stress, was dramatically alive, engendering the problems and thoughts that form the material of his writings. After Julia's death the work he produced was either repetitive or without its earlier quality.

His letters to Ethel, many of which are delightful in tone and style, are all written on a more ordinary level of human experience. Very readable, they are more of a personal account, including references to daily events and problems. They display no tension, no concentration, no condensation; sometimes they are prolix.

On receiving the news of Julia's death, Henry James, from Torquay in Devon, wrote to H.B. forthwith:

I lose not an hour in assuring you my deepest participation. Your news deeply touches me – I had preserved of your wife a recollection so vivid, an impression so fine! I am extremely glad to have acquired that knowledge of her which those days in Rome gave me – a really exquisite memory. The general sense of this

[257]

difference made in your life by the passing out of it of such a personality – to say nothing of the difference in that of your children – this sense is lively within me. But I won't say more of what vaguely prompts me to say than that I think of you with very friendly sympathy. The world will be other for you than before – but how far better you know that than I – and that it already – the difference – has begun. I am glad that you are coming to England and that I shall see you. But, you see, I am not in London; and my rooms being in the hands of painters, paperers, electricians etc., I shall not be there till the first days of November. I have been spending a series of weeks in this really exquisite place – the prettiest in England – in delicious quiet (as it is only winter; and even then a meagre season) ever since the middle of July and through this quite divine September. The Paul Bourgets have been here for a month – they depart tomorrow. I wonder if there is not a chance that you will come down for a few days. It is utterly peaceful; and this small hotel is very clean and comfortable, on a blue bay of its own with a charming waterside, lawn and trees. I could get you excellent rooms. Give me of your news again – tell me of your possibilities.

No, I shall never forget your wife's singular grace and quality. Tell your daughter and your son that I lay my hand very kindly on their hands. *Je serre bien la vôtre* and am yours, my dear Brewster, very constantly,

HENRY JAMES

Whether H.B. actually went to Torquay is not recorded. But he did take Christopher with him to London to have him coached for Trinity College, Cambridge.

[258]

22

Julia

Before me on my desk is a photograph, taken in about 1865, of a girl of eighteen or nineteen, a profile view down to her shoulders. A profusion of fair, long, wavy hair is done up in a kind of bun, at the same time falling back in a net over her nape. An almost lobeless, quite full ear is delicately framed; the left eye – the right one is invisible – set under a clearly delineated eyebrow has a pensive penetrating look. The nose is finely cut, almost aquiline and rather large in relation to the whole face. The lips and chin are rounded and soft, but the mouth has a firmness or stubbornness which matches the look in her eye. Her shoulders are wrapped in a knitted dark shawl from which the white collar of her dress emerges.

I also have another photograph in front of me, that of a marble bust down to the waist. The same features are represented, but those of a woman of about forty. The hair is likewise long though now pulled clean above her neck with a whisk of severity and piled not on the crown of her head but slightly to the back, leaving a fringe over her forehead. The eyes are more meditative, the aquiline nose more accentuated, the cheekbones more prominent. The marble neck is long and firm, but most remarkable are the hands, rather large, which repose crossed at the base of the bust. The veins are visible, you can feel them beneath the skin, the fingers are long and delicate. This bust, which Hildebrand made of Julia in about 1883, is one of his foremost masterpieces, until recently at San Francesco but now in a Cologne museum.

Indeed there was something marmoreal about Julia's personality. With all her lifelong pursuit of metaphysics and abstract disquisition, there was a measure of asceticism and withdrawal from life; with her Spartan character and the Spartan upbringing of her children, with her strict adherence to principles, with her aristocratic pride and aloofness, one might assume not only a rigidity of mind but also frigidity of heart. One would be wrong.

Julia was a woman whose distinction, refinement, intellectual interests, sensibility and lively conversation made her extremely dear to her friends. They were enchanted with her. Yet there were not many of them, because she shunned the world and was extremely selective about her circle. Pride comes into it, perhaps, but to a limited extent. Her health was uncertain and because of it she was very conscious of the passing of time. The few friends she had were very close to her – Irene in particular, who was so different from her in many ways. When Julia died Irene mourned her departure as that of her best female friend.

To her children she was unsparingly devoted though always strict, a strictness in keeping with the age in which she lived and the social class to which she belonged. She loved her children and they were respectfully devoted to her without any sort of reaction or rebellion – and both of them were far from being meek and mild. Clotilde, totally unrepressed and with a rare zest for life, was temperamentally closer to her liberally-minded father, but there was never any friction between her and her mother, though now and then a touch of mutual forbearance may have been required. Christopher, on the other hand, took mainly after Julia: not inheriting her mystical bent nor her tendency to withdraw from the world, but sharing the same passionate fire below a surface of rigid self-control.

Julia's book, *Via Lucis*, gives the clue to how totally introverted and spiritualized she was. Her heart was far from frigid, she could love most intensely, but that rigid integrity and purity of purpose could be emotionally limiting, a spiritual idealism, rationally conceived, conditioning the sensual forces. This way of thinking and looking at things fascinated and ultimately captivated her husband, despite the difficulty of reconciling his own liberal, free-thinking nature to her form of theocratic outlook. H.B., too, had an introspective, mystical and contemplative facet to his character, which coincided with Julia's entire being. But there was also a less cloistered side that Julia feared would cause him to disperse his intellectual energy by indulging in more general social, Epicurean intercourse, and compromise his intellectual and spiritual standards. The tendencies Ethel was encouraging Julia determinedly opposed. It was not only for its disruption to the Brewsters' married life that Julia resented Ethel's influence.

Julia and H.B. had in common a deep-seated longing to push

[260]

beyond the limits of the ego. With H.B. it was a sort of Oriental detachment deliberately free from theism, with Julia a persistent, if questioning, longing for God, sometimes abstract, sometimes personal. The collected *pensées* she left are self-revealing.

He who would remain alone in dialogue with God, has he really stepped beyond the limits of the self? . . .
    Our beliefs, are they not vivifying only when appearing to us no longer our own, after we have discovered that what we have painstakingly elaborated is the possession of every soul by virtue of its primitive nature?

Sometimes the threshold of Christian faith is almost crossed:

Acclamation d'un redempteur, humilité, vassalage; communion avec le mystère, participation aux forces et aux faiblesses d'autrui: la foi implique tout cela. Elle n'est ni crainte, ni rivalité, ni abdication.

Her understanding of the sacramental content and significance of religion was profound.

When religion is not the whole of life it is already a form of specialization, though less narrow than either art or thought. Owing to the need of synthesis which its rites and ceremonies disclose these are not simple commemorative acts: they belong to the miraculous.

She also showed considerable insight into the value of religious symbolism.

Aren't the symbols of faith born from the very needs of our own perception of its ultimate rhythms and aren't such needs so fully blended with historical traditions that they become incarnate and dogma? This implies not only individual perception wherein religious adventures are reduced to the expression of metaphor, but a popular consciousness where whatever belongs to one belongs also to the other and where the line of demarcation is uncertain between the interior adventure and the exterior fact.

And the full significance of liturgy is open to her:

[261]

Who will give us a calendar where everyday is a feast, where every hour has its rites and echoes, where every instant emerges out of the infinite and plunges back into it?

Philosophic thought formulates life and declares it to be single with a multiplicity of forms. But religion is life itself, accomplishing itself whilst at the same time proclaiming itself. It is love.

Though she might seem on the verge of Catholicism, her soul had its pagan or agnostic elements, instinctive doubts in the face of certain aspects of Christianity:

It is in the very nature of the Christian soul to accept suffering in view of future beatitude. For after all the Christian, though believing in the reality of this world, does not love it; he spies the moment to outwit it, to return and dream of things divine, to depart to Paradise.

There follows a voice she doubtless shared with H.B.:

There is another humility, that of the pagan who drinks the light of the sun, who vibrates at the slightest contact with nature, who never feels banished as a stranger in this nether world and who asks nothing of life hereafter.

But she veers away again with religious longing:

I should have a bad conscience if I denied the earth. And yet are we pagans? There is a Job missing to declare himself vanquished, who perceiving the Eternal from the bottom of his nothingness passes over to His side.

Then further questioning:

What are our doctrines? For some they are the symbolical expression of an urge which needs to be strengthened, the sign of a need for ecstasy, adaptation or renewal: for others it is a stressing of personality in relation to the world, or the universe in relation to the self; but for nobody the rehabilitation of the naive animal in us.

Like Julia, H.B. had been feeling the need for the rehabilitation of the naive animal in us, in the Victorian age long overdue. Both equated it with simplicity and spontaneity; Julia indeed regretted never having lived without sophistication. But in spite of her doubts about the value of specific doctrines and aspects of established religion, in spite of her tendency to a certain brand of pantheism which a lifelong dialogue with her husband kept alive, in spite of her love for metaphysical freedom, towards the end of her life she felt the presence of God impinging upon her with inexorable insistence:

Je m'assoupie en Dieu comme on abdique sa propre conscience auprès de celui qu'on aime. Tous mes désirs, tous devoirs meurent dans cette plènitude de sensation; toutes mes souffrances et tout mon orgueil. Qu'importent nos ambitions? C'est de Lui qu'il s'agit et non de nous, qu'il porte, qu'il enveloppe, qu'il opprime, qu'il ravit. N'est-ce pas là l'endroit de la halte que j'ai cherché toute ma vie?

I think it was this spiritual world, the *Innerlichkeit* as the Germans would say, coupled with deep earnestness regarding the ultimate values of life, that was the bond between Julia and Irene, who in other respects were so different. Though happily married, Irene was throughout her life paired with a husband whose prodigious activity and vitality were channelled first and foremost into his work. Hildebrand's unsophisticated approach to life, despite his shrewdness, gave him that spontaneous youthful freshness which so delighted his friends, yet at the same time it could stir up a kind of impatience in him, almost irritation, at any indulgence, or even interest, in problems of the soul. It created a void between him and Irene who, though fully participant in his way of life, had an introspective side to her nature which, as years went by, played an ever more important part. It is not surprising that she looked to her friendship with Julia to fill the void. Julia's death was a loss deeply felt.

Ethel never understood Julia, though she could hardly help recognizing in her a strong personality with exceptional intellectual gifts. Their respective temperaments were far too dissimilar, quite apart from the fact that Julia was the wife of the man Ethel loved. She saw Julia as the unbending dialectician as well as the possessive wife who would keep her husband imprisoned in an ivory tower of metaphysical disquisition. As time went on Julia seemed to harden into an unreasonable, not to mention inconvenient, opponent, adducing awkward metaphysical arguments such as that H.B. was not really in love with Ethel, he only thought he was – and marshalling the

[263]

very weapons of convention and social opinion that were incongruous allies of the freedom of thought she claimed to uphold and the theories on marriage she had shared with her husband. Doubtless Julia had her inconsistent sides: there was a Spartan conventional facet which, notwithstanding her introspectiveness, could lead her to pronouncements such as the following:

> It is not enough to analyse yourself; for you then lose yourself in meanness and pride. It is necessary to control yourself, to ask yourself which are the tendencies that display themselves in the customs of the day and to question history. Respect of tradition and consideration for fashion are the required correctives of inward life.

And here is a cry from out of Julia's own experience and life:

> Away with free contracts! Free contracts and private agreements dissolve or transform themselves into individual ideals persuasive perhaps, but incoherent. Law, such as it is elaborated and adopted by public conscience, Law, which holds men and masters them with the fear of dishonour, with the fear of exile and excommunication, that is the Sovereign, the Protector.

We can now see where she and H.B. clashed. But within the whole that Julia was, there were contradictions: witness her somewhat unbiblical decalogue:

> Is there another decalogue?
> 1 Thou shalt see.
> 2 Thou shalt hear.
> 3 Thou shalt touch.
> 4 Thou shalt feel.
> 5 Thou shalt taste.
> 6 Thou shalt breathe.
> 7 Thou shalt move.
> 8 Thou shalt eat.
> 9 Thou shalt drink.
> 10 Thou shalt love and sleep.
> But to dare! If only we dared obey such commandments!

Moved by the same spirit of rebellion and regret she cries out towards the end of her life:

I am guilty! Guilty of ingratitude and lukewarmness. I know now that work and striving are unable to satiate. What haunts me, what torments me is the need to say: *I have sinned*. I have sinned not at such a time, in such a way, but with all my soul, with my entire being, because I knew not how to open my arms like a child and live without sophistication.

Ethel could not understand her precisely because she herself lived through the late Victorian and Edwardian age in a spirit of moral conformity. For all her eccentricities and unpredictable actions, she lived in a spirit of propriety, convention and respectability, even more so than Julia. Ethel's effusiveness and dynamic drive were no part of the candid unsophistication Julia dreamt of with such longing and regret. Ethel keeps referring to Julia in her autobiographical books with a certain bafflement, for she was unable to perceive in her and comprehend the passionate wife, the desperate lover behind the wall of reserve, the thinker, meditator, worshipper, sinner and poet which made up her complex personality. For Julia a whole world stretched out in a direction Ethel was not born to behold, let alone follow. Her behaviour till Julia's death – or almost till then – was, from the standpoint of moral propriety and the customs of the day, beyond reproach.

In her turn Julia maintained a wonderful aloofness, a marmoreal purity and pride, a dignity of presence and appearance, her natural passions restrained within a carapace of self-control. She relied on her friends and the armoury of metaphysics – perhaps a little out of place on the battlefields of love. Irene managed it differently and with success; but she was no Julia and had a very different husband.

After her death H.B. devotedly collected her *pensées*, a selection of which he published in book form under the title of *Via Lucis* in 1898. Perhaps the deepest and richest in poetic quality are her reflections on death which are to be found at the end of the volume. I quote a few here in the original French. The significance of death cannot be felt unless the fullness of life has been grasped and appreciated. Ethereal though she was, Julia never turned away from life.

La vie est belle et la mort nous est promise – la mort en qui se consume le moi mensonger.

La vie est multiple et mélodieuse. Penchons-nous plus avant vers celui qui se nomme l'omniprésent.

[265]

Viens! toi qui donnes tout-à-fait sans réticence du regard et du sourire, toi qui guéris du mensonge et de l'hypocrisie, des marchandages, des atermoiements, toi qui détruis jusqu'au sentiment de toi-même, toi que est toute-présence et le rajeunissement, toi qui reposes comme l'épaule du bien-aimé.

It was probably these last meditations that specially moved Henry James when he wrote to H.B. on 11 February 1898 about Julia's *pensées*, shortly after the publication of the book:

I have read them with much appreciation and with a vivid recall of her so distinguished and exquisite personality, as I see it again, framed in the great rooms on the June afternoons of your high palace on the Corso. This recollection makes me sorry that you weren't able to prefix to the volume a photograph of Hildebrand's bust. There is scarcely a page of this little book that doesn't seem to me exquisite. What a delightful kind of soul, after all, to have – especially when so lovely an instinct of expression has come with it! I find your wife, on her scale, a veritable artist – and the air with which she moves in the immensities is what I envy her the possession of. It's a most strange and interesting mind – and how removed from the personal of life, the material and the accidental. Full of beauty, ingenuity and serenity I find, in short, the volume, and quite extraordinarily fine. It's like a small, delicate antique funeral vase – filled with ashes that are, somehow, also like dried rose leaves.

Yet Henry James's understanding of Julia was only surface deep. Far from dry the rose leaves are still fresh; her utterances are eloquent and moving. Nevertheless it is not easy to break through the surface. Ethel was at a loss:

So mystical, so diaphanous, so terribly abstract is the thought behind these exquisitely turned French phrases. But the beauty of expression, the altitude of soul, the profundity of emotion (whether you catch its nature or not), that was in the heart of the author, this much is manifest even to metaphysical dunces like the present writer.

The final words Julia left behind before she departed are again

[266]

close to H.B.'s way of thinking: 'Parole disjointe et perdue, je me reintègre dans le poème divin.'

23

As Time Went On

One late September afternoon in 1896, on the hill of San Donato a Scopeto, H.B. and Irene Hildebrand sat talking, looking across to where the city of Florence lay in its encompassing past. Their own past seemed now part of it. Until that afternoon they had neither seen each other nor communicated by letter for more than ten years. Throughout that time the break Ethel exacted had endured unrelentingly.

Much had happened in those years: close relations and friends had died, Julia had just died, Lisl had died, Fiedler had died. Only a few months previously Irene had lost her eldest son by her first marriage; he had strained himself in his military service training and had died of heart failure. Such moments revise our perspectives. H.B. and Irene felt the time had come for reconciliation, for gathering and tying up those threads of friendship they had strung together in youth and then somewhat rashly severed. Mutual understanding had to be re-established. Ethel was raising no objection and, besides, 'Understand, understand, do everything to understand' was an underlying principle of H.B.'s philosophy. So he had come back to San Francesco on a visit from Rome, to reopen closed doors.

Immediately after this meeting Irene wrote to her children who, for a short while, happened to be away from San Francesco:

> For two days you have had no letter from me – it is annoying, but the guests and the strange meeting again with Brewster after twelve years have allowed me no time to write. Killy and Glehn are still here, but Brewster leaves today. It is a strange chapter in the book of my life, this coming together again with him. We had a great deal to tell each other and were both very glad to have met again.

Glehn was Christopher's tutor at Cambridge and the two of them struck up a lasting friendship. They had evidently come to San

[268]

Francesco with H.B. – no surprise, since Christopher, as well as Clotilde, had remained on the closest of terms with the young Hildebrands.

H.B.'s account of the reunion, which he gave Ethel in a letter some days later, is more detailed than Irene's but also more restrained. The question now was whether or not Ethel herself should take steps to overcome the estrangement. After all, she had nothing against Adolf whom she had liked immensely and for whom she retained a lifelong admiration.

> Darling, I have been to San Francesco di Paola; dined there on Saturday – Berenson was there too, and another guest – and returned yesterday for tea and the inevitable *Besprechung* with Frau Hildebrand. She wished to make a clean breast and it all amounts to a confession of passionate jealousy in the past, the present and the future, of every woman to whom her husband might feel attracted or who might prefer him to her. She must be sure that she ranks first in the sympathies of any female friend they have in common. She repents of a letter she wrote in former days and in which she lied – goaded on by Frau von Stockhausen and her own jealousy. She believes that with that exception she has always spoken well of you; seems to have a really warm appreciation of you as soon as Adolf is out of her mind; wonders if she would be jealous again; is sorely perplexed; rather wishes and rather dreads a renewal of relations, and in her uncertainties seems disposed to trust to chance and *Gelegenheiten*. She has still her very genial attractive manner and all her German *Schwärmerei*. He has improved; much quieter, less professorial; is growing stout. The house and the children charming. One of the girls, Lisl, the one who paints frescoes, has the sweetest face one can see; and they have got a refinement of a peculiar kind which is not that of the world but is not less excellent.

One has to wonder whether H.B.'s condescending attitude towards Hildebrand was tinged with jealousy. It would have been out of character, though no more so than the 'professorial' manner imputed to Hildebrand, which directly contradicts almost every other account. Significant, however, is H.B.'s enchantment with the young girls. The five of them were becoming a colourful feature of San Francesco in the 1890s: some years later, Lisl, the second daughter, who made such an impression on H.B., was to marry Christopher. She was taller, more handsome, more impulsive and more stubborn than the rest, and artistically, at least as a painter, the most gifted. In many respects she was the one who most took after her father.

Eva – 'Nini' as they nicknamed her – was the eldest and the most intellectual. She was eighteen by then, played the piano well, was self-possessed, reasonable and well-read, interested in literature and philosophy without too much sophistication. She was on close terms of friendship with Clotilde, H.B.'s daughter, who was more or less the same age.

Third in age came Irene, nicknamed 'Zusi', the most exuberant and warm-hearted of the lot. She, like Lisl, painted but preferred sculpture. She was the daughter most interested in people, talkative and inquisitive. A story survives of her reaction when San Francesco was suddenly shaken by an earthquake one hot summer night in 1895. It was not the first nor the last to strike the vicinity, but it was particularly severe and prolonged, leaving scars in the walls still visible today where cracks had appeared and bars had to be applied to hold the masonry together.

The house rocked and the family in alarm came rushing out into the garden for safety, virtually unclothed because of the intense summer heat. No sooner had they settled down on the lawn under the pine tree to face the fall of San Francesco than Zusi, in sudden agitation, sprang to her feet again, wringing her hands and exclaiming, 'Emanuel's letters! His letters! I can't part with them!' She darted back into the house while the rest of the family waited helplessly for her return as the roof swayed between the cypress tops. San Francesco held up and Zusi re-emerged with a little casket. She sank to the ground with it clutched in her arms and soon fell asleep in the grass.

Fourth there came Sylvia, or 'Vivi' as they called her, perhaps the prettiest after Lisl. She was the most tolerant and the most tactful, always anxious not to impose herself upon others. At the same time she was no realist and found it hard to come to terms with the harsher aspects of life. Her approach was rather over-earnest, and because she attached the utmost importance to any form of commitment, she found it difficult to make emotional decisions. The man she was to fall in love with had to woo her for years and in the end had to sell his villa, threaten to quit for good and stage an elopement before he could win her hand as well as her heart. They were arrested on the Italian frontier by the police, who had been alerted by Hildebrand, and were brought back handcuffed to each other.

Bertha, or 'Berthele' as she was called, was the fifth, still a little girl at that time, but already remarkable for her intelligence and musical gifts – she was the most musical of all the sisters. She and Sylvia kept very much together and tended to take charge of their little brother Dietrich, or 'Gogo' as everybody called him.

The three older girls had reached an age where their conspicuously attractive looks were drawing in the young men. They dreamed of romance but their idealism and self-assurance made them particularly choosy. Achilles, Alexander the Great and Napoleon all featured at one time or another as heroes, but rather more accessible was Emanuel, the successful, good-looking Italian actor of the day whose hand they could sometimes press.

During the mid-nineties Emanuel played centre stage in the lives of the three girls. He had his own company, excelling in the production of Shakespeare and taking the principal male roles himself. The Hildebrand girls doted on him, scarcely ever missing a play in which he took the leading part. After the performance they would besiege him in his dressing room or invite him home the next day. Their hero-worship seems to have been a collective effort; they were all three equally in love and whatever feelings of jealousy may have developed between them his tact or skill in dealing with them was evidently consummate – there seems to have been no breakdown on his account in good-sisterly relations. Besides, Irene would have seen to her daughters' forbearance in matters of propriety, although she allowed them a freedom which went beyond the conventions of the age. But in any case, from the records and accounts available, it would seem that strict control was scarcely necessary since the girls' enthusiasm was pure hero-worship – and nothing else. Emanuel himself must have been conscious of this; moreover, much as he liked the beautiful girls, he was deeply involved in a love affair which dominated his life and was leading him to despair.

The Hildebrands were aware that he was having trouble with his leading actress, or *prima donna* as he would refer to her. Irene hinted at the matter in a letter to her husband in Munich. Then one day at San Francesco, under the sway of uncontrolled emotion, Emanuel burst into sobs and told the story of Virginia to his friends:

[271]

It was seven years ago in a small town of the Abruzzi where we were playing. She was an exquisite though still immature-looking girl of about fifteen. I saw her sitting at the door of a modest house. Her father was a cobbler; her mother was dead. I gave her a ticket for a seat at the performance that night. Her intelligent reaction, her enthusiasm and interest led me to see her several times in the next few days and soon I realized that I had found in her the material of a first-class actress ready to be moulded by proper training. I had no difficulty in persuading her to come with me – we were already in love – nor did I have any trouble with her father, seduced as he was by the picture of his daughter's future career. He was too poor to let himself be worried by her loss of respectability. So I set myself to work. I taught her everything in the next few years. I taught her elocution – how to produce her voice – I taught her how to walk on the stage, how to hold herself, how to change posture, movement, expression, looks, and yet appear perfectly natural – everything I taught her, with painstaking patience and love because I knew she would succeed, as indeed she did. . . She said she owed me everything, was immensely grateful, but that her art came first; it was time for her to go, it was important she should set out on her own as an actress, that she should be able to stand on her own feet and not in the limelight of my reputation. So she has left me ruthlessly. . . I've created her; she is my creature, she's my work of art, she belongs to me. What can I do now without her? I can't find a proper female partner or even the material that can be made into one. If only I had Duse, I might do something with her. She is the rising star of the day and she'll go far. But so would my Virginia if only she had me still as a guide.

The girls sympathized wholeheartedly; Irene felt sorry but wondered whether Virginia might perhaps have done the right thing to extricate herself from a Pygmalion mould.

For a while the girls went on lionizing their cherished actor, but the time came when their enthusiasm suffered sudden deflation. Lisl used to tell the story many years later, when Emanuel was long dead:

He was playing King Lear at Verona. He had failed to find another Virginia and his success with the public was on the wane. I must have been seventeen by then. We decided to take

[272]

the next train in time for the evening performance. We left with our mother's consent, subject to our being under the charge of a chaperon, who as usual was our manservant Fiore, though Nini was by then responsible enough to keep an eye on us younger ones. I thought Emanuel wonderful again – my feelings for him soared as they always did at every performance of his I had seen.

We arranged to go for an outing into the country with him next day. He was pleased to see us and, though tired, agreed to come after some cajoling. We wreathed ourselves with ivy, hired a trap, took a picnic and drove away with Emanuel without Fiore, who had been persuaded to stay behind. There was scarcely room for the four of us but we managed. After a cheerful picnic in a green field under Lombardy poplars we drove back by roundabout dusty country roads. It was a hot afternoon and Emanuel didn't seem in the best of spirits, so to cheer him up we sang *stornelli*, as we drove on slowly, the tired horse kicking up a lot of dust. We sang the popular ditties we knew best and when we couldn't think of any more we made jokes and laughed. But he wasn't his usual self, he remained somewhat morose. Then, as fate would have it, or rather the dust, Emanuel noisily cleared his throat and spat. I can still see the yellow spit coagulate in the dust. The image has remained impressed upon me these thirty years. I was amazed. It came as a terrible shock. So Emanuel could spit and actually did – like any other Italian, was it possible? Yes it was. We all saw it, we had seen the spittle in the dust. And of a sudden, as we drove on, my picture of him was torn to pieces; the spell was broken. I looked at him objectively for the first time. How could I ever have been in love with such a man? He was not so good-looking after all; he was like any middle-aged Italian with a paunch as a result of too much spaghetti; and he was growing bald; his hands were too fat; he hadn't made a single interesting, intelligent remark throughout the afternoon; he hadn't responded to the architecture, the churches, the villas, the view I had pointed out to him on our drive. Had he ever said anything intelligent? I couldn't remember. We drove back rather glumly – the *stornelli* died away and so did the jokes. Evidently my sisters were suffering from the same trouble. We took a train back to Florence that same evening. 'What was Lear like?' my mother inquired as soon as she saw us. 'I can't quite recall; not particularly good,' I think I said. And so Emanuel faded out of my mind and life. I forget whether I ever saw him again. I believe as he got older he took to character parts and he was no longer spoken about in the papers, or perhaps he died soon after.

The Hildebrand girls were famous in Florence, but more for their looks and their intensely individual, if not eccentric, way of living than for any great involvement in the city's social life. Their world was San Francesco, where they were free to follow their pursuits within its seclusion, undisturbed by any amount of coming and going around them.

It was in the spring of 1897 that Mary Berenson visited San Francesco and wrote to her children about them:

> After lunch he [Placci]* took me to call on Mr Hildebrand, who is, I think, the greatest living sculptor. He lives in a beautiful villa on the other side of Florence, with his lovely, lovely wife and a huge family of daughters and one little son. Some of the daughters are just getting grown up, and I couldn't help wondering what you would be like at their age. We talked a lot about it on the way back, for although those girls are brought up what I call perfectly, Placci says he doesn't like them! They are brought up in just the way I should like to bring you up if I had you all to myself – they have never read anything but the finest books (in all languages), never seen anything but the greatest works of art, never heard anything but the best music. And they like all these things – fine books, great art, beautiful music – very very much. And yet, and yet – it isn't the same thing to have it all *given* to them as to have fought for it and won it for themselves. I have often noticed it with perfectly brought up children, their taste is good, but it is a little tame. So I consoled myself for your awful books of adventure and the dreadful art your blue eyes gaze upon and the trashy music your little ears hear, thinking that when the day comes for you to take hold of things *for yourselves*, you will make everything you learn glow with your eagerness.

She was wrong to call them 'tame'. The Hildebrand girls were
*See p. 277

[274]

anything but that. They were full of carefree impulsiveness. Each girl had her own grove of ilex trees in the garden which had been planted for her by her mother and which she was encouraged to look after. Lisl not only took an interest in her own grove but developed an impetuous managerial urge towards the whole park and farm. This sometimes led to trouble. On one occasion, after having planted an avenue of cypress saplings leading to the house, she had a section of the wall pulled down which held up the garden terrace in front of the façade. This was supposed to improve the prospect and provide access to the avenue. Her father, who was away for a few weeks in Munich, had incised some figures in the plaster of that wall. It took all Lisl's charm to defuse his wrath when he returned to find what had happened.

There were, of course, quite a number of young men who came and courted the girls, but few met with any response. Often we find Irene complaining in her letters about the inadequacies of the young people from outside. Certainly they needed perseverance to prevail. One who had it was Sylvia's young man, who waited and waited and finally eloped with her. The scandal resolved itself in a happy marriage. Less fortunate was young Willy Furtwängler, the future orchestra conductor, who often came to stay at San Francesco. He and Berthele, the youngest daughter, fell in love with each other and were engaged for ten years. In the end she married another musician.

Sons of old family friends were also among the wooers and two of them were successful. At fifteen Christopher was in love with the eldest daughter, two or three years his senior. On his return to Europe after Cambridge and a spell in the pampas as a cowboy, he successfully wooed Lisl and married her.

By the end of 1896 most of Hildebrand's old friends were dead – Marées, Fiedler, Grant, Karl Hillebrand, Lisl von Herzogenberg, Julia. Jessie Laussot was still alive but getting old and spent. Hildebrand himself, on the other hand, was only forty-seven and bursting with energy and creative activity. Fiedler's death would have shaken him and one may assume that he was not insensitive to Irene's grief at the loss of her eldest son. But he was a man who lived with all his powers in the immediate present; it was not in his nature to dwell on fate's inevitable trials. His circle of new friends widened and the influential ones – those who could prove a source of advancement for his work – assumed an increasingly important part.

[275]

Royal visitors from the old princedoms of Germany, not to mention the likes of William Gladstone, kept putting in an appearance at San Francesco, regarding it as something of a curiosity or hearing it was somewhere worth visiting as a postscript to the historical monuments of the city. Some of these worthies became not only encouraging patrons but also real friends – among them the Duke of Saxe-Meiningen and later Rupert, Crown Prince of Bavaria with whom Hildebrand kept up a lifelong correspondence, much of which was later published.

When the Empress Elizabeth of Austria planned to have a sumptuous villa built for her in Corfu she came to San Francesco in the hope of persuading Hildebrand to take on the sculptural embellishment of the place. He declined – her worship of Achilles made him feel uneasy. So she recruited a Neapolitan sculptor instead.

This was the period, too, when Hildebrand's friendship with Cosima Wagner matured. Now that Wagner himself was dead, Hildebrand put his aversion to the composer behind him and yielded to Cosima's intelligence and remarkable personality. He made a fine relief portrait of her and exchanged numerous letters. The relationship, however, was never anything but a lively friendship; Cosima had long passed the age of physical dalliance.

Another visitor to San Francesco, from out of the opposing camp in the world of music, was Clara Schumann. She let herself be taken round the sights of Florence by Hildebrand who also sculpted a portrait bust of her. John Singer Sargent came too in the 1890s and early 1900s. There seems to be no evidence of his having met the Hildebrands in his early youth when he was living in Florence. It is more likely that his acquaintance with them came about later in life through his friend (and co-national) H.B., whom he visited several times in Rome.

At the Freer Gallery in Washington D.C. there is a fine painting by Sargent showing the San Francesco loggia in a mellow light. In the foreground, sitting at a table well laid with food and drink, are two ladies, the one on the left clearly Irene von Hildebrand. The painting is called *Breakfast in the Loggia*, seemingly a misnomer, since the meal appears to be rather more substantial and the light is a late afternoon light when the sun comes round to the west of the loggia.

People came and went – relatives, friends and acquaintances,

[276]

royalties, artists and writers, teachers and tutors. The old Italian friends, the Cini, Pasolini, Rasponis and Guerrieri, continued to play an important part. And Carlo Placci was constantly on the scene. He knew everybody, was everybody's friend and brought with him all the gossip of Florentine and Roman society. He would tell one what Eleonora Duse was doing, how d'Annunzio's love affair with her was getting on, all about Giulietta Gordigiani's hopeless love for d'Annunzio and so forth. Irene was busy not only with the running of a large household, including the farm, but also as a hostess receiving and entertaining visitors whose intellectual standard demanded some intelligent attention. The records as well as the anecdotes that have been handed down show that she accomplished this task with skill and serenity.

One day, for instance, Richard Strauss called at San Francesco and Irene received him alone for tea – Adolf was away in Munich. They talked about music, but after a while she got up, poured him another cup of tea, gave him a book to look at and, excusing herself, left the drawing-room. She went to the adjoining bedroom and gave birth to Gogo. When this was over we don't know whether she came back to have another cup of tea with her guest.

Hildebrand was reaching the apogee of his success as a sculptor and commissions were beginning to pour in, not only for busts, reliefs and figures but also for fountains, memorials and monuments in Germany. Some of these works are excellent, others not so satisfactory but always far better than most of the output by his competitors and contemporaries. He was awarded medals, orders, various honourary titles and in the end a hereditary knighthood. First came the important commission for the Wittelsbachbrunn, the largest fountain in Munich and on the whole a splendid work, dynamic and harmonious at the same time. This task and others of comparable size or complexity which were to follow necessitated, from the middle of the nineties onwards, increasingly long periods of sojourn in Germany.

Though there was no waning in Hildebrand's activity as an artist, there came a change in the life of San Francesco after 1895. With Hildebrand absenting himself in Germany often for more than six months in the course of the year, it made for a new regime. The children, who were growing up and who disliked living in Germany, contrived to remain in Florence for most of the year. Their mother, though apprehensive at having to leave Hildebrand alone for excessively long periods, managed to stay with them very often when he was away. But whether she was present or not, little by little the era of the Hildebrand daughters set in.

In looking back to this second age of Hildebrand's San Francesco one cannot help feeling that in spite of its prosperity, activity and the promise of youth it constituted a silver age compared with the preceding twenty years, which saw perhaps the sculptor's best work. Quite apart from the fact that after 1895 San Francesco was no longer in the same way the home it had been, the earlier period stood closer to the romantic world of Germany, a world into which the phoney respectability and the bourgeois nationalism of the late nineteenth and early twentieth century had scarcely penetrated. By the end of the century extreme nationalism was making swift progress in Germany and in a form arguably even more objectionable than in other European countries subject to the same complaint. On the whole San Francesco was not affected, but the shadow of a more unsettled world was beginning to extend to it. Some letters exchanged between Hildebrand and his wife on the subject are interesting. Apparently Irene was endeavouring to excuse or justify these trends in a new nation like Germany, whereas Hildebrand recoiled from them. When finally the First World War came, a whole era was swept away. Hildebrand survived the upheaval by only three years.

[278]

24
A Widower's Free Life

The palace I was born in consisted of

> a high house in the very heart of Rome: a dark massive struc-
> ture, overlooking a sunny *piazzetta* in the neighbourhood of the
> Farnese palace . . . a domestic fortress, which bore a stern old
> Roman name, which smelt of historic deeds, of crime and craft
> and violence, which was mentioned in *Murray* and visited by
> tourists who looked disappointed and depressed, and which had
> frescoes by Caravaggio in the *piano nobile* and a row of muti-
> lated statues and dusty urns in the wide, nobly arched loggia
> overlooking the damp court where a fountain gushed out of a
> mossy niche.

This is how Henry James described it in *The Portrait of a Lady*,
calling it by the fictitious name of Palazzo Roccanera to suit the
picture. It is a faithful description, however, of the real palace, except for the Caravaggio frescoes which it did not contain. The rooms
my parents occupied, and my grandfather before them at a time
when Henry James was a welcome visitor, were certainly in keeping
with 'a large apartment with a concave ceiling and walls covered
with old red damask'. But oddly enough H.B., who obviously was
not Gilbert Osmond, moved into the Palazzo Antici Mattei by the
piazzetta fifteen years after *The Portrait of a Lady* had been written.
   Henry James had often visited him in his 'high palace of the
Corso'. I have no recollection of that, since it belonged to a period
many years before I came into this world. But later, whenever he
happened to be in Rome, Henry James would visit H.B. at his new
dwelling in the palace I still remember from my early childhood.
H.B. had transferred himself there in 1896, occupying the floor above
the one where Osmond lived, if fiction could be reality. There was,
as it happened, a sinister rich American living there, on the *piano
nobile*, who, as H.B. wrote to Ethel in May 1896, had evidently

[279]

sworn to keep him out and 'would hire the apartment himself and have it empty as he does the *mezzanino*'. The obstacle was overcome, however, and the agreement signed for three years with the right of renewal on the same terms. 'I am glad. And I am glad too that you know the apartment and like it. We discovered it together.' Now he began doing it up at his own expense, including various structural alterations, as his letters to Ethel disclose.

> You will see how nice it will look after the repairs. But do you know it is not nearly so big as we thought at first sight. After throwing down the partition between the two rooms, I only get four bedrooms, drawing room, dining room, billiard room and library; which after all is quite enough. Particularly as my bedroom will have a huge dressing room attached to it. And the terrace will be a bower of roses.

In fact the apartment was more spacious than he suggested, according to another letter he wrote shortly after, in which he enclosed a plan:

> The kitchen, servants' rooms etc. are not shown on the plan as they come on the *mezzanino* below. Splendid garrets above. The billiard room is large enough for my French table. Notice that one had to pass through the W.C. to get to the terrace! I have changed that by adding a staircase. The terrace is eight metres by twenty! And I have added steps from the ante-room down to the drawing room. Electric light and wooden floors everywhere. It will look charming I think. Tomorrow I am choosing colours for the ceilings and walls.

The most vivid image I retain of the apartment is of the vast terrace where I spent my time playing, the tiled roofs stretching away below, over the whole of Rome it seemed to me, with baroque domes cutting the skyline and the swifts swooping down to pick up invisible midges in the golden air at sunset. But Henry James preferred to visualize H.B. wrapped in a more sombre Roman light, as we can see in the following letter he wrote on 17 June 1898 from De Vere Gardens, addressed to 1 Barton Street to await his friend's arrival there from Italy via Germany. This was a flat H.B. had taken for his daughter and himself.

[280]

All thanks for your letter from Weimar – and don't measure my appreciation by this rude form of response. Only bear in mind that certain kinds of rudeness are the very flower of our high civilization. I rejoice to know that you are soon to be in England, and though I gather – from your lingering leisurely *allure* – that you will not have reached London before I shall have quitted it, there will be possible rectifications of that that I am glad to think of. I shall certainly count on your coming down to see me at Rye. I shall have little else there but two chairs, two spoons and a Remington, but I shall arrange them so as to produce an impression on you. Then, when I see you adequately impressed, I shall try and give you a sort of inkling of how and why I never come to Rome. If it weren't for your two rooms and a nook – to say nothing of your daughter – I should suggest to you to come and live, in London, in *my* rooms. But I have four or five, and no nook, and no daughter: which are so many charms the less. I have seen the little place – Edward Warren has pointed it out to me; and I have stood spellbound by its promise of interior – well, what shall I say? – let me say perfection, and have done with it. It's a dear little 'dreamy', hansomless corner – for which, however, your palace of the Caesars, or at least of the Borgias, will have been an odd education. Perhaps you have had too much Caesar and too much Borgia – in which case it will be an absolute antidote. *Arrivez donc* and make me a sign as soon as you have done so. I shall be at Rye long and late, and hope you will come often. I send this where you tell me. Recall me, please, to your daughter's kindness – at some moment of your daughter's distraction, if any such there ever be – and believe me, my dear Brewster, yours always,

HENRY JAMES

Already two years before this letter was written H.B. had settled down in his Palazzo Antici Mattei apartment where for his last twelve years he was to lead an independent bachelor's life, surrounded by admirers, female admirers especially, and friends. But this pursuit of the worldly life expressed only one side of his nature, for not only did his aloofness remain but also the 'crypt', the turning inwards, the need for intellectual activity. Every morning he sat in his library, reading, writing letters and poems at his desk, working on a libretto for an opera of Ethel's or on a play of his own or on another philosophical dissertation.

Now that the Hildebrands had ceased to be a deterrent, he found himself visiting Florence from time to time. There he got to know Bernard Berenson more closely, whom he had already met in Rome. In a letter to Ethel he describes him as follows:

In the morning yesterday I lunched with Mrs Costello (who remains thin air to me; I am never quite sure if she is there or not though she is taller than I am and buxom in proportion) and with Berenson at Fiesole. This small weak Russian Jew, grown up in the United States, is unfortunately surrounded by people who never weary of telling that he is the greatest living genius and that he has explained everything, from the significance of the nude to the mystery of the universe. Creation and Procreation I suppose. Vain, timid and over-polite. Talks in a manner that makes one think of a lady putting on puff powder. And I fail to see the originality of his doctrine. Yet he is not quite uninteresting. I think he has an extremely delicate eye and he has trained it well. One can always have a certain respect for a man who makes you feel how obtuse one of your senses has grown or remained. . .

Then, with a touch of teasing sarcasm, he gets on to Violet Paget, 'Vernon Lee', the writer on aesthetics and other topics with whom Ethel had become enthusiastically intimate:

In the evening I dined at Palmerino with Vernon Lee and the rather beautiful Sellers, who has actually dressed well! And I had coffee after dinner. What do you say to that? Sellers's gown and Vernon's coffee! Where is Don Juan's diminished head? Only the wine kept my elated self-complacency within reasonable limits. During the dinner there was desultory chat; then we sat out till half past eleven near the little gate and I had a long discussion with Vernon Lee on the nature of truth. She was very aggressive and brilliantly intelligent, and after two hours succeeded in proving triumphantly the very statement she had undertaken to combat; at which she seemed gently surprised but not otherwise put out; and it all ended good-humouredly. The intense Sellers opened not her lips, but took short-hand notes all the time, as she expressed it. If you go in for acquiring culture, you must do it seriously. 'Nous ne sommes pas ici pour nous amuser,' as the whist player said. It was a lovely starry night and I walked back all the way in pleasant silence.

During his stay in Florence in that spring of 1896, where Ethel had joined him for a while, he felt the need to guard himself against the city's nostalgic allure.

I walked about Florence after you had left, dear one, and loved the old place. If the stage decoration were everything I should return to it and leave Rome, which is an acquired taste. Florence is the instinctive love; but it is dead. I should collect intaglios and manuscripts there and wander even further from the living than you accuse me of being now.

He went on seeing Vernon Lee, who interested him in spite of her capacity to irritate.

Now I know what she quarrels with in my writings. She says the words are well chosen and the phrases good but the conducting of the thought un-English, not *literary* in English, for this reason. The French disentangle their web of thought, go straight to the main ideas, formulate them as neatly as possible and then illustrate with happy similes. Which is also my method, says Vernon Lee. But the Englishman never (except in science) stands outside and in front of what he wants to say, it remains part of himself, he does not reduce it to an intellectual skeleton draped with illustrations and attended by minor personages on a similar pattern; he struggles blindly in a certain direction with all his brain at work at the same time so that the main thought is not expressed at all but one is pushed in its direction by a throng of metaphorical associations, all appealing to the eye, the touch and everyday experience. It is the rich hodge podge that constitutes the literary material in her opinion. I am completely 'out of it' because I begin by disentangling as carefully as possible bones from flesh and skin, which is the scientific process; so that whatever imagination and skill I may show in the detail only irritates one as borrowed feathers.

I was delighted with this very clever criticism. All I can say in reply is that it accounts for there being so to speak no good

[283]

English prose. The process V.L. describes and admires seems to me that of poetry; it needs the severe discipline of rhythm and rhyme to make up for the evasion of the chief difficulty which is precisely to curb and master associations, to bring out the essential and tone down the accidental, to avoid the volcanic blusterings of Carlyle (or Carlisle? How is the name spelt?) and the aromatic vapourings of Pater, both of whom V.L. quotes as the greatest literary champions of England. Such prose seems to me simply shocking, though I like what Pater has to say. I don't see why a new prose should not fight its way to the front – a prose that must hold its own in the long run as psychologically sincere. There are vast tracts of speculative thought in which it is mere affectation to present one's self to the public like a volcano or a mist; and if they are out of the literary domain its frontiers must simply be extended.

There is no record in writing of Ethel's reaction, probably because they saw each other again not long after. But her letters seldom go into such matters. Their style is chaotic and mostly related to the events, people, problems, arrangements and details of everyday life – a very full life no doubt. There was no longer a conflict in their relationship to despair of, reflect upon and discuss. So H.B.'s letters to her, though always extremely well written and interesting, are now similarly focused on the outside world. They tend to abstain not only from introspection, to which he had been so prone in his relationship with Julia, but also from disquisition on intellectual topics beyond the mere exchange of views and impressions. There was one area, however, of regular discussion – and that was the librettos of her operas in the making, in which H.B. took a cooperative part.

He constantly revisited London where now, in his more social mood, there was no neglect of friends and acquaintances. From there, in September 1896, he wrote to Ethel who was staying at One Oak, her house in the country:

Thursday evening I went to Henschel's. The Kneivels repeated Dvorak's quartet – the one I like so much – and played better than ever if possible, at least it sounded better in Henschel's room; I cannot fancy anything more perfect. I made friends with Schröder, the 'cellist, and he spoke with enthusiasm of your mass; of you too, but that interests you less of course. Long conversation with Sargent, who is pleasant. Alma-Tadema was there, telling filthy and idiotic stories in every language and quite sickening both to behold and hear. . .

Yesterday was devoted to one of those undertakings which are not repeated in a lifetime but which one must brace oneself up to once. A whole day's excursion from 10 a.m. to 11 p.m. with nothing but men. Twenty-six of them at a table for dinner at the White Lion, Guildford, Surrey, singing 'For he's a jolly good fellow'. A novel sight. It is a strange world. We visited a delightful Elizabethan manor with moats and an old-fashioned garden where at last I discovered a young lady and discoursed with her of John Inglesant. There is a silver lining to every cloud. Onslow Ford, who had invited me, was a nice companion. The other Academicians did not attract me much. Too many of them perhaps . . . Tuesday I am going to Rye to see Henry James.

On his way back to Rome H.B. enjoyed Paris again. During those warm September days memories of the past came crowding back. Perhaps a hankering after the French language as a means of literary expression took hold of him again, although he does not yet say so in his letters. But two years later he was to adopt French for all his future output.

Somehow I am delighted to be out of London this time. I had grown depressed in those two little rooms. No more ground floors and no more Westminster or Pimlico for me. Next time I shall try St John's Wood or Campden Hill or something of that sort, if it has to be London at all. But why not Capel Garmon or Farnborough Park? I am full of tender fondness for the sky; the landscapes, the light of France, have stepped back here into summer; and the streets of Paris where I trotted till I was seven years old have taken hold of me again as the nursery rhyme took hold of you the other day. Rue Cambon, that suits me exactly at present; I like it and love you . . .

Then on to Geneva from where he wrote again to Ethel:

Rod is in one of his happy moods – subtle, soothing, musical. Brunetière (who wields a kind of moral and intellectual sceptre in France) has been staying with him and there has been much interesting talk. Brunetière writes like a pedant but is quite unaffected and very impressive in conversation; refreshingly naive sometimes I should say, to judge from the following quotation. They were discussing the great question of morals: whether nature knows best or not, if we are to express or repress. B. of course was all for repression and Rod for expression. Finally B. exclaims: 'Et bien je ne veux pas qu'il soit ainsi parce qu'alors moi qui a passé ma vie à combattre mes passions j'aurais été dupe, et je ne veux pas avoir été dupe!' One rarely hears the case stated so frankly.

On Maupassant's *Une Vie*, which both Ethel and H.B. were reading at the same time, he says:

To me it seems all wrong artistically notwithstanding the wonderful workmanship: the figures are reduced to a mere outline as though they had been looked at from one spot and from a great distance; and every little touch of the brush is done with the delicacy of a miniature work, so that you have to squint alternately with eyes converging and diverging.

But on the whole he did admire Maupassant whom he knew personally and whose complete works in their first edition he acquired for his library.

A few days later he received a letter from Sargent – 'very curious'.

He has sent enormous photos of his Boston Library paintings to Rome, to a friend with a vague address. Post Office writes address not to be found. He writes back: 'Wait another month and if not cleared deliver to Brewster.' And he writes to inform me: and would I care to have them, and will I excuse the manner of presenting them, and if I don't want them I can get rid of them by discovering his friend's address. But perhaps I shall not get them after all. Altogether I think it is a very shy way of offering me this present and I am rather touched. If his friend turns up he will have to send me duplicates now; perhaps only wants me to ask for them. An American lady here has told me an anecdote of his shyness. He was nearly a month in a house where there was a very pretty girl. As the day of departure drew near he grew more and more silent and nervous and finished by walking to and fro without looking at anybody. The lady of the house who seems to

[286]

have had her eyes open – said to him at last: 'Wouldn't you like to paint Miss X?' To which he replied: 'That is just what I am longing to do.' He hadn't dared to say so.

It was about that time that H.B. wrote to Ethel describing a stirring experience in connection with Rousseau's birthplace:

The other evening I was coming back late from Rod's through a nice quaint old street – rue Jean Jacques Rousseau, the one into which he was born – and suddenly I was transported into Greece the year 800 or so before Christ. The magic was worked by most simple and trivial means: some ten or twelve boys were making music in the street; most of them had Pan's flutes, one had cymbals, and a few of them blew in what looked like double flageolets – two straight pipes apparently fastened together, meeting at the mouthpiece and then diverging; but what did the miracle was the inspiration of the bystander who thumped on the metal wall of one of those little temples erected in the streets of the Continent for the convenience of men and into which ladies do not penetrate – even as the chapel of John the Baptist at the Lateran. The sound produced was that of the big drum with something ominous and dire and it is extraordinary how it blended with Pan's flutes. I never had such a weird archaic impression – fauns and nomads, leopard skins, roses and the temple of Paestum – a most noble transformation of the little one whose wall was being banged.

With letter after letter their correspondence goes on to comment on the books they were reading and to describe the situations in which they found themselves, as well as the people they met and kept seeing again. And there was an additional object of interest – the novelty of the bicycle. Bates the banker, for instance, went cycling all the way out from Geneva to southern Italy and back to Switzerland where H.B., who was visiting his friend Rod before returning to Rome, met him.

I do wish you had seen my friend Bates at Geneva as I saw him there the other day. I don't know anybody who can be alternately so tedious and so fantastically original and delightful. He was just back from a trip to Naples on his bicycle. Started with four men and strewed them on the road – one ill with

[287]

dysentery, another with constipation, a third with indigestion and the fourth a fraud who went all the way by train registering his bicycle from town to town. Now Bates does not know a word of Italian, had no map, no implements of any kind, not even a pump to inflate his tyres. But he had started for Naples and he got there, the friends keeping up with him by train or waiting for him in the chief towns. When he had to sleep, as was oftenest the case, in little places where no one spoke English or French, he would telegraph to his friends in order to see by the address on their answer where he was. Everywhere he found someone to blow up his bicycle for him and when there was no one he put his Humber on his shoulder and trudged on with it. He was enchanted with everything like a schoolboy; made friends everywhere. One thing only perplexed him which is too amusing not to relate. He wore no shirt but a sweater that stopped much higher than a shirt. And his drawers were tight so that they yawned and the draught felt cold and there was a shrinkage so that when he got to Naples he found himself in the museum peeping curiously under the vine leaves to see what the normal proportions are. In fact he said that it had come to this that when he had occasion to stop against a wall he had great difficulty in finding it (not the wall). He vows he will have a flap to his sweater next time. But you should hear the descriptions of the country – as fresh as in a savage's brain, with an inexhaustible fund of humour. I admired him. Think of the wild goose ride with only two words of Italian at his service: Quanto? and Napoli. And he went tearing down the Simplon and down the Apennines in the dark – often in the rain, all alone and as happy as a lark. Mind you this is a man who hates games and has a fire in the office at the bank all the year round, in the hottest summer days so that even I gasp and call for air; a physically lazy man when there is nothing that appeals to his imagination. But he does not think of going to look for his ticket. In short he is an American.

So was H.B., who took to his newly bought bicycle with almost equal zest. Ethel caught the enthusiasm and so did his daughter.

[288]

25
Worldly Rome

Now settled in his refurbished apartment of the 'high house in the very heart of Rome', H.B. carried on his new, more worldly, social life, with which years later his surviving friends were apt to associate him perhaps too closely. But to all appearances he became delightfully urbane. The following extract from a letter he wrote to Ethel on 17 February 1897 is self-revealing:

> I am floundering in dissipation just now. Dinners, luncheons and dinners. The day after tomorrow I give a function of that kind: Sargent of course and to meet him the Soderini, the Frankensteins, Mme Theodoli and Mrs Hill, one of the fascinating divorced ladies whom I gather round me as sugar gathers bees. Mme Pasolini will come in the course of the evening. Saturday I entertain a small party: Miss Tucker and Miss Mellenson, both formerly of Newnham College – classics, philosophy, archeology and sport; Frau Homberger, widow of a German *Kritiker* and *Kulturgeschichtsforscher* (pronounced as written), and her brother Dr Karo, an intelligent young man full of Etruscan lore and polished by familiarity with many literatures. High talk and no champagne. And so it runs on. In short at the present moment I am rather like the prodigal son. Occasionally I ask myself why and the only answer I can find comes in little visions of past days: the rooms in Paris where I sat for two months without speaking to a soul and where I used to strain my ears to catch the sound of human voices on the other side of the wall; the winter I passed in Bloomsbury Square; a visit every fortnight to the Melvills and one every three weeks to Henry James; *sonst nichts*. The pendulum has swung the other way. Perhaps I shall end on a desert island: you don't mind the sea, do you? Otherwise I will have a bridge built.

He had been leading a fairly social life already in his former

[289]

Roman dwelling; now in the Palazzo Antici Mattei there was a housewarming to add to the luncheons and dinners.

> The grand dinner went off splendidly. I placed my people all wrong, it seems, according to etiquette, with the result that after a moment's bewilderment they enjoyed themselves much more than they expected to. The cook surpassed himself and when the mousse de foie gras was served a kind of religious awe filled the room and the hush of great emotions preceded the outburst of enthusiasm with which he was proclaimed an artist. After that everybody talked at once till one o'clock in the morning; the mighty Sindaco himself has never been known to laugh so often.
>
> Tonight the Guerrieris dine here for the first time. Etc. I am getting tired of it but Clotilde of course is insatiable.

In fact he felt the need, he says, of getting some working discipline into his daily life. Letters 'are terrible thieves of time' – and he was in the habit of writing very many.

H.B. was in his mid forties, strikingly good-looking. The ladies that gathered round him were a varied lot, some accomplished and some attractive, some both. One of these was Etta, Marchesa de Viti, whom he had met two years previously. She was a Bostonian by birth, married to an able Italian economist who owned large estates in the south of Italy. She and her charming children were to become intimates of H.B. and his family for more than one generation. After meeting her for the first time he wrote to Ethel:

> I was seated between her [the hostess] and the lady you don't like, the Marchesa de Viti, who I assure you came out with flying colours. Not at all a goose. She had been reading Berenson's book and criticised it very cleverly. I was rather astonished as I had not suspected her of pensiveness. Her husband – the Jewish-looking man – goes in for political economy. They have asked me to lunch with them on Tuesday at the Palazzo Orsini, near the Teatro Marcello.

Then there was Lily, Marchesa Theodoli, also born American, who wrote novels and whose 'dramacule' Henry James had critically torn to pieces. She had been a close friend of H.B. for some years already. There was Mrs Winthrop Chanler, a gifted American writer, and Mrs Crawshay, 'Mamie' as she was known to her close

[290]

friends, an English lady who was to play an increasingly prominent part in H.B.'s life. As years went by and their friendship deepened, jealousy between her and Ethel was only to be expected. Others in the inner circle were Maria Contessa Pasolini, from all accounts a delightful woman of whom H.B. grew particularly fond and at whose dinner parties he was a frequent guest; Donna Laura Minghetti, wife of an Italian minister, whose daughter had married a cousin of Julia; and Bernhard von Bülow, the diplomat who was about to become Imperial Chancellor of Germany. Donna Laura's salon formed a brilliant centre of Roman social life and gossip; she was widely known for her accomplishments and wit.

I have also paid a long visit to Donna Laura whose big drawing-room was bathed in a golden light, a joy to the painter's eye. We talked of stuffs and colours; then of you; then she made me expound *The Prison* and its doctrines and it is a sign of her conversational ability that she made me make an effort and talk decently on the subject that dries me up at once usually. 'Madame, lisez mes livres and laissez moi déjeuner en paix,' as d'Annunzio so well expressed it. I gave her your message about the evening gown at which she laughed heartily. Then we took our harps and she began to psalm in honour of your vitality. After the first strophes I struck in no less brilliantly on the theme 'You are another', with variations up to date and a grand effect on the diminished seventh: 'You it is whom she praises that you praise for that which she praises you.' It was her turn. Naturally she passed on to the dominant: 'What an artist!' This I usually meet by bringing in Mme de Bülow, after which we work back to the Grand Duke as tonic. The tradition is then to smile at the little foibles of the high and mighty, whereupon we shake hands like two kindred bohemian souls and I am dismissed. We part on the assumption that I am completely fooled and with a pretty clear feeling, on both sides I fancy, that the assumption is a perfectly gratuitous one. This time for the sake of variety I left Frau von Bülow out and it succeeded. At least it was better fooling. I brought in immortality and she pounced on it to talk of death and Julia's book, and you again, and my too great reserve and coldness, and the value of a nature like yours for one like mine; and then we plunged into *The Prison* where we were found

[291]

sharing a crust of bread and a jug of water by some princess or other whose name as usual escaped me. And I left. It was all very nice. I cannot say that I have an impression of insincerity; certainly not as regard the pleasure she takes in you; for the rest I don't want people to be so desperately in earnest. When they are I complain of it. So I keep repeating to myself that I am quite satisfied. But somehow it does not get hold of me.

There was also Mrs Crawford, the wife of the writer Marion Crawford: 'She is very pretty in the American *fin de race* style and very musical.' Finally, a later addition, there was Ella Joshua, an extremely handsome English lady of German-Jewish extraction.

The men with whom H.B. consorted in this world of Roman society were Italian diplomats and politicians, and some of the husbands of the aforementioned ladies. He would meet them at dinner parties and invite them back. He was also on close terms with non-Italian friends, who were either temporarily residing in Rome or visiting from abroad – mainly American and English, such as John Singer Sargent and Maurice Baring, for a time attaché at the British Embassy; and, on account of his niece Anne Brewster, a Pole, Henri Frankenstein.

In the early nineties, when H.B. was still living in Palazzo Marignoli, his first cousin William Brewster had sent out from New York his pretty daughter Anne. H.B. took her under his wing until a husband could be found for her. An attractive American girl of affluent means stood a fair chance of contracting a socially advantageous marriage with a Roman prince, or at least with a *marchese* or a *conte*. The Italian aristocracy, always in need of money, regarded these affluent contestants with cynical approval. A marriageable foreign girl who was rich would be called '*una vacca da mungere*', a cow to be milked.

But Anne was not likely to fall for a title alone. Nor was she really rich. She was a sensible girl with a touch of romanticism about her. Besides, H.B. would not have encouraged a mere *mariage de convenance*. His letters on the subject are witty as well as appreciative of his protégée. In referring to her looks he wrote to Ethel: 'I have two cousins (one a daughter to a first cousin, the other more remote) who compare favourably with the prettiest maidens in America. Be they my bearers, rampant on azure.'

[292]

Anne had no shortage of smart suitors. She regarded them warily and, no doubt prompted by H.B., suspected their cynical scheming. But she was the girl of the season, presented to the Queen of Italy and guest at a succession of dinner parties (some given by H.B.) – with the Colonnas, Ruspolis, the mayor of Rome, Prince Borghese, the Duke and Duchess of Galese, Count Primoli, and politicians and diplomats galore. The *New York Herald* reported: 'Miss Anne Brewster's little blue frock was much admired.'

As the season progressed, three suitors emerged as front runners. One of these was the Duke of Colalto. Anne did not much like him; nor for that matter did H.B., who discussed him in a letter to his daughter Clotilde: 'The Cross of Malta he bears is of no avail, since this wretched man – who in any case has no money – looks like a little teacher in calligraphy and moreover is not in the least in love with her.'

The other two suitors were a Greek diplomat, Caratheodori, and Henri Frankenstein. Both had made their declarations of love and threatened suicide. H.B. was rather worried that the Greek might be chosen, to judge from a letter to Ethel in February 1894:

> Her social tact is wonderful. We exchange services. She teaches me how to deal cards (I mean visiting cards) and I help her to put her ideas in order. Notwithstanding which combination of talents she is going to make a fool of herself for a played out, penniless Greek who goes in for the sulphurous style of passion and makes her teeth chatter. She sees her folly – yet the genius of the species clamoureth.

Apparently the Greek diplomat was particularly unhinged as the result of his passion, as H.B. wrote to Clotilde, adding:

> He spends his time sharpening his cutlass on the soles of his patent leather shoes and is determined to kill everybody including himself. He still has a few teeth – for the time being. Soon, however, he will have a complete denture. But he is a diplomatist, a cultivated and clever man, and Anne takes him fairly seriously. Frankenstein, on the other hand, is young, nice-looking and rich, but not a diplomatist. Also in his case it would be a *mariage de raison*, for Anne is not really in love with him.

[293]

Frankenstein turned out to be not as rich as expected. His Polish background was said to be obscure and the title of 'count' a little suspect. There was a suggestion it had been bought from the Vatican. His sister was married to Count Soderini, a sort of lay *éminence grise* at the Vatican with considerable influence in the Curia. But Frankenstein was a handsome young man and perhaps Anne was in love with him after all, for a fortnight later, early in 1895, they were engaged. In another letter to his daughter, informing her of the engagement, H.B. wrote:

Have you ever seen him? I like him and am delighted that it was not Caratheodori, the Greek diplomatist. Frankenstein is tall, slim, dark, young (28), the crown of his head is well supplied with hair, his teeth are small and shiny like those of a little dog, in fact he is fairly good-looking, an excellent horseman, brave, distinguished – *genre salon* – not stupid, loyal, disinterested, a great hunter and somewhat of an explorer in Africa, and finally very much in love. So it is not too bad, it seems to me. But he is not rich, more or less the same as Anne, and they will have to live mainly on the strength of their social prestige. He will revert to the diplomatic service to make her happy. I was so afraid it might have been the Greek that I accept the Pole with open arms.

They were married in New York that same year and returned to settle in Rome, where they remained on close terms of friendship with H.B. Their daughter married Prince Barberini.

From 1897 onwards we find Sargent increasingly prominent amongst H.B.'s male friends. They saw each other regularly, both in London and in Rome. Referring to the painter's arrival in Rome in February 1897, H.B. wrote to Ethel:

Watts bores me to death – Sargent is coming here! I had a letter from him dated Palermo the 6th announcing his arrival in about a week. A very agreeable surprise. His obejct is to see the Borgia apartment in the Vatican, decorated by Pinturicchio; wrinkles I suppose for the Boston library.

In the same letter he describes an encounter with Paderewski:

I wish you had been here this week. Paderewski gave two splendid concerts (except a Polish fantasia of his own which I thought

[294]

atrocious) and played at Mme de Viti's where I dined with him and exchanged a few words with him across our common neighbour (Mme Pasolini); – enough to see that he is very wide awake, of ready wit, and apparently well read or at least 'in his bearings' – *orienté* as Lady P. would say, knowing which way north lies, which is rare. I forget if you knew him personally but I think so, He reminds me much of Hildebrand in former days.

A week later he wrote again:

Sargent is here; very nice and friendly. His first enquiry was about you. He finds your medallion by Thornycroft bad, I am sorry to say; and my portrait by Raussonet good; the apartment charming. This morning we visited together, under the escort and thanks to the protection of Soderini, the Borgia apartments at the Vatican which are not yet open to the public. . . Sargent who wanted to see them in view of his Boston library work was in rapture over them.

To Rod he wrote on 27 March 1897:

My sister and niece are here, and Miss Smyth and one of her sisters as well as her chosen brother-in-law. Sargent has just left and I am waiting for Henry James. The weather is lovely and it seems to me one doesn't get off one's bicycle but for eating and sleeping.

In England six months later H.B. wrote to Ethel again about Sargent:

Sargent asked me to dine with him Sunday evening at his club, the Reform, which I did after getting back from Eastbourne. He was much interested by the account of your Alpine feats; he has never been above 11,000 feet but loves the mountains and likes it better the higher he goes; the quality of the light enchants him. We talked well, chiefly about gothic architecture and Roman Catholicism, and he is coming here on Saturday for dinner.

At the Pasolinis' in Rome there were always curious people to be met. H.B. revelled in describing them and recording amusing situations and spicy exchanges. The Volkoffs, for instance, a Russian married couple settled in Rome, are mentioned in a letter to Ethel of December 1897.

[295]

I made friends last night at Mme Pasolini's with a young Russian lady... Her name is Mme Volkoff and her father-in-law is a terror of the dogmatic, rude, ever-lecturing genius species; but her husband seems a nice quiet little fellow. I dined with Mme Volkoff once before at Palazzo Sciarra and had not spoken to her on account of her nose, which enters the room a good long time before she does. It affronted me. Karo was also there and said to me: 'Mme Volkoff is nice.' 'Maybe, but I dare not go anywhere near her.' 'I quite understand the feeling,' answers Karo; 'but you see she is very tall and I am very small; the danger does not exist for me; I pass under it.' Last night I was braver and found Karo was right. She is nice; quiet, responsive, clever and very refined... Mme Volkoff says:'In Russia it is perfectly natural to be natural.' What an unnatural state of things! And how can it ever have arisen? It reminds one of Peter the Great who when the lady next to him at dinner took his fancy, did not even go to the trouble of leaving the room with her, but enforced immediate compliance to his wishes in the presence of all the guests and sat down again and went on with his dinner, and she with hers. Nothing could have been more natural. And for that reason he was called the Great. By the by Volkoff (senior) is the man whom Stroganoff invited to come and see his collection of works of art and bric-à-brac which he is very proud of. Volkoff walked round in silence and then uttered these words: 'C'est pour vous mo-quer de moi que vous me faites venir afin de me montrer des cochonneries comme ça? Jetez tout cela par la fenêtre, mon cher.' And they were only just acquainted with one another. Peter the Great!.

D'Annunzio was much in the social spotlight at that time on ac-count of his love affair with Duse. H.B. could not stand him. Any form of pretentious self-display irritated him intensely. D'Annunzio exuded panache, the very personification of the successful writer and poet. In this connection Ethel relates the following anecdote in her introduction to the 1931 edition of *The Prison*:

I recall an exceedingly heated controversy with d'Annunzio, who had been announcing that all poets are of the royal blood – the sort of remark H.B. would not have stood even from Shakespeare, only Shakespeare of course could never have made

[296]

it. I can still hear the sarcastic inflection in his voice as, with a mocking-respectful bow, he flung open the dining-room door and said, 'Passez, Prince!' By his look and manner he contrived, courtesy notwithstanding, to make the words sound perilously like an insult – and for a moment one half expected that d'Annunzio, who was known to be temperamental to excess, might go for him; but nothing further happened.

With evident distaste H.B. refers to the poet in a letter to Ethel of February 1897:

Mme Pasolini asked if you had received d'Annunzio's photograph. I learn, from another source, that he, this Gabriele, is more magnificent than ever. He has reached a degree of splendour in his personal adornment that no one, except perhaps a negro minstrel, can vie with; and he leaves a wake behind him wherein all the perfumes of Arabia are blended. Frankenstein, from whom I heard this, proposed Clotilde as architect for the theatre at Albano, and Duse, who would like to see women occupy positions other than those of fond dalliance (how I sympathize with her!), jumped at the suggestion. But I am afraid nothing will come of it on account of the patriotic opposition of other shareholders who demand that the architect should be an Italian. Duse I believe is in Germany, or just going there, and she hopes to interest the Empress Frederick in her Albano scheme – a temple of Greek and Latin art; a Bayreuth without Wagner; *finocchi* instead of sausages and Genzano wine instead of beer. But on the stage? Well there is Gabriele and Sophocles and others no doubt. I should propose *l'Angelin Bel Verde*.

Did Sargent play you his Venetian song about the green bird? You merely mentioned that he was my only rival.

Duse's popularity and the exitement she arouse are reflected in a letter H.B. wrote not long after:

Duse plays tonight for the first time; all the seats have been secured (mine included) for the last six weeks; but the delivery of the tickets for which one's name was booked meant a day spent in furious clamouring at the office: hundreds of people waiting and admitted at the rate of one every half hour; whence hooting, rioting and window smashing – the latter performance on a small

[297]

scale I confess, the damage being restricted to one pane broken by myself. The result was success for myself and for two parties of friends whose tickets I rescued with my own; but it took me the best part of the day. The explanation of the difficulty is that all seats not claimed within a certain time would be considered forfeited and could then be sold at fancy prices. Simple, ingenious and rascally. Enough.

And again a fortnight later:

I managed to call yesterday on Mme de M. We began at once, as every conversation begins here, by discussing Duse of whom she has a very poor opinion. Her grievances are various: firstly Duse is not a lady; secondly she cannot keep quiet for a second; thirdly her voice is horrid; fourthly her movements and attitudes are so ugly that she actually recalls Maria Pasolini. Thereupon I glowed with inward rage and declared firstly that I failed to see why one should necessarily be a lady nor how that quality, pleasant enough in itself, could at all contribute to making one an interesting and gifted creature; secondly that I admitted the reproach of restlessness; thirdly that Duse's voice though sometimes disagreeable was at other moments, particularly at the important ones, very musical; and fourthly that I considered it a great compliment to say that she reminded one of Maria Pasolini, whom I admired and whose lines and movements struck me as particularly graceful. Thereupon Mme de M. looked all of a sudden twenty years younger and was all amiability. But as she did not tell me why, I did not bother about it. 'But I have actually seen Maria Pasolini sit on the floor!' – 'It does not scandalize me in the least.' – 'Oh well, tastes differ' (good-naturedly). 'Very much so' (ditto). Then we passed to d'Annunzio's new play, *La Ville Morte*, that Sarah Bernhardt is about to produce in Paris; and we both disliked it – she because it is incestuous and I because it is idiotic. She would not object to the idiocy if it were not incestuous, and if it were not idiotic I should not mind the incest; but being as it is we caught hold of it each from his own side and worried it pleasantly.

A man H.B. got to know well in Rome and liked was the British newspaper correspondent Wickham Steed, subsequently editor of

[298]

The Times for many years. He became a real friend.

> Steed seems very devoted to me and wants me to know the peole he thinks most of here – in the way of brains – the Contessa Lovatelli (sister of Sermoneta) and Sonnino, not the prince, the Jew, ex-minister of finance. He (Steed) is coming to dine with me on Thursday next and will take me afterwards to the Lovatellis. ... The day before yesterday I dined at Mrs Chanler's, meeting there again Mrs Crawshay and Countess Feo, also Frau von Arnim, sister of Mrs Story, and various other Broadwoods, Mr H. Aide, Mr Secretary Johnnie Ford (you know the one I mean?) and Sazanoff, a mystical Tartar. It was a very pretty and successful dinner. I talked chiefly to Countess Feo, my neighbour, and much about Munthe and his book. She says he wishes he could buy in all the copies and burn them, looks upon it as hysterical and sentimental etc. So I was rewarded for speaking the truth. Mr Secretary Ford was very amazing; he said rash things about women and all the ladies present 'made for him' smiling and stinging like wasps; he smarted but kept up a cheerful face and got in some very clever answers. Yet I don't like him much.

Ethel would come to Rome from time to time and stay with H.B. in the Antici Mattei flat. Naturally everybody knew she was his mistress. Many years later Mrs Chanler's daughter, who lived on Long Island, wrote to her own daughter when she was a very old lady:

> I remember H.B. well in Rome when I was about twelve. He was handsome and elegant, and Grandma has two pages about him in *Roman Spring* ... Ethel Smyth used to come and stay with him and it was one of the only times I knew Grandma to be at a loss. She discussed it with me – should she ignore the 'liaison'? She did. Perhaps that was why Cardinal Merry del Val refused her absolution!

With considerable – though not total – inaccuracy Mrs Winthrop Chanler included in *Roman Spring* a few things about H.B.:

> He had a romantic past that was never mentioned by those who knew about him. We only knew that after his German wife, the beautiful Julia von Herzogenberg [*sic*], died he spent two years

[299]

in complete seclusion. Of those he told me something in one of our long quiet talks, but he never alluded to the tragedy that led to them. He had chosen Paris as his retreat from the world and had buried himself there, avoiding all human contact by living among strangers and speaking to no one. He would not go to the same restaurant too often lest someone should recognize him from having seen him there before, and break in upon his silence. It was out of this dark night of the soul that he wrote *The Prison*, a remarkable book, written in the form of a journal or long soliloquy describing his solitary *psychomanie*, the struggle of the spirit with the powers of destruction; a *de profundis* without faith in God, but deeply felt and beautifully written. . .

George Henschel, the first conductor of the Boston Symphony Orchestra, spent a winter in Rome; he was an old frind of Brewster and often at his house. He was a most genial musician and a charming man. He and Brewster were both great chess players; they continually played a game that was carried on in their heads. In the middle of a dinner party one would signal to the other across the table and tell him his next move, then continue the conversation with his neighbour, who may hardly have noticed the interruption. They told me a game often lasted several days.

A few years later, on hearing from Mrs Chanler that she was busy 'making propaganda' in America for his books and that she was quite exhilarated at her success, H.B. wrote to Ethel (in January 1902): 'Here is a deep question: may not a man be a prophet in his own country if he was born and bred elsewhere? Strange if the only people who would listen to him were those he had walked away from!' This, however, in spite of Margaret Chanler's efforts, was not destined to occur.

H.B. had a knack in his letters of illuminating awkward situations and society gossip. The following extract is from a letter to Ethel dated 31 March 1898.

What do you think our friend Mrs Ladenburg has gone and been and done? She issued invitations for a dance at Mrs Chanler's (who has now a large apartment in via del Tritone) and only told Mrs Chanler a few hours beforehand. Says Mrs Chanler: 'Very well, you may receive them, I shall go out. I am in mourning and

[300]

it is Lent; I will have nothing to do with it.' And off she went. Lots of men came but only four ladies, two of whom were Mrs Crawshay and Lady Randolph Churchill. One of the men, Thor, a very rich American, brought a huge pâté de foie gras with him and deposited it on the drawing-room table. Mrs Ladenburg, very pale from mortification, had to do all the dancing with each of the men in turn; three bars for each. On getting home Mrs Crawshay bursts into Countess Feo's rooms and exclaims: 'I am disgraced for ever!' But this morning she was full of pity for Mrs Ladenburg and wrote to thank her – lest she should feel too unhappy. It seems Lady Randolph Churchill had expected something rather gorgeous and characteristically Roman in the way of entertainment, and was much puzzled; the pâté de foie gras particularly, on the drawing-room table, quite hypnotized her. This is gossip, but you know the people, so let it pass.

Here again is gossip redeemed by wit:

Mme Pasolini tells me there has been a little row between Vernon Lee and Kit on one side and Berenson, master of arts, on the other. V. & K. have written an article in the *Contemporary* proposing a theory to the effect that the sense of form proceeds from the lungs and not as Mrs Costello maintains, from the knee-pan. They sent the proof sheets to Berenson who professes himself outraged at the impudence, for firstly the article is rot and secondly all the ideas are his. It seems Vernon wrote back a letter much more remarkable for its vigour than for its sweetness. No one would have called it emollient; and as a matter of fact Berenson was not mollified. Things went so far that it was a question of naming an umpire who would have been no less a judge than Countess Maria herself. Fortunately this extremity was not reached; counsels of moderation on both sides prevailed and it is hoped that time will exercise its calming influence on the irritable race of quill drivers – *vatum irritabile genus* as we scholars (and what scholars!) call it.

Here he pokes fun at himself as well as at others:

I made the acquaintance of Frau Wagner at Primoli's. It was rather droll. There is a young lady here, daughter of the Bavarian minister I think, who married Roccagiovine. I was introduced to

[301]

Mme Wagner, tried to connect the name with Rome and – happy thought! – recollected the little Roccagiovine. 'There is her mother of course.' I was on the point of asking her if she had been to the races (they are a horsey set) when she said; 'We have friends in common.' I cheerfully: 'Oh I am sure of it.' She: 'The Hildebrands.' I was not expecting the Hildebrands at that moment and so I suppose I looked vague. 'The Hildebrands in Florence,' she repeated. Instantly it flashed on me that I was mistaken. 'It's not Mme Wagner; it is Mme Wagnière, the widow of the Swiss banker who failed four or five years ago and who still owes me 157 francs. I will not mention them. Tact before all things. She is a nice-looking old lady.' So I jumped on the Hildebrands. Well, we discussed their new house in Munich, their old house at San Francesco; and when she told me she had seen her friend Levi's house in the mountains I began to feel quite chummy. I knew that Mme Hildebrand used to see the Wagnières but I did not know that Levi frequented them also. Then we talked about all the little Hildebrands and carefully compared our impressions of Zusi and Lisl and Vivi. There are so many children that we felt we had a good mine to work at. It struck me again: a very nice old lady, good-looking and an agreeable manner. We came to Mme Hildebrand; says the nice old lady: 'I like her very much and I think she is a remarkable woman.' I wavered for a moment, thought it over, and then said: 'Well yes, perhaps she is; but she has no particular gift.' 'Do you think that necessary?' Slowly but sincerely, having thought of Catherine Sforza, I answered: 'No.' There our conversation ended, quite pleasantly. There were a great many people in the room, among others Duse, for whose sake I had come, so I did not attach any importance to this meeting with a friend of the Hildebrands but I said to Primoli on leaving: 'You introduced me to a very pleasant old lady. I suppose she is the widow of the bankrupt Wagnière.' 'Mais non, mon cher ami, mais non! C'est la célèbre Cosima.' A chapter for 'The Celebrities I Have Met'. Duse was putting on her cloak to leave when I was introduced. She held out her hand: 'We have friends in common.' Good gracious, I thought, there are the five Hildebrand girls coming back again! But no, it was Mme de Viti, and your favourite Mrs Green, and Primoli of course. A few words; hopes of future

[302]

meetings, and goodbye; she was leaving for Cairo the next morning.

H.B.'s letters to Ethel over this period are a glimpse of international Roman society of those days, and of H.B.'s participation in it. This is the air or 'cosmopolite mixture' he breathed which Henry James was drawn to and yet shrank from so determinedly. But this is only one side of H.B., one curve of his inclinations. He had not totally committed himself to this rather superficial way of living compared with the previous years of introspection with Julia. She had extended him to a fairly high level of intellectual exercise and spiritual inquiry. Doubtless with the swing of the pendulum, as he himself points out, there followed a mood of reaction as well as a sense of relaxation. It lasted three or four years. Most likely it was these letters that prompted Virginia Woolf, appreciative of them though she was, to tell Ethel that she got 'a little tired of the lunches and dinners and Pasolinis and Contessa this and that'. She was sure the dining out and dissipation would vanish, so she correctly read the reasons behind them. 'That's why, I expect, I don't quite come to grips with him. Rather as if he were always in evening dress – white waistcoat and so on. I can't feel the grain he is made of – can't get the full impression on the slab of my mind, as I do when I've immersed myself in letters – generally. But of course this may be the result of some pane of glass between. Too different? I want more – no, what is it – just saying things as they come into one's head. I can't catch him off his guard. But this may be because he writes so well. And that of course adds to the sparkle and the fun, and the gliding in and out and the quips and cranks which are all very pleasing to me. Yes, I'd like to read the whole series through, and yours in between. Now I get the grain of you printed on the whole of my person.'

But then Virginia knew Ethel personally as well as through her writings. By H.B. she was intrigued but somewhat mystified: he was not easy to grasp from the letters she was given to read. Probably others were withheld from her that contain passages of a more personal nature or, where Ethel's operatic work and his own co-operation in it are frequently referred to, of deeper conviction.

Ethel had succeeded, at least for the time being, in bringing out the extrovert side of H.B.'s nature which had previously been denied an

[303]

outlet. The zest with which he plunged into living more socially is eloquently expressed in his letters to her of that period. And he must have noticed with pleasure that this urbane as well as serene side of his personality was meeting with gratifying success in society.

26

The Mystification of Life

For all the fashionable predominance of the bicycle, H.B. rode out on horseback into the Campagna Romana, still open, untouched and wild, as a diversion from the social life. Then he would withdraw once more to his library for hours of work and reading. Apart from his cherished French literature, Oriental as well as Greek literature and philosophy went on playing an important part in his life. He remained on good terms with Cazalis, the Orientalist, although Rod later supplanted Cazalis as H.B.'s closest friend.

Behind the more demonstrative preoccupation of the social life the mystical mood persisted. We can see it emerge most poignantly in a letter H.B. wrote to Rod at the turn of the century:

> If I could talk to you I would say nothing but what I feel today: an immense detachment as if I were living in eternity. Evrything endures: joy, pain, mirth, sadness – I feel them and yet they affect me no more. The inn remains, the customers are the same, the inn-keeper has vanished. The establishment goes on by itself.

As he ruminates further on this theme, the old H.B. emerges, echoing his former writings in style and expression.

Apart from his letters to Ethel, which betray none of the stirrings of his innermost self, the longest and most continuous correspondence to survive from the pen of our indefatigable 'epistolarian' at this later stage of his life are some hundreds of the letters addressed to Edouard Rod, all written in French. These have been deposited with the public library of Lausanne. They reveal a mind of a somewhat different stamp; they deal more directly with literature and other intellectual subjects, while retaining a very personal flavour – warm, affectionate and never lacking in humour and wit. At the same time they show that the dreamer, the meditative and mystical H.B., is not a final casualty to Ethel's boisterous epistolary salvoes.

He discussed the publication of *Via Lucis* thoroughly wiith Rod.

[305]

The Swiss writer appended a preface giving an outline of Julia's personality. When the book appeared H.B. wrote thanking him for enlisting the interest of newspapers and literary reviews, adding:

I don't know whether in Paris the volume has fallen into the hands of some predestined readers, but it has found them here. It has had an extraordinary success, I mean to say about twenty people really love it and the author through it. And I know the preface helps a great deal. The readers, female readers especially, are mainly cosmopolitan: English, American, Italian, Polish, German, a Greek lady – the very one Rossetti and Burne-Jones painted and whose husband went hunting with Emerson; there is an Italian lady who has been painted by Lembach and whose husband used to work with Cavour. Rightly does Bourget say: 'Here is Cosmopolis,' and indeed I like Rome so much that I wish to return for the month of May, but after Weimar. Well we shall see. London, Paris and Geneva.

He roamed further afield than usual that autumn of 1898, as far as Killarney in the south west of Ireland where he enjoyed stayng with the Killarneys themselves, and then to the north of Scotland where he spent some time before turning southward to London again and back to Rome. From now on, for the rest of his life, he adopted the pattern of spending the winter months and early spring in Rome, the summer in England, and the intermediate months in various other parts of Europe, visiting relatives and friends. He was not primarily a visual man, so that when he visited places, even new to him, his letters remain by and large undescriptive of landscape and architecture, perhaps because he felt that his friends were in any case well acquainted with them. He rarely bothers to describe what he sees, though when he does so, usually in a few words, the picture is vivid. For instance, he writes of Paestum in a letter to Ethel of 1893:

It was a splendid rush through sunlight to Sorrento and Amalfi and Paestum. Paestum hurts; it is the only place I know that would move one to tears. A desolate fever-haunted plain with wild shaggy bullocks roaming about in the brush; then lovely mountains; on the other side the sea asleep naked; and near the shore the temple of Neptune, the oldest thing in the world – impressionally at least; older than Greece and Assyria, as old as

[306]

the oldest Egypt; so solemn and serene and sweet that one burns with shame; what have I done with my life? It hurts and consoles one at once.

H.B.'s letters to Rod throughout this period are full of references to his friend's books, with comments and criticisms as well as allusions to his own work and state of mind, often containing introspective passages expressed with the aid of poetic metaphors and similes. On one occasion he says he finds it easier to concentrate, meditate and work in the quiet of the English countryside than in Rome where he knows too many people. Rome was becoming noisy. He was enchanted with Venice on revisiting it in 1904 and almost tempted to settle there – you were not pestered, he wrote to Rod, by 'tramways, omnibuses, motorcars, honking bicycles and advertisements'. But, he conceded, he loved Rome too much to leave it.

Of course Rome was still lovely, although the period of *sventramenti* had set in, the environmental kick in the guts. That the beautiful Villa Ludovisi and its grounds should have been swept away to make room for Via Veneto and similar developments is understandable. It was necessary for an expanding city. Sadder and quite unnecessary were the monstrous monuments and edifices of the period, such as the gigantic memorial of Victor Emanuel and the Palace of Justice. Nevertheless Rome retained its unique atmosphere even though excavations and the tidying up of the Forum were rapidly encroaching upon the world of Piranese. The Campagna Romana, that astounding wilderness of nature and ancient ruins that used to surround the city, was as yet intact.

H.B. took an understanding interest in the problems, emotions and experiences of his friends. It was primarily about them that he would write in his more serious moods. He was a master at getting straight to the spiritual core of a sad event. When Rod, for instance, lost someone dear in 1906, H.B. wrote to him as follows:

Apart from cases of physical ailment it seems to me that chosen natures are ennobled by grief that is really deep; the others are either crushed or bewildered. The divine essence of things emerges at such times. You know the ancients used to figure to themselves the stars as little holes in the canopy of the sky through which they could perceive the fire of the universe. The things imprisoned in us by intense grief find an exit through

[307]

similar openings and thereby have the same effect on us as that of great joys. For it is the universe revealing itself to our minute world. And it is at such times that the things that really matter come into focus. The rest is of no consequence. You arrange it as best you can according to your temperament in order to dispose of daily affairs.

Here is evidence again that in spite of not being a theist H.B. was at heart deeply religious.

With the passing of the 'Gay Nineties' a touch of melancholy began to tinge H.B.'s outlook. Christopher, after failing to pass his Cambridge tripos in spite of his being a brilliant linguist, went off to the Argentine as a cowboy in the pampas, but spent most of his time courting an attractive young lady at the Italian Embassy in Buenos Aires. A year later he came back to Europe and married in 1903 Lisl, Hildebrand's most beautiful daughter, whom H.B. was in the habit of calling 'Mona Lisa'. Less than a year later Clotilde married Percy Feilding, a young architect colleague, and settled down to a married country life at Farnborough. These developments did not affect the pattern of H.B.'s life: his children, after all, had been grown up and more or less independent for some time. The framework of his way of living remained unchanged – dinner parties, invitations, guests, outings in the neighbouring countryside during the winter months in Rome, followed by the same pattern of moving about elsewhere later in the season, often in connection with Ethel's operatic activities in which he was directly involved. But now there was greater con-centration again on his own work, a turning inward, a cultivation of detachment under the surface of sociability, a coming to terms with life – in fact a more faithful implementation of his true philosophy.

At the same time one cannot say that there was too much harden-ing of the social arteries as he passed into his fifties. On the contrary, new friends were made; Maurice Baring, for example, became very close on being posted to Rome as an embassy attaché in 1902. As a very young man he had met H.B. in England some ten years before and had already been impressed by his personality. In his memoirs he looked back to that encounter:

His appearance was striking; he had a fair beard and the eyes of a seer; *à contre jour*, someone said he looked like a Rembrandt. His manner was suave, and at first one thought him inscrutable –

[308]

a person whom one could never know, surrounded as it were by a hedge of roses. When I got to know him better I found the whole secret of Brewster was in this: he was absolutely himself; he said quite simply and calmly what he thought. Nothing leads to such misunderstandings as the truth. Bismarck said the best of all diplomatic policies was to tell the truth, as nobody believed you. But even when you are not prepared to disbelieve, and suspect no diplomatic wiles, the truth is sometimes disconcerting when calmly expressed. I recollect my first conversation with Mr Brewster. We talked of books, and I was brimful of enthusiasm for Swinburne and Rossetti. 'No,' said Brewster, 'I don't care for Rossetti; it all seems to me like an elaborate exercise. I prefer Paul Verlaine.' I knew he was not being paradoxical, but I thought he was lacking in catholicity, narrow in comprehension. Why couldn't one like both? I thought he was being Olympian and damping. When I got to know him well, I understood how completely sincere he had been, and how utterly unpretentious; how impossible it was for him to pretend he liked something he did not like, and how true it was that Rossetti seemed to him as elaborate as an exercise.[1]

In a letter to Ethel shortly after his arrival in Rome and dated 30 June 1902 Baring wrote elatedly of his new experiences:

Today I had luncheon with H.B., the guests being Rodd, Mme Pasolini, Bagot (right spelling? I mean the nets and fishes), and another man. I think H.B.'s apartment is perfection... the double staircase! After luncheon I drove with Mary Crawshay along the Appian Way. Oh, the Campagna! It was a grey day with a slight silver fringe on the tops of the blue hills, and in the desolate majesty of the plain a boy, dressed like a real shepherd, played on a pipe like Kurvenal in *Tristan*. I shall never forget it. . .

Maurice Baring's description of Rome and his life there before breaking away from the Diplomatic Service and embarking on his literary career is interesting because he moved amongst more or less the same people as H.B. About the Pasolinis, H.B.'s closest Italian friends in Rome, so frequently referred to in his letters, Baring writes in *The Puppet Show of Memory*:

Among the Italians, my greatest friends were Count and Countess

[309]

Pasolini, who had charming rooms in the Palazzo Sciarra. Count Pasolini was an historian and the author of a large, serious and valuable work on Catherine Sforza. His ways and his conversation reminded me of Hamlet. His dignity and high courtesy were mixed with an almost impish humour, and sometimes he would glide from the room like a ghost, or suddenly expose some curious train of thought quite unconnected with the conversation that was going on around him. Sometimes he would be unconscious of the numerous guests in the room, which was nearly always full of visitors from every part of Europe; or he would startle a stranger by asking him what he thought of Countess Pasolini, or, if the conversation bored him, hum to himself a snatch of Dante. Sometimes he would be as naughty as a child, especially if he knew he was expected to be especially good, or he would say a bitingly ironical thing masked with deference.

There follow a few examples of Pasolini's unpredictable behaviour, one of these being an account of his reaction on meeting Anatole France. Baring says Pasolini reminded him of some of the French novelist's characters and adds that those who knew him would often say 'If only he could meet Anatole France and if only Anatole France could meet him!' When the meeting did come off at a dinner party the result was not entirely a success. Pasolini knew what was expected of him and, looking at Anatole France, who was sitting on the other side of the table, said to his neighbiour in an audible whisper, 'Qui est ce monsieur un peu chauve?'

H.B. admired Anatole France's works but when he got to know the author personally, he recoiled from him. Rodin's character, too, seemed to H.B. dwarfed by his artistry: on making Rodin's acquaintance he came to the conclusion that he was not an interesting man though 'certainly one of the greatest living artists'.

After the Pasolinis, in the same chapter of Baring's memoirs, there comes an account of H.B. several pages long – his manner, his mind, his taste and his work. A couple of passages are worth quoting:

> At Rome I got to know Brewster very well. He lived in the Palazzo Antici Mattei, and he often gave luncheon and dinner parties. I often dined with him when he was alone. His external attitude was one of unruffled serenity and Olympian impartiality, but I often used to tell him that his mask of suavity

[310]

concealed opinions and prejudices as absolute as those of Dr Johnson. His opinions and tastes were his own, and his appreciations were as sensitive as his expression of them original. He had the serene, rarefied, smiling melancholy of great wisdom, without a trace of bitterness. He took people as they were, and had no wish to change or reform them. He was catholic in his taste for people, and liked those with whom he could be comfortable. He was appreciative of the work of others when he liked it, a discriminating and inspirited critic. While I was in Rome he published his French book, *L'âme païenne*; but his most characteristic book is probably *The Prison*. Some day I feel sure that book will be republished, and perhaps find many readers; it is like a quiet tower hidden in the side street of a loud city, that few people hear of, and many pass by without noticing, but which those who visit find to be a place of peace, haunted by echoes, and looking out on sights that have a quality and price above and beyond those of the market place. . .

Few people had heard of his books. He once told me that his work lay in a narrow and arid groove, that of metaphysical speculation, in which necessarily but few people were interested. He talked of it as a narrow strip of stiff ploughland on which just a few people laboured. He said he would have far preferred a different soil, and a more fruitful form of labour, but that happened to be the only work he could do, the soil which had been allotted to him. He was Latin by taste, tradition and education; a lover of Rabelais, Montaigne, Ronsard and Villon, but seventeenth-century French classics bored him.

A word of caution is here called for, in order to understand, in its proper proportion, H.B.'s 'Latinity', if I may use the term. What Baring says is true up to a point. H.B. loved paradoxes and liked to over-emphasize his Latinity when consorting with non-Latin friends (who outnumbered his Latin ones). It was almost a pose, though not quite; he was in love with France and everything French, the love being that of an outsider – the 'Gallo-American', as Henry James would call him. But it should be borne in mind that however Gallic his education had been and no matter how cosmopolitan he grew up, there was an indelible Anglo-Saxon element in him of basic importance, which derived from his parents. He went on being, and in a

[311]

certain sense feeling, American until the end; he was married to a German and then closely joined to a woman extremely English. He never became integrated in either France or Italy and throughout his life he continued to live as a foreigner in whatever country he resided, remaining in fact an expatriate, though once or twice removed as it were. He was at home in the cultural world of Europe of those days, in the upper echelons of society. He brought up his children neither as French nationals nor as Italians, but as cosmopolitans like himself, Anglo-Saxon culture slightly prevailing in their education, with French following close, then German and Italian.

Maurice Baring goes on to say:

> He disputed the idea that French was necessarily a language which necessitated perspicacity of expression and clearness of thought. He thought that in the hands of a poet like Verlaine the French language could achieve all possible effects of vagueness, of shades of feeling, of overtones in ideas and in expression. He admired Dante, Goethe, Byron and Keats, but not Milton, Wordsworth or Shelley. He disliked Wagner's music intensely, which had, he said, the same effect on him as the noise of a finger rubbed round the edge of a piece of glass, and he said that he could gauge from the intensity of his dislike how keen the enjoyment of those who did enjoy it must be.

Though virtually a generation younger, Maurice Baring had much in common with H.B. He was, like him, a brilliant linguist and culturally almost as cosmopolitan. They both relished the international feel of Rome. Baring wrote for H.B. the following poem, probably after having read to him his 'Tristram and Iseult'.

> I too have travelled in the unknown land
> And anchored by the unfrequented shore;
> I too have heard the Stygian waters roar
> And seen the foam of Lethe kiss the sand.
> I too have trampled the enchanted grass
> And seen the phantom hunters gallop by
> And heard the ghostly bugle and the sigh
> Of banished Gods that in the woodways pass.
> And as a traveller brings his spoil to him
> More richly graced in might and bravery,

So do I give to you these records dim
Of bright adventures in the realms forlorn:
To you who heard the blast of Roland's horn
And saw Iseult set sail for Brittany.

On 12 November 1902 H.B. wrote to Ethel:

Baring came last night to dinner and afterwards read me 'Tristram and Iseult'. The best word I can find for it is ... delightful. Attention is riveted at once; you can neither say when or how it happened, but you are floating quietly in blue space, and you cannot even hear the flapping of the wings.It doesn't seem to matter much what happens; you are as willing to go to the right as to the left when you glide through the air with such exquisite taste and the sky is a haze of gold. . .

In the early years of the present century Baring, like H.B., was engaged in writing plays or 'poetic dramas' as he called them. Whether this form of drama, detached from the theatre for which it is unsuited, can retain any enduring quality is a moot point. Both men were fascinated, however, by the exercise itself, as well as mutually appreciative. Baring was to become prolific and in other fields of literary output fairly successful. But at that time, when he left Rome at the end of 1903 to work for a while at the Foreign Office in London, he kept up a correspondence with H.B. dealing with the 'poetic dramas' he was then writing, asking for advice and expressing gratification at H.B.'s encouraging criticism.

I thank you for your long, delightful and most comforting letter. Your views about literary production are my views. But it is nice to hear them confirmed in so delightful a manner. I believe one only asks for advice when one knows the advice will tell one how to do what wants to do. On the other hand one may sometimes be making *fausse route* and then one's friends can sometimes lead one back to the straight path.

For instance you would surely agree with those of Vernon Lee's friends who urge her to write fiction in preference to psychology. In any case I like writing plays and mean to go on until I dislike it.

Sometimes he did have doubts. He would ask H.B., 'Am I to go on writing plays?' And H.B. would write back in terms such as these:

[313]

The demon of dumbness has been sitting on my shoulders, but I was grateful for 'Mahasena' and the lyrics, all of which I like and two of which delight me – 'Prayer' and 'Tristram'.

The play is beautiful. If you call it 'dramatic poem' instead of 'drama' it might do away with some objections that foolish people make. Definition seems to be the only intellectual amusement of the millions. Present them with a work of art; it is too fatiguing for them to find out if they enjoy it or not, so they rush to the easier pleasure of classification. 'Does this play correspond to my notion of drama?' 'Does this building fully realize my conception of a church?' 'If not, poet or architect may have blundered,' etc. Names! Names! . . .

Call your plays as you choose; I hope you will write many more of them. I see them as frescoes, and there are dozens of skilful writers who can turn a neat sonnet to one who can fling a great vision on the wall.

Here is Baring in return:

I have been spreading *The Prison* far and wide. Poor Balfour, who wanted to write an article on your books and was so carried away by *The Prison* that he read it three times running, has been very ill; in fact for a fortnight he was raving mad but they say he will get well.

Ethel herself, a keen admirer of Baring's literary gifts, had her doubts about his output in the field of drama. In the book she wrote on him after his death she made this relevant remark:

I am uncertain as to whether the author had or had not the question of their actability in view. At the time he was writing and planning a good many of them he was in intimate touch with Henry Brewster, a man of finest literary instinct but whose nature was not dramatic, and who in the case of these particular dramas would have probably have considered stage-effect a negligible matter.

I confess I feel differently . . . more like Rogers the poet, who, when told by the late Lord Lytton that Browning had written another play, asked if it was a *reading* play or an *acting* play, and when informed it was a reading play said: 'Then I shan't read it.'

But what of H.B.'s own literary work during these Roman years? *The Statuette and the Background* came out in 1896; it had been completed before he finished a play, 'Astray', that same year. This was his last piece of writing in English. Henry James praised it but felt that although the subject was good and the play well written it was unsuited for the stage unless most of the handling was revised. By then H.B. was moving in another direction and so lost interest in the play, which remained unpublished. He returned to philosophy for a while yet felt the need for a new medium. He also chose French as the language he would write in, perhaps, as Martin Halpern suggested in his dissertation, in the light of Vernon Lee's criticism that his style – or rather his method of disquisition – was unsuited to the English language, his conducting of thought un-English. In fact Vernon Lee was quite mistaken, for although the texts of his English books do contain an occasional Gallicism it was their style that particularly appealed to their admirers. The change to French was more likely in response to an urge to try his hand in a language which was as much his own as English and with which his education had been so closely associated. But first he was busy helping Ethel with a text of her one-act opera *Fantasio*, adapted from a play by Musset. Then, towards the end of 1898, he started work in earnest on a philosophical book similar in form to *The Background*, in other words a meditative essay (though much longer and in French) which was published three years later by Le Mercure de France. He proceeded slowly and laboriously, revising and polishing the text repeatedly. When the book eventually came out in France it sold, unlike his former writings, remarkably well and was reissued in France as well as translated into Italian and published in Italy. *L'âme païenne* is brilliantly written, crystal clear, recapitulating views for the most part already expressed in his former works but stressing, perhaps even more emphatically than before, his belief in detachment, disengagement from the ego and acceptance of the world such as it is, which can never be changed, in a spirit of cheerful resignation.

Throughout the book there prevails a throroughgoing acceptance of Eastern attitudes in a Western garb, of Lao Tse in particular, with a curious stand taken against bourgeois intellectualism – which reminds one of certain tendencies of our own times. But on the whole the book lacks the depth and poignancy of either *Theories of Anarchy and Law* or *The Prison*, which were written when his

[315]

beliefs were being put to the test by harrowing experiences in his life. Instead there emanates from the introductory invocation of *L'âme païenne* a challenge to the reader, kept up throughout the book, urging him to join the author in his brand of wisdom – detachment strangely coupled with anarchism – against the *bien pensants*:

> Muse de l'Amnésie, fais-moi tout oublier, toute leur philosophie, toute leur morale, toute leur politique!
> Muse de l'Inconséquence, protège moi contre mes vieux péchés; brouille ma clarté, confonde ma logique, arrache moi à tout système; pousse moi à me contredire afin que je suis simple et vrai!
> Soeurs divines et chéries, maîtresses des deux crépuscules, épaississez mon ignorance, donnez des ailes à ma légèreté!

Vernon Lee was enraged by what she regarded as the book's flippancy.
In spite of his principles it is amusing to note that H.B. was capable of passionate reaction when provoked where he happened to feel most sensitive. Such was his response, for instance, to a reproof from Ethel in 1901:

> I will accept and be grateful for any criticism tendered affectionately, but a very sensitive skin, and a French education, and all my childhood during which I was ruled with a feather and thought a mere look of disapproval a punishment hardly to be borne, and twenty-three years of married life with a woman of the gentlest possible manners, however stern the character may have been – have made me unfit to bear in a friendly spirit the rough kind of criticism which I believe is usual in English families. It does not affect me in the way it is meant; it affects me as an act of ferocious hostility and an assertion of arrogant superiority. It affects me as a blow straight in the face and mars my perception of the striker. I have not been trained nor have I trained myself to hit back and shake hands – a schooling the value of which I recognize. I belong to another school, Continental I suppose, old-fashioned perhaps, and possibly more artificial than the English one: 'Never quarrel. Drop discussion the moment the personal element is perceptible. Don't make personal remarks. Neither praise nor citicize people to their faces. Convey your praise and suggest your criticisms. The greater the affection, the more delicate the touch. Take your friends as they are:

[316]

forget their faults and remember their virtues. Never try to play first fiddle nor refuse to do so when requested.' Such are its precepts. They have their advantages; they are half way on the road to the *sourire japonais*. And they have a serious drawback, that of extending the domain of inner solitude. . . I shall never learn your trick; never be able to hit back because I could only hit with the sword.

In 1902 began the close cooperation between H.B. and Ethel which led to *The Wreckers*, perhaps her best opera. In the last instalment of her memoirs, *What Happened Next*, she gives a full account of how she came upon the subject and handed it over to H.B. for him to work it into a libretto. It was based on the story of the wild Methodist inhabitants of the Cornish coast, at the end of the eighteenth century, systematically plundering the ships that were frequently wrecked on their rocks and murdering the surviving passengers and crew. The libretto, with an interwoven love drama, was written in French by H.B., but the opera, which turned out to be Ethel's most successful work, was performed only in English and German with translated texts, never in French.

The French original has a strange haunting beauty which, as Ethel pointed out, could never be adequately rendered in translation. H.B. succeeded in infusing the subject matter with a high degree of dramatic intensity, contrasting with the lyrical passages and disclosing a surprising aptitude for drama and dramatic stage effects – which Baring evidently lacked. *The Wreckers* simply proves that a man can achieve unruffled serenity in his way of living, behaving and thinking and yet successfully conceive of dramatic situations which he can convincingly express in writing. This truth is brought out most explicitly in Martin Halpern's lucid analysis of H.B.'s libretto.

As regards the music, we find Ethel at her best in this opera, which during her lifetime was performed several times under the direction of Thomas Beecham and John Barbirolli. With her usual vitality she relates in her memoirs the initial vicissitudes of *The Wreckers*, its first performance and success at Leipzig and the subsequent fiasco at Prague on account of the disgracefully bad production – notwithstanding H.B.'s subvention of £1,000 which in those days was no inconsiderable sum. She tells about her feelings with the famous conductor Nikisch, with Mahler in Vienna and finally with Bruno

[317]

Walther, then a very young man, who was enthusiastic about the opera and years later was to conduct it himself at the Munich 1914-15 season.

Since Ethel's death in 1944 *The Wreckers*, though always well received, has only occasionally been revived, notably in America at a Newport Festival concert on 6 August 1972 and more recently in England at Warwick. On the former occasion the *New York Times* reviewer praised its originality in spite of its Wagnerian influence. Writing about the Warwick performance on 20 February 1983, the *Observer* showed much appreciation for the dramatic quality of the libretto and the inventiveness of the music, drawing attention also to the specifically English elements. It is curious that Ethel, who had been such a friend and supporter of the Brahms faction for so many years, should have been influenced by Wagner.

After *The Wreckers* H.B. applied his mind during the last years of his life to writing a drama of his own in Alexandrine couplets – *Buondelmonte*. The subject was based on the feud between the two dominating families of Florence in the thirteenth century – the Donati and the Uberti. The play is not without merit, containing poetic as well as dramatic passages which are excellent, but marred by unwieldy soliloquies, lengthy speeches and whole sections completely lacking in stagecraft, as well as defects in the text itself. Most of the defects can be attributed to the author's untimely death, for the text amounts to no more than a first draft, which was published posthumously by H.B.'s son. So it is not easy to guess what the play in its finished form might have been – certainly far better, for H.B. was in the habit of carefully revising his texts.

At the end of the volume which Christopher had published in France by Perrin & Co. in 1911 and which also contains *Buondelmonte* are to be found a number of poems in French which H.B. had written during his last years. They have a melancholy refinement, catching the atmosphere of Rome in those days as well as H.B.'s own philosophy of life. They are written in a mood of inner loneliness, the 'extending domain of solitude' which dominated his later years, echoing the past. It has been said that they categorize H.B. as a decadent romantic, a *fin de siècle* aesthete. This judgement is totally wrong, for H.B. was basically influenced by Oriental thought. His acceptance of life such as it is, without commitment to any particular cause, his participation and yet detachment, his emphasis on human values as the only things that really matter – these are qualities that have nothing to do with decadent romanticism or aestheticism. Kindness, gentleness, warmth of heart, generosity and helpfulness in his dealings with people were not characteristics that he lacked, as his correspondence testifies, despite his apparent reserve, aloofness and critical irony. Toleration and understanding – time and again he would repeat to himself and to his friends 'Understand, understand' – were fundamental to his character. This did not prevent him from holding very definite opinions on individual people and life generally. In the main he was naturally a product of his times, even though some of his views were well ahead of them. But he remains an interesting personality.

As regards his literary and philosophical work, *Theories of Anarchy and Law* and *The Prison* stand out as his masterpieces, on whose quality alone he should be remembered and better known. His remaining output falls short of that excellenec – save his letters, if letter-writing can be regarded as a literary genre. Undoubtedly he had a supreme gift for it – it is not for nothing that Henry James described him as 'the last of the great epistolarians'.

Two more extracts from his letters may be quoted which shed light on his mind:

> Dear one, I come to ask you for a cup of tea. I mean that I have nothing but very small talk close to the surface, and there seems to be no immediate occasion for me to strike an artesian well and squirt floods of eloquence to Scotland. The little people in my brain seem to be chattering newspaper gossip, when they are not playing Hamlet in the graveyard, which they do very decently I am bound to say; neither callously nor sentimentally; but why repeat their meditation? They are indoor voices and it is a German sin to let them go forth without artfully intertwining them. I wonder if it is also a sin to let the little newspaper imps chatter out loud? Perhaps they ought to be drilled to cunning chorus work. But I shall have time to see about that next time I live; provided of course I am promoted and reach the exalted level at which no one relaxes from perfection. Possibly the worst sin of all. Meanwhile I shall put my elbows on the table – sometimes – and smoke pipes and laugh at the burlesque – all things which Henry James for instance would never stoop to do. He has been promoted.

[319]

Just about ten years later, on seeing Henry James perhaps for the last time, H.B. wrote:

Henry James dined with me last night. I had an impression of great goodness and kindness, almost tenderness; of an immense *bienveillance* and yet of fastidious discrimination; something delicate and strong morally. But the fumbling for words is worse than ever. You know how patient I am; well sometimes I could have screamed. Surely this must be nervousness; it is not possible that he should talk thus with the people that he sees daily. And he has the puffy vegetarian look; and the spring, the flash of steel, has gone. You must pay a heavy price to be so good... He enquired with interest, real interest, about you and *The Wreckers*; wanted to understand everything, vibrated, responded. All joys, sorrows, hopes, trials and strivings find a prompt and delicate echo in him. He is going to send me his book on America. Oh how I wish I could be as good as that! without salivating, without vegetables.

Late in 1907 H.B.'s health begain to fail. On 13 June 1908 he died of cancer of the liver aged fifty-seven, bemoaned by a few male friends and mourned by a host of ladies, '*les veuves Brewster*', as they were then to be called.

Ethel describes the end of H.B.'s life in detail, how he came to England in May, a dying man and yet his usual self, up and about, talking to his friends as if nothing were the matter with him but knowing that he had come to the end of his days. 'Life is a magnificent adventure,' he would say, 'death probably a still more enthralling one.' He died at his daughter's house in the country, whispering to Christopher 'C'est fini! Tant pis.' His old friend Sargent had come to draw him on his deathbed.

He ws cremated and his ashes were taken to Rome by his son. They were interred in the Protestant Cemetery near the pyramidal tomb of Cestius which Shelley, who is buried there as well as Keats, described in a letter to Thomas Love Peacock as 'the most beautiful and solemn cemetery' he had ever beheld.

A few weeks after H.B.'s death Henry James wrote to a friend:

I am haunted by the tragic image of our fine inscrutable Brewster, who hadn't really half done with the exquisite

[320]

mystification he somehow made of life – or perhaps received from it! I had seen him little of late years, but feel him such a strange handsome questioning cosmopolite ghost.

Nevertheless H.B. probably died at the right time; and so did Henry James not many years later. The destructiveness and intense nationalism spawned by the First World War would have made him a very unhappy man in spite of his spirit of detachment. It was as a cosmopolitan in a positive sense of the term that Henry James looked back to him with nostalgic sympathy in his *Notes of a Son and Brother*, referring to his own early experiences of Rome:

I recall how in the air of Rome at a time ever so long subsequent, a countryman now no more, who had spent most of his life in Italy and who remains for me, with his accomplishments, his distinction, his extraordinary play of mind and his early too tragic death, the clearest case of 'cosmopolitan culture' I was to have known.

For Ethel there followed a period of empty bewilderment before she plunged into active feminism, becoming a prominent suffragette and thereafter resuming her career as a composer. The last volume of her memoirs, though written more than thirty years later, ends with the death of her friend and lover. It is a pity she did not continue her autobiography, except for intermittent flashbacks, to cover the subsequent thirty-eight years of her tireless life. As an autobiographer this self-centred, socially exuberant woman, so gifted in many ways, wrote brilliantly well.

She concluded her memoirs with a quotation on the subject of death from her rival's book, *Via Lucis*, translated by Maurice Baring, which reflects not only Julia's soul but also H.B.'s mind:

Who is he who comes with clamour through the deserted streets, and grants the quiet of which night was chary? Who is this toper who comes singing and shouting? His hoarse voice is sweeter than the lute, and the thrill which he gives is better than love.

Who is this vagabond who prowls about lamenting, who batters at the doors like a bailiff and a lover, like a tormentor and a deliverer?

Who is this invader who seems to triumph in his agony, and sets us free from everything, even from liberty?

[321]

APPENDIX

Germany in the 1860s

Excerpt from a letter, translated from the French, written from Dresden in December 1867 by H.B., aged seventeen, to his friend Georges du Buisson in Paris.

In one of your letters you ask me for particulars regarding Germany. Here are some that might interest you.

1 The working classes are on the whole content, hard-working and peaceful, even though quite busy with politics. The most striking aspect is the marked division between 'masters' and 'companions'. The companions have to tour the country, stopping in the principal towns, in order to get employed for work by the best-known masters before becoming *Meister* themselves. These trips are undertaken on foot. They start in groups of varying size, each with his walking stick, smoking his pipe and begging on the way to be able to pay for his mug of beer and kipper in the evening. This sort of begging is not called 'begging' but 'fencing' (*fechten*) and everybody feels obliged to lend the companions (*Gefährten*) a hand. These trips in the normal run of things are often extremely merry. Going along they sing in chorus songs for which the Germans are rightly famous. But sometimes the story could not be more tragic. It has to be said that most murders are the result of the travellers' privations.

2 The middle classes in Germany are the most bourgeois one can possibly imagine. The common type is the *Philister* or *Spitzbürgher*. He is the typical routine man, narrow-minded, set in his habits, who cannot be made to go out of his way for anything. This, almost by definition, is the man who on Christmas Day every year gathers his children round the traditional tree. He is the man who on Sundays goes out, not to mad Asnières or Meudon parties, but for a quiet walk in Grossen Garten if he is in Dresden, or in Thier Garten if he is in Berlin. You will see him with his wife on his arm, a Bremen cigar in his mouth, walking at a measured pace in the middle of the path. Or again you will find him in the evening at the so-called

[323]

Restauration (what a profanation of the French language!), sitting in front of a large mug of beer, the eternal Bremen cigar in his mouth and the eternal wife clutching his arm. The true *Philister* has three subjects of conversation – himself, his wife and his neighbour. If he has a fourth, it will consist of commonplaces on morality and philosophy. But besides this type of man there is another almost as common. He is the intellectual bourgeois who goes to the theatre and to concerts and has a subscription to the Kadderadatah (the Charivari of Berlin). He too frequents the *Restauration* and enjoys a huge mug of beer, but it has to be Viennese. He will smoke Hamburg cigars and join a small circle of friends to chatter away like a magpie. More often than not he talks about Bismarck, the demoralization of the French or the theatre. He will blurt out against Paul de Kock, whom he reads with great care so as to be able to castigate him with more conviction. *La pucelle de Belleville* disgusts and desolates him at the same time. He is conservative and avoids moral commonplaces in favour of pronouncements on political economy. Basically he is a good fellow.

3 Students are very prominent in Germany. The years spent at the university are the ones every good German recalls with most enthusiasm. In the student's life there are two basic things: one is to show off, the other to drink. The first of these two objectives is achieved by displaying the colours of the college to which he belongs, by wearing soft boots and by endless duels, the motive and attraction of which is to have his face cut open. As for drinking, I have to concede that students maintain a surprising as well as a sad degree of perfection. In fact there is nothing so stupefying as beer in the quantities these gentlemen swill down. Women play no part in a student's life – no Fridoline, no Rose, only disgusting female cooks and charwomen, restricted to feast days, three times a year. Their idea of the ultimate is to replace women with soft boots and champagne with Bavarian beer.

4 The situation is quite different with the aristocracy. Instead of that arrogance we hear so much about, I was very surprised to find the most pleasing courtesy, exquisite manners, cultivated and frequently unprejudiced minds, extensive knowledge of literature and perfect taste as far as the arts are concerned. Most noblemen say: 'Aristocracy is a stupidity, but we profit from those who have the double stupidity to believe in it.' Of course some are rather too

[324]

taken with their coats of arms, but they have the tact to conceal such feelings, at least when they are in the company of commoners. Morals, so strict in the middle classes, are on the whole laxer among the aristocracy, especially as far as the army and the diplomatic service are concerned. To find some Fridolines you have to get up there.

5 This brings me to German women. By and large they are ugly, sweet and good. Mentally extremely limited, they relish their ignorance, which they say renders them fitter for the household. The husband is the supreme master. This of course applies to the middle classes. The aristocratic woman is often charming, neither too lax nor inexorable, for she has the qualities of her husband. But with regard to women what predominates in Germany is the world of dressmakers and shopgirls, real Teutonic easygoing girls, a philanthropic institution which must have been founded specifically for the young. These girls are usually not particularly pretty, but they are modest and affectionate; they never ask for money and accept it with shame. Their idea of heaven is to drink champagne as they smoke little cigarettes made by Laferne or Jean Vouris. As for the courtesans, they are much less elegant than in Paris but much more modest.

6 To sum up, in general the Germans are *gentil* and polite. They frequent the *Restaurations* a great deal, where they all smoke cigars (pipes are smoked only by workers and students). All together it is a country where one can live very peacefully and agreeably.

Notes

CHAPTER 2

1 Archivo Diplomatico, Florence.
2 Giovanni Battista Lami, *Memorie Ecclesiastiche*, vol. 2, p. 301; *St Antonino's Histories*, tit. 15, ch. 23.
3 Archivio Diplomatico, Florence.
4 Archivio di Stato, Florence, *Coventi Soppressi*.
5 Aldo de Rinaldis, *Storia dell'Opera Pittorica di Leonardo da Vinci*, Bologna, 1922; G. Poggi, *Leonardo da Vinci*, Florence, 1919; H. Bodmer, *Leonardo da Vinci*, Stuttgart, 1931.
6 'I shall be saintly when you will be the Most Holy.'

CHAPTER 3

1 Bernhard Sattler (ed.), *Adolf von Hildebrand und seine Welt, Briefe und Erinnerungen*, Munich, 1962.
2 Ethel Smyth's memoirs, all published by Longmans, Green & Co., were as follows: *Impressions That Remained*, 2 vols., London, 1919; *As Time Went On*, London, 1936; *What Happened Next*, London, *1940*.
3 An ambiguous statement. Fiedler helped Hildebrand not by financial allowance as in the case of Marées, whom he entirely supported financially, but by promoting his reputation as a sculptor and by the sale of his works. Hildebrand received a small allowance from his father, enough for his immediate needs, until he married Irene Schäufellen, who was well off.
4 'Ille terrarum mihi praeter omnes angulus ridet', Horace, *Odes*, II, vi.
5 Letter to Georg von Marées, 30 May 1874.
6 To Melanie Taber, 1 July 1874.
7 Goethe's *Die Wahlverwandtschaften*.
8 At Beckley Park, Oxford, in the possession of my cousin Basil Feilding's heirs.
9 Now with Gerald Balfour's granddaughter, Mrs Anne Balfour Fraser, in Oxfordshire.

10 *Der Meister von San Francesco*, Tubingen, 1931.

CHAPTER 4

1 This story was told to me many years ago by my aunt, Clotilde Brewster Feilding, who as a little girl frequently played with the Hildebrand children and joined them in that assault.
2 George Henschel, *Musings and Memories of a Musician*.
3 Clothilde von Stockhausen, Julia's and Lisl's mother, was née Baudissin.
4 Bernhard von Bülow, *Denkenwurdichkeiten*, vol. 4, p. 186 ff.
5 *Johannes Brahms, im Briefwechsel mit Heinrich und Elisabet von Herzogenberg*, Berlin, 1907. Letter from Via de' Bardi, 22, 3 May 1880.

CHAPTER 5

1 Thomas E. Evans, *Recollections of the Second Empire*, London, 1906.

CHAPTER 6

1 *Selected Correspondence of Frédéric Chopin*, coll. Bronsilaw W. Sydow, tr. Arthur Hedley, London, 1962.
2 *Op. cit.*, to Domini Dziewanowski in Berlin, second week of January 1833.
3 *Op. cit.*, 30 November 1842.
4 *Op. cit.*, 26 November 1843.
5 *Op. cit.*, 24 December 1845.

CHAPTER 9

1 Letter of 25 December 1903, quoted by Maurice Baring in *The Puppet Show of Memory*, p. 25.

CHAPTER 14

1 *Adolf von Hildebrands Briefenwechsel mit Conrad Fiedler*, Dresden, 1927.
2 *Op. cit.*, letter to Fiedler from Florence, 4 October 1876.
3 Conrad Fiedler, *On Judging Works of Art*, tr. Henry Schaefer, Univ. of California Press, 2nd ed., 1957. See reference to Fiedler in Herbert Read's *Icon and Idea*.

[328]

4 Bernhard Sattler (ed.), *Adolf von Hildebrand und seine Welt, Briefe und Erinnerungen*, Munich, 1962.
5 *Stories of Naples and the Camorra*, London, 1897.

CHAPTER 16

1 Martin Halpern, PhD dissertation 'The Life and Writings of Henry B. Brewster', Harvard University, 1958.

CHAPTER 18

1 Cécile Delhorbe, *Edouard Rod*, p. 99 ff.
2 Letter published in *Botteghe Oscure*, no. xxix, Rome, 1957.

CHAPTER 19

1 Reissued by Heinemann 1931, currently out of print.

Index

Agoult, Comtesse Marie d', 51, 151

Alma-Tadema, Sir Lawrence, 285

Balfour, Arthur (later 1st Earl of Balfour), 143, 145

Balfour, Francis, 146

Balfour, George (later 2nd Earl of Balfour), 143-6, 314

Baring, Maurice, 82, 254, 292; to Ethel Smyth, on Rome, 309; memoirs quoted, 308-9, 310-11, 312 (on H.B.), 309-10 (on Pasolinis); poem for H.B., 312-13; 'poetic dramas', 313-14; Ethel's view of them, 314; promotion of *The Prison*, 314; his translation of *Via Lucis* quoted by Ethel, 321

Baronowska, Helen, 139

Baronowska, Mary, *see* Dohrn

Bates, M., H.B.'s banker in Geneva, 186, 249; bicycling exploit, 287-8

Bennet, Henry, 40

Benson, A.C., correspondence with Ethel Smyth, 233-4; on H.B., 233-4

Benson, Most Revd Edward, Archbishop of Canterbury, 199, 233

Benson, Mrs (wife of preceding), 199-200; friendship with Ethel Smyth, 220; objects to

'dethronement' of Julia Brewster, 233

Berenson, Bernard, 269, 282, 301

Berenson, Mary, 274

Bernhardt, Sarah, 250, 298

Böcklin, Arnold, 15, 148

Bourget, Paul, ix-x, 190; and wife, 240

Brahms, Johannes, 21, 29, 30, 31; and Lisl von Herzogenberg, 34-7, 230

Braunfels, Dr Sigrid, *Hildebrand*, 25

Brewster, Anna (*née* Bennet), H.B.'s mother, 40, 41-2, 45, 59, 60, 62; letter from H.B. in Dresden, 67-8; letters to H.B. in United States, 71-3, 75-7; 80; death in Vienna, 84

Brewster, Anne (daughter of H.B.'s cousin William, married Henri Frankenstein), 292-4

Brewster, Christopher ('Killy'), H.B.'s son, 32, 105, 156; letters from H.B. in the United States, 160, 161, 162-4, 165-70; from London, 194; school, 200, 235-6, in Freiburg, 251, 252; friendly with Hildebrand children, 225, 249; and Rome apartment, 229; mountaineering holiday with H.B., 251-2; coached for Cambridge, 258; at San Francesco, 268-9; fails

[331]

Cambridge tripos, goes to
Argentine for year, 308; marries
Lisl Hildebrand, 308; arranges
publication of H.B.'s
Buondelmonte, 318; death of
H.B., 320
Brewster, Dr Christopher Starr,
H.B.'s father, 40-8; death
described by H.B., 48; 55, 58, 69
Brewster, Clotilde (later Feilding),
H.B.'s daughter, 27, 55, 101, 111,
121, 122, 127; letter from H.B. in
Salt Lake City, 165; 200; friendly
with Hildebrand children, 225,
249, 269, 270; brush with Eva
Hildebrand, 249; and Rome
apartment, 229; Newnham
College, Cambridge, 235, 241-2,
250; liked by Henry James, 250;
studies architecture, 250, 252; in
London with H.B., 250-1; joins
mother at Freiburg, 251; 258;
bicycling enthusiasm, 288; as
architect, 297; marries Percy
Feilding, 308; H.B.'s death at her
house, 320
Brewster, Elder William, 40, 45
Brewster, Henry Bennet, 'H.B.', x,
xi, 3, 23, 26; early opinion of Lisl
von Herzogenberg, 31; 32, 37;
described by Ethel Smyth, 38-9;
parental background, 40-8; close
childhood contact with
Stockhausens, 55; Paris Lycée,
56-8, 59; professed atheism,
56-7; good looks, 57, 290, 308; in
Dresden, 60-8, *and see*
Appendix, 323-5; visits United
States, 69-78, 130-1, 156-70, 183-
4, 187-9; 'metaphysical
courtship' with Julia
Stockhausen, 79-85; in Spain, 80;
in Sweden and Norway, 80;
friendship with Henri Regnault,

82; marries Julia, 85; 93; early
years of marriage, 101-7; search
for an estate, 104-5; Avignonet,
105-6, legal problems, 107, burns
down, 112, 113, 119, finally sold,
200; 122; in North Africa,
109-12; involvement with Ethel
Smyth, 116-27; in France, 121-3,
200, 219, 249, 285; ultimatum to
Julia, 128; 'treaty' between
them, 129, reported to Ethel,
129-30; rebuffed by Ethel, 130;
lawsuit over uncle's will, 130-1,
159, 167, 184, 187; peripatetic
phase, 178 ff; correspondence
and arrangements with Julia,
179-89; declaration against life
of seclusion for his children, 180;
enthusiasm for London, 186-7;
Mrs Humphry Ward, 196-8;
meets Edmund Gosse, 198, 250;
Thomas Hardy, 199; James
Whistler, 199; Mrs Benson,
199-200; rents La Colline in
Switzerland, 200; Ethel
re-encountered, 219-20, religion
the main issue, 220 ff; apartment
in Rome, 227, 229-30, 234, 236,
238, 245, move from Palazzo
Cini to Palazzo Marignoli, 246,
bachelor apartment, 279 ff; Ethel
and Lisl's death, 230-1; in
London with Clotilde, 250-1;
mountaineering with son
Christopher, 251-2; criticizes
Ethel's *Fantasio*, 252; approach
to his own work, 252, confuses
Ethel, 252-3; sex with Ethel,
253-5; reaction to Fiedler's
death, 255-6; death of Julia,
256-7; publication of Julia's *Via
Lucis*, 265, discussed with Rod,
305-6; reconciliation with Irene,
268, and account of it to Ethel,

[332]

269; Florence, 282-3; London, 284, 285; reports to Ethel on Rod, 285- 6, Brumetière, 285-6, Sargent, 286-7, Bates the banker's bicycling, 287-8; 'worldly Rome', letters to Ethel, 289, 290, 291-2, 293, 294-5, 296, 297, 297-8, 299, 300-1, 301-3, to Clotilde, 293-4; and Anne Brewster, 292-4; meeting with Paderewski, 294-5; dislike of d'Annunzio, 296, 297; enthusiasm for bicycling, 288, 295; friendship with Wickham Steed, 299; recalled in Margaret Chanler's *Roman Spring*, 299-300; encounter with Cosima Wagner, 301-2; mystical mood persists, 305 ff; writes of Paestum to Ethel, 306-7; children marry, 308; involvement with Ethel's operatic activities, 308, 315; opinion of Anatole France and Rodin, 310; his 'Latinity', 311-12; reaction to Ethel's criticism, 316-17; writes to Ethel of last meeting with Henry James, 320; last illness and death, 320; ashes interred in Rome, 320
and Maurice Baring, 82, 292, 308-9, 310-14
and Henry James, 149, 194-8, 238, 239, 285, 289, 290, 295, 311; James's view of H.B., 199, 241, and of *The Prison*, 199; James's letter to H.B. on Marchesa Theodoli's play, 239-40; James writes from Venice, 246-7, 247-8, 249, from London, 281; last meeting with, 320; remembered by, 320-1
and Edouard Rod, 190-4, 285-6,

287, 295, 305-6, 307-8
and John Singer Sargent, 199, 250, 292, 294, 295, 297, 320
reading, 57-8, 63, 64, 123, 182, 183, 185, 189, 286, 305, 311; of Oriental literature, 103, 305
writings: *The Theories of Anarchy and Law* (1887), 123, 171-7, 182, 221, 319; *The Prison* (1891), 176, 194-5, 199- 200, 221, 300, 319; Maurice Baring on, 311; analysed, 201-18; Ethel's introduction to 1931 edition quoted, 296-7; plans for 'Animal Religion', crucial strand in all his writings, 188-9; 'The Statuette', 242, 243-4, 244-5, merged with *The Background* (1896), 245, 247, 314; adopts French for future writings, 285; *L'âme païenne* (1899), 190, 311, 315, compared with *Anarchy and Law* and *The Prison*, 315-16; 'Astray' (unpublished play), 315; text for Ethel's *Fantasio*, 315; libretto for Ethel's *The Wreckers*, 317; *Buon-delmonte* (1911), 318-19
Brewster, Julia (*née* Stockhausen), 3, 26, 29, 30, 31, 32, 33, 35, 37; described by Ethel Smyth, 39; piano lessons from Chopin, 51-2, 56; early friendship with H.B., 55-6, 64, 68, 70; 'metaphysical courtship' with H.B., 79-85; 93, 100; early years of marriage, 101-7; relationship with H.B. under strain, 108 ff; opposition to 'trio', 123-4; 'treaty' with H.B., 129; 149; letters from H.B. in United States, 156, 159; correspondence and arrangements with H.B., 179-89, 193; attachment to

[333]

Florence, 179, 180; at Berchtesgarden with children and Herzogenbergs, 181-2; receives first draft of *The Prison*, 194-5; letter from H.B. describing Mrs Humphry Ward's party, 196-8; La Colline in Switzerland as summer residence, 200; objects to H.B.'s meeting Ethel, 223; deterioration in health, 227, 253; advised against staying in Florence, 227-8; illness and death of her mother, 228; proposed book, 236-7; reclusive, 245; at Freiburg, 251, 253; in Rome, 252; reaction to Fiedler's death, 255; death, 256-7, 300; bust by Hildebrand, 259; *Via Lucis*, 261-7, 305-6

Brewster, Katherine, H.B.'s sister, *see* Terouenne, Baronne de

Brewster, Louis, H.B.'s brother, 45, 46; accompanies H.B. to United States, 70, 77; remains there, 78; 80, 82

Brewster, Seabury, H.B.'s grandfather, 40

Brewster, Seabury, H.B.'s uncle, 70; ambiguous will, 130-1, 157, 159, 160-1, 184, 187

Brumetière, Ferdinand, 285-6

Bülow, Prince Bernhard von, 30-1, 51, 292, and wife, 291-2

Bülow, Hans von, 149, 151

Cazalis, Henri, 79, 82, 83, 103, 185, 194, 200, 220, 305

Chamberlain, Basil Hall, 58-9

Chamberlain, Houston Stewart, 58

Chamberlain, Lady, 43, 47

Chanler, Mrs Winthrop (Margaret), 290, 299, 300-1; *Roman Spring* quoted, 299-300

Chopin, Frédéric, describes Paris demonstration, 49-50; friendship with Stockhausens, 50-4, 56

Churchill, Lady Randolph, 301

Churchill, Winston, 226-7

Crawford, Mrs Marion, 292

Crawshay, Mrs ('Mamie'), 290-1, 299, 301, 309

d'Annunzio, Gabriele, 277, 291, 296-7; *La ville morte*, 298

Dew-Smith, A.G., 140, 144

Dobson, Austin, 233

Dohrn, Dr Anton, 17, 137

Dohrn, Mary (*née* Baronowska), 139

du Buisson, Georges, 59; H.B.'s letters to from Dresden, 60, 61, 62, 63, 64-5, 65-6, *and see* Appendix, 323-5; with H.B. in Italy, 82; 83; death of, 84

du Buisson, Mme (mother of preceding), 84, 105

Duse, Eleonora, 250, 272, 277, 296, 297-8

Eugénie, Empress, 224-5

Evans, Dr Thomas W., 41, 42-3

Feilding, Percy, 308

Fiedler, Conrad, 15; Ethel Smyth on, 15-16; 18, 20, 24, 25; on Ethel Smyth, 28; 29, 32-3, 88-9, 90, 93, 95; marriage, 98; 100, 115, 125, 129; friendship with Hildebrands, 132, 134-5, 137, 149; attitude to Wagner, 134-5; death, 135, 255; philosophical works, writings, 135-7; and Charles Grant, 141, 142; 145, 152, 184, 225, 230

Fiedler, Mary (*née* Meyer), 16, 28, 32-3; marriage, 98; 125, 129;

[334]

friendship with Cosima Wagner, 132; character, 133; 135, 225, 230
Filtsch, Joseph, 53
Filtsch, Karl, 53
Florence, ix, 1-2; Via de' Bardi, Hildebrands' and Brewsters' apartments in, 2-3; 101 ff; Julia's attachment to, 179, advised to leave on health grounds, 227-8; H.B. visits again, 282; *see also*, San Donato a Scopeto, San Francesco di Paola
France, Anatole, 198, 232, 310
Frankenstein, Henri, 293-4, 297
Furtwängler, Wilhelm, 275

Geneva, as Rousseau's birthplace, H.B. to Ethel Smyth, 287
Gladstone, Helen, 146
Gladstone, W.E., 146, 276
Gonzaga, Carlo Guerrieri, 149
Gosse, (later Sir) Edmund, 198, 233, 242-3, 244, 250
Grant, Charles, 17, 23, friendship with Hildebrand, 137-44; his drinking, 13, 141, 142; literary output, 138; and Helen Baronowska, 139; death, 142; letter to Marées, 142-3; 145, 151

Halpern, Martin, 176, 177, 315, 317
Hardy, Thomas, 199, 233
Henschel, Sir George, 27-8, 29, 284
Herzogenberg, Elizabeth von ('Lisl', *née* Stockhausen), 21, 26; Ethel Smyth on, 29-30; von Bülow on, 31; letters to Ethel Smyth, 31-2, 33; marries, 34; and Brahms, 34-7; 39, 56, 68, 100; on sister Julia's lack of sympathy for her childlessness, 114; view of H.B., 114; alienated from Ethel Smyth by Irene

Hildebrand, 125-7; Brahms faction, 133; 149; at Berchtesgarden, 181-2; death of, 230; Ethel's desolation, 230-1
Herzogenberg, Heinrich Freiherr von, 30, 31, 36, 68, 83, 100, Brahms faction, 133; 154; with Julia Brewster at Berchtesgarden, 181-2
Hildebrand, Adolf, 2; birth and early years, 15; in Rome and Naples, 16-17; visits Florence, 17; acquires San Francesco di Paola, 18-20; breaks with Marées, 21; Ethel Smyth on, 21-3; evaluation of his sculpture, 24-5; sculpts Ethel Smyth, 26-7; 30; bust of Lisl von Herzogenberg, 31; appraised by Lisl, 33; 35, 36, 86, 88, 89; involvement with Irene, 90-7; confronted by Koppel, 94-5; marries Irene, 98; 99, 103, 104, 111, 112, 127, 129; the circle at San Francesco, 132-55; views on Wagner, 134; and Gerald Balfour, 144-6; and Liszt, 151; children friendly with H.B.'s children, 225; sculpts relief for Lisl's tomb, 230; bust of Julia Brewster, 259; H.B.'s suspect view of him, 269; widening circle of friends and patrons, 275-6, 277-8; work in Germany, 277-8; resemblance to Paderewski, 295; discussed by Cosima Wagner, 302
Hildebrand, Bertha ('Berthele'), 271, 274-5
Hildebrand, Bruno, 14-15, 18
Hildebrand, Dietrich ('Gogo'), 271, 274, 277
Hildebrand, Eva ('Nini'), 99, 249, 270, 274-5; and Emanuel, 272-4

[335]

Hildebrand, Irene (*née* Schäuffelen), arrival in Florence, 2; 21, 26; appraised by Ethel Smyth, 27; 28; engagement and marriage to Franz Koppel, 86-7; leaves for Florence, 88-9; involvement with Hildebrand, 90-7; marries Hildebrand, 98; character and influence at San Francesco, 98-100; 103, 112; blamed by Ethel Smyth for break with Lisl von Herzogenberg, 126-7; 129; friendship with Mary Fiedler, 132-3; on Charles Grant, 141-2; her relationships with Julia Brewster and Lisl compared, 154-5, 260; reconciliation with H.B., 268; and daughters, 271; 277; discussed by Cosima Wagner, 302

Hildebrand, Irene ('Zusi'), 270, 274-5, 302; and Emanuel, 271, 272-4

Hildebrand, Elizabeth ('Lisl', later Mrs Christopher Brewster), 269-70, 274-5, 302; and Emanuel, 272-4; 274

Hildebrand, Richard, 30, 154-5

Hildebrand, Sofie, 99, 100, 141

Hildebrand, Sylvia ('Vivi'), 270-1, 274-5, 302

Hillebrand, Jessie, *see* Taylor

Hillebrand, Karl, 93, 150-1, 152, 153

James, Henry, viii, 38, 56; and Hildebrand, 149; 176, 195-9; and *The Prison*, 201; 226, 234, 235, 238; verdict on Marchesa Theodoli's play, 239-40; fortunes in the theatre, 241; H.B. the 'Gallo-American', 241; and H.B.'s 'The Statuette', 242, 243, 244-5; writes to H.B. from Venice, 246-7, 247-8, 249, from London, 281; working on 'The Coxon Fund', 248; liking for Clotilde Brewster, 250; on Julia Brewster's death, 257-8; response to *Via Lucis*, 266; and H.B.'s apartment in Rome, 279-80; 289, 295, 303, 318; qualified commendation of H.B.'s play 'Astray', 315; last meeting with H.B., 320; H.B. remembered, 320-1

James, William, influence of *Anarchy and Law* on, 177; 195

Joachim, Joseph, 28, 146

Joshua, Ella, 292

Koppel, Franz, 86-90, 93-5, 97

Kurz, Isolde, 23, 140-1

Laussot, Eugène, 150

Laussot, Jessie, *see* Taylor

'Lee, Vernon', *see* Paget

Leonardo da Vinci, *Adoration of the Kings*, 6-7

Levi, Hermann, 100, 133, 226, 302

Liszt, Franz, 51, 140, 151

Mallarmé, Stéphane, 200

Marées, Hans von, 15, 16-17, 18-21, 86, 87, 88, 89, 90, 91, 93, 100

Maupassant, Guy de, 200; H.B. on *Une vie*, 286

Minghetti, Donna Laura, 291

Minims, friars of St Francis of Paola, 9, 10-11, 12

Meyerbeer, Giacomo, 53

Naples, Hildebrand and Marées in, 16-17

Paget, Violet ('Vernon Lee'), 282-3, 283-4, 301, 313, 315, 316

[336]

Paderewski, I.J., 294-5
Papadopoli, Contessa, 246
Pasolini, Contessa (Maria), 277, 291, 295, 296, 297, 298, 301, 303, 309-10
Pater, Walter, 233, 237, 242, 250, 284
Perthuis, Comte and Comtesse de, 51
Placci, Carlo, 149, 274, 277
Ponsonby, Lady, 126, 226, 255, 295
Primoli, Conte Giuseppe, 234, 249, 293, 302
Prison, The, see Brewster, H.B., writings

Rasponi, Angelica, 149, 277
Rasponi, Giuseppe, 149, 277
Read, Sir Herbert, 25, 135, 173, 176
Regnault, Henri, 82, 83
Renan, Ernest, 80-1
Rod, Edouard, 190-4, 220, 234, 235, 238, 295, 305; letters from H.B., 306, 307-8
Rodin, Auguste, 22, 310
Rome, Hildebrand and Marées in, 15; Brewsters leave Florence for, 200, 228, 229-30, 234, 236, 238, H.B.'s reactions to, 245-6, 307; H.B.'s apartment in, 279-80; H.B.'s life in, 289 ff
Rothschild, Baron (James), 50, 51, 52
Rothschild, Baroness (wife of preceding), 50, 51, 52, 53

St Francis of Paola, friars of, *see* Minims
San Donato a Scopeto, Florence, 4-8, 9, 268; 'Scopetini', 5-8; 18, 99
San Francesco di Paola, Florence,

history of, 4-13; acquired by Hildebrand, 18-20; 36, 90, 92, 96, 98-100, 'house and friends', 132-55, 270-8
Sand, George (Mme Dudevant), 52-3, 53-4
Sargent, John Singer, 199, 250, 254, 285, 292, 294, 295, 297; draws H.B. on deathbed, 320
Sattler, John, 147
Schäufellen, Irene, *see* Hildebrand
Schumann, Clara, 36-7, 92, 276; and Brahms faction, 133, 230
Silvani, Gherardo, 9, 11
Smyth, (later Dame) Ethel, x-xi; on Fiedler, 15-16, 134, 255; on Hildebrand, 21-2; 24; meets Hildebrands and Brewsters, 26; on Irene Hildebrand, 27; described by Henschel, 27-8; by Fiedler, 28; on Lisl von Herzogenberg, 29-30; 35; on Brewsters, 37, 38-9, 109; 57; religious views, 79; letter from H.B. on Renan, 81; 100, 112; on H.B.'s reaction to Avignonet disaster, 113; stays with Brewsters, 115; triangular predicament, 116-21; with H.B. in Leipzig, 122; plea for H.B.'s silence, 123; stance of propriety, 124-5; change of heart over Mary Fiedler, 133; cut off from H.B., 178; reaction to *The Prison*, 201; H.B. re-encountered, 220-1, religion becomes chief issue, 220 ff; friendship with Empress Eugénie, 224-5; desolation at Lisl's death, 230-1, 254; turns on Julia, 232, 254; relationship with Bensons soured, keeps up correspondence with their son, A.C.Benson, 233-4; and H.B.'s

[337]

'The Statuette', 242; *Fantasio*,
252; confused by H.B., 252; loses
virginity, 254-5; H.B. writes on
Julia's death, 256-7; lack of
understanding of her, 263-4, 265;
letters from H.B. about Rome
apartment, 280, Rod and
Brumetière, 285, Sargent, 286-7,
Rousseau's birthplace, 287,
Bates's bicycling, 287-8,
Paestum, 306-7, Henry James,
320; Sargent deplores
Thornycroft's bust of her, 295;
on Maurice Baring's 'poetic
dramas', 314; H.B.'s response to
her criticism, 316-17; *The
Wreckers*, 317-18; describes end
of H.B.'s life in memoirs, 320;
later life, 321; concludes
memoirs with quotation from
Via Lucis, 321
Smyth, Robert (brother of
preceding), 226-7
Steed, Henry Wickham, 299
Stockhausen, Baron von (Bodo),
34; friendship with H.B.'s father
in Paris, 41, 43; friendship with
Chopin, 50-4; marries Clothilde,
51; 55; transferred to Vienna, 56;
Dresden, 59, 63; 101
Stockhausen, Baroness von
(Clothilde, *née* Baudissin), 23,
43; marriage, 51; *The Memoirs
of Countess C*, 51; and Chopin,
51-2, 54, 55; in Dresden, 59, 63;
160; death of, 200, 228; dislike of
Ethel Smyth, 228-9
Stockhausen, Ernst von, 54
Stockhausen, Julia von, *see*
Brewster
Strauss, Richard, 277

Taylor, Jessie, 93, 133, 140, 149-53,
276; marries Hillebrand, 150

Terouenne, Baron de, 103, 156-7,
180, 186
Terouenne, Baronne de
(Katherine), H.B.'s sister, 58,
70-1, 103-4, 121, 130-1; visits
United States with H.B., 156,
161-3; letters to H.B. from
France, 157-9; preoccupation
with hunting, 156, 157-8; visits
from Ethel Smyth, 159; dispute
over uncle's inheritance, 159,
167, 184, 187; 180, 186;
pregnant, 194; 220
Theodoli, Marchesa (Lily), 239-40,
241, 289, 290
*Theories of Anarchy and Law,
The, see* Brewster, H.B., writings
Thoma, Hans, 147-8
Tovey, Donald, 146

Viti, Marchesa de (Etta), 290, 295,
302
Volkoff, M. and Mme, 295-6

Wagner, Cosima, 92, 100, 132, 149,
151, 152, 276, 301-2; Hildebrand
on, 152-3; Wagnerite faction,
133-4
Wagner, Richard, 16, 34, 58, 134,
135, 150, 152, 153, 276, 312;
Lohengrin, 226; *Tristan und
Isolde*, 250-1, 309; influence on
Ethel Smyth's *The Wreckers*,
318
Wagner, Siegfried, 153
Ward, Humphry, 198
Ward, Mrs Humphry, 195, 196-9
201
Whistler, James, 199
Wilde, Oscar, 198, 250
Wittelsbach, Rupert von, 23
Wittgenstein, Princess Caroline,
151
Woolf, Virginia, x-xi, 303

[338]